MENDACITY & MOURNING

JAN ASHTON

Copyright © 2019 by Jan Ashton

All rights reserved.

This is a work of fiction. Names, characters, businesses, places, events, locales, and incidents are either the products of the author's imagination or used in a fictitious manner. Any resemblance to actual persons, living or dead, or actual events is purely coincidental.

No part of this book may be reproduced in any form or by any electronic or mechanical means, including information storage and retrieval systems, without written permission from the author, except for the use of brief quotations in a book review.

Edited by Gail Warner and Ellen Pickels

Cover Design by Diamondback Covers

ISBN 978-1-951033-29-3 (ebook) and 978-1-951033-30-9 (paperback)

For Emma and Sam, who make everything more fun and more wonderful

TABLE OF CONTENTS

Chapter 1	1
Chapter 2	9
Chapter 3	18
Chapter 4	27
Chapter 5	37
Chapter 6	49
Chapter 7	65
Chapter 8	80
Chapter 9	93
Chapter 10	111
Chapter 11	125
Chapter 12	137
Chapter 13	153
Chapter 14	168
Chapter 15	182
Chapter 16	200
Chapter 17	218
Chapter 18	234
Chapter 19	249
Chapter 20	265
Chapter 21	280
Chapter 22	299
Chapter 23	315
Acknowledgments	329
About the Author	331
Also by Jan Ashton	333

CHAPTER ONE

It is a truth universally acknowledged that a gossip in possession of misheard tales—and desiring both a good wife and an eager audience—need only descend upon the sitting rooms of a small country town in order to find satisfaction.

And thus it was that Mr William Collins—in spite of his generous height, insatiable appetite, and slovenly manner—found himself a welcomed guest in many of the five and twenty households of Meryton. It was fortunate that as much as he enjoyed his own voice, he could also listen because he could not tell his own story in full truth. For reasons he did not understand—and at a time when his patroness should have the most need for him—Lady Catherine, reeling in shock and horror, had ordered him to vacate her lands and leave her in peace.

No one need know that the man of God had unwittingly insulted or shamed the great Lady Catherine de Bourgh. Or, perhaps, that by exiling her clergyman, she had ensured that the true reasons for her distress and disgust remained veiled behind a series of half-truths and twisted meanings.

At least until the mongrel child of her daughter—and the lowly man who had stolen her away from Rosings—was born.

Fitzwilliam Darcy, gentleman of Pemberley and haunter of ballroom walls, was, like the good parson, outside the circle of knowledge of his aunt's behaviour and his cousin's true fate. As he understood things, his cousin Anne—to whom only Lady Catherine, Mr Collins, and assorted long-suffering servants had believed him affianced—was dead. Dead of the pox these two weeks and buried at Rosings before any family members could be notified and roused to her bedside. And now her mother, railing in anger and grief, was installed in London and surrounded by sympathetic family, all the while seething in secret and publicly demanding that no stone be ordered and no family journey to Rosings be commenced.

"I am bereaved; I am lost!" she cried.

"And quite red faced with bellowing," Richard murmured, rolling his eyes.

Darcy knew the second Fitzwilliam son, nearest in age to him and the closest he had to a brother, did sympathise with his aunt's loss. Richard had cared for Anne, cared for her happiness. He had related to Darcy that there had been a moment a year or three ago when lying atop a dirty blanket and nursing a head wound and two broken fingers on the outskirts of Burgos, he had considered offering for Anne himself. The comforts of home and a deep purse, however, could not overcome the spectre of sad, angry, spindly Anne in his bed while the World's Most Knowledgeable and Imperious Mother-in-Law hovered outside the door shouting instructions on proper limb management and correct rhythms in the most private of marital realms. "I am not so devoted a cousin and nephew," Richard had said bleakly. "And I am a breast man."

Darcy, being a good and proper younger cousin, reacted somewhat differently. Somewhat. When the news arrived of Anne's sad yet unsurprising demise, he had worried, wondered, and written letters seeking the particulars. While he had been troubled, the malaise that struck him over the loss of Anne was less from bereavement than relief. *Guilty relief.*

Anne had been…difficult. She was moody, used to supplicants, and resembled a younger version of her mother. He never would have married her, a fact for which Anne had said she was grateful. They were of similar age, and when she had striven to kiss his twelve-year-old cheek and seen him shrink away, she proclaimed that he had passed 'the test' and they were indeed free of each other's spell. "I prefer a whiskered cat to pet and purr to a boy who cannot hold still and eats too many sweets," Anne had insisted. Darcy chose to focus on the blessing of self-determination over the insult.

Still, before he left for Cambridge five years later, he had gone to her and asked whether she remained unencumbered by her mother's deranged marriage plans. "I do not think we were fixed for one another while still in our cradles, Anne. Do you?" He had hoped his desperate aversion to such a conclusion did not seep out in his solemnly voiced query.

She had laughed in her wheezy way and cut him to the quick. "You are not meant for me, Cousin. Nor I for you. Go off and read books and ride horses. I shall marry another."

But she had not, and now she was dead.

Darcy sighed. He felt some pangs of remorse for not spending more time with Anne, but she, like her mother, had been a hard lady with whom to converse. Since her death a fortnight ago, he had not been dutiful enough to have dismissed his aunt's wishes and run off to Rosings to investigate what had happened or to lay flowers on the still-fresh grave. He in fact felt quietly relieved to have the onus of a mythical engagement gone away and intensely guilty about feeling so. Neither he nor Anne had ever taken seriously her mother's claims and threats, but they had also spent little time together since he had reached manhood and Anne's health had declined. He had been a poor cousin and a poorer friend.

Never once had he given honest consideration to marrying his cousin. He cared for Anne as he might have cared for a piece of fruit. She had been enjoyable when in season, but when her temperament turned dark and surly—as it so often had—Anne had a sour bite to her personality. The apple did not fall far from the tree, his uncle Lord Matlock would grumble.

Occasionally, Darcy wondered whether his family's reliance on fruit metaphors for ill-behaved relatives did not mask some deep-seated resentment of the French vineyards the D'Arcys had abandoned some three centuries earlier. Years ago when he had mentioned this supposition to Richard, all he had provoked in response was a raised eyebrow and a reminder that no Fitzwilliam had any envy of the frog-tainted D'Arcy blood. "Just our gold and our art collections…" a thirteen-year-old Darcy had mumbled under his breath, but he had refrained from ever repeating it aloud after Richard bloodied his nose.

No, he knew there was much to envy about the Darcys—all two of them. He and his young sister, Georgiana, were wealthy, their reputation excellent, and their servants loyal, and they had the great joy of living in perhaps the most beautiful home in England. Pemberley and its grounds were the envy of all who saw them. It was also, he had thought over the last few years, rather large and lonely and far too quiet. It was a house made for generations to share: for parents, children and grandchildren, aunts, uncles, and cousins to fill with laughter and music and to scatter with stray ribbons, tin soldiers, and muddied boots, tiny and large. While not bleak, worn down, and lacking warmth as Rosings had always been, Pemberley needed more liveliness. Much as the two remaining Darcys treasured their time together in Derbyshire, their home felt happiest and most vital when parties of friends and family gathered and filled its eight and twenty bedrooms.

Fortunately, the sprawling Fitzwilliam clan of Matlock House and Mayfair was happy to lay claim to Darcy and Georgiana. Lord and Lady Matlock and their sons were as well established as any family could be in the scheme of things: comfortably situated in London's social and financial spheres, rich in good health, and not overly prone to apoplexies, painful shyness, or horrific childbirth dramas. Darcy enjoyed these hale and hearty relations, tolerated those frail, angry ones at Rosings, and worried that as his sister came of age, her Fitzwilliam blood would be her undoing. No Fitzwilliam woman seemed free of poor health, fragile demeanour, or imperious disposition. Now, with Anne dead and the family in some mutually unspoken state of bewildered yet relieved mourning, it seemed the dark fates loomed ever closer to the youngest girl with Fitzwilliam bloodlines.

Oh, Georgiana. He worried endlessly about his younger sister. She appeared far older than her fifteen years, but she lacked the worldliness and wiles of other girls her age. Her quiet, shy deportment masked her immaturity.

Their cousin's death was just the latest example of Darcy's struggles as not just an older brother but also a father figure.

Even as witness to Anne's years of illness, his sister refused to believe her sole female cousin and sometime correspondent could be dead. When she protested that Anne seemed lively enough in her recent letters, Darcy shook his head sadly. Georgiana had had similar difficulty letting go of broken dolls and a dead pet rabbit; the loss of both parents before age twelve had likely prompted such denial. He hugged his sister, patted her head, ordered her new sheet music, and asked Cook to serve her favourite desserts.

The realist in him warred with the romantic. His sister's protests that 'Anne cannot be dead; she is likely hiding from her mother' evoked rueful smiles but did not budge him or Richard into going to Rosings and inspecting the mouldering pile for all the places that Georgiana speculated Anne might have concealed herself. The estate was full of the pox after all, and his aunt's steward, bumbling though he might be, was maintaining it with the little bit of oversight he had been granted.

Whatever festered at Rosings could be perilous to his sister. Darcy's hair could turn grey from his fears for her. So many dangers: the pox, rabid dogs, highwaymen, a fall down the stairs, or a kick from a startled horse. And she had just faced down an unexpected and startling peril at Pemberley—a brush with disgrace narrowly averted.

Who would have thought it would be a footman—a doughy-cheeked, bran-faced footman who was overly solicitous of a lonely young girl's desire for conversation? Which is all it was, he reminded himself again and again. No more than conversation with a 'friend.' A friendly footman.

In his heart, Darcy knew it was not quite as bad as it might appear to outsiders, nor was Georgiana as horribly wicked as she supposed. Her recent 'downfall,' such as it was, had led to her removal from Pemberley and her current situation with the Fitzwilliams in town. There, surrounded by her boisterous uncle and cousin, her ever-occupied aunt, and a stable with two newborn foals, she would be safe from footmen who were too eager to assist her and stupid enough to be found alone with her in a small, dimly lit room. Nothing untoward had occurred, Georgiana had haltingly and hysterically told her companion, Mrs Annesley. But the mere appearance created by her misjudgment, and the social isolation imposed by Pemberley, had compelled Darcy to remove his sister from the sprawling estate and ensconce her with family for these final weeks of summer.

He would have preferred his uncle's country estate, but Anne's death had compelled the Fitzwilliams' return to London, where Lady Catherine now dwelled. He dreaded London's foul air and water and worried for his sister's health. Worried more than usual, according to Richard, who had determined Darcy needed to fence. Or tup. Or both. Well-regulated man that he was, he chose fencing, and they set off in the carriage to have a match or two. Richard's glower was a mixture of pity and annoyance.

"You continue to act like a hysterical woman, Darcy. Georgiana is not a baby to be swaddled nor a teacup to be handled. She is with my mother. Leave it—leave *her*—be."

The glare Darcy shot him would have felled Bingley; the younger man's buoyant vulnerability to Darcy's moods was one of the attractions of their friendship. Richard, however, simply cocked an eyebrow and frowned.

"Leave Georgiana be? Should we have let Anne be? Did we leave her *be* too long and fail her?" Darcy pulled out his watch and looked at it. "I spent many hours staring at Rosings's clocks, wishing the hands to turn faster so I could get away from the place. Imagine how Anne felt; can you?"

Richard seemed to feel true guilt over his cousin's death. "She was not like us, you know. She seemed…content. Accepting."

"Of her fate? Yes." Darcy pulled his attention away from his watch and stared out the window at those they passed who were scurrying, strolling, or standing idly. *All living lives of which I know nothing.* "Was her fate assigned at birth? Was mine?"

"Of course. You are the master of Pemberley. You rule lands and lives and make your elder cousin miserable with your endlessly dour philosophising." Richard sighed. "And this poor, put-upon cousin must listen and nod for he is dependent upon you for good brandy, a hot meal, and a decent fencing match."

In spite of himself, Darcy laughed quietly. "Put that way, mine is not too sorry a fate."

Still, he thought there was more than what fate might assign a man. He considered the notion of changing his fate while facing what lies ahead. He would return to Pemberley for the harvest and its accompanying celebrations before settling into Darcy House for the long winter season. He wondered whether Christmas at Pemberley would be too lonely and they should forego their sleigh and skates this year and stay in town. He wondered why it was easier to decide between barley and wheat for the upper fields than to make the best, happiest choices for himself and his sister. He was unable to even define best or happiest, so perhaps settling was the simplest resolution.

Settling the question of his aunt's future was one on which he tried not to dwell. He prayed it was enough for now that she had her home in London and seemed content to rule and grieve from her bed. He knew his aunt blamed him for Anne's death.

"If only he had married Anne, she would be well and Rosings's future assured!"

Darcy wondered which of those mattered more to his aunt. Much as he mourned his cousin, the future of Rosings was not a subject he wished to consider. Darcy was preoccupied with his own. Lady Catherine now refused to allow him in her presence—a blessing he should appreciate, according to Richard.

He did not care for the black curtains and dark clothing, all the accoutrements of death that seemed too common to his family. Georgiana liked yellow whilst he preferred green—the colours of life, the colours of their mother's sitting room. He was twenty-eight years of age and tired of wondering whether death and mourning would always determine his path. Death could come suddenly, and fate held surprising turns. No matter one's wealth or happiness, it could be cut short in an instant.

An entrapment by a desperate, scheming lady would be even worse. At a few estates, Darcy had evaded some well-laid plans by avoiding oddly darkened rooms and balconies and bolting his door. So little was within his control. Wary fear and vigilance were exhausting.

And then, in the work of a moment, he was decided. He would determine his own fate. He would get through this mourning period for Anne and find himself a wife and Georgiana a sister, and they would fill the cavernous, echoing halls of Pemberley with children, noise, and laughter. He could not bear to go back to that house without such happy assurance, yet he could not imagine meeting such a woman, now or ever, in London. Here ladies preened and smiled; they nodded and touched his arm. Their dresses plunged and their intelligence seemed to follow. Not one had caught his eye in nigh on two years, and none had ever made him catch his breath. His heart remained untouched. But for his sister's sake and for some grasp of future happiness, he would try. He would exert an effort beyond any he had before, and he would find himself a wife.

With the summer season of country living still in full swing—and London host to only those most grasping of families who lacked a country house or who, like the Fitzwilliams, were managing a grieving, obdurate relative—Darcy thought it more likely that he could become acquainted with a young lady by visiting his friends' estates. Prior to the news of Anne, he had accepted three invitations, and he determined to follow through with abbreviated visits. After a farewell to his sister and another attempt to pay his respects to his aunt, he would journey off on his assignment. There was little chance he would meet a young lady of quality in a place called Meryton, but he could enjoy Charles Bingley's happily infectious spirit.

CHAPTER TWO

"My friend Darcy is to arrive tomorrow," Bingley said, happily and heedlessly interrupting the tea his sisters were hosting for their neighbours, the two eldest Bennet sisters.

The lively young man, already half in love with the angel known as Jane Bennet, was as pleased to share his news as he was pleased to please his new friends. He gazed dreamily at her while disregarding a few mild concerns over the reception of the announcement by Netherfield's other occupants. He was certain Darcy's letter would enliven Caroline's mood. His sister had never been known for her pleasant demeanour, but her mood these past weeks in the country had been miserable, even *ugly*. It was clear she did not have a high opinion of the townspeople nor of the shops and their merchandise, but must she be so expressive with her opinions? Did her arms need to fly about when she gesticulated? Her tantrums behind closed doors were of no help to her aspirations for a good marriage to a landed gentleman. Darcy had once caught a glimpse of an argument's angry aftermath, and Bingley had seen the disgust in his friend's eyes.

Bingley remembered childhood summers at their great uncle's farm collecting eggs, plucking daisies, and riding ponies. Louisa and Caroline had been such agreeable playmates then. Now, with the former married these four years and the latter looking towards her *fifth* Season, they seemed merely grumpy and greedy. Not even the pretty countryside of Hertfordshire and the happy company of the two eldest Bennet sisters could delight them. *My sisters are such unpleasant girls. Some people are not formed for happiness.*

"Mr Darcy!" A squeal of delight brought him back to the moment. As he had expected, Caroline greeted the news with great enthusiasm. "Oh, how wonderful! Finally, a taste of intelligent conversation and news of the *ton*."

The Bennet sisters exchanged looks. Jane, the elder by two years, reached for her tea. Her eyes widened, her smile compensating for the narrowing of her sister's expression. Miss Elizabeth looked up at her host and spoke in a cheerful voice. "Finally, Mr Bingley, with the arrival of your friend, you and Mr Hurst will have the advantage in numbers. Your friend brings you intelligent conversation, and you will reward him with the calming joys of Netherfield?"

Bingley, already conversant with his angel's sister on the paucity of volumes in Netherfield's library, chuckled. "Well, yes, I shall, Miss Elizabeth. We have fields to explore, fine steeds to ride, and at least a few birds to shoot and fish to catch. And if I know my friend, he will bring a box or two of books with him. He will likely carry a volume in each coat pocket as well."

Miss Elizabeth seemed pleased by this intelligence. "So, Mr Darcy is a wise gentleman who makes good use of his leisure."

Now it was Caroline's turn to narrow her eyes. "Mr Darcy is the finest gentleman of our acquaintance. His estate in Derbyshire has no rival, his library no equal."

"He would appear to be quite the fine gentleman," Jane agreed.

Louisa gave her a tight smile. "He is, indeed. And suffering such a grievous loss."

"Oh no!" Jane's eyebrows furrowed and her hand went to her heart.

Bingley smiled sadly at the stricken beauty before glancing at his sisters and clearing his throat. "Darcy's cousin, Miss Anne de Bourgh, died a fortnight ago. He has been assisting his aunt in her bereavement. Miss de Bourgh was her only child."

"Oh, how tragic," Jane gasped. Bingley winced and went to sit across from her. Her blue eyes looked so sad.

"So he is joining you here as a respite from his mourning," Miss Elizabeth said. "That is kind of you to relieve him of his burden." At the indelicate sound of a snort, her eyes shifted from Mr Bingley to his eldest sister.

Louisa wore an amused expression as Caroline sipped her tea. "Yes, poor Mr Darcy did lose his cousin, but his aunt lost her daughter and her chance for landed greatness. Uniting the fortunes was a great lure, and his aunt is reputedly quite persuasive."

Elizabeth wondered whether Miss Bingley's insincere smile resembled those in the etchings of Ceylonese crocodiles of which her uncle told tales to her little cousins.

"Oh, it was not a mercenary move by him," Miss Bingley added. "Mr Darcy is the master of Pemberley. He is too good to form a false attachment."

And apparently too rich. Elizabeth thought that Mr Bingley's sisters were *the* authorities on falsity.

"His cousin...she was said to be loose in the head."

"Caroline!"

"Oh, Charles, everyone knows she was not well. Lady Catherine simply wished for the match, and the Darcy lineage must continue on."

Mr Bingley jumped up from his seat and stalked over to the fireplace. He shook his head and spoke in a sharper voice than Elizabeth had imagined him capable.

"I must defend my friend from Caroline's assertions! Darcy

grew up with his cousin and was quite fond of her. In spite of her ill health, they were close friends. He and his family are grieved by her death."

He smiled tightly, and glancing at Jane, his eyes softened. "I hope you will excuse me, Miss Bennet. Darcy has been a great friend to me, and I hope he will feel welcome here and take as much pleasure in the company as I have."

"Please bring Mr Darcy to call at Longbourn. My family will make him feel welcome," Elizabeth said warmly. She felt Miss Bingley's eyes on her, but she maintained a steady smile for her host.

Mr Bingley nodded and bowed slightly, and after apologising that he had left his steward waiting too long in his study, he left the room.

The sisters of Longbourn sat quite still as they absorbed the looks exchanged between Mrs Hurst and Miss Bingley. Small talk on future events in town filled the minutes until the clock rang half past five, and Elizabeth and Miss Bingley swiftly sought their escapes.

As the Bennets rode home in Netherfield's carriage and raindrops splashed on the roof above them, Jane shook her head. "Oh, Lizzy, I believe this Mr Darcy is the same gentleman mentioned by my cousin."

"Mr Collins, the man who will not leave?" Elizabeth muttered under her breath. Oh, how she wished the olive branch he was extending to her family would snap and send him tumbling back to his parsonage.

"He told us about his patroness's daughter who was betrothed to her cousin, the master of Pemberley. The poor, heartbroken man must be Mr Darcy."

Elizabeth took Jane's hand. "It is sad, Jane. We know so little, though, about the situation, and Miss Bingley had quite a different point to make."

"Lizzy, be kind! Mr Bingley's friend is in mourning. He has lost his cousin, his betrothed."

Elizabeth gave her sister a weak smile. Although she could not help her aversion to Miss Bingley, she recognised that she had been harsh in assuming any gentleman the fashionable lady admired must be of similar character. Her eldest sister saw only the good in their neighbour, and Elizabeth knew their arrival home would bring a deluge of questions from another sister about the 'lovely and fearsome Miss Bingley.'

Elizabeth marvelled at Kitty's fascination with the lady. Yes, she granted that Miss Bingley was a rather pretty woman who dressed in expensive, well-tailored gowns and had access to, and relied on, every manner of feather, bead, and trim to emphasise her charms. But Kitty had not stopped praising the lady's 'most handsome appearance' since the moment they were introduced a few weeks prior. Elizabeth recognised that Kitty was young and had not been exposed to the larger world of society, but to Elizabeth, her younger sister's object of admiration was not worthy of such esteem.

In fact, she felt it curious and unfortunate that Kitty was so taken with Miss Bingley because Elizabeth had formed a quite different opinion. She had taken note of the lady's eye rolling and flared nostrils when others extolled the virtues of country living. She had listened patiently to the lady's observations on grass and foliage, tea service, window views, cheeses, animals, fashions, merchants, society, and the tradespeople of Meryton and its 'inferior' countryside.

London, of course, held all that was of interest and importance: the shops and tea rooms, the promenades and society. Even the flowers and trees of the city's parks were brighter, larger, and more colourful. Elizabeth was sceptical that Miss Bingley would spare a glance for nature's beauty, but perhaps she judged her unfairly. She did feel sympathy for her brother's friend; after all, Mr Darcy had suffered a great and terrible loss. Yet Mr Collins had provided them with a slightly different view of the dead bride-to-be and her heartbroken groom.

Indeed, since his arrival three days earlier, their cousin had regaled them with tales of the great and wondrous Rosings and its excellent and revered occupants. He had spoken at length—yet with a curious lack of detail—of the demise of Lady Catherine de Bourgh's only daughter. He had described the lost heiress as the jewel of Kent, a beauty of vast talents who was to be married to her illustrious cousin and to unite their great estates.

He mourned for his extraordinary patroness who, left alone and bereft, had cried out, "She is dead to me!" and refused his attempts at pastoral counsel. Mr Collins intoned solemnly that Lady Catherine chose to grieve alone. "Leave me and the parsonage to grieve in peace," she had ordered him. And so he had. He carried little to recommend him to his relations but platitudes and parables, rambling biblical references, harsh admonitions, and a huge appetite for whatever emerged from his host's kitchens. He paid for the hospitality by sharing the minimal knowledge he had gleaned, sprinkled with ill-considered speculations and hypotheses, about the sad end of the future mistress of Rosings and Pemberley.

Meals had become a test of endurance for some members of the Bennet family. Rather than receiving enlightened titbits and stories from a cousin who had seen a bit of the world and spent time with people of quality, the family's patience was burdened with discourse about Mr Collins's palate and digestion, the food that filled his plate, and details on meals enjoyed in the past and hoped for in the future.

It was in reality rather mortifying. Since his arrival after a fortnight of visiting his spinster aunts in Epsom, Mr Collins had conspicuously been unable to contain his effusions over the meals produced in Longbourn's kitchen. His raptures—which ever so awkwardly skirted insult to the efforts of his aunts Millicent and Lavinia and to the cooks labouring for the great Lady Catherine—seemed to increase with his girth. He was a large, imposing young man and growing larger. Lydia predicted that a violent, untidy explosion would occur at any moment as a result of his appetite.

When the sisters arrived home from Netherfield, they espied the dreaded Mr Collins hovering near the kitchen doorway. *From one grinning reptile to another.* Elizabeth had felt trapped during the past few days of rain with nowhere to go for undisturbed thought or private conversation. When a visit to the Lucases' or tea with the Bingley sisters proved the zenith of intelligent discussion, she knew things were dire. A glance at the tired, angry expressions on her younger sisters' faces made it clear that their afternoon had been spent in close company with their eager-to-converse cousin. Mary, even paler than was common, was bent over a hymnal. Lydia looked more vexed than usual; her nostrils flared alarmingly like Miss Bingley's. Kitty's face spoke of weary melancholy. Elizabeth sighed quietly at the smallness of her company.

As Elizabeth and Jane put away their pelisses and hats, Lydia and Kitty drew near. Kitty enquired after Miss Bingley, whether the lady had asked after her, what colour dress she wore, and what was served at tea. Elizabeth provided short replies that Kitty greeted with enormous sighs.

"I wish I too had been invited to tea with Miss Bingley."

Jane and Elizabeth traded looks. They had noted Kitty's plaintive expression when the invitation to tea arrived addressed only to them and agreed it was best to let Kitty's interest run its course. After all, she had always loved fashion and frippery, and she rarely saw such fine examples of it in Meryton. When Miss Bingley went back to London, Kitty's life would resume all its ordinariness.

Their youngest sister had other concerns to share. Mr Collins's buttons, noted Lydia the Wise, were near to popping. Elizabeth reminded her *again* that a young lady's eyes belonged elsewhere—in a *proper* place. Thus commenced more whinging about the ache in Kitty's neck and the strain on Lydia's eyes from looking up at the tall, ungainly man.

Lydia seemed particularly displeased with the small size of their cousin's head set atop such a large body. She had made the mistake of mentioning it the day before in the presence of her Aunt Philips, who had tittered for five minutes on how a small-headed man boded well for both his mother and his wife. Mrs Bennet had joined in the hysterical, knowing laughter while her daughters exchanged the uncomfortable glances of innocents. Elizabeth despised the few moments when her mother and aunt held the advantage in knowledge. It occurred rarely, but when it did, the Gardiner sisters relished their superiority. Elizabeth had tucked away a sudden, unnerving recognition of their resemblance to the Bingley sisters.

Mr Collins smiled upon seeing Cousins Jane and Elizabeth enter the house. He had considered both as suitable for marriage—one kind, serene, and beautiful; the other charming, bright, and frightfully clever—but until he knew when he could return to his parsonage, he feared raising their hopes. *'Tis a better thing in the eyes of God to be true and kind.* And to enjoy the gustatory glories of Mrs Bennet's table.

Already he could hear her voice rising above the others. "Mr Bingley's particular friend is arriving tomorrow. He comes to our neighbourhood for rest and sport." She nodded at her husband, who maintained a steady focus on his book. "He is said to be a great man of the *ton*. It speaks well for us and for him that he visits Hertfordshire even if he will be dull with all of his resting."

"A great man?" Mr Bennet exclaimed. "Would that make him a learned man, a man with whom I can play chess, or a man of great capacity for drink and riding? I wonder at your definition of a great man, Mrs Bennet."

"Papa," Jane said softly, as close to a reprimand as Mr Collins had heard her speak. "Mr Bingley says that Mr Darcy is a gentleman in mourning, in need of quiet diversion."

"Indeed," her father replied. "Sadly, we've nothing to Almack's, but our hills roll gently, Mr Piper's shop carries every shade of hair ribbon, and there is many a bird waiting to be shot for the supper table."

Cousins Lydia and Kitty snickered while Elizabeth lowered her head to hide a smile. Their mother looked peevish from Mr Bennet's words but remained silent, observing Hill as she carried in the trays.

"Mr Darcy? Mr Darcy is coming here, to Hertfordshire?" Mr Collins's eyes gleamed in excitement. "How singular." He eyed the platters of meat and roasted turnips being set just an arm's length away. "As he is Miss de Bourgh's cousin, his mourning period is over. As the bereft betrothed, however, he will be in need of my counsel. I must go to him. Ecclesiastes is in order."

Jane spoke and saved him from further musings. "Sir, you made the acquaintance of Mr Darcy at the funeral for Miss de Bourgh?"

"Uh, no, I did not, Cousin Jane. There was no funeral service."

"You did not conduct one?" Elizabeth asked. "There was no more than a simple gathering of the family?"

Mr Collins lowered his fork and shook his head.

Mary, listening intently, seemed especially grieved. "Was there not a Christian burial?"

Mr Collins frowned. "A troublesome infection, Cousin Mary. Not a soul entered Rosings, and no family members were permitted to honour the memory of the dear, departed Miss de Bourgh. I believe she is laid to rest in the family tomb with prayers said by a visiting bishop."

"Did you meet this bishop and discuss scripture, Mr Collins?" Mary enquired.

He glanced away from her piercing stare. "No…the infection of course affected proper social calls."

"But…"

"How dull this conversation has become, Mary, with all this talk of death and mourning," Mrs Bennet said with disinterest. "More potatoes, Mr Collins?"

"Mama, have you been listening?" Lydia interjected. "Mr Bingley's friend is very rich, and he may be very handsome."

Mrs Bennet looked at Mr Collins. "Mr Bingley's friend is the widower you mentioned?"

"Mr Darcy is the master of Pemberley, Mama, the man of whom our cousin has spoken," Elizabeth said while Mr Collins piled another slice of roast on his already full plate.

"The Grieving Groom?" Mrs Bennet asked, her eyes alight with wild fancy.

"Groom-to-be," Mr Collins corrected, pausing in his exertions. "He loved his cousin dearly, but her heart gave out and broke his before the banns could be read."

"Her heart?" Mr Bennet enquired. "Was it not a troublesome infection, as you said? Or was it the pox? Or mayhap scurvy?" He leaned back and surveyed the table, his eyes resting on Elizabeth. "I sense a mystery on our doorstep."

CHAPTER THREE

The streets of Meryton were quiet when Darcy rode in. He glanced about at the shops: the milliner, the apothecary, the blacksmith. Nothing here was remarkably different from any other small country town. There was a beautiful grouping of chestnut trees down the way and benches for conversation placed under the arching branches. He heard the voices of laughing children and turned to watch two small boys chasing a butterfly.

"Thomas! Henry! Stop!"

Darcy observed a woman hastening after the pair. "That might well be the last butterfly of the season," she admonished them in a cheerful voice. "It lives so short a life; let it fly freely and enjoy this day."

He smiled. When she was a little girl, Georgiana had loved to chase butterflies as well. He did not recall scolding his sister for it, but *he* had not been a maternal figure, and *she* had always been a well-behaved, obedient child.

"But we wish to capture it for our collection!"

"Not while it is still alive, Henry," the lady said gently. She brushed some dirt off the smaller boy's sleeve, re-settled the older one's cap, and took their hands. "Your father will be waiting for us. I wonder whether he might have filled his pockets with a sweet or two for his clean, well-behaved sons."

"Oh yes, hurry up!"

Darcy watched the youngsters pull the woman quickly towards the dry goods shops and admired her clever maternal management. As they neared him, she glanced up and warned, "Mind the man's horse now." He nodded and touched his hat. Her dark eyes sparkled with the exertion of holding onto the two boys, both redheads under the age of six. She was young herself, he realised, not much more than twenty years of age.

"Lizzy, my dear, I see you have wrangled some wild tigers!" cried a deep, jovial voice. Darcy turned his horse and saw a well-dressed man perhaps ten years his senior emerge from the shop.

"Papa, did you buy us sweets?" asked the younger of the boys.

The man laughed. "One for each of you boys and two, of course, for my dear Lizzy."

He stooped to pick up his youngest son. The other boy accepted a package from his father and took the hand of 'Lizzy.' As the group disappeared around the corner, Darcy heard the young lady say gaily, "Now, Thomas, you had best hide them unless your father has enough for a houseful of women."

Darcy turned his horse back in the direction of Bingley's estate. North to the trio of willows and then he would see the house—at least he *believed* that was what Bingley's inkblots had detailed. Idly, as his horse trotted beneath him, he thought on the family he had just observed and wondered whether all the people of this town exhibited such warmth towards one another.

It took little time for him to forget this speculation. Two days into his stay at Netherfield, Darcy was reminded that good manners and kindly ways rarely extended upwards in the social sphere. His hosts did try to be considerate in their own peculiar manners of effort, but they were exhausting rather than enlightening. He tired quickly of Bingley's concerned glances, Hurst's offer to pour a glass to relieve his pain, and Mrs Hurst's reminders that many flowers grow in a field and not every rose will wilt to the air—or sun or shears or whatever it was she was striving to say metaphorically. Richard would laugh at the lady for confusing dying flowers with rotting fruit when it came to summing up the flaws of the Fitzwilliam family.

Why did they feel that they must patronise him? Was he quieter than he had been in the past? Softer from all the sad events of the past few months? Could he not just *be*? Apparently not.

In an effort to escape Miss Bingley's suffocating expressions of sympathy that seemed to compel her into far more intimate contact than was proper, Darcy found himself enjoying his explorations of Netherfield's sprawling, undisciplined lands. He took Charles in hand, and they scouted the estate on horseback, drawing a rough map of what they observed to match against the one shown to Charles by his lending agent. In the interest of learning the estate's flora and fauna, they fished in the stream and fired guns in the air, securing—all by Darcy's hand—three trout and two grouse. Hurst, a frustrated angler, said loftily that he would show them how to hunt wild boar, but he insisted a new stock of brandy and gunpowder should be laid in first.

It was a merry time, a respite from worry and guilt. Darcy realised rather smugly that after three days without encountering any of the town's denizens, he had been correct in assuming a visit to Bingley would bring no chance of meeting an eligible bride. Mayhap things would be different in a fortnight when he journeyed to Hadley's estate. The man was beset by well over half a dozen female relations and their friends.

Still, the company at Netherfield had grown rather stifling.

"I believe we could garner a better sense of the wood here and the reason that certain buildings are so oddly situated," Darcy said at breakfast, "if we were to speak to your neighbours. Whose estate lies closest to Netherfield's eastern edge?"

Bingley looked up and beamed. "Well, that would be Longbourn. That is a fine idea, Darcy. I suggest we go right away." He paused and looked significantly at his friend. "That is, if you are up to company."

Darcy bit back the glower he felt slipping across his features. He felt…well…coddled by his younger friend whenever they were indoors. Did Charles actually think he was in such deep mourning for Anne? He was sad about her passing, grateful for her relief, and annoyed at and confused by her mother, but that was all. If he had learned anything from these years without his parents, it was how to mourn, when to mourn, and how not to let mourning rule one's emotions.

He cleared his throat, which compelled Bingley to look even more concerned. "Charles, my mourning has passed. Let us go and meet your neighbours."

Miss Bingley, entering the dining room, drew in a breath. "Are you off to Meryton?" she asked in a falsely gay voice. "I should wonder whom you would meet there."

The men, who had stood upon her entry, moved towards the doorway. "We are off to Longbourn, Caroline. Estate business." Bingley's chest puffed up ever so slightly.

"Charles, are you sure that is wise? Perhaps Mr Darcy does not wish to mix with the people there." She enunciated in a hushed voice, "It is a delicate time."

Bingley cleared his throat. "Darcy will enjoy meeting the Bennets, Caroline. All of them."

As they withdrew, Darcy noticed the vexed expression on Miss Bingley's face. Rather perversely, it made him anticipate their visit to Longbourn all the more. *Hic sunt dracones.* He stifled a chuckle.

As they mounted their horses, Bingley said, "My sisters are invited to Longbourn for tea tomorrow; otherwise, I am sure they would have joined us."

"So they are friendly with the…Bennets, is it?"

Bingley sighed. "Caroline and Louisa lack patience for the slower rhythms of the country and seem to despise the genteel manner of the people here. The Bennets are a good family. Mr Bennet is a gentleman."

"Is it Mrs Bennet who troubles them?"

"Um, yes. A bit," Bingley admitted. "She is proud of the society here, and although a bit fulsome on the subject, she has a kind heart and sets a fine table."

Darcy laughed. Some things never varied with Charles.

"And their daughters are fine girls, especially the two eldest."

Ah, we get to the heart of the matter. "No sons?"

"No, but soon a son-in-law. Mrs Bennet has mentioned an understanding with a gentleman. A cousin or some such relative."

"I see. This understanding is not with the Bennet sister you fancy?"

"No, thank goodness," Bingley replied dreamily before suddenly wheeling around to glare at his friend. "Ho there! I have said nothing of fancying a young lady."

"But you do."

"I do, I believe I do," Bingley agreed. "But how did you know?"

"Charles, do you not recall your algebraic equations?" Darcy said wryly. "Caroline's vexation multiplied by your eagerness to dispel her reasons for vexation, added to your lovesick expression, divided by the quantity of food you left on your breakfast plate in order to ride more quickly to Longbourn…it all adds up."

Bingley's horse slowed as his rider considered the steps in Darcy's calculation. "Um…"

"Come on, man. Let us ride." Darcy tapped his friend's mount and both horses sped off at a canter. Neither noticed the slight figure looking down at them from atop Oakham Mount.

When Elizabeth walked into her home a few minutes later, she was discomposed to find two gentlemen in the doorway. Mr Bingley stood near Jane, both of them blushing and averting their eyes. The other man was taller and darker and bore a look of studied indifference as he suffered one of her mother's heartfelt monologues on loss and lace and the glories of Meryton society. Kitty and Lydia stood on the stairs, smirking. When he noticed Elizabeth's entrance, the man appeared shocked and peered at her closely.

Am I such a fearsome creature? Do I have mud on my face and leaves in my hair?

"Lizzy! Off on a walk again? We have visitors." Mrs Bennet gave her daughter a peevish look.

"Yes, Mama. The clouds were especially glorious today."

Her mother sighed. "But if you are always looking up, you cannot heed the mud!"

Elizabeth glanced down self-consciously at her feet. *Oh, indeed. Mud on my nose, mud on my boots...banishment must be next.*

Jane spoke up. "Lizzy, this is Mr Bingley's friend, Mr Darcy. Mr Darcy, this is my sister Elizabeth."

The two strangers nodded to each other. *The Grieving Groom.* Noting his eyes still fixed on her, Elizabeth blushed and spoke first. "And how do you find Netherfield, sir? Does it measure up to the excellent reputation Mr Bingley has proclaimed?" She cringed a bit at the brightness of her tone. He *was* grieving after all.

"Of course it does," Mr Bingley protested.

"It does, indeed," Mr Darcy replied in a solemn voice.

Mr Bingley smiled and nodded vigorously. "Perfect in every way."

Mr Darcy eyed his enthusiastic friend. "It is quite a suitable house albeit the library is in great need of refurbishing. The shelves groan for want of books."

Elizabeth nodded knowingly. "Oh, that phenomenon may be blamed on the previous owner. Mr Eggleston was known for his parsimony, and when the winter of aught-seven blew fiercely for so long, it is said he burned his books for warmth."

"Surely, you jest, Miss Elizabeth!" Mr Bingley glanced uneasily at his friend.

She frowned at Mr Darcy's look of mortification. "I am sorry to bear such news, sir, but the words of Milton and Cowper, Homer and Shakespeare are said to be in the ashes that fertilised the fields that spring."

Mr Darcy's eyes moved away from hers and settled on some point behind her shoulder. He nodded slowly. "A fine yield come harvest time, was it?"

Mr Bingley stared at his friend, aghast at his response.

"Indeed it was, Mr Darcy. The turnips and potatoes became vegetables of legend. Some were said to be as large as a man's head." She gazed at Mr Darcy's amused expression and tried not to show her own mirth. She could hear Lydia behind her, whispering to Kitty. "Lizzy has made a joke about a man's head!"

"Lizzy!" Mrs Bennet cried. "Mr Darcy did not come to Longbourn to be teased. Go change your boots."

"Yes, Mama." Elizabeth nodded to the two men. "Are you waiting for my father? I had best knock to gain his attention." She walked a few steps to the library and rapped thrice quickly on the oak door, followed by two slower knocks. They could hear a voice behind the door offering them entry and then the door swung open.

"Mr Bingley," drawled Mr Bennet. "And who is this tall, sombre fellow?" He adjusted his glasses and looked up at the man in black.

"My friend Darcy has accompanied me to enquire of some estate issues. Have you a few minutes to indulge our questions?"

As the two men turned to follow Mr Bennet into his library, Mr Collins emerged from the kitchen, a dusting of sugar on his collar. "Cousin Jane, did I hear visitors?"

Jane blushed. "Yes, Mr Collins. Mr Bingley and his friend Mr Darcy are here to see my father."

The cleric's eyes widened, and he took a hurried step towards the retreating backs of the two men. Elizabeth grimaced and bent to remove her boots.

"Mr Darcy?" he cried. "I do most humbly say I am sorry for your great loss and wish to aid you in your bereavement."

Mr Darcy stared at the man, a rare combination of height and girth that nearly outstripped his own impressive physique. *Nearly.*

"Have we been introduced?" he asked coldly.

"My good sir, may I introduce myself—"

Jane interrupted. "Mr Darcy, this is our cousin Mr Collins, lately from Hunsford in Kent. Mr Collins, I believe you have met Mr Bingley of Netherfield Hall. This is his guest, Mr Darcy."

Mr Collins leaned closer and looked expressively at the master of Pemberley. "I saw your aunt, my benefactress, Lady Catherine de Bourgh, but a fortnight ago and shared my distress over her loss of the most estimable Miss de Bourgh. A more exceptional and accomplished young maiden has rarely been found on England's shores."

An ominous silence hung over the room as Mr Darcy stared at the man before him. Mr Collins placed his hand on his chest. "Mr Darcy, I share your remorse and your grief for your cousin and be—"

"I thank you," Mr Darcy replied, turning away.

"If you would care to unburden yourself of your sorrow and require a companion in prayer and solace, I would be happy to—"

Mr Darcy's attempt to hide his practised glower was less successful this time. "I thank you, no."

Elizabeth wondered at the quicksilver artist who went by the name Mr Darcy. From sly humour to cold dismissal. Had she provided the man with some diversion from his sorrow only to have him reminded quickly of his loss by her clumsy cousin? This, she determined, required deeper contemplation, as did the reason for his startled look at her entrance and at the mention of the exceptional and estimable Miss de Bourgh. Her father was right: a mystery had not only arrived on their doorstep, he had crossed the threshold and walked into their home.

On the ride back to Netherfield, the two men reviewed their conversation with Mr Bennet. By mutual agreement, they parted ways when they entered the house through the servants' entrance. Bingley hoped to elude Caroline and pay a quiet visit to the kitchen for a biscuit or a scrap of bacon. Darcy had other considerations and strode towards the library. He needed to look again at those empty shelves, ransacked for warmth by a desperate—nay, stupid—man. What a tale recounted by Miss Elizabeth Bennet! It was tragic and unfortunate, but he was happy to know the story, especially in the drily humorous manner in which she told it.

The Bennet family should not have taken up a second thought, not with that jabbering mother and those spoony younger sisters, yet he could not stop thinking on his brief interaction with Miss

Elizabeth. Perhaps he had been trapped, suffocating, for far too long in the conversational quagmires of Miss Bingley and her ilk, where faded tapestries, family portraits, and feathered bonnets formed the background for meeting social obligations and solving the world's great evils.

This was different. It had proved a brief but refreshing change from Netherfield and its practised conversations, social scheming, and gratuitous character disparagement. Longbourn was in need of attention, its grounds neglected, its rugs a bit faded. But he had been impressed by the book titles lining the walls and stacked on the floor in Mr Bennet's library. And he had not missed the sight of the ivory chessboard on the table by the window.

The man was a little too droll about his neighbours and dispassionate about his estate, but he had a mind for the elegantly written word. Although without a son, he had said that he often shared his library with his daughter, the same one who would likely beat him in chess that very afternoon. The same one, Darcy suspected, whom he had seen playing with those boys in the town square and who missed the family breakfast in order to walk out when the dew was fresh.

The cost of returning home in muddy boots was minor indeed when a walk brought such a blush to her cheeks and a lilt to her laugh. Her actions did not merit censure from her mother. She was intelligent, interesting, and clever. It was little wonder that she was the soon-to-be-betrothed Bennet sister. The giggly ones were too young to be out, and obviously, the eldest Miss Bennet had captivated Bingley. Miss Elizabeth must indeed be the sister who had an understanding with a gentleman. *That* gentleman, a man nearly twice her age.

Her liveliness was a rare thing. Those young boys to whom she would be mother would enjoy her spirit. Darcy pondered whether their father believed in a well-stocked library. Then he recalled himself and wondered why, in his busy life with so many demands on his time, he was standing in the middle of Bingley's woebegone library and thinking on a near stranger's understanding with a gentleman of no acquaintance. He turned around and walked to his bedroom in search of his boxes of books.

CHAPTER FOUR

The sisters worked quietly in the still room, sorting flowers, separating the blooms from their stems, and crushing their petals. Elizabeth stole glances at Jane, who appeared to be glowing with happiness.

Elizabeth was perplexed by Mr Darcy's unexpected good humour. It was quite odd. While he carried an air of melancholy, she had seen no signs of grief, no dark smudges of sleeplessness under his eyes. He was quite handsome, she acknowledged, his appearance solemn but not ravaged by pain. Although his betrothed had been sickly—according to Mr Collins, their perhaps not wholly accurate source—she also was accomplished, remarkable, estimable, and beautiful. Perchance it had been an engagement of true love, but it was more likely one of family obligation, convenience, or tied to some entail or pecuniary agreement. Yet, judging from his manner, it seemed there had been no abiding love and he was free and happy. It was a puzzle.

"Lizzy? Did you hear me?"

Elizabeth looked up from her pile of crushed rose petals.

"Lizzy, those petals are near powder. I believe our work is finished."

Elizabeth gathered the pulverised blooms and poured them into a jar as Jane watched quietly. "I do not think I am the only sister busy wool-gathering. Is your mind still in the clouds you enjoyed this morning?"

Elizabeth smiled. "Nearly so. I was thinking on our visitors. Your Mr Bingley was reluctant to leave. Longbourn has some allurements that Netherfield does not?"

"You mean books, Lizzy?" Jane said, blushing. "He is not *my* Mr Bingley…"

"And books are not what lured him here for a visit." Elizabeth dusted off the table and walked to the door. "Jane, he takes great pleasure in your company. Do you enjoy his as well?"

"I believe you know the answer to that, Sister. He is all a young gentleman should be. I hope my father's advice will help him see the promise of Netherfield."

"Agreed. His friend seems inclined to offer sage counsel as well."

Jane nodded "Yes, he does. Mr Darcy seems an intelligent gentleman and a kind friend to have thrown over his mourning to aid Mr Bingley."

They went out into the bright sunlight, and Elizabeth shook her head. "I did not detect any signs of grief. He appeared put out by our cousin's comments."

At her sister's silent, reproving look, she continued. "Jane, Mr Collins annoys most people, and his words were rather impolite." *In fact, he is a positively pompous panjandrum.* Elizabeth bit her lip before she could laugh aloud.

"They were indeed ill-timed. Do you believe Mr Darcy might be of service to Mr Bingley?"

Stealing a glance at her older sister, Elizabeth smiled and slipped her arm through Jane's. "I believe Mr Bingley will be eager for advice from both his friend and my father. His friend is close by, but I believe all the enticement is at Longbourn."

Jane blushed again, and in a soft voice, she said, "He is coming here in two days to walk the gardens and see what blooms we have that he might grow at Netherfield."

"Ah. You know, Jane, flowers must put down roots."

Church service revealed Mr Darcy as a sturdy tenor and a steadying influence on his friend's attentions to both the sermon and his handling of prayer books. Elizabeth noted Mr Darcy's focus on Rev. Miller's words and Miss Bingley's focus on him. The lady's behaviour puzzled her. Miss Bingley had known Mr Darcy for a number of years and was aware of his engagement and his heartbreak, yet she spoke almost caustically of the arrangement and quite carelessly of Miss de Bourgh's death. Had there been bad blood between the two women, or was Miss Bingley simply seizing a new opportunity to win the prize she so obviously wanted? There were so many layers to peel away from the enigma who had arrived at Netherfield.

Darcy, while not listening to a sermon he found rather too influenced by Fordyce, added a few more lines and shading to the mental portrait he had been sketching of the Bennet household. He noted that their party included the two little boys he had seen earlier with Miss Elizabeth, as well as a sister he had not met at Longbourn. A plain, narrow-nosed girl, she kept her head bowed to her prayer book and sang with a great enthusiasm that reduced one spoony sister to less than saintly eye-rolling. The other kept stealing furtive glances towards Miss Bingley. They were a decidedly ill-behaved, odd pair of girls.

Further, he saw that Mr Bennet was not in attendance nor was the boys' father. *Miss Elizabeth's betrothed.* Idly, it occurred to him that he needed to ask Bingley about the man. *Why is such a lively young lady to marry a man nearly twice her age? Is he a local or a Londoner? Is it possible she—?*

No! None of this was his concern, and he bit back his curiosity.

Mayhap, it could arise more naturally in conversation.

The lady's gown was a lovely shade of blue, rather like the colour of this morning's nearly cloudless sky. The collar of her yellow spencer created a palette for the dark locks of hair peeking through her matching bonnet. In spite of the dullness of the service, her eyes shone brightly, as though amused by the grave piety of the parson's words. Darcy wondered whether her boots were freshly muddied. It took the loud smack of a prayer book hitting the floor behind him to bring him to his senses and pull his eyes away from the young lady. When Miss Elizabeth was not leaning over to listen to the concerns and complaints of one boy or the other, the object of his attention kept her eyes straight ahead. Observant though he was, Darcy failed to note how her neck blushed under his notice.

When the service ended, Mr Collins moved to speak with Rev. Miller on his interpretation of Corinthians. The Netherfield party waited outside for the ladies of Longbourn and their two young charges. The boys tumbled down the stairs with Miss Catherine, ready to race ahead until Mrs Bennet and Miss Mary each seized a hand. The older woman bent over and said something to the youngsters, who squealed in delight. Miss Catherine called over, "Lizzy! We are taking Thomas and Henry to Aunt Philips's house to say their goodbyes."

"Thank you, Kitty. Boys, mind your manners, please."

"Yes, Lizzy!" they cried in unison, spinning in circles and nearly toppling Mr Collins as he approached the group.

"The sky is most beautiful today, is it not?" Bingley said cheerfully.

"Cerulean, I believe," Darcy agreed. "And nary a cloud."

Miss Elizabeth smiled. "All the better for keeping my eyes to the ground."

Miss Bingley peered at her. "One should observe one's environs, Eliza, and take in nature's beauty."

"And its dangers," Hurst added drolly. "One never knows when there might be a snake in the grass."

Miss Lydia snorted, diverting Bingley from his perusal of the sky. He offered his arm to Miss Bennet, and together they led the group towards their respective homes. Darcy cringed as Miss Bingley seized his reluctant arm and began tugging him to follow her brother.

With Miss Lydia's unwilling arm already captured by Mr Collins, Darcy offered his spare arm to Miss Elizabeth. She smiled and accepted.

He sought to take advantage of the opportunity to converse and sate his curiosity. "Those are lively young men who escorted you today, Miss Elizabeth. But they were quite well-mannered in church."

"Yes, they are wonderful boys. They are excited that their father returns tomorrow."

Darcy's smile slipped. "You must be happy as well."

"Relieved, I would say."

"'The just man walketh in his integrity; his children are blessed after him,'" Mr Collins intoned.

Miss Lydia scowled. If one strained one's ears, she could be heard muttering, "Beetle-headed vicar."

"'Tis true. Children should be seen and not heard," Miss Bingley said. "Louisa and I were terribly accomplished at sitting still and listening to our elders. Charles was indulged by my mother and aunts."

"It was those curls, Caroline," Mrs Hurst replied. "My mother loved his curls."

Darcy saw Miss Elizabeth glance at the sisters' wisps of dull brown hair escaping their Sunday bonnets then turn to espy Mr Bingley's dark blond curls peeking out from under his hat. When she looked up at Darcy, her eyes sparkled in shared amusement of the picture the sisters painted of a beloved but envied younger brother.

"Mr Darcy, have you been reading the volumes left you in Mr Eggleston's library?" she asked.

"Not those left behind, no, Miss Elizabeth. I unpacked a box of my own books. In honour of those lost to the flames, I am re-reading Milton."

"Paradise Lost?"

"Of course."

She smiled. "Will these volumes find a permanent home in Netherfield's library?"

He returned her smile and replied in a solemn voice. "And chance a cold night and another man desperate for warmth? I think not."

"Mr Darcy, my brother would never burn your books!" Miss Bingley cried. "Eliza, you must not be so impertinent. Mr Darcy has a library to be envied at Pemberley, with hundreds, mayhap thousands, of books housed floor to ceiling."

"Oh, that is to be envied and admired," Miss Elizabeth replied. "When I have a house of my own, I shall be miserable if I have not an excellent library."

"'A room without books is like a body without a soul,'" Darcy said.

"Yes, Cicero had it right," she responded brightly. Darcy stared at her and nearly guided Miss Bingley on his other side into an overgrown buckthorn bush. "Some say that eyes are the window to one's soul," Miss Elizabeth concluded, "but I suspect that books provide another view in."

"Cousin Elizabeth!" Mr Collins looked affronted. "Mr Darcy, please forgive my cousin. She has forgotten Matthew 16:26. 'For what is a man profited, if he shall gain the whole world, and lose his own soul?'"

Darcy rolled his eyes. "Mr Collins, I believe that Miss Elizabeth meant it as a metaphor."

Miss Lydia snorted. "Perhaps it went over his head."

"Nothing flies over my head," Mr Collins said indignantly. "I have a butterfly net."

Thus, at a metaphorical impasse, the two groups parted ways.

Darcy sighed as he gazed on the large packet of letters delivered the following morning. *Enjoy your angel, Charles. The dullness of duty ties me here.* During the course of the long hours, he was distracted only a few times by wondering what topics might be canvassed during his friend's visit at Longbourn.

Should he have sent over that book he had discussed with Miss Elizabeth? No. It was not proper behaviour in London to forge such a friendship with a lady, most particularly one promised to another. Nor was her open friendliness to him quite right. Yes, they shared a fondness for books and the morning air, but her openness was not...done. It was neither correct nor suitable. He should maintain some distance, should he not? Though perhaps he was safe as she was betrothed and he posed no threat. Or did she eye him as a better choice? No, he would not believe that of her. She was simply a friendly sort of person: open and happy and so...fascinating.

Good lord, she knows Cicero.

Damn it! His head hurt. *Stop thinking on it. On her. Your business is not here. This is nothing but an interlude in the country, a brief time away from responsibility.*

A knock on the door and the delivery of an express from his cousin rescued him from his musings. He was summoned to London.

Darcy was strangely reluctant to leave Netherfield, but the express was not one he could disregard. In spite of the sympathy he felt towards his aunt, honouring her commands remained rooted in duty and obligation rather than love. The intent of the gathering laid bare similar feelings among his cousins and uncle.

With her immediate shock diminished and her grief set aside, Lady Catherine convened a family council *not* to reveal further details of her daughter's death or her burial but to have Anne's will read and the funds dispensed. The fact that all funds would be dispensed to *her* was obvious, as Anne had had no close friends and would have inherited Rosings in ten days when she turned nine and twenty. Lady Catherine said she wanted to take care of the papers before facing that dreadful day.

Her brother, Peter, and the three nephews in attendance had seen no reason to fight her wishes, though Darcy had quietly sent a letter to Rosings's steward asking for more details on the condition of the estate amid the current situation. He was *that* dutiful, he reminded himself. Or at least he was more properly dutiful than his rather annoying cousin, who joined him at Darcy House after the meeting.

"So how goes your tour?" Richard grinned slyly. "I do salute your efforts, Cousin." He waved a glass of brandy in his beefy hand.

"My tour?"

"Your wedding tour—your search for the future Mrs Darcy. That *is* the idea behind this parade of book boxes and pressed linen waistcoats you are leading from estate to estate, is it not? You have deserted town in search of a real girl."

Darcy stared across the room at his all-knowing older cousin. For a man of few handsome features and little inheritance, his cousin's familiarity with society was impressive, and he was a clever observer of Darcy's romantic entanglements and social life. More than once, Richard had saved the younger man from an eager seductress; Darcy still insisted that because the first instance occurred when he was but seventeen, it was no compromise but instead an opportunity. And it had been his *first* opportunity. His bitter protests had had no effect even these ten years later. And although far from an innocent now, Darcy still wished to know what exactly it was that the Thompson girl had whispered she could do with her tongue.

"Town is full of pretty girls with pretty ideas," Darcy finally replied. "I wish for something different." He poured himself a tumbler of brandy and refilled his cousin's empty glass before sinking into a chair.

"Is this about Anne? It seems a bit rash."

"Her death has affected me, yes, though not as severely as it might have in years past when we were close friends; rather, it has made me recognise the brevity of life, of the precious time we have here bearing this mortal coil."

Richard stared at him, his moustache twitching. "Have you been reading those bloody romance novels my mother hides between the cushions?"

Darcy rolled his eyes. "Marriage should be more than a duty,

Richard. If I am to take a wife back to Pemberley and spend months only in her company and Georgiana's, would it not be best if we were friends with interests in common? If we talked of more than who was seen with whom at Almack's, which family was not invited to which dinner, and whose hat featured the finest feathers?"

His cousin cleared his throat. "I believe you are mocking my mother."

"No, I believe you did that earlier when you disparaged her choice in reading."

Richard drained his glass, sat up, and leaned towards Darcy. "So...you have planned visits to three estates. Have you had any luck at Bingley's place...uh, Featherfield?"

"Netherfield...and not luck, no. But I have found it to be an interesting spot."

"I knew you would come to your senses and steal that bedizened Bingley woman away from me!" Richard slapped his knee. "Has she been mending your pens?" He fluttered his eyelashes and rocked with laughter.

Darcy grimaced and glanced at the nearly empty carafe of brandy. "Just how long were you in here before I arrived?"

"Long enough."

"Where is your brother? I thought Robert would join us."

Richard's cheeks coloured. "Today is Thursday. He must be home for dinner with his wife."

"They have an engagement?"

"So to speak. Not that he speaks of it." Richard found a thread on his waistcoat of great interest.

"I fail to understand. He has to be home because it is Thursday?"

"Yes, young man." Richard sighed. "He and Harriet have a standing engagement on Thursday. At home. Alone."

"But you just said..." Realisation dawned, and Darcy's cheeks reddened as well. "They arrange their...?"

Richard nodded, a bemused expression on his plain face. "Is that not true of every couple wedded more than half a year who has not yet produced their heir?"

"I…this is common practice? Arranging relations with one's wife?" Darcy sat back in his chair and nursed his brandy, shock warring with sadness. *Once a week? On a set date? The passion already gone?*

Richard stared at the horrified look on his cousin's usually impassive countenance. "Darcy, can you name which day of the week you were born?"

"Um, I believe it was a Friday," he said after a moment's thought. "Yes, a Friday."

"Most mothers and fathers also could tell you the day you were conceived." Richard smiled grimly at Darcy's expression. "Truly, this is news to you?" He shook his head. "You have stayed out of society for too long."

Oh no, I have come back too soon. Darcy sighed. "There are things I wish I did not know of society—or of my friends' lives."

Richard raised his empty glass. "Some things need to be known. How many times have I saved you from the intentions of a scheming mother or maiden?"

Darcy silenced him with a dark glare. "And to think I was worried that I could cause insult to Anne's memory or to Lady Catherine by venturing out on this—"

"Quest for love?" Richard roared with laughter. "You are a knight in search of the Holy Grail! True love, not to mention two eyes, two hands, two breasts…"

Darcy scowled. "You are a strange and lonely man, Richard." He took a sip of his brandy. "I no longer think my actions offensive for their speed or their intent. I am firmer in my conviction that only a love match is worthy of making a marriage." He laughed bitterly. "And in spite of this, I like your brother, and I like his wife."

"He liked her once as well. The way he was eyeing her earlier, I think he might like her twice tonight."

"Shut it, Richard."

"He needs an heir." Richard's eyes twinkled. "And practice makes perfect."

CHAPTER FIVE

The Bennet sisters waved until the carriage pulled out of sight.

"It was grand to meet your uncle and cousins," Mr Bingley said.

Mary disappeared into the house while he and the four remaining Bennet sisters walked towards the garden.

"Longbourn will be far quieter and our kitchen supplied more fully now that the boys have gone home," Jane said, smiling.

It may be quieter, but Longbourn will not be peaceful until Mr Collins leaves as well, Elizabeth thought. A glance at Lydia proved they were of like mind.

Jane continued, "My sisters and I are fond of Henry and Thomas, and we rarely have the opportunity to enjoy their company without their sister."

"Mrs Gardiner has been hosting the ladies of her family?" Mr Bingley enquired.

"My uncle and cousins return to a houseful of ladies, babies, and wedding purchases," Elizabeth averred. "I had hoped Thomas would exchange families with Kitty; she is a great lover of babies and enjoys long discussions of lace and romance novels." Kitty's protests went unheard as her older sister squeezed her hand. "But the poor boy wanted his mama."

Lydia laughed and ran ahead into the house.

"Smart lad," Mr Bingley agreed. "As an only son, I endured many a tea room conversation centred on lace, bonnets, and proper baby rearing."

"Oh, Miss Bingley must know everything about bonnets," Kitty asserted. "She is so very fashionable."

He gave her a stiff, confused smile. "Yes, well, to Caroline, babies are another matter."

"I do not like babies and romance novels," Kitty mumbled. "The first is always sticky and the other always so sweet."

"You are wise to discern the difference, Sister," Elizabeth soothed.

"Kitty, would you be so kind as to investigate whether Thomas or Henry left anything behind in the house?" Jane asked. "I worry a piece of sticky candy or a wooden horse might surprise us."

"Oh! Lydia or Mr Collins may be already searching!" Kitty cried and hurried through the doorway.

The trio watched her and then turned on a path away from Longbourn and its gardens. They walked in silence for a few minutes. Jane and Mr Bingley navigated while exchanging smiles, and Elizabeth lagged behind, finding fascinating bits of nature to ponder. *Miss Bingley would be proud of my observant eye. I shall tell Kitty, so she might sing my praises to her heroine.*

"I hope you do not mind our slow pace, Miss Elizabeth," Mr Bingley said, "or that we leave you no escort. I had hoped Darcy would have returned by now. His business in London is taking longer than I had anticipated."

"Quite serious business, Mr Bingley?" Elizabeth smiled. "It has been but two days."

"Is that all?" he replied with some surprise. "Well, yes, it is serious. I believe he had to meet with his aunt and her solicitors about his cousin's will."

The Bennet sisters grimaced at this reminder of Mr Darcy's loss.

"Of course, he also will spend time with his sister."

"Oh, how wonderful for him," Jane said.

"Yes," Mr Bingley agreed. "He misses her greatly, and as her guardian, he worries much about her welfare."

Guardian to his sister? The mystery deepens. Elizabeth had spent too much time thinking about Mr Darcy and his many complexities. Much as she loved the families of Meryton, they held no mystery. *One new face with a life and history so removed from my own, and my curiosity is piqued.* One new *handsome* face, she admitted a little reluctantly.

Noticing that Mr Bingley and Jane had moved ahead on the path, Elizabeth hurried to follow. Her sister would not mind her lingering; Jane was also curious about the dramas of Mr Bingley's mysterious friend.

"His mood will lighten even more upon seeing her. He has raised Georgiana by himself for these past five years, and a fine job he has done. She is a lovely girl." Mr Bingley glanced at Jane and hurriedly added, "Close to Miss Catherine's age, I believe. She has been spending time with an aunt as consolation for her recent disappointment. She was fond of Miss de Bourgh."

"A great loss for her as well," Jane opined. "Miss de Bourgh must have been a lovely person."

Mr Bingley paused as though unable to render an opinion on a lady he had never met. A lonely bloom on a neglected rose bush caught his attention, and he leaned over to snap off the flower. He handed it to Jane and smiled. "I have been pleased to see Darcy enjoy himself here. He always has been a serious fellow and not one to spare a grin when a grimace will do. Of course, that might be because my sisters are around so often."

Elizabeth bit back a smile, but Jane held to her manners and overlooked his lapse. "Mr Darcy cared deeply for his cousin."

"Well, yes, he did. Duty and all," Mr Bingley agreed. "But I believe he feels relief in some sense."

Relief? Elizabeth was puzzled. *That she is dead? His betrothed?*

"Miss de Bourgh had been sickly ever since childhood," Mr

Bingley continued. "I suppose her death was less a shock than an event for which he was prepared."

"So, sadness and looming tragedy haunted the two of them?" Elizabeth asked.

Mr Bingley looked a bit startled, as though he had forgotten Elizabeth's presence. "Er, yes, I suppose that is true. He once made mention of a family curse, what with losing his mother when he was but a boy and his father not five years ago. But he is as light in spirit as I have ever seen him—a bit of a surprise since he is in mourning."

"I am pleased he seems to be finding so much here to please him, Mr Bingley," Jane said.

"Not near as much as I, Miss Bennet," Mr Bingley replied, his eyes earnest upon hers.

His mother died when he was a boy, then his father, and now his betrothed? It is heartbreaking. I might agree—a family curse, indeed. Elizabeth slowed her step and left the aspiring lovers to their own joys as she wondered further on Mr Darcy. What did she know of him? He had revealed little of himself besides a love of books and pride in his estate. He had a fine seat on a horse and many family responsibilities, he sang well, he had a younger sister but had lost his parents, and he owned a library she could only imagine and envy from afar. Truly, why should she know any more of a man that she had met on merely two or three occasions? It was not her place to question him about such a delicate thing as the death of a lady to whom he was betrothed.

Even Mr Collins, who liked to speak at length and with inflated proficiency on nearly every subject, had shed little light on the matter. The glories of Rosings and the wonders of its windows and chimneys were topics on which he could expound for hour upon hour. And he did, which irked even her Aunt Philips. Elizabeth feared his attentions soon would land on her or one of her sisters, and his much vaunted olive branch would turn into a weapon. She doubted both his fencing skill and his ability to please a woman. *Or anyone.*

When the trio returned to the house, they found Lydia and

Kitty sitting on the bench. Kitty looked glum, but Lydia had a gleam in her eye.

Elizabeth spoke first. "Any wooden horses or stockings left behind, Kitty?"

"Not a one, Lizzy." She sighed dramatically.

"La, it will be so dull now that the boys are gone," Lydia trilled, shooting a sly glance at Mr Bingley. "What are we to do?"

The object of her gaze met her eyes and smiled. "Miss Lydia, what say you? Would a ball be a pleasant diversion?"

"A ball, Charles! Here? With these people?" Caroline gripped her well-worn issue of *La Belle Assemblée* and glared at her brother. "What are you thinking?"

"He is not thinking, Sister," said Louisa.

"Oh, he is thinking," her husband interjected. "He is thinking of his happiness and the happiness of some pretty young ladies, and of us, of course. We have dire need to fill these long, dull hours."

"That is hardly true, Mr Hurst," his wife sniffed.

"No? These past two days without dear old Darcy have been interminable."

The portly man rose slowly from the chair and strolled to the looking glass. He peered at himself then turned to his family. "No one with a taste for billiards. No one with the quiet talent for fishing or shooting." Charles eyed him, an affronted expression dawning on his face. "No one to flirt with or tease…or to mend pens for. A ball is a happy thing. It requires shopping, does it not?"

"Here? In Meryton?"

"Yes, Caroline, in Meryton." Bingley grimaced.

"A ball?" said a deep voice. Its owner stepped into the room, brushing dust off his coat.

"Mr Darcy! Thank goodness you are back." Miss Bingley rose abruptly from the settee and strode to his side. As was her habit, she clutched his arm, and her voice took on a peculiarly wheedling tone. "Please talk some sense into my brother."

Her captured prey took a deep breath and scolded himself for not sending a footman ahead to scout the territory for unwanted prowlers. "Miss Bingley, this is one of Hertfordshire's largest estates. A gentleman is expected to host events at his home, and Charles is doing his duty by his neighbours."

"But you are in mourning, sir."

"No longer," Darcy replied, extricating himself from his eager shadow and strolling over to the window. He was pleased by Bingley's news of the ball. He would soon be leaving Netherfield for his visit to the Hadleys, then it was off to Marlbourn to see the duke and duchess. Both houses would overflow with suitable young ladies. Cecilia Hadley would have a house full of sisters and friends, all of them eligible and eager to make his acquaintance. And he knew that the duchess had invited her three younger sisters and a number of her unmarried friends, and she had been disappointed when he had written that Georgiana would not accompany him. Travelling with his younger sister on his search for a wife seemed a terrible idea, and her experience with Pemberley's errant footman made firm his decision to keep her with family.

He knew he should be looking to his prospects in the weeks ahead, but at the moment, he was wondering about the proper way to ask an engaged young lady unrelated to him to dance a set. Would her betrothed be there? Did he, a stranger to the man, need his permission? And worst of all, why did a dance with Miss Elizabeth mean so much? It had never *once* mattered to him to dance with a particular lady, and certainly not one from the country who was promised to another man. He had met her but two or three times and conversed for mere minutes. *Why does it matter?*

Thinking on the significance of his impulse made his head hurt and reminded Darcy of other duties he should perform, such as reading letters that had arrived in his absence. He was due to play chess with Mr Bennet in the coming days; perhaps he should look at Netherfield's board and plan his tactics.

Tactics—that was it! Yes, he was decided. He would dance with her, say good-night, and journey on his…his 'quest for love.' Damn Richard. He hated when his cousin had it right. *He knows me far too well.*

When Darcy and Bingley set out to inspect the estate the next morning, only one stated his intention to visit the Bennet home. The other smiled indulgently, his eagerness hidden deeply under layers of denial. After an hour's perusal of fence posts and tree lines, it appeared their impending call at Longbourn beckoned more interest than did poor drainage and dangling limbs.

"I admire Miss Bennet, Darcy. She is so kind, so lovely."

"Like an angel?"

"You know?"

"I believe I always do." Darcy glanced at the other man and waved his hand to dispel Bingley's protests. "You have admired many ladies since we became acquainted, my friend."

"She is different, Darcy." Bingley looked at him, a great depth of feeling emanating from his being.

"She is indeed a wonderful lady," Darcy replied gravely. "But she is here. Will you be staying on? You cannot excite her hopes and then hie off to London. How deep are your feelings?"

"I am courting her."

"Well, then…" Darcy stared ahead, the outline of Longbourn coming into view. "After a month in the country and mere weeks of acquaintance?"

"Yes." Bingley sighed quietly then spoke in a firm voice. "Love is simple, Darcy, when it comes into your heart."

Darcy's eyes widened as his throat tightened. Together, they rode in silence towards Longbourn's gates.

Ten minutes later, they were strolling into the gardens in pairs. Darcy wished to give his friend some privacy with his angel, and he wished to learn more about Miss Elizabeth.

"Is the walking pace to your liking, Miss Elizabeth?"

"Yes, thank you, Mr Darcy."

"Good. As chaperons, we must keep pace with Bingley and

your sister, but it appears we both tend to a faster stride. Perhaps as admirers of nature and clouds, we can slow our steps to enjoy what beauty surrounds us?"

"Eh, yes." She turned away and gazed at the greenery in the distance.

He gestured with his hand at the cumulus clouds above their heads. "I recall your fondness for the skies. That is as white and happy a cloud as I have ever seen."

What did I just say? She thought him daft; he knew it. Here he was, spouting insensible soliloquies on puffy white masses, and she knew Cicero. She appeared…wary. *Bloody hell.*

She was evidently too intelligent to reply to his nonsense as she instead enquired, "Will you be staying much longer with Mr Bingley and his sisters?"

"Er, no. I'm off to visit friends soon in Warwickshire."

"I see. Your mourning period is over?"

"Two weeks is the accepted length of time for a cousin. It has been three." Darcy glanced at her and noted that her errant eyebrow was once again acting up. "You understand that Anne's death was not a shock to anyone save her mother? That she had suffered greatly for years from ailments no doctor had ever adequately treated?"

"Yes, Mr Darcy." Miss Elizabeth frowned. "Again, please accept my family's sympathies on your loss. I am sure you have had much thinking to do on your altered future as you dwell on your loss."

"I…um. Yes? I mean, yes." He frowned. *My altered future? Could we not talk of clouds?* He needed to redirect this conversation again.

"Miss Elizabeth, you too have some alterations ahead? You will not always be at Longbourn."

She smiled. "Yes. I should be gone within the month."

"Before the ball?"

"No, sir. A few days after."

So soon? "To where?"

"Why, to London."

"Oh. I should offer you my best wishes." *I should but I do not wish to.*

Darcy offered her a fleeting smile and looked at the ground. *A gentleman cannot ask a young lady about her engagement. I must speak to Bingley—if I can get him to notice anything besides his angel. Elsewise, this is the best confirmation I shall receive.*

Yet he could probe, could he not?

"London is where Thomas and Henry live? With their father who was visiting you?" He refrained from asking the more pertinent questions preying on his mind.

"Yes, I shall be happy to join the family and share in sensible conversation that does not centre on ribbons and dancing slippers. A houseful of sisters can be quite…trying at times. And I have been promised an excursion to Pidock's Menagerie. The boys tell of a man-eating tiger from India residing there. Have you seen it?"

Damn, the subject has turned again. She is determined to keep the conversation to less personal matters.

"No, I have not. My cousin Colonel Fitzwilliam has attended the exhibit. He tells the tale of a fierce cat with teeth the size of his sword, sleeping on its back atop a rock."

Miss Elizabeth laughed. "Oh no! Not as fearsome as promised."

"I believe my sister was disappointed as well by this disclosure. Still, we are to venture to Pidock's when I return to London."

"Do take care, Mr Darcy. I should hate to see your name splashed across the newspapers from an unfortunate encounter with a large orange cat."

Darcy, struck by the image of a fearsome Caroline Bingley, began laughing. The lady beside him stared at the sight.

"Pardon me, Miss Elizabeth," he finally managed to say. "I promise you will not see my death notice as a result of such an event."

A shadow crossed his face, and hers, from the reference.

"Mr Darcy, I am sorry to have made light of such a serious subject. I am so sorry about your betro—your cousin."

Blast! I want to talk of books, music, anything but Anne.

"I too apologise for making light of such a thing," he replied quickly. "Truly, might we discuss Mr Eggleston and his bonfire of books? Have you read Defoe or Swift? What think you of Wordsworth?"

They continued on their walk, talking of books, poetry, and

news from abroad while keeping pace with Bingley and Miss Bennet for a good thirty minutes until Miss Bennet became winded and all throats were parched. They strolled to benches in the garden and sent a summons for lemonade. Miss Catherine accompanied the refreshments, and Darcy was prompted by Bingley to tell stories about Georgiana's delight in naming the horses, cows, dogs, cats, sheep, and even the mice at Pemberley.

"She seems a lovely girl," Miss Elizabeth said.

"She is, indeed," Darcy affirmed, fondly.

"What age is she?" Miss Bennet asked.

"She will be sixteen come March."

"As will Lydia, come June!" exclaimed Miss Catherine.

"Do you know the girl has even drawn lineage charts for their milk cows, horses, dogs, and cats?" Bingley said in amazement. "She has a head for numbers like her brother and draws a pretty line as well."

"As do I! I like to draw. Horses are the most difficult things to capture. Their heads are long and their bodies so oddly curved. They often resemble dogs in my drawings. Or cows."

Once again, when Darcy stifled a smile, he felt his eyes drift towards those of Miss Elizabeth. She too was biting her lip, but her eyes were glowing with laughter. *She is beautiful*, he suddenly realised. Her eyes held such warmth and intelligence. He enjoyed her company and conversation, and he would miss sharing it. It was fortunate he would be leaving soon and that she was promised to what he hoped was a good man; otherwise, he might be in danger of feeling too much affection for a country girl without title or connexions. He already thought about her more than was wise. He pulled his eyes away and drew inward. It would not do to allow the lady to think he paid her too much notice. He was trying to find a bride, not confuse young ladies or entangle those promised elsewhere. He spoke scarcely ten words more to her that day.

That night, Elizabeth found sleep elusive, her mind full of Mr Darcy.

His eyes on her during their walk had been a familiar sensation, and she had hoped to puzzle him out. But as they strolled on the grassy lane under the warm sun with a soft breeze blowing, she found herself enjoying whatever direction their conversation led. Now, tucked in her bed, so many impressions demanded her attention.

He was a handsome man, he was Mr Bingley's friend, and he treasured books. It pained her to realise that it made her want to think the best of him. She enjoyed his company far better than she should. It bothered her to find herself thinking so often about this man who came to Hertfordshire to forget his dead bride-to-be and soon would journey on to richer company at finer, larger estates. She had amused him at a time when he needed to be amused. She would know him briefly, and then he would leave and she would never see him again. In only a handful of meetings, they had talked of books and music, of history and nature. She had never had such conversations with a gentleman who was not her uncle or father. She had never had such conversations with a woman either.

In these few meetings, she had forged many different portraits of him. She still wondered at Miss Bingley's uncharitable comments and remained confused over this serious man's lack of profound grief or open mourning. She did not know the intimate particulars of his relationship with Miss de Bourgh but admitted she would carry her mourning quite lightly if she had suffered the loss of Mr Collins, a cousin of short and intolerable acquaintance. But Mr Darcy had grown up with *his* cousin and, despite knowing her to be ill, had been promised to her. He was her betrothed—that was the material point! What was the story of their connexion and their engagement? Were his sentiments so shallow, his love so tenuous? Was his grief buried so deeply that it did not show, or had he even loved Miss de Bourgh? Mr Darcy was rather topsy-turvy with his emotions. Could he perhaps be in denial of his loss and in deep pain?

At times during their walk, Elizabeth had seen her companion look angry, or at least irritated. At other moments, he had laughed, a rich and sonorous sound. He was a handsome man, made handsomer when his eyes crinkled and his cheeks dimpled. He was like no man she had encountered before and so dizzying. She should not notice him or his…handsomeness. Her theories on deep-seated grief were cast off as easily as his so-called heartbreak.

He is the Grieving Groom; he should not be handsome nor should he be laughing. And I should not be noticing.

Elizabeth shifted under the covers and sighed. It seemed impossible that she would miss a man she barely knew or understood. They had spent a lovely time conversing until he withdrew and turned formal in his behaviour as the afternoon waned. Perhaps something had reminded him of his mourning or recalled him to his place in society and the company with whom he was spending time. Perhaps he had realised that their friendly familiarity was an ill-conceived lark, hardly appropriate for the master of Pemberley and a girl from Hertfordshire. It mattered little, she knew, but he confused her, and she badly wanted to figure him out.

Her father was amused merely by the mystery of it all. It was a distance Elizabeth found herself envying.

CHAPTER SIX

Darcy watched as Louisa Hurst ushered her sister from the drawing room. Wine dripped from Miss Bingley's bodice and angry epithets spilled from her lips. The younger woman's attempts to secure a dance or three with him for the ball had both exhausted and disgusted him. She had simultaneously disparaged the propriety of mourning while encouraging him to commit himself to her by ruling out the eligibility and reputation of any lady in the area with whom he had become acquainted.

According to Netherfield's all-knowing social arbitress, Charlotte Lucas was old and plain while her sister Maria was young and possibly cross-eyed. The Bennet girls were cited one by one: too taken with her own beauty (and with Charles); too proud a bluestocking; too plain and pious; too silly and rheumy-eyed; and too stupid and crass. How, Miss Bingley had sniffed, their cousin could ever choose among them for a bride was quite the mystery.

Her oblique reference to Mr Collins's plan to wed one of the sisters caused Darcy some confusion. To overhear her telling it—and Hurst seemed to overhear everything and relished in the retelling to Darcy—'the Dreaded Bennet Sisters of Longbourn are akin to Hercules's multi-headed hydra.' None of the five girls—after some thought, Darcy *had* determined there were five Bennet sisters although it seemed the middle one was always missing from the group—appeared to even like the vicar. While that was not a necessity for marriage, he thought himself a keen enough observer to have noticed whether an understanding existed between the man and one of the Bennet ladies.

Miss Bingley's disclosure about an entail, however, had raised an alarm. If the man was heir to the estate, then of course it would be advantageous for the Bennets to secure him as a husband to one of their daughters. But which one? Darcy realised that he wanted to protect the Bennet sisters. Collins was ill-suited for at least three of them, and based on his own resistance to his aunt's wishes, he disliked the idea of marriage forced on any man or woman.

But Collins certainly was not a man to keep news of an engagement to himself. Darcy realised he might have missed some intimations by assiduously avoiding the obsequious parson. The last topic he wished to canvass with anyone, let alone an idiotic parson, was the life and odd circumstances surrounding the death of Anne de Bourgh. And that was the *only* topic Hunsford's absent vicar seemed to speak about when in his presence. Darcy refused to enquire about the man's knowledge of the situation at Rosings —it was fairly clear that Collins had left Kent quickly and without being taken into any family confidence.

After the sound of Miss Bingley's ranting died out, the three men filed into the library. Bingley shut the door and groaned. "I have warned Caroline again and again about her gesticulations! She has knocked over vases and puddings since we were children. Once she bloodied my nose when I unthinkingly wandered into her fist."

Hurst laughed. "And how she turned on Miss Catherine, whose 'rheumy eyes' can only be so from staring adoringly at your sister."

"Say what?" Bingley gasped.

"'Tis nothing but a young girl idolising a fashionable lady," Darcy explained. He found Miss Catherine's fascination with Miss

Bingley to be frightening yet refreshingly naïve. "Your sister cuts quite a swath in a small town while cutting the townspeople to the quick."

"Oh." Bingley's face flushed.

Chuckling, Hurst collapsed onto the settee and announced himself done in by the combination of Caroline's angry soliloquy and the evening's finely done partridge. "Superb shooting, Darcy. If it is not too much to ask, I have a taste for pheasant tomorrow."

Even Darcy had to smile. He leaned back against Bingley's sparsely filled bookshelves and asked his friend whether he had enjoyed his afternoon with Miss Bennet.

"I did." He sighed contentedly. "I have secured the first dance with her *and* the supper dance." He stood up a little straighter.

"And the courtship? She is aware of your intentions?"

Bingley flushed. "I...um...I thought requesting two dances *and* confirming her feelings on my courtship might be too much for one afternoon."

"*You* thought that, Charles?" Hurst sniffed. "Are you certain Caroline had nothing to do with this decision?"

"Lord help me. She is so fierce. I worry for Jane...um, Miss Bennet." Bingley took a deep breath and rubbed his neck. "Caroline was unhappy to hear about the Bennets' relations in Cheapside, and she disparaged the connexion so much this morning that I felt hesitant to secure the...to make such a..."

Bingley glanced up and saw Darcy's disapproving stare.

"I think I have heard you say that their uncle is an attorney in Meryton."

"Yes," Bingley acknowledged, "but they have another who lives somewhere near Cheapside."

"That is capital," Hurst murmured. "Your sisters could hardly visit there, let alone claim an association."

"If they had uncles enough to fill all of Cheapside," cried Bingley, "it would not make them one jot less agreeable!"

"But it must materially lessen their chance of marrying men of any consideration in the world." Darcy was appalled with himself even as he spoke the words.

"It matters not to me. They appear to be good people. Mr

Gardiner has a number of warehouses, and Jane...um, Miss Bennet told me about her aunt's recent activity in securing items for her niece's wedding wardrobe."

Darcy felt a sudden chill.

"We men know so little of what women go through to prepare for weddings," Bingley continued. "We ensure the banns are published, draw up the settlement papers, and are fitted for a new waistcoat, all the while dreaming only of the wedding night."

"Charles!"

"Well, most men do, though perhaps not you, Darcy."

Hurst snickered. "Always so good and proper."

Bingley smiled weakly at Darcy and shook his head. "I apologise, my friend. I should not make jokes at your expense, considering..."

"Considering what?" Darcy croaked out.

"Your cousin Anne. I know you were not truly engaged, but I fail to grasp whether you had some understanding with her. By the time you both reached a certain age, perhaps?" He picked up the brandy bottle and began pouring them each a generous serving.

"Of course not. Whatever schemes her mother claimed, none would have come to fruition." Darcy was beyond tired of thinking on the topic, let alone explaining it. Again. Yet he continued.

"My father made it clear that my aunt's claims were nothing short of deranged and imparted the importance of a healthy wife in providing an heir."

"Well, that is quite romantic, my friend." Hurst laughed and took a hearty gulp of the brandy.

"You could put Cupid into the poorhouse." Bingley offered a brimming glass to Darcy, who shook his head in refusal.

"Shut it, Bingley," he growled. "You find beauty and loveliness wherever you go."

"And you are a far harsher judge of your own needs, Darcy." Bingley glanced at Hurst as though making a private joke. "A pretty girl with a happy disposition, a dislike of dancing, a love of books, and patience for your dark moods and odd ramblings on Greek philosophy and chess manoeuvres should be easy enough to find, eh?"

Darcy pretended not to hear Hurst's roar of laughter. "Right."

"After all, your friends have likely lined up a multitude of eligible ladies at their estates. I wager you will be betrothed before me." Bingley smirked. "However, if you meet no one, do remember there is always my sister waiting in the wings."

"Good lord," Darcy muttered. "Charles Herbert Bingley, I believe I must call you out."

"What?" Bingley's voice cracked.

"Pour me half a glass, and I shall find it in me to forgive you," Darcy grumbled. He pulled a book off the shelf and strode over to the windows.

Bingley prepared a nearly full glass, walked over to his friend, and handed him the drink. "You will stay until after the ball?"

"Yes, of course. The following afternoon, I shall be off to Kenilworth. I have delayed my visit already, and my friends await." He sipped the brandy and placed it on the table near his favourite chair.

"As do their sisters, I have no doubt."

Darcy glared at him then sighed. "Yes, as you have already stated. Their sisters *and* their sisters' friends." He sat down, stretched out his legs, and stared out the window. Black clouds were rolling in, and he could feel the temperature dropping as a cooling breeze blew. A rumble of thunder could be heard in the distance.

"You seem less than enthusiastic, my friend." Bingley fell into the room's other reading chair and stared at Darcy. "Do you wish to keep to your practice of avoiding eligible young ladies? Or would you like to find love and happiness as I have?"

Both men disregarded Hurst's snort of laughter. "Cupid's arrow indeed!"

"Bingley…"

"What harm can come to you? It is a late summer sojourn. You may meet a pretty girl or two."

"Yes. This has been a comfortable respite." Darcy's eyes moved back to the window and the roiling clouds outside. "I am not averse to enjoying the company of intelligent young ladies." *I have already enjoyed the company of one and can only hope to find another to match her wit and beauty.*

The clock chimed. Hurst looked over and squinted at it, then stood up a bit straighter and adjusted his waistcoat. He took a final gulp of brandy and set down his empty tumbler. "Excuse me, gentlemen. I rely on you not to drink all the brandy. I shall return at a later time, undoubtedly in need of a glass or three."

Darcy and Bingley watched him stroll briskly out of the room.

"Where is he off to?" Darcy asked. Hurst rarely moved with much intent and never with such speed.

Bingley's cheeks reddened. "Er, Louisa." He stood up and walked to the doors, closing them firmly before returning to his seat. "It is Thursday."

"Thursday..." Darcy repeated, his face reddening as realisation dawned.

"Have another brandy. He should be back within the half hour. Or quarter hour."

Darcy's eyebrows rose as far as they could.

"I know," Bingley cried. "It is an absurd amount of time. The walk up the stairs alone..."

"Bingley."

"Every so often, he does not return. Most often, though, he is absent for at least thirty minutes." Bingley looked beseechingly at his friend. "I do not care to think on it."

"But you do like to talk on it."

"It is just...not quite the way I foresee marriage. If that is all the time I can give my wife, or she give me, I can handle things faster by myself."

"Bingley! For goodness' sake, shut it."

"The ball!" Lydia cried. "Lizzy and Kitty have flowers sewn on their gowns! I need some as well! And feathers for my hair and bodice!"

"Lydia, we need not look like peacocks," Elizabeth said sharply. "Mr Bingley's sisters are unsettled enough at hosting a ball so soon after Mr Darcy lost his cousin." *And quite peeved to be hosting one in the wilds of Hertfordshire. Perhaps I should not have mentioned the legend of the family who kept pigs in the house.*

Jane looked at Elizabeth. "This might be a difficult evening for Mr Darcy, Lizzy."

"He will bear up. He seems less than wholly melancholy."

"If Mr Darcy wants to be unhappy, he should just go back and sulk in London," Lydia sniffed. "He only talks to his friends and Lizzy. No one wants to dance with him." Disregarding the exasperated stares of her sisters, she began fitting feathers into the lace on her dress.

"Hush, Lydia," Kitty ordered. "I think Mr Darcy is nice. Miss Bingley thinks so as well. He is handsome. He has dimples and a cleft in his chin."

Yes, he does. And he is. He smiled less often than Mr Bingley, but he often did so when in *her* company. She was not sure whether it was appropriate for her to have noticed, and she declined to dwell on whether it was common for him to smile so frequently around a young lady. Did she remind him of his sister, the girl who liked to name animals? *Georgiana.* She sounded charmingly sweet, if a little innocent.

Elizabeth glanced around the room at her sisters. Lydia and Kitty squabbled over ribbons, and Mary squinted into the mirror while Jane brushed her hair. She loved them all in spite of their imperfections, and she would miss them when she journeyed to London. The change would be refreshing; she would enjoy her relations there and encounter many new, interesting, and strange people. And if she were fortunate, she might hear the roar of a man-eating tiger.

Miss Caroline Bingley may not have encouraged her brother to host a ball. She may even have disparaged nearly everyone to whom her brother had extended his hospitality. Although word of their generosity and humiliation was unlikely to seep across county borders and reach the ears of Those Who Truly Matter, she was not a lady to shirk her commitment nor miss the opportunity to display and provide the finest foods, entertainment, and decoration that Meryton had ever seen.

Unwilling in spirit though he was, Darcy knew his manners, and manners required that he partner Miss Bingley to open the ball. Bingley jumped in heart first and led Miss Bennet to the floor with the Hursts behind them. Darcy extended his arm, and with his eyes focused over Miss Bingley's head, he smiled, bowed, and performed the steps drilled into him at a young age. He listened to her comments and complaints, and he nodded and congratulated her on her wise choices in flowers and cheeses. Nothing betrayed that his attention was elsewhere, watching as Collins misled Miss Elizabeth and bungled his way through the dance. He saw her cringe and witnessed her tight-lipped smile and brief expression of pain when the parson's foot made contact with hers. *Gadzooks, the man is an atrocious dancer.* Add that to Collins's growing list of sins against Darcy's refined sensibilities.

As he stared at the cleric, Darcy felt others' attentions on himself. He sensed that the people of Hertfordshire viewed him slightly askance. He was accustomed to the deference and respect owed to him as a Darcy, but the kind and sometimes sad expressions his presence had generated during his stay were unusual. Bingley attributed it to word having spread of his cousin's tragic death. Now, as he stood near the punch table and looked around the room, he noticed several looks of disapproval, mayhap of judgment. For having danced with the sister of the ball's host? Was that, in the phrase overused by Hurst, 'quite singular'?

He was appalled. His ears felt hot, as if they were burning. Darcy turned to his left and saw the mothers of the town, their names forgotten, gathered in a circle with their eyes on him. Talking about him, by the looks of it. *Me? For doing my unpleasant yet necessary duty? Or is it my house in town you covet?* Each lady wore a look of injury, with her face severe and her lips downcast. The plump one in purple was speaking loudly and rapidly to her rapt audience. Frowning, Darcy counted Mrs Bennet among the group.

"Mourning appears to be observed quite differently among the *ton,*" the society expert lectured her listeners. "Here, when Mrs Miller passed, the family wore black for a year. No assemblies for them, and young James had to put off his courtship of that girl in Barnet."

"Proper though James was, the girl went off and married another, did she not?" voiced another matron of Meryton. "Tragedy and heartbreak. He lost his mother and the girl he loved."

Heads bobbed and eyes narrowed. Darcy turned away, displeased by the ladies' disapprobation. His musings were interrupted by the arrival of Sir William Lucas, which only compounded his displeasure. Aggravated as he was by the sympathetic sighs he received as a grieving cousin, and now by the offended glances of Meryton's matchmaking mamas, he had to admit that he also was guilty of exaggerating his mourning to avoid certain social obligations. His brief encounter with the knight and a few other townsmen had tapped his reserves of patience and good will.

Beyond Hurst and Bingley, he had found only the company of Mr Bennet and his chessboard to be of any comfort and interest. They played a day ago in a spirited match that ended in a draw. Miss Elizabeth sat at her father's desk watching the men, and with a quick inhale or exhale of breath, she judged their moves. Her father questioned her loyalties only once, when Darcy's bishop threatened his king and Elizabeth had hidden a smirk. "Et tu, Lizzy?" her father had cried.

The traitor herself now watched Marc Antony don that imperious mask she had seen at Longbourn; it was the face he wore whenever Mr Collins came near. She certainly did not blame Mr Darcy for evading her cousin, for the vicar was far too proud of himself and his oft-discussed list of talents. He spoke of his beekeeping and gardening, his raptures in observing the heavens, and his skills in discerning spices. Elizabeth thought his greatest talent was speaking of himself and his patroness. On this night, he was a most proficient gossip. She did not wonder at his lack of good manners, but she did marvel at his lack of sense

Although Mr Darcy's aloofness had stilled Mr Collins's tongue while at Longbourn, when the town's other families played host, the chattering cleric appeared freer to share his sad and terrible tale of heartbreaking loss. It was perverse yet expected that the mothers of Meryton appeared to enjoy his company.

During the weeks of his stay at Longbourn, Mr Collins's recitation of his tale ensured the master of Pemberley received his due as the Grieving Groom, and that the majesties of Rosings, the tragic beauty of Miss de Bourgh, and the brilliant courage of her beloved mother were well known throughout the county. Mr Collins appreciated the meals served and the sympathies expressed for the loss he had experienced. Mourning was sad, but his pain was assuaged by custards and spice cakes.

During their dance, Elizabeth wished that Mr Collins were focused on counting his steps rather than expressing his shock and amazement at the events of the evening. He seemed to be so busy pondering the wisdom of Mr Darcy's presence at the ball and his shocking lack of propriety in dancing that Elizabeth surmised it likely her awkward cousin would require her mother's salts.

But Sir William was a sweet man, pleased with himself and nearly everything and everyone around him. Elizabeth thought it enviable to find joy in the simplest of things and serenity in the worst of times. Maria Lucas and her brothers were much like their father, but Charlotte's practical contentment was a rare quality, one she finally appeared to accept. She was prepared now to settle for any happiness, but no man seemed prepared to settle on her. Elizabeth felt a twinge of melancholy for her dear friend. Aside from this ball and perhaps an assembly or two come autumn, at seven and twenty, Charlotte had few opportunities left and no family to visit in London—family who would show her the delights and promise of life outside of Meryton.

Elizabeth shook off her malaise and looked around the room. For all of her hostility to the idea of hosting the town's families, Miss Bingley did know how to throw a ball. She tapped Charlotte's arm and gestured to the flower boughs over the windows. Then her eyes drifted back to the pair across the floor. Mr Darcy was raising his eyebrows and nodding his head at whatever Sir William was saying. He appeared to be tolerant of—if a bit bemused by—the older man's effusive speech and gestures.

"Lizzy," said Charlotte, "my father seems to be enjoying Mr Darcy's company, much as your father has."

"He does, indeed."

"In spite of his tragic loss, Mr Darcy seems much improved in mood. He danced with Miss Bingley."

"Charlotte, she is acting as host, and he is a guest in her home. It was expected. It is unlikely we shall see him dance again tonight."

"Is it? He stares at you quite often."

Charlotte had more than five years of ballroom seasoning over Elizabeth, but the younger woman could not mistake the meaning behind her friend's words. Eager to change the conversation, Elizabeth weighed her response.

"He knows few people here, Charlotte. We have discussed books." She gave an arch smile. "To hear you speak, all it takes is an evening with stars overhead and punch overserved for Miss Bingley—or any lady—to mistake something that did not belong to her as a promise to be claimed."

"Or not take notice of what could be hers, Lizzy."

Elizabeth blinked and pulled her eyes away from Charlotte. She was startled to find the two gentlemen approaching.

"Good evening, Miss Elizabeth, Miss Lucas."

Sir William beamed at the ladies. "Mr Darcy and I have just had an enlightening conversation about the Prince Regent and the coming Season. You are for London soon, Lizzy?"

"In three days, sir."

"We shall miss you, my Charlotte especially." He turned to Darcy and chuckled. "I used to find these two perched in trees, reading their books and hiding from their mothers."

"Father!"

"Ah, Charlotte. I suppose it was mostly Lizzy, our princess of the trees." He beamed at Miss Elizabeth and nodded to Darcy. "Jewel of the county, this one. We all shall be sorry to lose her." He turned to his daughter. "Your mother has requested your help, my dear. Maria's slipper has had a bad turn and is in need of your deft helping hands."

The Lucases wandered off. Darcy turned to see Miss Elizabeth biting back a smile. She glanced at him and shrugged. "Charlotte is a dutiful sister."

"Yes, I...Miss Elizabeth, I hope I am not..." he faltered, trapped by her laughing eyes. "May I say you look quite handsome tonight? You and all your sisters, of course."

"You may say as many pretty things as you like, Mr Darcy, though I warn you, I practise discernment in my acceptance of such compliments."

"Oh." Darcy paused. She left him tongue-tied and confused—again. "In the same manner as you judge a chess match, I assume?"

Her eyes met his, sparkling and full of laughter, and he felt dizzy. This mere slip of a girl with flowers in her hair and a yellow gown that seemed to highlight her dark eyes was captivating. *Lord, I will miss our conversations.*

"Why, yes. Exactly the same manner." She tilted her head and stared at him. "Mr Darcy, I believe conversation is far easier if one breathes in and out."

He pulled his eyes away from hers and turned to watch the movement on the floor. "Have your toes not recovered from your last dance, or do you choose to sit out this one?"

She was caught between a smirk and a blush. "My toes will be well enough. Two days ago, after Mr Collins secured my hand for the first set, my sisters and I devised a use for our old handkerchiefs. They make for wonderful protection when stuffed into one's dancing slippers."

Darcy coughed back a laugh. "You are indeed a chess player, Miss Elizabeth. Pray, will you require the stuffing for your future partners?"

"I think not. I am familiar with the dancing skills of my other partners, and none frighten me."

"Ah." He looked at her from the corner of his eye. "So, all your sets save this one are taken?"

"No, I have the supper dance open."

She blushed. It was charming.

"Might I secure your hand for that set?"

"I find I have no reason to say no."

"I thank you, Miss Elizabeth. Until then…" He gave her a small smile, and eyeing the approach of Miss Lydia and two young men, he moved away. He was aware that the supper dance was 'La Boulangere,' and he looked forward to watching her step to and remark on that joyful music.

He was leaving tomorrow. She would be gone two days after that. They would begin new lives: she, soon to be a bride, and he, to find one. One dance seemed a fair way to say farewell.

Elizabeth was faring less well two days later.

"I did not realise the militia was to be at my aunt's card party," she murmured to Charlotte and Jane. She was tired from a sleepless night and keenly feeling the absence of a good conversationalist. She was annoyed with her sisters, her cousin, her mother, and her Aunt Philips. If only she had stayed home with her father and his chessboard. If only it had not rained much of the past two days, keeping her inside and away from her walk and her solitude. If only Mr Darcy had not left Netherfield. If only that last thought did not plague her.

"I believe they leave within the week," her friend said quietly.

"Ah, well. At least they provide new ears for Mr Collins's many exciting tales and proverbs."

Charlotte gave her a sharp look. "Not everyone finds him so tiresome, Lizzy. He would make a suitable husband to some in spite of his tendency to talk overmuch and expound on the savoury goodness of every meal."

"I am not certain he is wife hunting with his own parish currently in flux," Elizabeth said slowly as understanding flared.

Charlotte sees him as desirable in whatever desperate sense that makes. She should not fear Jane or me standing in her path to such happiness.

"He is a good man," Jane said in her ever-agreeable way. "And this is a fine night."

"It does provide a last hope for certain ladies to secure themselves a redcoat."

"Oh, Lizzy, be good." Jane glanced worriedly at her sister, who now wore an impish grin.

"No one can be as good or as happy as you, Jane. I am sorry Mr Bingley is not here this evening."

"As am I, but there will be much to occupy us."

The threesome listened as Mr Collins completed his compliments of the room and said that it favourably recalled to him a similar yet much larger and grander room at Rosings. After a rather upset Aunt Philips deserted his side, he began a perambulation, strolling slowly and introducing himself to those he deemed most presentable.

Elizabeth noted that he had stopped by Lydia and Mr Wickham—a man they had met the day before in Meryton and who was now wearing regimentals as he had joined the militia. Feeling unselfish, Elizabeth tugged on Jane's hand and led her, followed by Charlotte, to the group. Mr Wickham welcomed them with a broad grin, but his greeting was interrupted by his admirer's oration.

"The nephew of my generous benefactor, Lady Catherine de Bourgh, has been in the area of late, sir." Collins folded his hands across his expansive chest. "We have spent some time in conversation, and I have offered him my pastoral counsel."

Wickham's eyes had narrowed on hearing the word nephew and now widened as his face paled. "Her nephew? Colonel Fitzwilliam…?"

Met with blank stares from his audience, realisation dawned. "Do you mean Darcy? You have made the acquaintance of my old friend?"

Jane's attention was sought eagerly by her mother, and she drifted away. The other women remained, keen to forward the conversation.

"Yes, we have, Mr Wickham," Elizabeth said. "He was visiting a friend."

"And mourning his beloved," Mr Collins asserted.

"Darcy? Mourning his beloved?" Mr Wickham repeated slowly.

The vicar nodded gravely. "His betrothed, Miss de Bourgh, has gone to her maker."

"She is dead," Lydia assured him.

Mr Wickham nodded and looked away for a moment before adopting a concerned expression. "He is mourning the woman he threw over?"

Elizabeth stared at him. "Pardon me?"

He laughed softly before giving voice to bitter-sounding sentiments. "I grew up with Darcy at his family's estate. My boyhood chum was indeed betrothed to Miss de Bourgh. They were promised to each other from the cradle, but he was less than inclined to actually wed her. The lure of joining the estates was great at one time, but I believe he met another beauty whose charm and fortune equals his own, and he ended the engagement mere weeks ago."

When gasps erupted, Mr Wickham leaned closer, his blue eyes moist. "And now you tell me Miss de Bourgh is dead? Dear lord. She was a delicate flower on the cusp of her bloom. That man has no right to mourn. He broke her heart."

"Oh, this cannot be, yet it explains it all!" Mr Collins cried. His face was pale, and his hands shook as he brought them to his chest. "Poor Lady Catherine!"

"Truly tragic. Lady Catherine should rely on your wise counsel," Charlotte said quietly to Mr Collins. She placed her hand on his arm.

"Mr Darcy is a monster," Lydia voiced, her jaw slack.

"Unbelievable," Elizabeth whispered. "Mendacity and mourning…"

She stepped away, stunned by what she had just learned and appalled at the man who freely defamed another man she thought she had admired. One man was a dissembler, the other a scoundrel. Or was one man both of these things? Was it the man she had known for mere weeks and with whom she had conversed and laughed, or was it the man she had just met? Did it matter? The former was gone, off to meet other ladies at other estates. Or was it to rendezvous with the 'beauty whose charm and fortune equals his own?'

None of it made sense—not the accusation made by Mr Wickham nor the feelings she had been quashing since meeting Mr Darcy. She had held his hand and matched his steps, met his eyes, and, it felt at times, met his mind during their dance two nights earlier. He had enquired about which books she and Charlotte had read up in the tree branches. *"Were they stolen from your father's shelf or were they deemed appropriate for curious young girls?"*

He had been flirting with me right in the middle of the ballroom floor! It had not felt that way at the time; it had been a spirited discussion of books, music, and the ruins in Rome they both wished to see. But he had charmed her. Was this behaviour common to men of his station at small country balls? Was it common to *him*? Was Mr Darcy a rake and a scoundrel?

Her head ached; her eyes stung. She was as stupid and silly as her younger sisters. She spoke of clouds and wishes and books with a man doing nothing more than whiling away his time with a country girl. *All of those important nothings about which we had conversed.*

She had allowed Mr Darcy into her heart a little, knowing nothing would come of it. He was a flirt at best, a cad at worst. There was nothing in between.

What a joke she was.

CHAPTER SEVEN

It took but a day with the Hadleys in Kenilworth for Darcy to relax and push away any lingering regrets about his time in Hertfordshire. The shooting was good, the conversation lively, the sprawling estate rife with good trails and rides.

As much as he had enjoyed his time at Netherfield, achieving as always a comfortable amity with Bingley and Hurst, he felt a sense of himself return whenever he was with the companions of his youth. John Hadley had been with him at Eton and then at Cambridge. He was familiar with more than the outlines of Darcy's life; like Richard, he had helped sketch and colour them in.

Hadley knew the loss Darcy had suffered with his mother's death and the struggles he had faced when suddenly becoming the master of Pemberley and parent to his sister. He understood the complicated relationship Darcy had with his aunt and the frustration he had felt—and family battles he had fought—when he had denied any intention to marry Anne.

Tall, broad, and ruddy-faced, Hadley lived the life Darcy imagined for himself. He had taken the grand tour while Darcy was burying his father and consoling his sister. Upon his return, Hadley met a pretty young lady from one of London's best families and married her while Darcy lurked near the walls of the few ballrooms he had ever entered. Now, Hadley and his wife lived happily with their two young sons on a fine, well-situated estate not far from his parents' land and the dower house where his mother resided. Hadley had everything that could make a lesser man jealous. While Darcy could admit to a few moments of envy, he mostly felt admiration for the way his friend had managed his life, and he hoped his own would follow a due course. Soon.

It was apparent Cecilia Hadley had the same hopes for her husband's quiet friend. Three days after Darcy's arrival, her two younger sisters and their friends descended upon the estate and destroyed his equanimity. It was as Miss Bingley had feared: he was surrounded by pretty young ladies, each of whom thought Darcy was all that was handsome, intelligent, manly, and perfectly suited for *only* her.

Cecilia's sisters were pleasant, lively, and rarely stopped talking, though mostly to each other. Their friends were not dissimilar. Miss Copley had blonde hair and blinked her eyes more than seemed normal. Miss Eakin had large teeth and a sceptical demeanour. Miss Upton tittered or gasped at everything he said, and the Misses Edwards enjoyed Shakespeare and pantomime. It was…exhausting. Miss Bingley had nothing to fear, but he might. Darcy told his man, Smith, that he would be locking the door to his rooms. And perhaps wedging a chair or two against it.

It was after a long afternoon of providing identical answers to similar queries on his preference in cake, partiality to tea, opinion on ladies' novels, and favourite horse names that the 'Darcy disappearing act'—first established during his third year at Eton—occurred.

After a search of the library, the study, and the conservatory, Hadley found him in the stables, preparing for a hard ride. Together, they rode silently out through the wood and up to the property's highest peak, where they dismounted and strolled over to see the view.

"I know you prefer the rough, untamed looks of the north, but I find at least as much beauty in Warwickshire," Hadley said quietly.

"It is more civilised here, more cultivated," Darcy agreed. "That does not lessen the beauty. You have not imposed yourself or any French sensibilities on your land."

Hadley chuckled. "No. But I believe I have imposed on you."

Darcy glanced over at his friend. "I beg your pardon?"

"I owe you an apology. Cecilia and I never intended this as a hunting party with you as the prey."

"I know that, John."

"You have had enough of that, I think."

"Yes…" Darcy tamped down a memory of a recent ball and the lady whose laugh and spirit haunted him at the most unexpected times. "I do not wish to be hunted, yet…" he continued, his voice low, "I believe I would like to be found."

Hadley glanced at his friend staring unseeing out at the valley below.

"Found? Are you lost?"

Darcy shook his head. "Not lost at all. Searching, perhaps, for the happiness you have found and that your parents and mine enjoyed."

The two men stood in silence. In the comfort of being with a friend who understood his meaning, Darcy's mind wandered. He deliberated on the lack of easy conversation to be had with young ladies not named Elizabeth Bennet. He wondered whether she would retain that name for a few more days or weeks.

What will be her name after her marriage?

He had never thought to ask her this or many other questions. He had been content and safely happy to enjoy her witty observations and intelligent comments. He had never pressed Bingley to fill in the details about her intended husband and those two boys she would mother or the exact arrangement that Collins man had with another of the Bennet sisters. Another small oversight to be added to his regrets in life. He sighed. He needed to stop thinking about Elizabeth Bennet. Hadley's voice broke through his dullness.

"This is unseemly, hosting you here with all these young ladies and Georgiana back in London. Rather the reverse of things, don't you agree?"

"I do."

Hadley laughed. "See, my friend, you *can* say those words. We simply need to find you the right lady to say them to."

While Elizabeth could admit Mr Wickham was all that was handsome and charming, she could not admit she liked him or felt him a proper gentleman. Although she had limited acquaintance with gentlemen outside her family and those she knew in Meryton, none had ever spoken of another person's behaviour to her with such familiarity. She was accustomed to the gossip of the town being delivered with undue haste by her Aunt Philips and quickly digested, interpreted, and passed on by her mother. For a man to behave in the same manner was unseemly. She could not admire him.

Mr Collins presented a greater dilemma. He had mortified her with his observations on her sisters' dress, conduct, and piety, and since hearing Mr Wickham's pronouncement on the alleged Grieving Groom, the vicar had shared many opinions on the worth of Mr Darcy. He spoke of character with as much force and enthusiasm as he had previously employed when sharing the merits of a dish seasoned especially well. Twice she had reminded him that Mr Darcy remained his ladyship's nephew and presumptive heir, and Mr Collins had reined in his tongue. Still, she suspected him of continuing to cast dark calumnies on Mr Darcy and wondered at any whispers she heard in the shops and sitting rooms.

More than once, while visiting or walking with Charlotte, she alluded to her concerns. Her friend had seen little of Mr Darcy or Mr Wickham, but she was more grounded in a charitable view of Mr Collins than Elizabeth anticipated.

"The study of God's word and the practice of piety may not make a man wholly wiser than other men, but Mr Collins has been in the world, Lizzy, and he knows Mr Darcy's family."

"Thus he must be believed and allowed to spread gossip and rumour about a man not present to refute it?" Elizabeth was aghast.

"Perhaps Mr Darcy's friends should do their duty by him."

No matter her growing feelings of hurt and confusion, and her frustration over her shrinking circle of confidantes, Elizabeth was exasperated with what seemed to be a mounting hostility towards a man not in residence to defend himself. She quietly reminded her mother that any stain spreading across Mr Darcy's name would only harm Mr Bingley and thus, Jane. Wide-eyed with shock, Mrs Bennet began silencing the conversation when Mr Darcy's name arose among her friends and daughters. Her sister, however, remained an eager confidante and audience for Mr Collins's conversation, and the trio spent much time at the Philipses' table, though no further slanders were spread at Longbourn.

Elizabeth took her concerns to her father. Mr Bennet closed his book, leaned back in his chair, and looked amused. "Now, Lizzy, what has Mr Collins said that defamed Mr Darcy? A week ago, he raved about the man's intelligence and worth, riches and family lineage. Now, after hearing from Mr Wickham, he is calling him a scoundrel, a deserter of his bride, and the cause of her tragic death? What is the truth?"

"One or the other, I suppose." Elizabeth frowned. "My inclination is to believe better of the man with whom I am acquainted than the one who smiled and shared his thoughts so freely." She thought much better of the former while acknowledging that both men vexed her in different ways.

"I agree. I rather enjoyed Mr Darcy's intrepid proficiency at chess. He was a worthy opponent."

Saddened, Elizabeth looked at her father. "Yet we may never know."

"'Tis true. Is the story of death and deception better suited for a novel, or is it one for the history books and society pages?" He smiled, and his familiar droll expression lit up his face. "It surely is a better story at the hands of Mr Wickham and Mr Collins than the many novels your sisters claim not to be reading."

Elizabeth laughed softly. "I suppose that is true." She shook her head and referred to the other matter weighing heavily upon her.

"Papa, how much longer will Mr Collins stay at Longbourn? I leave tomorrow. When I return in a few weeks, will he still be under our roof?"

Mr Bennet gazed at his daughter, happy to be sparing his favourite from the truth and intent of Mr Collins's prolonged visit.

"I should think that he will soon return to his parsonage."

Elizabeth nodded, choosing to agree with her father. She already had grasped more than he realised. She knew of the entail, and she had seen the way Mr Collins regarded her and her sisters. Jane thankfully received only chaste, polite glances; Mr Bingley's attentions could not have been better timed. Elizabeth supposed herself safe from the vicar. She upset him with her opinions and her chess playing, and she frightened him with her demands that he cease speaking about Mr Darcy. Mr Collins appeared conflicted about her easy conversations with that gentleman. Just yesterday, he had walked with her to the rose garden, admonishing her and the blooms in equal measure.

"Cousin Elizabeth, Mr Darcy's understanding of gentlemanly behaviour is in question, but he remains the master of Pemberley and the nephew of the great Lady Catherine de Bourgh."

After snapping a wilting rose from its stem, he had lowered his voice. "You are not his equal, and he is not to be trusted."

Elizabeth's valiant protector had glared at her with a severe expression of questionable intent. She had pondered him, wondering on his awkward, often venal stupidity. He liked to gossip and cast opinions and judgments. He easily exhausted others' patience and hospitality, and he smelt of fish and never appeared thoroughly washed. Yet she could appreciate that he would someday be a father who strove to provide guidance—however dull and misdirected—to his children. She hoped he would have more to offer his wife and that the poor woman would curb these tendencies and ensure he bathed at least once a fortnight.

"I have neither fear nor expectations of Mr Darcy. When thrown into company, we have discussed books and made simple but intelligent conversation—much as you and I are doing at this moment."

Raising her eyebrows, she had shifted her basket to her left hand. "Not once did Mr Darcy besmirch the name of any person, but he only spoke in admiration of a singing voice or a well-turned phrase."

Noting the vicar's confusion, she had concluded, "That is certainly more gentlemanly behaviour than I have seen of late among other men of my acquaintance."

Ha! Her cousin had understood her meaning. He would not dare think her a proper wife nor consider presenting her as his bride to the fearsome and marvellous Lady Catherine; she was sure of it.

Her youngest sisters were also free from his admiration. Mr Collins was appalled by Lydia and confused by Kitty's fascination with Miss Bingley. While he seemed pleased and flattered by Mary's piety and discipline, his eyes quickly shifted away from her, apparently relieved, whenever someone else entered the room.

He had not dared to court any of them; even Charlotte's murky hopes seemed unlikely to garner attention. *So why does he linger here?* Was it the tragedy of Rosings that delayed the inevitable? And why was her father so silent on a matter of such importance? She could only hope that during her weeks away with her aunt and uncle, the man would take his leave as alone as when he arrived and life could return to a common, quiet pace.

Elizabeth finished packing and readied her bed. One more day at Longbourn, and she was not just frustrated: she was angry and confused. Overhearing Lydia whispering to Kitty about Mary King's overtures to Mr Wickham and how that man's open handsomeness was so in contrast to the dark evil of Mr Darcy infuriated her. Kitty's indifferent response—she wondered whether Miss Bingley frequented the fabled Almack's and favoured pink or yellow rosettes on her green dance slippers—came almost as relief. Almost. Once again, Elizabeth told Lydia to mind her business and her tongue. Lydia laughed and claimed her older sister was green tinged with envy for losing the charms of two handsome would-be suitors.

Elizabeth was beyond pleased to be leaving Longbourn for the home of her aunt and uncle, where intelligent conversation took precedence over casting aspersions on character. But leaving Jane behind and floundering in the bubbling stew made her unhappy. The night before she left, the two sisters sat on Jane's bed and pondered the looming questions.

"Lizzy, can Mr Wickham be truthful in what he says? Mr Darcy is a good friend to Mr Bingley, yet Mr Wickham has known him far longer."

Elizabeth brushed a thread from her nightgown and sighed. "Oh, Jane, Mr Wickham confuses me. He has all the appearance of happy charm but with so much ire beneath."

"Ire?" Jane's pretty face wore an unfamiliar, sad expression. "So you doubt him?"

"I question his reason for telling such tales, true or not. A young lady is dead, a family is in mourning, and Mr Darcy may be a dastardly cheater, or he may be a truly bereaved groom. What sort of man is he? He confuses me too." Elizabeth flung herself back on the bed.

"He was glad of your company." Jane lay down beside her.

"He was," Elizabeth agreed in a hushed voice. "More than was proper, according to Mr Collins."

"And now he is off, enjoying his friends at another estate party. It is curious."

"He showed no signs of cruelty nor any lack of feeling. Mr Wickham was swift to tar his reputation with cruel accusations."

"Yes, he was quick to tell his tale. However, it is true what Mr Collins said: Mr Darcy gave his betrothed only a short grieving period."

Elizabeth bit back another sigh. *All behaved badly, and all are equal?* She wished her sister could give an opinion, pronounce a verdict, or say aloud what she truly thought of a person, a gown, or an idea. Their cousin certainly had no such hesitation—nor did she. She shuddered to recognise their shared trait.

"So, Mr Collins is in the right?" Elizabeth felt her face flush as her anger flared. "For a man with little grasp of what occurred behind the walls of Rosings and no apparent knowledge of Miss de

Bourgh's 'spurning by the Judas,' our esteemed cousin has claimed a high moral ground on which to proclaim judgment."

"Lizzy!"

"Jane, he passed judgment on me to our neighbours, faulting my friendly conversation with Mr Darcy."

"He *has* been rather verbose on others' behaviours, especially those of Mr Darcy." Jane had a perplexed look on her usually serene face.

"Indeed, he has. He claims to be a man of God, yet he forgets that which he studies and professes. Does not Proverbs tell us, 'Accuse not a servant to his master, lest he curse thee, and thou be found guilty'?"

"Defending Mr Darcy brings out the Mary in you." Jane giggled and peeked at her sister. "Oh dear, I am so awful!"

Elizabeth tossed a pillow at her sister. "Oh, Jane, I shall miss you."

His cousin's appearance in Kenilworth two days later lessened some of the pressure felt by Darcy. Richard attracted all the attention due a distinguished but amusing, brave, and moustachioed officer of the King's army. Every female fluttered after him, seemingly unmindful of his status as a second son. He was manliness and courage personified, and he wore his uniform (and the scar on his cheek) quite well.

None of the ladies need know the scar came at the hands of his deceased cousin Anne, when the outraged fourteen-year-old had thrown a fork at him for an impertinent comment about her ill-fitting gowns. A stern lecture from his father followed, and his advice on how to properly observe a lady proved itself valuable in years to come. *"The Fitzwilliams are breast men, boy. Take care with where your eyes land so that your hands and lips might later roam."*

The earl had a way with words.

Three days after Richard's arrival, an afternoon thunderstorm found the sexes scattered indoors enjoying separate pursuits. The ladies were practising a pantomime or playing duets while the men used their idle time to perfect their skills at billiards. Richard and Darcy, respectively the victor and disgruntled loser of the previous match, conversed quietly on the other side of the large room and watched Hadley play his older cousin.

"Ah, Darcy, defeated again. All the pretty ladies will swoon when the news reaches their ears. I believe it past time that I teach you a favourite game among military men."

Darcy rolled his eyes. "Richard, I do not wish to fence or play mumblety-peg or compare…*things*."

His cousin laughed so hard he began to wheeze. "Gadzooks, Darcy. You are no fun. You need relief. Let's off to London for a night or two and visit—"

"No."

"It has been ages for you."

"And it will remain *ages*, Richard, until my wedding night. I have had my…sport, my education. I do not…that is not what I wish any longer." Darcy stared at the window, watching the rain droplets run down the dark glass panes.

The colonel's silence spoke more than would a joke. Darcy looked away from the window and saw Richard stroking his moustache. That was never a good sign. *He is thinking hard, peeling away my layers. Damn it.* Darcy determined to take control of the conversation.

"So, if you must, tell me about this military game. Does it require swords or pistols?"

"Neither." Richard's eyes were focused keenly on Darcy. "You see, men at war spend hour upon hour with nothing to do. They are on watch, they are on alert; it is tedious, and they are frightened. They miss their mothers, their wives, their lovers, their whores."

"This is taking a dark turn, Cousin."

"So, when men imagine what they are missing, they idealise what was left behind."

"Yes? That would seem a natural consequence of such hardship and solitude." Darcy shifted in his chair. He felt his cousin's eyes still boring into him.

"So, in their minds, they see only beauty, grace, and love. And a soft, round set up top and a lush pink—"

"Richard!"

"Darcy, you truly need to drink more." Richard leaned over and filled his cousin's glass. He sat back and waited for him to drink.

"The *game*, Fitzwilliam? Please finish this excruciating exposition of your game."

"All right then, you impatient lout." Richard stroked his moustache and smirked at Darcy's annoyed mien. "The game is the men constructing their perfect mate. The *perfect* woman. It begins with a conversation. Hair, eyes, smile…everyone has the time to think and be specific. Is she a woman who loves to sing or loves to laugh? What are her favourite foods, her best recipes, her arts and allurements? What children would she bear you, and what would be their names?"

"This, I agree, would fill an idle hour."

"And the men compare these women, debate over attributes. Why, one might ask, would a loud man favour a quiet girl? Why would a fat soldier prefer a plump woman? It would appear to make certain…um, positions more difficult."

"Richard…"

"Well, a woman's disposition for such activities is of course a major share of the conversation. Everyone has a preference." Richard took a long drink and stared at his reddening cousin. "Do they not?"

Darcy sipped his brandy. "Tell me about your *perfect* woman, Richard."

"I have spoken enough, Cousin. Tell me of yours."

Darcy hesitated. Some small part of him wished to pursue this conversation, to wrestle out his confused thoughts.

"Beyond books and eyes to read them, and a mouth that speaks words with too many letters, of course." Richard laughed. "Tell me what I cannot guess about the woman who frequents your dreams."

Only Hadley's cry of victory saved Darcy from further interrogation.

Tigers. Wolves. Which was worse? The menagerie was full of foreign creatures, some of them frightening, all of them fascinating. But when Elizabeth saw the tiger pacing in his small cage, he looked less fierce than weary. Trapped, stared at, unable to roam and run the lands from whence he came. Her excitement to see such a wild creature was tempered by sadness that the magnificent animal's life was reduced to an iron-barred box. Her little cousins shouted and gasped, their excitement not tempered by the crush of awed onlookers nor the dull anger in the big cat's eyes. She wondered what Mr Darcy would think of it and when he would bring his sister to see the menagerie.

Suddenly, the words of Mr Wickham, repeated to her the day after their encounter at the card party, returned. He and his friend Mr Denny had gone to Longbourn for tea, invited by Lydia and Kitty. The memory of his visit and their conversation nearly made her shudder, and she remained angry that it had tainted her last day at home.

She had tried to enquire about his life in the militia and to make observations about the weather and local lore. Mr Wickham's interest centred on learning about the neighbourhood families, Longbourn, and Mr Collins's prolonged stay. She had spoken few words on the last subject for the man himself was nearby, hovering over a platter of ginger cake, and she instead let her raised eyebrow express her opinion. Elizabeth wished to learn a bit more about the lieutenant's statements on Mr Darcy, but he had waved away her enquiries.

"I have said too much. Suffice to say, he is a charming but venal man—a man whose bride is dead, whose sister is locked away… Did he dance at Bingley's ball?"

"Yes." *His sister?*

"With more than one lady?"

"Yes. Two, I believe."

"While in *mourning*?" There had been disgust in his voice.

"Mr Wickham, I am confused about Mr Darcy's sister. You say he has locked her up? How can that be?"

"Georgiana suffers, as her late cousin did, from a weakness of the mind. Miss de Bourgh was a shy, retiring sort, but Georgiana is a bit...forward in her affections. Darcy locks her away to keep the family safe from scandal."

Elizabeth had recoiled in horror.

"She is a pretty girl but too young to display her arts and allurements. Darcy has failed her as a parent. She is too much like her mother."

She had felt sick and infuriated. "Mr Wickham, the business of the Darcy family is no business of mine. Nor is it of yours to discuss at a card party or while enjoying the hospitality of the families here. We all have sad stories and human weakness, but to air them to the world as you have done is more a disservice to your name than to the Darcys'."

Wickham had stared at her, his eyes narrowed. "Are you defending Darcy? Is there more to your *friendship* with him than you let on?" He leered at her, then strolled over to Lydia and Mr Denny, and Elizabeth had been grateful to be in her own home, surrounded by family.

"Lizzy! Lizzy! Come see the furry beast!"

Elizabeth shook off the memory and turned to see her young cousins jumping up and down. Thomas and Henry held the hand of their baby sister, Lily, and they were pointing at a peacock strutting in front of the cage where a great wolf howled at the sky.

Perfect, a preening peacock and a braying wolf.

Stubbornly, perhaps stupidly, her sympathy remained with the tiger.

The cousins were not able to sit alone again for conversation until nearly a week into Richard's stay.

"Hadley is not about, I take it?" Richard asked, pouring them a generous serving of their host's brandy.

"Business with his steward."

It was time for a conversation about the family, and Darcy broached the topic he dreaded.

"How is Lady Catherine?"

Richard frowned. "Damned quiet. She has moved into her town house and admits no callers save my parents. She will not speak of Anne."

"Will not or cannot?"

"It seems a choice, as though mourning comes easier if she pretends Anne never existed." Richard shook his head. "Sometimes it seems she did not. I rarely thought of her once I donned my uniform. She was neither a faithful correspondent nor an eager host when we visited Rosings."

Darcy nodded sadly. "She was a shadow of life much of the time, most often when her mother was in the room. Yet she had a brain and wit and asked me for books."

"You were of use."

"Ha." Darcy leaned forward in his chair and stared at his cousin. "Did we fail her, Richard? Did I, by not marrying her?"

"She did not want you. She did not want marriage. Anne's temperament was often foul and unpleasant, and her health was never strong. You deserve more, far more. She deserved more as well; however, what more that was, I do not begin to know."

Darcy closed his eyes and nodded. "Right, then."

Richard cleared his throat. "What she does deserve is to have her death announcement printed in the *Times*."

"What?" Darcy sat up in his chair. "Do you mean to say no formal announcement of her death has yet been published?"

"That is correct. No family service, no funeral, no announcement." Richard rubbed his jaw. "Lady Catherine ran her household differently than most do, and she is not accustomed to her commands being questioned. But all of this is quite odd."

"What are you saying?" Darcy asked. "That Anne died under mysterious circumstances? Of unsavoury reasons? That our aunt had something to do with her death?"

Richard shrugged. "I do not know. That is why I went to Rosings before journeying here."

"You did what?"

Richard shrugged. "My father was concerned. His sister is obstinate on every issue and refuses to leave her London home, yet she threatens daily to return to Rosings." His eyes narrowed in disgust. "His instincts were correct. The place is a disaster. Lady Catherine dismissed the entire household. The doors are barred, and I could not gain entry. Whatever happened to Anne, things are not right."

"No…"

"Bloody Fitzwilliam women! It is probably best I not marry and curse my wife with my name."

Georgiana.

Darcy's silence roused Richard from his musings. "Forgive me, Darcy. I am an addle-pate. I meant no slur on Georgiana or your mother. I apologise. It is all that strain. I should rightly blame the de Bourghs."

Richard rarely babbled, so Darcy knew he was sincere. Still, his cousin had roused his deepest fears. He needed to see his sister.

CHAPTER EIGHT

Within an hour of settling their scheme to ride to London for a meeting with Richard's father before travelling on and demanding entry to Rosings, Darcy had advanced a new plan. "We shall stop at Netherfield to rest the horses." He was unable to fully recognise, let alone express, the root of his idea. He never discussed the nocturnal wanderings of his mind and certainly not those that touched on a young lady—such thoughts needed to be locked firmly away from his most inquisitive cousin. All Darcy knew was that he wished to stop again in that place and learn whatever news there was of Elizabeth Bennet. He had stared at trees and imagined her perched on a branch, a book in hand, the entire time he had spent at Kenilworth. He needed to do something—anything—to exorcise her from his mind.

After emitting a dramatic sigh, Richard agreed that a night at Netherfield was a fine idea as it was but an easy morning ride from there to London. "Sharp minds and fresh cravats seem a wise idea for the operation we plan. But do not lie to me, Darcy. I know this is all a ruse to see your true sweetheart, the enchanting Miss Bingley."

The next sigh, this one from Darcy, was more affected. He had not thought of Charles' sister in more than a fortnight, a period spent evading younger, less jaded versions of her. In particular, he had worried about Cecilia Hadley's young cousin, Miss Upton, who seemed to lower her bodice further and place herself more closely to him as the days passed. The manor was smaller than Pemberley and with fewer forgotten rooms and hidden nooks. Darcy had found solitude only in his rooms or by riding out, until ten days into his stay, an observant butler showed him the hidden lock on the library door. Netherfield would be far easier; he knew the house and was wise to Caroline's tricks. *Another house, another night, another locked door.*

Behind those doors, he found books could not hold his interest. Instead, he had focused his time pondering the question that Richard had planted in his mind. What *was* his idea of the perfect woman? Darcy knew the kind of lady his friends and family supposed for him: beautiful of face and born to the right family; comfortable in his social sphere and fluent in manoeuvring its demands; able to give him sons, paint a screen, ride a horse, and compliment the right people at the perfect balls she would host because such things were expected.

Expected. How I hate expectations. His entire life revolved around fulfilling expectations and doing his duty by his family and by society. *What of my duty to myself?*

Much as he tried to repress it, there was but one likeness that came to mind when Darcy thought of his perfect woman. *One voice that teased and laughed and quoted dead Roman poets. One face that smiled with warmth and wit and exhibited an innocent, intelligent, irresistible charm.* She was not born to the right family, did not mix in the right society. He had heard her admire the talents of those who could paint screens, but she preferred books to brushes. She did not like to ride but admired the gentle beauty of horses. She enjoyed dancing even at risk to her toes. *She was a tactician there, with her slipper stuffing.* He smiled at the memory.

Yet she did not scheme to place herself in the way of a man like him who could fall in love with her and take her to a new life. She had no need; she had chosen, with all appearance of happiness, her life's future companion. He should be pleased for her, but such sentiments failed him. For the first time in memory, Fitzwilliam Darcy wanted something he could not purchase with his family's wealth, earn through hard work, or acquire through use of his rusty charm. He wanted Elizabeth Bennet, and he did not wish to exorcise her from his mind. He wanted to imagine her as his.

He laughed at himself. *I am not in love with her.*

Surely not. Even if his perfect woman would be small and dark with fine, laughing eyes and an impertinent spirit. She would smell like wildflowers, autumn leaves, and sunshine. She would push him to think more deeply and talk of subjects he had long thought uninteresting to anyone else. She would tease him until he quieted her with a kiss. And she would taste of all that was good and be soft and lush and receptive to his words, to his lips and hands. To all of him. There was no woman like her.

Damn it! He could never tell a soul of his foolishness, and he must remember the company he was keeping. His cousin could enjoy a woman and charm a lady, but Richard would never be vulnerable to a member of the opposite sex, and Darcy could not lay himself bare to his taunting banter. He must forget about Elizabeth Bennet's future and think of his own.

On the following day, Richard ceased his teasing about fawning young ladies when Bingley led them into the sitting room at Netherfield. One lady leapt to greet them while three others looked up expectantly. Darcy would have smirked at his cousin's stunned response to the ethereal beauty of Jane Bennet, but his own admirer was quick to her purpose.

"Mr Darcy," Miss Bingley trilled. "We are so pleased to have you return to Netherfield. We welcome you as well, Colonel Fitzwilliam." She slid her arm through that of her favourite and pulled him closer to her side.

Richard greeted Mrs Hurst, and he was introduced to Miss

Bennet and Miss Catherine. He shot a questioning glance at Darcy, who studiously disregarded him as he busied his energies extricating himself from Miss Bingley's tight embrace.

"I regret I did not accompany my cousin here last month." Richard sat where he could stare at Miss Bennet, apparently unmindful of the frown creasing Bingley's face. "He neglected to inform me of the native beauty of the region."

Miss Bingley's sharp intake of breath provided Darcy a brief window of opportunity. He slipped his arm from hers and celebrated his freedom by dropping down forcefully onto a chair suitable for one. He readied a cutting response for his cousin's insolent flirting, but Miss Catherine spoke first.

"Oh, we have loads of pretty flowers and shrubberies, sir! 'Tis a shame Lizzy is not with us. She knows all the walking paths and the best views, and she can name nearly every bud." Miss Catherine smiled prettily at the colonel, her expression faltering only when Miss Bingley sat beside him and cleared her throat.

"Yes, well. There is the rare native prettiness here, I suppose, but I believe a higher quality of beauty can be found in the greenhouses and conservatories of London. Or at Pemberley! There, the beauty lasts the entire year rather than fading and withering." Caroline turned to Darcy and smiled, and not for the first time, he was struck by the cold and waspish cast to her expression.

"Yes, the conservatories are host to beauty and are of great value in wintertime," he replied, "but at the height of the season, nothing is grander than the splendour of autumn leaves or the spring gardens full of colour. I have seen many fine examples here."

As he finished his soliloquy on Hertfordshire's landscapes, Darcy noticed Miss Catherine's eyes darting worriedly between him and Miss Bingley. *Odd.* The younger girl looked displeased. He recalled that she admired Miss Bingley's style and manner of dress. *Truly odd. Why would she not emulate her older sisters, who dress and act as proper ladies should? Why would a young lady with such fine examples—* A sudden vision of his own sister, dulled by loneliness and reaching out for friendship to a chubby-cheeked footman, clouded his thoughts.

Bingley began speaking about grasses or horses or some such thing, and Darcy's attention faded. He felt exhausted of conversation and drifted back to examining the pair of Bennet sisters before him. He felt Elizabeth's absence quite keenly as the discussion of nature changed to one of the militia and his cousin's adventures on the Continent. Bingley's angel was a lovely creature if one wished for kind assurance on every topic canvassed. Miss Catherine was a sweet, enthusiastic girl, if rather limited in her interests and objects of admiration. Neither one was a match for their fine-eyed, well-read sister, who appeared to be happily ensconced in London.

How is it that I can find so many adjectives to draw upon when describing her? When is her wedding? How do I divert the conversation back to her? He sighed quietly as the person he wished not to think on kept intruding. *Elizabeth Bennet is so very vexing!*

As had happened to him more than once since leaving Hertfordshire, Darcy recalled the final time he had seen her. It was the ball, where after enjoying the supper dance and her small hand in his, they had continued a merry conversation over the meal about the merits of Boswell and the sights to be seen in the Lake District. It had been, he realised now, the last intelligent conversation he had had with anyone save Hadley.

No! he reminded himself yet again. He must not think of her nor wonder about her marital felicity. Married or not, it simply did not matter. *She* did not matter. Their separate societies were different and ill-fitting. They might meet again as friends—as brief acquaintances from a month spent in the country. That was all. Despite her perfection, there were flaws in his thinking.

Their ease with each other resembled a puzzle piece fitting into a carefully carved dissection: with perfect ease, it would help clarify the whole picture being created. But as was clear from even this short visit to Hertfordshire, the piece was truly an ill fit, uncomfortable and rubbing the edges raw from abuse and unhappiness.

Or was it so clear? Why does thinking of her always make my head hurt? Blast! He had confused himself. He wished she were here.

"Darcy? Are you with us, man?" Richard's voice interrupted his reverie. "Miss Bingley was enquiring about Georgiana."

Darcy sat up a little straighter. "Pardon me. My mind had drifted to an issue with the harvest at Pemberley, and I recalled I must send a letter to the duke about our change in plans. My visit will be delayed at least a week."

Miss Bingley looked pleased by his news. "How is dear Georgiana?"

"My sister is quite busy with her aunt. During our stay in London, I hope we shall attend the menagerie. In her letters, Georgiana has written of a collection of foreign animals. The tiger and the constrictor are of particular interest."

"Oh, Lizzy saw the tiger!" Miss Bennet's face lit up in excitement. "She said it was quite fascinating, if not a bit melancholy."

While Darcy absorbed the happy news and began forming a query about Miss Elizabeth, he heard Miss Bingley titter.

"A wild cat prone to melancholy? A fierce and bloodthirsty beast such as that has no such feeling."

In a cool voice, his eyes fixed firmly on Miss Bingley, Richard replied, "I have seen animals feel many things: fear, excitement, joy. Dogs are happy creatures. Horses love to run, but in the face of danger or loud noises, they are frightened. A wild, untamed creature cannot be happy in the city with the cries of children breaking the peace and the eyes of the multitude upon him."

"Oh, this makes me sad," Miss Catherine said in a small voice.

"It does, indeed," Bingley exclaimed. "But to see it makes it real and not a creature of myth and legend." He smiled when Miss Bennet met his eyes and nodded.

"Yes, Mr Bingley," she said softly. "It does."

Darcy watched as his cousin's eyes roved over the couple as though assessing the field that lay before him. Shrugging, Richard sat back and enquired as to the whereabouts of Hurst.

Mrs Hurst averted her eyes as her brother revealed that her husband had met a hearty ragout he deemed the finest of his life but lost the battle. Richard chuckled. "He best not be in the militia or the navy if his stomach is so delicate."

"Ah, I believe it was the quantity he ate rather than the quality of the dish," Bingley asserted. "Four servings. And soup, a pudding, and a tart."

"He is resting upstairs," Mrs Hurst added.

Richard coughed out a laugh. "Well. He stands tall in my esteem, even while lying abed."

"Where is our tea?" Miss Bingley asked abruptly. "Charles, the servants here are negligent." She stared at her brother as though waiting for him to address the situation.

Bingley, an uncomfortable look on his face, glanced at the door. "I apologise for the wait. I am sure that any moment—"

"Finally!" Miss Bingley exclaimed as the door opened. But it brought forth only a footman, a salver in hand, his eyes fixed on the letter it held. He nodded to Bingley and walked towards Darcy.

"Sir, the express rider said he was re-directed here from Kenilworth."

Darcy picked up the paper and stared at the direction inscribed on it. The handwriting was familiar, but he could not place it. He rose, excused himself, and headed to Netherfield's study. Miss Bingley followed into the corridor, calling after him, "I shall send your tea, Mr Darcy!" Her voice drifted away as she began questioning the footman about the letter.

After the trio disappeared, Mrs Hurst sighed. "Poor Mr Darcy. Business with his estate, troubles with his aunt, the loss of dear Miss de Bourgh."

"He needs a wife to help him tend all of his responsibilities." Kitty's bold statement was met with silence until the courteous colonel came to her rescue.

"That he does, indeed, Miss Catherine. As do we all. The situation with my aunt and cousin is most lamentable, and we do mourn Anne. Yet as tragically difficult as it is, Darcy was rather fortunate that the supposed arrangement came to naught."

Kitty shook her head sagely. "So it did. Might Miss Bingley now succumb to Mr Darcy's charms? Have you seen how he gazes at her? Will he pursue her now that his mourning is ended?"

Four sets of incredulous eyes focused on Kitty. The spell was broken when the doors flew open and Miss Bingley entered. Two maids followed with tea trays.

She paid no heed to the chill enveloping the room and sat down swiftly on the settee. "Mr Darcy's correspondent has such beautiful handwriting," she sniffed, turning to glare at the colonel. "Mayhap yet another lady with fine eyes has tickled his fancy?"

Darcy sat down, tore open the envelope, and gasped. "Anne?"

Cousin,
I understand that you believe me dead. I am not. Mother has told quite a tale with which to cloak the truth. I am alive, I am married, and I am with child.

I am so very happy.

My husband, Peregrine Dumfries, is a wonderful man, a painter who creates beautiful pictures with his hands and brushes. He is dearly handsome and cares deeply for me. None of that matters to my mother—for he is not you. My marriage to Peregrine has ruined her, she says, and destroyed Rosings and my future. I fail to understand why she has denied our marriage and lied about my death. I fear for you and imagine she has berated you quite viciously for your failure to marry me. I apologise that my happiness has caused you pain or tainted future prospects for Georgiana.

We are residing in the Hunsford parsonage at present. Mother turned us out of the dower house after she locked up Rosings and the stables and dismissed most all of the servants. Poor Mrs Jenkins is with us at the parsonage, tending to our necessities and our kitchen. I confess, Cousin, that I miss Cook and my abigail, Daisy, who was dear to me.

I have no access to my inheritance nor do I fully understand the terms of my father's will. I need and I beg for your assistance, Fitzwilliam. If each of us has failed my mother, then together we must succeed in ensuring some victory. My happiness is enough for me, but I need more than a full heart to provide for my husband and child.

Your cousin,
Anne de Bourgh Dumfries

He folded the pages, slipped them into his pocket, and stared unseeing at the portrait of Mr Valentine Eggleston, legendary burner of books. After a few moments' reflection—though, in fact, he could barely think—Darcy rose, poured and drained a large glass of port, and summoned a footman to fetch his cousin. When Richard entered the room, Darcy thrust another full glass at him.

"Sit. Drink. Read. And then tell me what in hell we are to do."

Richard did more than simply read the letter and stare at the wall.

"Alive!? ... Married!? ... With child!? ... Peregrine! What kind of blasted name is Peregrine?"

Richard threw the letter to the floor and drained his glass. "That meddling, decrepit cross-patch! She's more brim than soul."

"Anne or her mother?" Darcy asked drily.

"One would rather die alone in self-righteousness than show affection and compromise to those she presumes to berate and bully. And she dares to call it a duty of love," Richard growled, his eyes afire with anger. "And the other? She has been compromised by a scurrilous leech! *Peregrine?* Bloody hell."

"Yes, well, it would seem." Darcy sighed and sipped from his half-full glass.

Richard sat up and stared at him. "This is astonishing news: that our cousin could so deceive everyone and her mother could double the bet with layer upon layer of deception."

"Your father always says that the apple does not fall far from the tree."

"Yes, rotten fruit, bad to the core. He is going to enjoy all the fruity metaphors to be had from this calamity." Richard shook his head. "You appear oddly calm, almost unsurprised."

Darcy set his glass aside and rubbed his hand across his face. "It is simple. I *am* unsurprised by any of this. Shocked, sickened, and horribly angry. I am of course happy to learn that my cousin is alive and well. But Anne's susceptibility to a clever poacher surprises me less than does our aunt's web of deceit."

"Hmm," Richard mumbled mirthlessly. "Thus the larger mystery is not Anne's 'undeath' but how our notoriously suspicious relation allowed a scoundrel so near her pride and joy."

"Indeed." Darcy sighed. "Georgiana kept telling me she did not believe Anne to be dead. I recall her words: 'Anne cannot be dead. She has fled her mother and burrowed in the closet.' I blamed it on those novels your mother reads, but mayhap she knew something…?"

He looked over at Richard, waiting for him to refute the notion. Instead, his cousin appeared deep in thought. Darcy sat up quickly, brows furrowed in outrage. "Richard! Are you thinking my sister is in on this appalling scheme?"

"Good lord, man, of course not! I was thinking that Georgiana spent a week at Rosings last spring when you were on your first round of wife hunting." Richard was braced for Darcy to strike him, but he paid no attention to the jest. "I would not imagine Anne opening her heart to her, but Georgiana might have seen or heard something."

Darcy's face paled. "Possibly. But she would not have confided in me, not after the incident with the footman." He sighed. "I frightened her. I was angry, and she felt I was blaming *her*."

"Were you not, just a little? She showed extremely poor judgment."

"She did, indeed. She was lonely and allowed herself to speak to a servant as she would to a friend, though I do not understand why she did not turn to her lady's maid or Mrs Reynolds." Darcy tapped his fingers against his knee, his tension too great to rein in. "A footman," he spat.

"What did they talk of?"

"Dogs." Darcy rolled his eyes. "And a rainbow that occurred on a day she was sad." His frown grew deeper. "They spoke of the disaster on Runton Bridge when she was a little girl. He—the footman—claimed he was witness to it."

"It was nothing but innocent conversation until she stumbled on the ladder. He was helping her in the library?"

Darcy nodded.

"Then his presence in the room was not inappropriate. Bear that in mind and do not forget the cavernous echoes of Pemberley." Richard looked down at his boots and sighed. "Rosings is half its size, but Anne was truly all alone and far lonelier than you or I knew."

"My sister befriends a footman and my cousin marries a portrait artist. Shall we worry next for the attentions of the blacksmith?"

Darcy felt himself a hulver head. He had asked so few questions after Anne's death, and now all was turned on its head. He had been an indifferent cousin and brother. He wished to punch something, to feel pain and punish himself for his stupidity. Instead, numb and angry, he stared at his cousin who was sunk deep in his chair and brooding.

Once the shock and disgust wore off, Darcy realised their behaviour was entirely too reasonable for two men coping with the problems of a looming scandal that involved a mysteriously alive cousin wedded to a stranger and carrying his child; a lying, scheming aunt; and a less than trustworthy young ward. Darcy suddenly felt exhausted.

Elizabeth set aside her book and sighed. London was full of wonders in spite of the October rain. She yearned for the countryside but felt it her duty to help her aunt in these difficult early weeks of her pregnancy. There were months until her confinement, but Aunt Gardiner had been overtired with this, her fourth babe. The children were thriving in the small lessons Elizabeth prepared and the outdoor activities she planned. The boys had a natural curiosity that her father had encouraged in her and been disappointed to find lacking in her sisters.

Mary's interests had narrowed as she grew up and found her sisters and friends shifting their allegiances and attentions; her reading and her Bible remained her only true companions. Kitty flitted about, captivated one month by flower presses and the next by drawing fashionable clothing; now her attentions were settled on her true model, Miss Bingley. Elizabeth repressed a snort, amused that her sister idolised the lady who coveted Mr Darcy, or at least Mr Darcy's houses and social standing.

What a tangled web of mistaken passions, soon-to-be shattered illusions, and futures thwarted. Mayhap, I should write a romantic novel full of intrigues and impassioned conversations. But what do I know of romance?

Lydia, the Wise and All Knowing, would think herself an expert on such a topic as she did on so many things. At least she was one of steady interests: laughing and dancing had always been her fancy. Jane, ever serene, did what was needed and kept her dreams and intrigues to herself.

Elizabeth kept her secrets quiet as well, confiding small thoughts to Jane and Charlotte but entrusting no one with her deepest concerns and hopes. It would appear to her family that she enjoyed everything and never stopped posing questions and challenges. Her mother would exclaim, 'Lizzy, you wear my patience,' and her father would usher her to the chessboard or to his bookshelves. Her uncle had done the same for her and, just the previous day, had shown her *On the Modification of Clouds,* a treatise on the skies that he had procured for a customer in Devon. The book was to be sent out in a day or so, but before then, Elizabeth was determined to memorise and perhaps teach the Latin names for all the cloud types to her young cousins. She picked up her pen and resumed work on the lists and drawings she was copying from the volume. *Who knew there were species of clouds?*

Mr Darcy did. Suddenly, she recalled a moment on one of their walks with Jane and Mr Bingley when he had pointed at a group of peculiar, curly white tendrils in the blue sky. '*Cirrus uncinus,*' he had said. 'Like a grouping of fish with their tails flapping.'

She realised that he must have this volume. He would be just the man to own and read it. She wished they had had an opportunity to discuss it. He would be amused, perhaps impressed, by her endeavour here. But such a conversation was unlikely to occur, and if they met again, it would be at a wedding between his friend and her sister—an event as far away and delicate as the clouds she wished to discuss.

Clouds. Elizabeth shook her head. *I am lost in the clouds.* How everyone at Longbourn would laugh if they saw this work. Even Jane and Charlotte would sigh and exclaim, 'Oh, Lizzy…'

And so she was alone in this pursuit.

CHAPTER NINE

At dinner that evening, Darcy spoke barely a word. Neither cajoling by Miss Bingley nor queries about his visit to the Hadleys and the nature of his business in London could pry more than a word or two from his lips. Indeed, it was not until the sexes separated that Bingley—and a large bottle of port—could jar him from his stupor.

"I say, Darcy. You have gone into a funk. What on earth could have happened? Is everything all right with Georgiana?"

"She is quite well, thank you."

"But your express…? I understand you did not wish to be open with your news at dinner, but you are among friends. Is all well with you?"

When Darcy remained impassive, Bingley cringed and cried, "Oh no! Was dinner a reminder of Miss de Bourgh, perhaps, with the mutton? I recall a story of her love for mutton."

Richard stared at Bingley, an incredulous smirk spreading across his face. "You recall *that* but not the total yield of your fields nor where you left your favourite waistcoat?"

His face flush with embarrassment, Bingley admitted the waistcoat—one the colonel had admired a few months earlier—was not missing but rather had been hopelessly stained by gravy and deemed by his valet as unworthy of wear. "It was such a fine shade of grey," he said sadly.

Richard seemed to be grasping for some bit of humour to leaven the mood and raised his glass. "Lost to the eternal battle of sloppy table manners."

Darcy finally stirred and sighed heavily.

Bingley cleared his throat. "Apologies, Darcy. Whatever has happened, I do not wish to laugh at your worries."

"Would that I could laugh, Bingley." Darcy waved his hand dismissively. "Anne is alive. She is married. My aunt did not react well to her daughter's choice of a husband, and she invented a tale to hide the truth."

"Good lord, Darcy!" Richard nearly shouted. He turned to Bingley who sat with mouth open and eyes round with shock. "This does not leave this room. Do you understand?"

Bingley, looking half-terrified, nodded mutely. Richard turned and glared at Darcy. "What are you thinking, telling him our family secrets?"

Darcy smiled grimly. "I am sick of lies and duplicity. Anne is alive, and that is my focus."

Bingley leaned forward to pour his friend a drink. Then, hand shaking, he raised his own glass. "To Anne?" he ventured in a hopeful tone.

There was no response. Darcy had his own questions, and his disgust at his family—the family that had guided his choices and decisions—behoved him to think selfishly for once. If he closed his eyes, he saw Elizabeth Bennet smiling at him, urging him to share his burdens. He was determined to keep them open and drink more port.

"Bingley, why is Jane Bennet here?" he asked abruptly. "Why is she not in London with her sister, preparing for her nuptials?"

Charles laughed. "Whose nuptials?" Glancing at Richard, he added, "I am courting Jane but not yet betrothed."

"Ah, so you finally did take the fateful step and confirmed her attachment? Good man." Darcy closed his eyes and then quickly opened them to see Richard raising his eyebrows and shrugging at Charles, apparently indicating his disinterest in the topic. Darcy sat up a bit straighter.

"I did, indeed," Bingley replied. "Whose nuptials, Darcy? I know Mr Collins has been…um, hovering about Longbourn and a few other houses. Has there been a proposal?"

Darcy shook his head and stopped when he realised it hurt to do so. He had imbibed a bit more than was usual. He should stop drinking; he needed to think, not lose himself in endless, angry musings. Clearing his throat, he declared, "Mr Bennet would never allow Collins to have Miss Jane or Miss Elizabeth. Both are spoken for…"

Bingley appeared confused. "Miss Elizabeth is spoken for?"

"Yes, the gentleman with the boys? She is off with them in London."

"Ah. Mr Gardiner. Wonderful man."

Is that his name?

The doors opened and Hurst, who had been absent from dinner, entered to loud greetings and gibes from Bingley and the colonel. The topic of his health was canvassed, which required another serving of port. Darcy nodded to all of it, lost in thought. After he drained his share, he stared into the empty bottom of the glass. He almost laughed aloud. The woman he had been determined *not* to wed and the first woman he might *possibly* consider marrying were both taken and tied to men they loved. Men who were definitely not like him—and more than likely beneath him—in social standing for Anne and in everything he could imagine for Elizabeth.

What man could be good enough for such an intelligent, lively, lovely woman? This 'wonderful' Gardiner man, apparently. Darcy hated it. *He* knew her, while knowing so little. But there was more he must learn before he could dull the pain of knowing he would not see her again without a band on her finger and a bonnet on her head. *All that beautiful hair covered up by a dowdy marital cap…*

"So Miss Elizabeth is soon to marry this Gardiner?" he asked, his voice as dull as his mind. "Will they be in London?"

"What?" Bingley sputtered. "Miss Elizabeth is not betrothed. Mr Gardiner is her uncle."

Darcy looked at him, shocked. "Her *uncle*? The man with the boys?"

"Yes, yes. He is her mother's brother, the one in Cheapside. Mrs Gardiner had been hosting her sisters and their daughters at her home while they purchased wedding clothes, so he was here with their sons." He smiled wryly. "You know, to escape the happy noise of excited ladies choosing lace."

"But Elizabeth is now with them in London?"

"Yes, Mrs Gardiner invited *Miss* Elizabeth and Jane to visit after her relations left. Jane chose to remain at Longbourn." A blush rose on Bingley's cheeks.

Darcy gazed at him, slack jawed and unaware of his cousin watching him closely.

"You thought her betrothed to her uncle?" Bingley asked, laughing a bit. "Were words ever exchanged to create such a wrong impression?"

Darcy sat still. How had he so convinced himself that she was spoken for? Because he saw her familiarly engaged with the man and his sons? Or because it made him safe from considering her as…as more? As a possibility for himself? He knew he was vulnerable to her with her wit and her walking and her shining intelligence and lovely eyes and… *Oh damn!* She was his perfect woman. He was already in the thick of it.

"I…there was some confusion in my interpretation," he said quietly.

"Obviously," his cousin supplied in an amused voice.

"Well, she was certainly confused about you as well, my friend," Bingley said. "In fact, the whole town is rather confused. It seems harmless enough to tell you now, given your latest news." He glanced furtively at Hurst. "Do you know that all of Hertfordshire thinks of you as the Grieving Groom?"

An hour after the tin soldiers were packed away in the nursery on

Gracechurch Street, Elizabeth was overjoyed to receive three letters from Longbourn. She chose to first open Mary's letter, determining it would contain less news than admonitions and reminders of ways she could best spend her time and enlighten the children. Instead, she found a terse note.

Sister,
Mr Collins has left us to return to his parsonage. My mother had given me notice that I might expect a courtship with my cousin, but it was for naught. He is gone, with few words to explain his hasty departure.

I would wish to be with you at Gracechurch Street and forget my loss.

Your sister,
Mary

Elizabeth shook her head in disbelief and again read the short missive, all meaning and emotion in four scant lines. Mary sounded heartbroken, expressed in the manner that only Mary could. *Oh dear. Her loss is painful, but over time, considering her escape should lessen the hurt.*

She turned next to Kitty's letter, anticipating small drawings of barn creatures and flowers and mentions of bonnet trimmings and young men. Her disappointment was hardly felt.

Lizzy,
Disaster has struck! We are free of the terror of Mr Collins, but he has set forth ghosts and fears all over Hertfordshire!

The man lurked where he should not have, and he eavesdropped when I told Lydia what Miss Bingley overheard a footman tell a maid that Mr Darcy told Mr Bingley: the long-dead Anne de Bourgh is speaking from the grave as a ghost or a vengeful spectre!

Miss Bingley, whom you know I consider a friend and counsellor in my striving to be a more thoughtful person of style and art, says rumours of Miss de Bourgh's return to the living are untrue. She denies that Mr Darcy tried to murder his cousin and the poor lady is in hiding. Miss Bingley is furious, and she has declared the servants at Netherfield to be thieves and liars.

I know not what to think. Lydia consulted with Mr Wickham, and he expressed no surprise at the story. Did you suspect Mr Darcy of such nefarious doings? You danced with him and were friendly with him. I would think Mr Collins capable of bad things, but Mr Darcy is so handsome. Not so much as Mr Wickham, but I think him a finer looking gentleman than any around Meryton, even Samuel Lucas, who is beneath my notice. Miss Bingley advised me so.

Mr Collins deemed himself a protective knight and said he must return to Hunsford to assist his patroness, Lady Catherine de Bourgh. He left us this morning.

Mary is sad. Mama is angry. Papa is amused. Lydia is greatly relieved. She felt Mr Collins's eyes lingered too long on her neck and below. It is true, Lizzy. They did linger, as did his odour. He smelled of fish and sweat. I am relieved that Aunt Gardiner, who is especially sensitive to such offenses, was not here to faint.

Please write as you may with your news and advise me on how best to think on these matters. Also, do you agree that Samuel Lucas is beneath my notice? He smiles at me a great deal.

Your sister,
Catherine

Elizabeth set down the letter and drew a deep breath. A new crop grew in Hertfordshire: insanity. She turned to her final envelope and pulled out the page.

Dearest Lizzy,

I live in a madhouse. Truly, dear sister. Mr Bingley has revealed a startling truth about Mr Darcy. He thought you betrothed to Uncle Gardiner!

Further, Mr Collins has left, declaring himself necessary to the aid of Lady Catherine and her daughter, who is rumoured by Mr Collins and at least one footman to be alive!

I wonder whether this means that Mr Darcy will now be married to Miss de Bourgh? Or has he found a new bride on his estate visits? He and his cousin were recently at Netherfield, pausing on their journey from Kenilworth to London. The cousin, a Colonel Fitzwilliam, indicated that Mr Darcy had been relieved not to wed Miss de Bourgh. They were gone before the news had spread of her supposed re-emergence among the living.

As Mr Bingley and I are courting, I hesitate to ask too many questions of him. I confess, I have not spoken to him about the gossip Mr Collins perpetuated and which has so angered Caroline. With our cousin gone, the whispers about Mr Darcy's friendliness towards you have quieted a bit. Mr Darcy did ask after you; I believe he missed your conversation. Did he never question you about your supposed nuptials? It is a puzzle, Lizzy, though his mind has been much occupied with his mourning. Unless his betrothed is alive.

Mr Bingley's sisters have little tolerance for gossip. They fired the footman and at least one lady's maid and requested to return to London. Mr Bingley assures me of his plans to stay on at Netherfield. I am confident enough in his affections that his concern for his friend worries me not. If Mr Darcy requires his aid to sort through the confusion in Kent, Mr Bingley has my blessing. And, Lizzy, he has my love. There—I have said it. I do love Mr Charles Bingley.

You and he are my stalwarts. I hear Mama calling for her salts and Lydia laughing in relief. Kitty remains in thrall to Miss Bing-

ley, and Mary is quieter than is usual. *I found her in the garden today, staring at the beehive. I wonder whether she had some affection for Mr Collins.*

Oh, Lizzy, I have gone on so long. Do write to me and tell me of your adventures.

Your loving sister,
Jane

Elizabeth sank back into the pillows. There was much to think on. Jane loved Mr Bingley, and he appeared to love her. Miss Bingley was a spying shrew, with Kitty her worshipful acolyte. Lydia was confiding in Mr Wickham, and Mary was staring sadly at beehives. Mr Collins was gone—his truth-twisting and dastardly aspersions with him—and only two in the Bennet household were bereft.

Miss de Bourgh might or might not be dead. Mr Darcy might or might not be a murderer or a grieving groom, but he was most certainly a simpleton. *He thought me betrothed? To Uncle Gardiner? He is indeed an idiot, or Mr Bingley was confused in conveying the information.*

Unable to determine an event or conversation with Mr Darcy that would have created such an impression, she preferred to think the latter. *Mr Bingley is a kind man, but he is prone to misinterpretation and susceptible to his sisters' opinions. He is mistaken in his understanding.*

Then another thought occurred to her: perhaps Mr Wickham was right about Mr Darcy and his motives. He was ever friendly to her in spite of thinking her promised to another. *What was that about?* He had trifled with her, and he was careless with her emotions and reputation. Then he returned to Netherfield and asked after her. How singular.

She pulled her knees up under her gown and rested her chin on them as she measured what she knew of the man. A valued and helpful friend to Mr Bingley. A skilled chess player whose conversation was enjoyed by her father. A hearty voice in song, a learned dancer and reader. And a man determined to find a rich, young, well-placed wife. He was handsome, vexing, and possibly—perhaps likely—badly behaved. And he was no longer bereaved if Miss de Bourgh was indeed alive.

Unless he had truly hoped her dead.

Anne was alive and married. Elizabeth was not attached and within reach. The shock had worn off more quickly than the effects of the port. Darcy found himself unable to sleep, overwhelmed by thoughts and emotions, and unable to think of anything beyond the lady whose existence posed a problem to be delicately addressed—and the other whose existence was now the forefront of all that truly mattered.

He was aggrieved at his stupidity, but he could forgive himself for being too preoccupied with the not-quite-true death of one young lady to fully think on the marital status of another. Of course, it appeared everyone else in town was equally confused about him.

The Grieving Groom, indeed. How mortifying.

He was accustomed to deference and respect wherever he went; why would he pay heed to the way a handful of families in a provincial town perceived him? Or imagine that they thought him betrothed, bereft, and boasting of the burdens of seeking a wife? At least Elizabeth was sensible. They had conversed and learned about each other. *She* knew he was a good, honest man, not one rebounding from a loss by charming young ladies for sport.

Elizabeth was in London. He could find her there; he *must* find her there. Duty, he acknowledged painfully, tugged at him. He had neglected to fully oblige his family duty when the news of Anne's 'death' first arrived. Now he and Richard must seek out answers, and they must assist Anne, the man she called her husband, and the child she carried.

Anne, with child. Good lord! Darcy rubbed his temples. He had never imagined Anne employed in the mechanics of coupling. His mind shifted easily to thinking of Elizabeth and imagining her beauty and liveliness gracing his bed. He had much work to do if he was ever to see her there.

She is not attached and thought me in grief over my own attachment. I am a fool. But far worse, to her, I appear careless in my affections.

The first thing to do—when he returned from this godforsaken journey to the ninth circle of hell—would be to seek her out. Society be damned, there had to be some way to see her. She was his friend, and he wished her to think well of him. More than well —he wished her to admire him as he did her.

The cousins slowed their horses and stared at Rosings Park. The grounds, always trussed and tamed into some approximation of a French estate, now showed signs of falling into a native wildness, with odd stalks and stems growing out of topiary ears, wildflowers and weeds emerging from between cracks in the mortar, and what appeared to be a herd of deer enjoying a patch of clover.

"It has been but seven weeks," Darcy mumbled. "The land is reclaiming the place."

"It is reasserting the natural order of things," Richard replied, staring at a large squirrel. "See that? In her absence, her enemies are encroaching. Lady Catherine despises deer and rabbits, any and all manner of furred creatures."

"Vermin, every blasted one."

"Except for the dead ones wrapped around her neck."

Darcy shook his head, an all too common physical response to his aunt's behaviours. He hated being here, hated Rosings and all the memories it held and the burdens it placed upon him. Burdens and mistruths, lies upon lies. Occasionally, when his aunt behaved especially awfully, he would wonder how his mother, the loveliest, kindest lady who ever lived, had considered Lady Catherine such a sweet, dear sister. Had she prevaricated, hoping not to sully her son's ears with tales of sisterly malevolence? It must be that—his mother had not been stupid. After all, she would remind him to hide his cat when her sister paid a visit.

The cousins rode on to the dower house where they

dismounted and made a circuit around it, knocking on and rattling doors and peering in windows.

"It is as tight and closed off as our dear aunt's mind," Richard growled. "There are spiders overtaking both houses. It is October; why are they not all dead?" He shuddered and climbed on his horse. "Anne said they were turned out of here. Let us be off to the parsonage."

They were less than a mile away from their final stop on what Darcy thought of as a thankless endeavour. After leaving Netherfield, the men had stopped briefly at Matlock House to divulge the contents of Anne's letter to Richard's parents. Darcy's aunt was speechless, his uncle apoplectic. In a voice hushed only by his son's reminders of the eager ears of hovering servants, Lord Matlock demanded to lead the investigation at Rosings. Then his wife broke her shocked silence.

"Anne fears you, Peter. She always has. Her cousins are her friends. Let them meet this Dumfries and choose whether he deserves a welcome or a sound thrashing."

Darcy was darkly amused that the voice of reason was, as usual, not a Fitzwilliam by birth.

Darcy also was full of regrets. He missed his sister and had had time only to inform her of the urgency of his journey, make promises to return within the week, remove her to Darcy House, and visit the menagerie. At Richard's urging, he had refrained from revealing the truth of Anne's life among the living until they knew more. Through a well-formed query, Darcy had discerned that his guileless sister knew nothing about Anne having a friend or suitor.

"I spent all my time in the music room or riding, and Anne kept to her rooms," Georgiana had said. "I saw her rarely. She preferred her solitude."

"Solitude, indeed!" Richard laughed.

Suitor, Darcy thought bitterly as guilt and frustration warred within him. *A title I did not want with Anne and failed to earn with Elizabeth.* He was heartsick over his misunderstanding of Anne's character, and he censured himself over his missed opportunities and stupidity with Miss Elizabeth Bennet. He was an idiot. He was a tight-lipped one as well and avoided answering any of the constant questions put to him by his amused and curious cousin. Darcy would not speak her name until he had sorted out his feelings and his future actions.

Now at Hunsford, the two men dismounted slowly, with no small amount of trepidation for what awaited them. Indeed, the newly wedded couple greeted them at the parsonage door.

"Cousins, welcome!" Anne's face was alight with joy. "Please come meet my dear husband." She stepped aside to allow them entry and turned to smile at a figure approaching from another room.

"Peregrine, these are my cousins, Richard Fitzwilliam and Fitzwilliam Darcy." She stared adoringly at a slightly built man. His thick blond hair was arranged excessively and rather oddly, and his jutting chin was marked by a prominent mole. (Or perhaps a beauty mark, Richard would later ruminate at length, at least until Darcy threw his boot at him.)

The two men, tired and still aghast by their aunt's behaviour, did their best to maintain decorum and school their manners. The couple tested their patience and exuded smug satisfaction, though the smudges on their clothes, their unkempt hair, and the cramped accommodations belied their attempt at full contentment and cleanliness. Clearly, the parsonage had not been well cared for under Mr Collins, but with his removal went the few servants assigned to do even the simplest tasks, such as wiping the table, rinsing the privy bucket, and washing the linens. A dull stink hung in the air, prompting Darcy to fling open the nearest window.

"My brother recommended fresh air, but Annie is affected by the blowing dust," Dumfries said.

"What dust? There are puddles on the ground; there is no dust." Richard looked closely at the couple. "Or is it the damp that affects her? Anne, you are much swollen."

"Damn it, Richard!" Darcy glanced at the lady. "Forgive him, Anne."

"My good sir! You speak of my wife!" Dumfries face was red, his eyes narrowed.

"She was my cousin before she was your wife," Richard

responded, glowering, "and none of the current situation sits right on the pot."

"She is my wife and the mother of my child." Dumfries smiled at the cousins, not grimly, as they did at him, but with an odd dash of insouciance. He peered closely at Darcy and gave a quick nod before extending his hand. After a long moment, he clasped Richard's as well. It was, the good colonel would later say, the dampest handshake he had borne since leaving the Continent.

"I am so happy for my family to meet at last," Anne exulted, her eyes fixed on Dumfries. Neither cousin had ever seen his erstwhile sickly relation look quite so…pink. Buxom and glowing with health and happiness, Anne was near giddy. She kept stealing glances at her husband and then would peer curiously at her cousins as if seeking their approval. Instead, they stared in shock as she sighed and leaned into the fancy man at her side, prompting Dumfries to speak in a quiet, singsong voice.

"My dearest, after all of this agitation, it is time for you to rest. Let me escort you upstairs and speak to the gentlemen, and then we shall take our tea."

As the couple left the room, it struck Darcy that Anne had likely no opportunity to introduce her husband to anyone whose approval mattered. Although the man had received no blessing before the vows, he still was due their interrogation. And that was not all.

"By the looks of him," Richard observed acidly, "the beau nasty might have benefited from a bit of advice before the wedding night."

Darcy scowled in reply. "Have you not seen Anne's…um, figure? They have been wedded but six weeks, and that babe she carries is much further along. She has had the…what is it called… the quickening?"

"Damn it to hell! We are trapped in a parsonage filled with books, cobwebs, and page after page of discarded sermons but not one bottle of brandy?" Richard looked to Darcy. "Gadzooks, we are spending the night here. I must forage for supplies."

Darcy watched through the window as his cousin mounted his

horse and rode off. When he turned, Dumfries was standing behind him.

"Sir, I believe we are due a conversation," the man said, peering up at him with narrowed eyes.

Darcy flushed with anger. "Do you? I believe you have a long list of past due conversations. Let them begin with me." He strode into the study, which was filled with reminders of Collins's dull piety and lacking any warmth or comfort—though it smelled faintly of fish. Darcy leaned against the desk, folded his arms, and faced down Anne's husband.

"Who are you? How is it that this series of events has unfolded—my cousin with child, married, and turned out of her home, and her mother telling wild tales of her death?"

Dumfries sank onto the small, worn settee and stared up at his wife's angry, imposing cousin. "If I might begin at the beginning?"

"Oh, I think the beginning and the middle would be advisable. Only then shall we determine whether there is a reasonable ending."

Dumfries nodded.

"How did you meet Anne? Who is your father, your mother?"

His father, Dumfries said, was a surgeon who, years ago, had consulted on Sir Lewis de Bourgh as his health failed. Peregrine and his older brother, Percival, had accompanied him. Percival was now a surgeon as well, and he, Peregrine, worked with him as an illustrator for a book of surgeries. Earlier this year, Percival had examined Anne during one of her bouts with fever and cough. She was especially ill with a lung ailment at that time, and the two men spent more than a fortnight at Rosings. As Anne's health improved, she took an interest in his drawing.

"I gave her a few lessons. I made sketches of her." He smiled in a manner that recalled a milk-sated pup. "Some are only for my eyes."

Darcy bit back the bile rising in his throat. *Thankfully, Richard is not here. There would be blood on his fist by now.*

"And over the course of a few weeks, we fell in love."

"In love. With Anne." Darcy peered at the man. "Forgive me, but this is incomprehensible."

"You have known your cousin all her life. Do you not see her intelligence and wit and how those manifest into beauty?" Dumfries rose and stalked to the window. "You, sir, have not valued my Anne."

My Anne? Darcy stared at the man's back. "I have always esteemed Anne as my friend."

Dumfries whirled around, his colour high and voice pitched sharper than seemed natural. "I have to ask you, sir. Are you here to challenge me, or is it as Anne assures me? That you never planned a proposal."

Darcy's jaw dropped. "What kind of jest—?"

"Anne's mother. Her fury was directed at me, and among her accusations was that I compromised her daughter in order to steal her from you, her promised suitor."

"He was never Anne's promised suitor," growled a grim voice. Richard entered the room carrying a bottle in each hand. "You, Mr Dumfries, are the only suitor our cousin has ever known. And a skulking one at that."

He set down the bottles, pulled three glasses from his coat pocket, and poured them each a generous serving. Darcy took his gratefully but Dumfries demurred. Richard gave him a bemused stare.

"The larger question is: Why Anne? Her fortune?"

"Her fortune?" Dumfries sputtered. "No, her mother controls that. It is her eyes—her lovely eyes—her dimples, and the glow of her gentle spirit." He looked at them solemnly. "I am a painter. She is a goddess. Neither of you sees this?"

Neither did. They tried, earnestly, as the evening wore on, replete with lovesick murmurings, tepid tea, and a tasteless dinner. Anne was sorely correct in missing Rosings's cook. Mrs Jenkinson had little talent in the kitchen and relied upon the help of a local girl to put together simple meals. If there was one dish an army man never wished to taste on a night out of uniform, it was mutton stew.

Richard, never at a loss for words, made clear to Anne that her cousins might not fully understand her current entanglement but would do nothing to contest it. Wedded, consummated, in whatever haphazard order, it was futile to fight it.

"We must get you back in your mother's good graces so your child can have a decent meal."

Anne beamed and laid her head on her husband's shoulder. "You see, Peregrine? They are wonderful boys."

Dinner behind them, the two men chose to forgo further conversation with the couple and retired to the chambers they would share. "Ye gods, I could swear that was bow-wow mutton in that broth," Richard muttered. "Awful stuff. I wonder whether all the dogs have gone missing."

Darcy chose not to think on their thin, foul-tasting repast. Tomorrow would be another dreadfully long, unpleasant day. There were papers to be examined and decisions to be made here, then violent arguments to be had back in London. First, he needed sleep. "I never knew our cousin so cared for her possessions," he said after peeking into the spare room packed floor to ceiling with crates, boxes, and trunks of Anne's paraphernalia. "I feel I never knew her at all."

Settling into the room, they tiredly removed their boots. "What are we to do, Darcy? Our cousin is happy, never mind that she is immodestly in love with, and married to, a fop."

"And carrying his child." Darcy's voice strained with disgust as he struggled out of his jacket.

Richard groaned. "Please, no more! How is it that our aunt shirked her duties and did not call out instructions through the doorjamb? Mayhap, she left a note?"

"What did you say?" Darcy asked in a tired voice, pulling off his cravat and unbuttoning his waistcoat.

"I had always imagined her hovering about on the wedding night."

"You did what?"

"Er, nothing." Richard threw his vest and cravat on the chair and looked around for an extra blanket. "Good lord, they are an awful pair. They never stopped touching each other in our presence. Imagine their behaviour when alone."

"Oh, I think I shall not." Darcy shuddered. "It is remarkable how much Anne is under his sway, and her mood is far more pleasant than I can recall since…ever."

"What has he done to her, besides the obvious?"

"Love?" Darcy folded his trousers and slid under the covers. *Blast!* The mattress was, as he had anticipated, from a prior century and had rarely seen re-stuffing.

"Hardly. He is a saucy bugger, is he not?"

"That hardly bears comment, Richard. You are the more knowledgeable military man."

The colonel's eyes widened, and he chuckled. "Aren't you the filthy one?" He uncorked the remaining brandy and took a swig. "I shall need to be drunk to sleep in this house."

Darcy agreed but declined the liquid assistance. "By the way, how did you get to town and secure brandy so quickly?"

"Oh…I had forgotten that one of my secret hiding places was close by." At Darcy's raised eyebrows, he rather sheepishly explained. "Lady Catherine would always have our rooms searched for liquor and engagement rings, you know. I have found hollow trees to be extremely useful things while visiting her."

Too tired to be shocked any further by his aunt's behaviour, Darcy laughed in understanding. He shifted under the thin blanket and observed aloud that Dumfries's chin mole slipped while he chewed, which sent Richard into a coughing fit of laughter.

"The man is an artist. He needs to study his paints a bit better or find a bigger mirror!"

"Think on it, Richard." Darcy held up a hand to quiet his cousin. "It was good of God to let Anne and Dumfries marry each other, thus making only two people miserable and not four."

Richard sighed. "If they get a foothold back into Rosings, it is likely that the steward, housemaids, and footmen will be miserable as well."

"Yes, but they at least are recompensed for their misery. I would assume a happy Anne and a sweet baby would alleviate some of the gloom for the servants." Darcy heard Richard's chuckle. "We must ensure to raise their wages from whatever Lady Catherine was paying them."

"Darcy, what was that woman thinking, closing the house and lying about her daughter's death? How do we fix this?"

Suddenly, both men heard high-pitched squeals of laughter, followed quickly by a prolonged guttural moan and the creaking of springs. Within seconds, the wall behind them began to take abuse from an oak headboard.

"There is not enough brandy in two counties to erase this night from my memory," Richard groaned. He threw a pillow over his head.

CHAPTER TEN

The meeting with Peter Fitzwilliam, Earl of Matlock, was only the first of three *colloquium horribilis*. Lady Matlock and Georgiana were visiting the shops when the two cousins arrived at the house, allowing them to be as frank and, in Richard's case, as bawdy as necessary. Lord Matlock, not a man known for repressing his anger, sat completely still as his son and his nephew told the long, twisting tale of their cousin Anne: her secret swain turned husband, her delicate yet oddly robust condition carrying the impending heir, the couple's less than luxurious living conditions, and the pitiable state of Rosings.

Richard watched his father carefully for signs of apoplexy. Anne's presence above ground and her stomach swollen with child belied long-held notions about the weakness of the Fitzwilliam constitution. It was a shocking turn of events, and his father was known for his volatility. The fireplace was swept often for shards of the brandy glasses thrown there during arguments with his sons, friends, peers, and neighbours. Only his wife's calm presence could mollify him once his wrath was fully engaged. At times,

Richard wondered whether his father was cognisant of his similarity to his only living sister.

However, this time, his response was unexpectedly delayed. Cool and collected, Lord Matlock asked for the specific details of their journey.

"Did you see the wedding licence?"

"Yes, sir. Legally, all was as it should be."

"So…" The earl leaned back in his chair. "We have a wedding licence and no death notice."

Richard saw Darcy glance at the table where a decanter and two glass tumblers awaited their sacrifice to the fireplace bricks. He seemed uneasy with his uncle's tranquil demeanour.

"So…"

Oh, this is truly odd. Mayhap he will simply fall over. Richard braced himself.

"Anne has found herself a husband—a man of a lower social sphere who proclaims to love her but married her in secret and impregnated her."

"Yes, sir."

"And thus Anne—wan, sullen, sickly, sneezy, wheezy Anne—will bear the first Fitzwilliam grandchild." The earl looked hard at Richard.

"Sir, if you recall, I am unwed. My brother, however, married these three years, could be called to task on the issue. Or, mayhap, the lack of an issue."

He smirked. The fuse was lit. His father jumped out of his chair.

"Damn it, Richard! Anne was left vulnerable to the arts and allurements of a foppish painter. Rosings Park lies exposed to the machinations of whatever this man might have planned." The earl paced the floor, one fist punching the air, the other free to arm itself with glassware. "He busies himself doing the rumpity-pumpity with Anne in that rotting excuse for a parsonage, and my sister has fled, rejecting the marriage, denying the child, and claiming her daughter dead. This is madness!"

Never a small man, the earl loomed over the two men who were three decades younger and made smaller by hunger and fatigue. "Could neither of you boys do your duty and marry her? Beget an heir or two and take a mistress who has the fleshy figure and pointy dugs any man craves?"

"Uncle, you know that is not fair." Darcy cringed, seemingly aware that he sounded like a ten-year-old boy.

"From the *cradle*, Darcy, as my sister claims. You could have honoured that promise, and we would not be in this bloody predicament!"

Richard's head spun; his father's much-anticipated apoplexy seemed imminent. But Darcy was livid.

"I did *not* honour it," Darcy spat, his hands fisted and shaking, "as it was neither my mother's promise nor the truth! It was another of your sister's prevarications. You know this, and now all of this matters. All of it." He glared at his uncle, obviously furious that the blame for choices and mistakes made by Anne and Lady Catherine were being laid at his door.

"Father, what is done is done. Anne is married and has consummated her vows. Repeatedly." Richard closed his eyes for a moment, willing away the sickening memories of the cries, moans, and thumping springs that had kept him awake the night before. *Whoever thought a cock robin could enjoy a woman—a woman like Anne—so robustly? Or that she would enjoy it so loudly?*

"Those facts, and these, are before us," he continued. "She is carrying the child of a popinjay and appears bewilderingly happy. Rosings is in disrepair with no servants to care for it. And Lady Catherine has spread lies and slander across the countryside about her daughter's death."

"It is wretched, I tell you," the earl growled, glaring at Richard. "I fear your mother's wrath on my idiot sister."

Darcy grimaced and implored his uncle to calm down. "We need to address those concerns that have a resolution and determine a way forward through the lies and mistruths."

The older man nodded, but when he eyed the glass tumblers sitting a few feet away, Darcy sat up quickly and spoke with great urgency. "We have directed Mr Beeker, Rosings's steward, to rehire the servants or find new people as needed. He was in possession of a key to the kitchens, and he will open the house for Anne and Pe...her husband."

"Peregrine," Lord Matlock said sourly. "Did the girl we thought was frail as a bird truly marry a man *named* for a bird?" The earl looked at the two exhausted men seated before him. "My sister is mad. Why did she not announce that Anne is off to the seaside or to Scotland? Why claim her as dead? She has placed the family in an impossible position!"

All three could agree on that point. The earl, saying he wished to drink and sulk and consider his next steps before facing his wife, dismissed Richard and Darcy until dinner the following evening. He had meetings with solicitors and lords filling his time, and he declared they would confront Lady Catherine two days hence.

Darcy said he wished for nothing more than to go home and take a bath. He smelled of fish, mutton, and perhaps spilled brandy. Richard pleaded a desperate need for sleep, sustenance, and the avoidance of his parents once his father told his mother the sordid tale, and he joined Darcy for the half-mile ride to Mayfair.

As they rode slowly towards Darcy House. Richard's mind focused on the larder there and the good care Mrs Hopkins would give to 'the poor boys.' *Yes, we few, we happy few. We band of brothers who avoided entanglement with Anne. So she caught herself a peregrine. A bird of prey.* He chuckled quietly.

Darcy spent the few blocks thinking on his family's present circumstances and wishing he had had a moment with his sister. He had left her a note requesting that she spend the following day with him at the menagerie. That thought brought a smile to his face. One small, happy thing amid all of this rot, decadence, and destruction.

And then he saw her. *Elizabeth Bennet.* Just as the first time he had laid eyes on her, she was holding hands with small children and laughing. Her eyes sparkled with joy as she swung their hands with graceful energy. *The other woman holding hands with the older boy—Henry, was it?—must be the aunt, Mrs Gardiner. The boy had her light eyes, not Lizzy's flashing dark ones.*

The small party turned the corner and disappeared from sight. *Lizzy?* He shook his head. *Where did that come from?* But he knew. It hit him with all the force of the moment and the emotions that had been roiling in him since he had heard of Anne's 'death.' Darcy knew he had been searching for one thing, one source of happy constancy. He had found her, paid her no serious attention despite enjoying her company, and assumed her to be promised away. What a rum-ned he was. But she was here, so close now. It was time, finally, to talk of more than books and ideas and butterflies. It was time to talk about love.

I love her.

The thought startled him. Warmed and frightened him. He had not spoken to her for well over a fortnight. He had gone off to Kenilworth to see his friends and left her to her nuptials. Oh, the happy confusion, needless worry, and misunderstanding! She could be his. She would be his. Tired and in need of a hot meal but jubilant with love and hope, Darcy kicked his horse and galloped around the corner after her.

Richard followed at a slower pace.

"Miss Bennet? Miss Elizabeth?"

As he approached, he saw Elizabeth, apparently startled by his fast-moving horse, pull the children tightly to her side. When she heard her name called, she looked up in alarm, which quickly turned to utter shock.

"Mr Darcy?"

Darcy jumped down from his horse and bowed to Elizabeth and her aunt. The children stared at him, wide-eyed, and he suddenly remembered that he had neither bathed nor shaved that day. Only his shirt was clean. *I must look a sight.* He reddened but forged on.

"Miss Elizabeth, this is an unexpected pleasure," he said eagerly. "I had wondered whether I might see you while I was in town."

"Ah yes. London is a large city, so this is rather…fortuitous."

Elizabeth turned to her aunt. "Mr Darcy, may I introduce my aunt, Mrs Gardiner?"

"Very nice to meet you, madam," he replied and ventured cautiously, "I believe these young gentlemen are your sons, Thomas and Henry, visitors of late to Longbourn?"

Mrs Gardiner smiled. "Yes, returned with Lizzy and reunited with their sister, Lily." The little girl squirmed and turned her face into her mother's skirts.

"A pleasure to meet you, Miss Lily."

"Darcy?" Richard's voice cut through the awkward silence.

Darcy turned around and glared at his cousin. "I shall be but a moment. Please meet me at the house."

Richard said nothing. He smiled, tipped his hat, and rode off.

Darcy turned back to Elizabeth. His eyes softened as he gazed at her. "Please, forgive my appearance. My cousin and I have just returned from a visit to Kent, and our lodgings were rather…um, less easy than we had hoped. We are now for Darcy House to refresh ourselves."

Although her eyes betrayed confusion, Elizabeth nodded sagely. "Not a bedroom to spare at Rosings? Mr Collins claimed at least sixteen bedrooms, and the closets are more than commodious. He often has mentioned the impressive shelves."

"Your cousin is well versed in the glories of my aunt's house." Darcy bit back a smile. "Uh, there were complex circumstances in this particular visit."

"Indeed." Elizabeth's voice lost its teasing tone. "I hope Warwickshire was more to your taste and comfort."

Mrs Gardiner interrupted. "Lizzy, I must take the children to the carriage. Will you join us shortly?"

Before Elizabeth could reply, the boys had run ahead to a fine-looking, well-maintained carriage. "I shall be there in a moment," she cried as her aunt, Lily in hand, followed her sons.

Darcy realised he had little time. "I apologise for the intrusion, Miss Elizabeth. I wondered whether you… You see, I am joining my sister here in London. May we call on you? Or, perhaps, would you join us at the menagerie exhibition? I understand from your sisters that you quite enjoyed it, and I hoped you might lend Georgiana and me some of your knowledge."

Darcy watched a myriad of emotions cross her face. *Confusion, anger, indecision... What preoccupied her?*

"Miss Elizabeth?"

"I would be happy to join you at the menagerie," Elizabeth said in a halting voice. "I had hoped for another visit to see my new friends in all their furred and feathered glory."

"Splendid, splendid." Darcy smiled at her and said no more.

"Mr Darcy, I must join my aunt. If you will excuse me."

Darcy shook himself out of his haze and walked with Elizabeth towards the carriage. "Forgive me, I am not quite myself, and I am in great need of sleep."

"Your invitation, then, was it sincere or the product of a rattled mind?"

"Oh, quite serious. Quite serious indeed." Darcy looked at her intently. "My sister and I shall call for you tomorrow at, say, half-past eleven?"

"Tomorrow?" She paused before responding, "Yes, that will do."

"Good," he said cheerily. "Um, Miss Elizabeth? Where would we find you?"

Halting next to the carriage, she smiled archly. "Gracechurch Street, sir. In Cheapside. The house with the blue door."

He did not flinch, she thought later, only because he was so tired.

Elizabeth had spent the rest of what felt like an endless day avoiding her aunt's inquisitive glances and wondering what Mr Darcy was thinking. *What does he want?* To while away a few more hours before heading back on his bridal hunt? More talk of books and clouds and tree climbing? Did he think she was a convenient companion for him and his sister? What was it that Mr Wickham had said of the girl?

She had found refuge in a game of pirates with the boys and a book on naval battles that she only stared at blankly. Now, with dinner over, she sat at the writing table in her room. For nearly a week, she had managed not to think on that which again so preoccupied her: *Who is this man? Which version of him, which shadings, are correct, and which stray outside the lines of truth?* Thinking about Mr Darcy was both exhausting and fascinating, though she chastised herself for the latter.

He was betrothed, or he was not. His promised bride was dead, or she was not.

Regardless of whether Anne de Bourgh lived, he had deserted her. Or he had not. He was unkind to his sister. Or he was not.

Her sources were less than impeccable. In her recent experience, men were creatures of deceit and confusion. Although a self-professed learned man of the cloth, Mr Collins proved himself a greedy, opinionated, even naïve observer of the human condition. He had the temerity to judge her a bit wanton for her open friendliness to a man she thought bereaved. Mr Wickham made a handsome man in uniform, but he appeared too eager to share his tales, to soak in sympathy, to rest his eyes on unworldly country girls.

As for Mr Darcy, Elizabeth felt chastened in her openness to him. She had enjoyed his company, but now she felt the disparity in their status, in their friendly conversation, in her buried hopes and expectations. No more than comfortable repartee had ever been assumed, but his leaving for another estate party had hurt—she hated to admit it—and left her feeling more alone at Longbourn than ever before. She had no claim on his attentions and no right to feel his absence.

Those who had noted her friendliness to Mr Darcy failed to see the effect his departure had upon her. Jane was so occupied with Mr Bingley that she did not see how her sister had grown quiet. She was accustomed to an Elizabeth who listened to, asked questions about, and expressed enthusiasm over Jane's exultations on her wonderful gentleman of Netherfield. Papa seemed to miss his chess-playing friend but observed no more. Her mother regretted the departure of a rich man in spite of his possibly scandalous and blackguard behaviour, but she appeared more concerned over the loss of Mr Collins as a suitor for her daughters. While quite pleased with Mr Bingley's steady attentions to Jane, Mama was satisfied when Mr Wickham, often accompanied by a friend or two from the militia, came to tea. Elizabeth, loath as she was for *that* man's company, had forced herself to attend in order to police her mother's eager ear and loose lips for gossip and aspersions on Mr Bingley's absent friend.

It was insufferable to feel this way, to have regret and hope and anger warring within her heart. Elizabeth did not lament that little had passed between them, but she was steeled against resuming Mr Darcy's friendship. Even though his eyes sparkled with amused intelligence...and that lock of hair fell in his eyes...and his lips curved in that soft smile when discussing the stars or listening to her light-hearted stories about her neighbours.

They should not be friends; but now, he was here in London and requesting she meet his sister. She could not imagine his motives. Was his sister made dull here as he had been in Hertfordshire, and would a country girl's company serve as a useful diversion? Was she little more than an unpaid companion for tired, jaded Darcys? Did the girl know the true fate of Miss de Bourgh? Did Mr Darcy? Why had he gone to Rosings?

For all that she wished to know, Elizabeth could only arrive at a single conclusion: Mr Darcy remained a mystery. However much meeting his sister might allow her some further discernment of his character, the prospect of making her acquaintance raised ever more worries and questions.

Will a girl accustomed to London society and a great estate in the north lower herself to allow this country gentleman's daughter as her guide among the wild beasts in the menagerie? Will she suffer my company simply to satisfy her brother's intentions?

What are *his intentions?*

Elizabeth sighed and stared at her reflection in the wall mirror. Miss Bingley would find the request for her company perfectly apt. *The wild girl of Hertfordshire would of course have cause for familiarity with the wild, untamed animals of Africa.*

Throwing herself down on her bed, Elizabeth wondered how the next morning would pass. She could talk of books and children and ribbons and grass, but her cache of such anecdotes was near empty. She would not enjoy herself overmuch. It was a good thing the man would not be long in town. She was in no danger.

"I shall break you, you know."

Richard smiled in the coldly amused manner that so disturbingly resembled Miss Bingley. Darcy turned away and filled his plate.

Richard's moustache twitched. "Darcy, who was that young lady? Miss Elizabeth Bennet? You have neglected to tell me how you know her and in what connexion."

Settling himself at the table, Darcy maintained his silence.

"Come now." Richard appeared annoyed. "You virtually vaulted off your horse, and I must say, Orlando was one unhappy steed."

Darcy took a bite of the cold roasted pheasant and nearly sighed aloud. A bath, a shave, clean clothes, and now this vast repast. He had done his time in coaching inns and once, while at Cambridge, spent a night in the stables after failing to return before the gates were locked. But he had never felt quite as… dreadful as he had a mere two hours ago. His spirits were low, disturbed, and chaotic after learning of Anne's new status—and made worse after their visit there—but they had improved remarkably upon seeing Elizabeth. He despised importuning her while in his state of vileness, but it had to be done. She had been placed in his path as a stroke of good fortune or as reward for his endeavours. He had to seize the moment and secure some time with her.

Now he felt himself again: Fitzwilliam Darcy, master of Pemberley, man of decisive action. A good meal, a short nap, and he and Richard would resolve how to best address Lady Catherine and peel back the remaining layers of deceit. They would need Richard's mother to help mend the social damage, which they could hope would be confined to 'that unpleasant, eccentric branch of the Fitzwilliam family.' Never before had the family's happy, comfortable situation in society been so imperilled. They had earned favour as supporters to their friends, hosts of grand parties, and timely payers of their bills. All would be well, eventually, if all would cooperate.

He consumed half his dinner before turning to Richard. "Miss Elizabeth Bennet is the sister to Jane Bennet, whom Bingley is courting in Hertfordshire. She and I often served as their chaperons while I was at Netherfield."

"Ah, of course," the colonel replied.

But Richard wished to know more, to know the story behind his cousin's odd behaviour. His own reconnaissance of the tempting armful whom Darcy had chased down raised puzzling questions demanding deliciously detailed answers. *Darcy's object of pursuit has a lovely set underneath that pelisse, though something tells me that pair is the lesser of what fascinates him.* Not that he would mention this particular observation to his repressed, possessive cousin, but he anticipated an interesting conversation ahead, preferably over brandy not poured from moss-covered bottles.

Richard sat back and watched Darcy stab another bit of creamed potatoes. Apparently, the man would not break easily. *Pity.* He was tired and less inspired to play than usual. No matter, he would interrogate him further. It was his cousinly duty, after all. He had never before seen Darcy eager to solicit female attention, and this one did not fit the portrait of a lady he had imagined for him. Not that he thought too much on such things, of course. It was all that damned time waiting for battle with nothing to do and his blasted imagination running wild. Hence, those cursed visions of Anne as his bride. Thankfully, he could leave those thoughts behind—and the dreadful visions as well. *Please!*

He stroked his moustache to clear it of crumbs. "There is more. Speak, Darcy."

"I enjoyed her company. We discussed books and history, and I wished to greet her. It would have been rude to pass her by."

Books and history. Of course. Richard rolled his eyes. "She passed you by and never saw you. But you saw fit to pursue her while in a most wretched state and greet her?" He chuckled, sat back from his empty plate, and stared at Darcy. "I have seen you at balls and dinners, done up to the nines with a freshly shaven face and a ruffled silk cravat tied around your neck. Not once have I seen you pursue a woman for conversation. Ever."

Later, Darcy would attribute his moment of weakness to fatigue. He was tired and in need of sleep. But he was also tired, so tired, of half-truths, lies, and deceptions in his family and in society. So when Richard pushed him again to explain his attentions to Elizabeth Bennet, he did. Briefly.

"She is the only woman of my acquaintance whom I can imagine marrying."

It was a rare thing to leave the all-knowing Richard Fitzwilliam speechless. Darcy would like to do it more often, and he suspected that Elizabeth was just the woman to manage it on a frequent basis. He left the dining room and headed to his rooms, where he pulled off his boots and stretched out on his bed. He would close his eyes for a few minutes before attending to the post and returning to his uncle's house to see Georgiana. He would tell her about the plans for tomorrow and ensure that she felt able to make a new friend. She would like Elizabeth straightaway, he was certain, if only his sister would put forth the effort. And Elizabeth would draw her out and make her smile as she had done with him within moments of their introduction. Thinking back on it now prompted the same response.

They had met barely two months ago—and had immediately become friends, he thought, over the story of Mr Eggleston's burned books. In ensuing weeks, their conversations ranged over terrain he had never covered with a lady and quite rarely with a man. Bingley and Richard certainly did not care for books as he did. Since Cambridge, he had found friendships in his fencing school or at his club, and none of them had ever once touched on Milton's musings on Dante or the curious shape of a cloud that resembled a chicken.

There is no one like her. Not another woman in England on any estate or in any house. She was like no one he thought he would fall in love with and marry, but she was everything he wanted that person to be—except for the unmentionables, of course, such as social standing, family name, and wealth. And those unmentionables *would* be mentioned by his family in spite of proving no real obstacle; she already had risen above the people of her town and her family, and his wealth was enough for their comfort. He would have to suffer her mother, but had he not suffered for years under the tantrums and smothering demands of Lady Catherine? It might be best if Lady Matlock never met Mrs Bennet, but Elizabeth was reasonable. Some arrangement could be worked out to lessen the effect her mother could have on their happy felicity.

Her father was an intelligent man, a dry conversationalist, and an astute player of chess; but whether from disinterest or indolence, he had neglected his estate. Clearly, there would be little or no dowry. He thought with some pride that he had done a fine job these past five years ensuring that Pemberley and his other estates and investments thrived. All was well. She need bring nothing but her charming, beautiful, intelligent self to the marriage. And to the marriage bed. He groaned. It had long been an effort to suppress his more rapaciously intimate thoughts about her, but she enflamed him. His skin tingled when she was near; he felt hot, itchy, and fully alive. He ached for her, but it was more than lust—he was sure it was love.

She would be overwhelmed by it all, but he would guide her. He would lie beside her and teach her about all they could share. *Good lord.* Darcy closed his eyes. *There it is again.* Visions of her beside him flooded his mind. Her hair, loose around her shoulders, her bare shoulders… He had repressed such feelings for so long, but once he saw the first and only woman to tempt him in years—or ever—he had to redouble his efforts not to think of her *that way.* It was safe to think of her brains and her beauty and her eyes—always her eyes. But by all that was holy, he had to fight his observations about her figure—her lovely, heart-pounding, trouser-tightening figure.

Darcy sighed heavily. In spite of the entreaties of his friends and cousins to enjoy himself, he had not touched a woman in better than three years. Lying abed at Hunsford, trying desperately not to hear—let alone laugh or scream at—the sounds emerging from the room next door and trying to block dreadful images of Anne in ecstasy from imprinting themselves on his sex-deprived brain, had been exhausting and sickening.

Had he and Richard ever been as dull as they had been that morning? They rode away tired, hungry, unshaven, and unbathed from that sorry excuse for a love nest after making promises to pry open both Lady Catherine's mind *and* Rosings's doors. They could not make eye contact with Anne or her preening husband, who grinned at them like the cat who ate the canary. Just the vague memory of those torturous hours now softened his desire and his traitorous body's urges.

Tomorrow. He would see Elizabeth tomorrow and re-capture that charmed amity they had shared in Hertfordshire.

He closed his eyes and fell into a dreamless sleep.

CHAPTER ELEVEN

Georgiana was full of questions about their detour to Cheapside. She wondered about this new friend her brother had invited on their excursion, and she seemed dissatisfied with his explanation that Miss Elizabeth Bennet was a neighbour to the estate Charles Bingley was leasing.

"Fitzwilliam, do you know her well? Is she much older than I am? Will we share interests? Why has she not called on us, and why has my aunt not mentioned her?"

Darcy gave his sister a soft smile. *So many questions, only half of which I can answer.* He recognised that she had lived under the Fitzwilliams' roof for some weeks now, and being an intelligent girl, he had anticipated her suspicion that their aunt and uncle knew nothing about this new friend. In fact, he had to ask for Georgiana's help in this subterfuge.

"As I mentioned, Miss Bennet is visiting her aunt and uncle, and she has been to the menagerie. When I saw her sisters at Netherfield a few days ago, they made reference to how delighted she was to see the wild animals." Darcy glanced at his sister.

"When I unexpectedly encountered her yesterday, I enquired as to her interest in showing us her favourites. She was well-informed about the flora and fauna around Netherfield and her own estate."

Georgiana nodded. "She is a new acquaintance, then, who has met the Bingleys?" She paused a moment. "Does she claim Miss Bingley as a friend?"

Darcy cleared his throat. "Um, I believe she would refer to Miss Bingley as an agreeable acquaintance." He wondered how much to say. "Her elder sister, Jane, has formed a stronger friendship, I believe, due to Charles's interest. Have I mentioned he is courting her?"

"Oh yes," Georgiana sighed. "Is Jane…the sister…is she beautiful and blonde?"

She knows Charles far too well. "Yes, she is, Petal. Miss Jane Bennet is quite handsome."

"So you have noticed as well?"

"Only when asked by Charles," he replied a bit irritably.

"And Miss Elizabeth?"

"Lovely as well, but with darker colouring. In her hair and eyes," he quickly added, not wishing his sister to think Elizabeth a country girl tanned by the sun, although of course she was. "She enjoys walking a great deal."

"She sounds interesting, unlike the girls and ladies in town. If she is not often in London, is she not among the countess's acquaintances?"

"No, dear. Miss Elizabeth is but a few years older than you are, and I should think she would make you a fine friend. She is very kind to her sisters."

"Sisters? She has more than the one? How happy she must be!"

Darcy turned away to hide his expression. Elizabeth's sisters were, to borrow Georgiana's phrase, 'interesting.' He knew little of the serious one who never spoke. The younger two were more high-spirited than was truly proper but cleverer than he had first assumed. "I believe her to be a happy person. I think you will enjoy her company."

His sister gazed at him intently, tilting her head as though considering his words. "I hope so, Fitzwilliam. I will follow your direction as to what I might tell Aunt about our excursion."

Elizabeth watched from her window as the Darcy carriage pulled up to the Gardiners' home. She looked closely at the tall man who emerged from the fine equipage, wondering how he would react to the modestly sized but neatly maintained house. His expression gave nothing away, which neither pleased nor angered her. She observed his careful handling of his sister as he guided her to the door. *The girl Mr Wickham said was locked away, too forward with her attentions, and delicate in the head.* She peered more closely. The girl was decidedly cowed by the neighbourhood, she decided. Or by her brother. Or perhaps it was by fear of meeting a stranger who would show her creatures of the wild. The idea that she, Lizzy Bennet of Longbourn, was supposed to be an expert observer of the animal kingdom made her smile.

It took but a moment after they were introduced for Elizabeth to disregard everything Mr Wickham had claimed. She recognised Georgiana's resemblance to her own sister: quiet in company and kind-hearted, as evidenced by her shy delight that young Henry Gardiner eagerly wished to join them on their jaunt. The boy was immediately enthralled by the young woman, and he called Georgiana 'the golden-haired princess.' Elizabeth could see that his fixed adoration enchanted her. Speaking to Henry seemed to alleviate much of her nervousness and lessen her need to look to her brother for guidance.

During their carriage ride, Henry puffed out his chest and asserted that he knew all the best views in the menagerie and would show them to Miss Darcy. He looked to Elizabeth and Mr Darcy for approval. The man nodded his assent at his sister's besotted, waist-high suitor, as did Elizabeth.

At their destination, Darcy helped the ladies from the carriage and fell into step with Elizabeth. She knew she was in trouble when he leaned over and shared his observation on the burgeoning friendship between their young companions.

"Does Henry play chess and read books in trees?"

Elizabeth looked up at him in surprise.

"Pardon me," Darcy said quickly. "Please know that I admire that story of your childhood." Seeing her wry smile, he went on. "I have a confession to make. The first time I saw you in Meryton, you were with Henry and his brother, discussing butterflies."

She gazed away from him, deep in thought. "Yes, I recall giving them a small lecture on allowing the poor creatures a few more days to flutter in the breeze." Her eyes moved to his. "You witnessed this?"

"I was riding into town. You were laughing, and the boys' father came to join your group."

"I remember now. You were on horseback. That was my uncle, Mr Gardiner."

Darcy sighed. "Yes. I...I have learned that I made a grave mistake. Together, you all formed such a happy portrait that I misunderstood." He breathed in deeply. "I took you...I thought you to be his wife, or rather, due to the boys' ages, his betrothed."

Elizabeth froze. "My uncle?"

He nodded, his cheeks reddened. "I apologise. You were so familiar and happy."

"You thought us engaged? My uncle and I? That we were a family?"

So he was truly confused; it was not Mr Bingley who misunderstood. How disappointing. I thought him smarter. Her shock faded into mirth. "Oh, to have thought such a thing! My uncle and aunt will be so amused."

"Must you tell them?"

"I think I must."

"Your father as well?" Mr Darcy looked chagrined. "He will use it against me in the future. I shall never again best him in chess."

In the future? Her thoughts muddled, wondering exactly when Mr Darcy had determined she was not in fact betrothed. Elizabeth glanced away and watched Henry pull Georgiana towards the cage with the two monkeys.

"Henry is not the tree climber in the family. That would be his younger brother, Thomas."

Darcy smiled softly. "I meant it in fun as it seems another friendship is born between our families."

"Yes, your sister is all kindness to an inquisitive little boy."

"She is pleased to make his acquaintance—and yours, of course. Georgiana has little experience with young children but enjoys their company. She has had less freedom to make new friends of late."

"Although she has been in London, surrounded by society?"

"Um, yes. My aunt and uncle are often in society, but this is an unusual time for them to be in town. They have business here."

"With solicitors and the like, with your other aunt?" Elizabeth knew she was on the precipice of rudeness, but there were so many pieces missing from her understanding of this man.

"Yes." He clearly did not wish to discuss what appeared to be an endlessly complicated family. Watching his expression, which stiffened whenever he looked towards the passing throng, Elizabeth again wondered about his ephemeral moods. He could be kind to her and her family but then turn formal and distant in a flash.

Mayhap, he was uncomfortable walking alone with her and they should move closer to Henry and Georgiana. He was not a man used to public excursions with eligible young ladies; he was more accustomed to meeting ladies at private estates. Yet, Elizabeth realised his current actions would indicate the opposite—he did not hide the fact that they walked together as a couple. She had seen the tipped hats and fluttering eyelashes that greeted the gentleman; he was recognised wherever he went but did not deign to speak to any of his peers and devotees. It was a bit dizzying to watch him in his element.

Was he always this way, and our comfortable conversations at Longbourn were out of character? Why could this man not be simple to understand? Why had he been to his aunt's estate? To grieve a dead woman or to visit a lady he might marry?

As they neared the tiger's cage, she watched Henry gesturing wildly to Georgiana and heard her excited cry. Elizabeth glanced up at Mr Darcy and gave him a solemn look as he watched the animal yawn.

"It is magnificent," he said quietly.

"He is indeed a fearsome and beautiful sight from a distance." The animal's eyes rose to hers and began to pace.

"Mr Darcy, I believe this creature reminds me of you. He dislikes his cage and the stares of the people who are fascinated by him. You dislike the city at this time of year and wish for your estate where the people know and respect you."

Mr Darcy's eyes widened, and he chuckled as they stood in front of the large cat's prison. "*I*, akin to that creature? I will not speak to my preference for places where I am respected, but I do favour Pemberley, where things are familiar and the skies are clear. The city is quite foul."

"Indeed, the country is preferable no matter the time of year."

He took a breath. "He is a fine-looking animal, so handsome yet so terrible in his savagery."

"Yes." Elizabeth's eyes shifted from the pacing cat to the man beside her. She felt a slight softening towards Mr Darcy, and she prepared to ask after his visits to Kent and Warwickshire before realising she had lost his attention. His eyes, searching out his sister, had fallen on a young man who appeared to be approaching Georgiana and Henry. He stiffened and began to move in their direction.

The gentleman handed Georgiana an item, bowed, and moved away.

"Georgiana!" Mr Darcy hastened to her side. "What was that about?"

She turned and looked up at her brother, a frightened expression on her young face. "I…I dropped one of the soldiers Henry had given me. I put them in my purse, but I had dropped one."

When her brother remained silent, Georgiana said in a pleading voice, "Fitzwilliam, please. That is all that occurred." He nodded, expelled a breath, and squeezed her hand.

"Are these redcoats or navy men, Henry?" he asked, kneeling in front of the boy.

"Oh, redcoats, but I would like navy men, sir. My father has everything in his warehouses, all from the big ships." Henry gestured with his arms wide, his eyes sparkling with excitement.

"I would like a giraffe as well," the boy continued, "but Mama says we cannot fit one into our house. They live in deepest Africa."

Before Mr Darcy could reply, Henry turned and pointed. "The peacock is over there, miss! It has such fine feathers. Come, Lizzy!"

The small group began moving towards the bird, Henry leading Georgiana by the hand.

"I should never leave her side," Mr Darcy murmured softly. Elizabeth heard his words and turned to see the dark expression on his face. She appreciated his protective nature towards his sister, but how sheltered had the poor girl been? The man seemed to enjoy *her* friendly, expansive nature but feared it in his sister? It was as she had suspected: the Darcys were intent on a day out amid London's dangers and savage animals, chaperoned by the amiable country folk.

Darcy regained his senses and asked a few questions on the animals they had yet to see. As he listened to Elizabeth's recital of facts and impressions, Darcy wondered whether his mood was affecting his sense of the lady beside him. He was perplexed by her behaviour. Their conversation, so easy at Longbourn and Netherfield, was strained. She seemed cooler and more formal than before. Where was the friendliness, the open humour he adored?

Was she shy at seeing him again? She seemed uncomfortable and only a little amused by his confession of his former confusion. He had been mired in thoughts of marriage and his need for a wife when he had laid eyes on her with her cousins and formed an erroneous idea in his head. A foolish, ridiculous idea.

He hoped she would see the levity in his mistake. Was she perhaps insulted that he had thought her suitable for an older gentleman? He must convince her otherwise—that, in fact, he found her suitable only for himself. If his frustration was not spent, his patience was at an end. He must speak.

Her voice interrupted his thoughts.

"Were your travels fruitful in Warwickshire?"

Fruitful? Puzzled by her question, Darcy agreed only that he enjoyed his visit. "But I was happy to leave and return briefly to Netherfield. My friend is quite happy in his courtship."

"As is my sister." Elizabeth smiled, and he felt more at ease. "I need never wonder of Jane's whereabouts. Her happiness fills the air wherever she goes."

"As does Bingley's."

"Miss Bingley has proven more amenable to the relationship."

"Has she? She did appear more cordial when I saw her the other day."

Elizabeth laughed. "I believe my younger sister Kitty is owed for that. She believes Miss Bingley to be the arbiter of all that is wise and beautiful."

"Wise *and* beautiful?" His gaze drifted to her, and he willed her to notice while fearing she would. "An enviable combination."

"Or so thinks her acolyte," she said in an arch tone. "Four sisters around her, and Kitty finds her perfect lady in Miss Bingley. Jane finds her perfect man in Mr Bingley. There simply are not enough Bingleys to go around."

She sighed dramatically. They shared a look and smiled.

She is so lovely.

"I believe Georgiana may have found her acolyte in Henry." Darcy gestured at the two sitting on a bench deep in conversation.

"Mr Darcy, you have already misjudged one Gardiner's felicity. Beware of another mistake."

Biting his lip, he noted the arched brow above flashing eyes. "Acknowledged, Miss Elizabeth."

"Henry loves his mama, of course, but he confides his secrets to his rocking-horse, and his tin soldiers follow him everywhere."

Darcy smiled shyly. "My mother said the same of me and my soldiers. At least one was always sitting atop our supper table in danger of falling into the soup."

Elizabeth returned his smile. "The fancies of young boys differ greatly from young girls. I wonder how the conversation at our table at Longbourn might have been altered had we a brother or two. My father would appreciate far less talk of lace."

"I think you would have liked a brother," Darcy said gently, "with whom you could climb trees and debate clouds."

Elizabeth looked up quickly, her cheeks red. "I did have Charlotte and her brothers for the tree climbing, but you are the first to have engaged me in the scientific consideration of clouds."

"As you are for me." He stared intently at her.

"Mr Darcy, I wonder if you have read—"

Suddenly, Henry was at her side, wailing. "Lizzy, a bee has stung me!"

Georgiana joined them, distraught and beset by guilt. "Poor Henry. The bee wanted his sweet. I am so sorry I gave it to you, Henry."

Elizabeth knelt and enveloped the boy in a hug. He showed her the red spot on his hand. "I think we had best go home, Henry. We can pull out the stinger and find you a bit of ice."

"No, I am well, Lizzy. Truly." The boy sniffed. "May I have a lemon ice?"

Darcy waited for Elizabeth's nod before assuring Henry that a lemon ice would cure all ills. He smiled, led the group to a bench, and strode off quickly to a vendor.

"I am so sorry, Miss Bennet," Georgiana said. "It is quite late in the season for bees, and I did not see it buzzing about us when I gave Henry some honey candy." Georgiana stopped and bit her lip. "I apologise. I should have asked you if he could have sweets."

Elizabeth laughed and gave the girl a reassuring pat on the arm. "I am his cousin, not his mother. You are his friend. What is the joy of an adventure with a small boy if not to spoil him? He is well, and this is a fine day—bee or no bee."

Georgiana returned her warm smile. "It truly is."

"And you must call me 'Lizzy.'"

The Darcys dined with their aunt and uncle that evening; Georgiana's presence ensured lighter conversation and no mention of the de Bourgh disaster. Instead, their aunt questioned Darcy on the young ladies he had encountered at the Hadley estate and those he might meet when he visited the duke and duchess. He hesitated, unsure whether to disclose his cancellation of those plans.

"I had thought, with so much else transpiring, that I instead should attend to affairs at Pemberley." He noticed the shift in Georgiana's posture.

"Darcy, you must go to Marlbourn," his aunt insisted. "Propriety demands it, and you must make a marriage—soon."

Georgiana gasped, and her brother immediately understood her fear. "Petal, this is not about you. It is about the impatience of your aunt and uncle to see a wedding for your wayward brother."

She stared at him, eyes wide.

Richard smiled at his anxious cousin. "Your brother speaks the truth, Georgiana. My parents are tired of us old men rattling about and dilly-dallying in choosing our brides. My mother misses cooing babes in her arms."

Georgiana nodded and broke contact from her brother's intent gaze. "I like babies as well. I look forward to a niece or nephew of my own."

Darcy relaxed and smiled. "Have you not had your fill of wild, untamed creatures?"

"What is this?" Lord Matlock exclaimed, his eyes alight. "No matter his bad habits and insolence, that is an impertinent way to speak of my son."

Richard glanced at a worried-looking Georgiana and crossed his eyes to prompt a smile. "Father, you misunderstand Darcy—though 'untamed' would well describe my older brother."

Lady Matlock levelled a severe look at her younger son. "Do grow up, dear. Robert is well married and esteemed."

Darcy coughed. "Uncle, we viewed Pidock's Menagerie earlier today. The tiger proved quite fearsome."

"The monkeys made me laugh," Georgiana added.

His uncle's tone became serious. "You and your sister may have your fun, but we must settle our business tomorrow afternoon. And your aunt is correct, Darcy. You must continue to Marlbourn."

"Uncle—"

"Take Georgiana if you wish. She will make friends there. I might even spare you Richard for a fortnight."

"Father—"

"But you *will* go, and you will do what is necessary."

"He is *your* father, Richard, not mine. I will not throw myself on the marriage market to divert attention from Anne's folly and her mother's lies." Darcy stared out the window, his hand twisting the cords on the heavy brocade curtains.

Richard remained silent, watching his cousin work out his frustration. These were the first words Darcy had spoken since the two of them had left the Fitzwilliam house, and granting the man time and space to vent his anger seemed only fair.

"*I* am the one without parents, so yours and Anne's believe they have the right to order me about. 'Fix this, Darcy. Go here, Darcy. Marry her, Darcy.'" He stalked from the window to his favourite chair and flung himself into it. "I have lived my life clean of scandal, resisting temptation, and taking care of every bit of estate business and more. Yet it is not enough?" He looked up at Richard, his face angry and confused. "Does my life of so-called privilege extend only to enjoying rich foods, fine tailoring, and good horseflesh?"

Richard sat down across from him. "Neither of us wished to marry Anne, and neither of us wishes to give up having our choice of bride. I would take your place in a moment; you know that. But I offer little to society as a second son."

Darcy leaned over, his head in his hands. "Damn."

Sometimes being the kindly older cousin was exhausting. It had been far easier when they were mere youths; all that was expected then was to teach Darcy how to box and flirt and encourage him past his mourning for his mama. But then, as now, Richard recognised that Darcy supported *him* in everything *he* did, and beyond relying on him for advice with Georgiana, his cousin always asked so little of him in return. He took a deep breath.

"You said you wished to marry this girl from Hertfordshire. Tell me of her."

Darcy sat up, his eyes ablaze. "Does it matter, Richard? Does it matter that she sets my soul afire, that her mind is alive with ideas and thoughts and sweet comments that leave me paces behind, attempting to keep up? That she was kind to Georgiana? That she is beautiful, witty, and playful?" He paused a moment before adding, "That I love her?"

Love, not lust? Richard nodded. "Yes, it matters. If you have found yourself the perfect woman and you are dead sure of it, then you must marry her. It may do you well to court her first, of course," he added wryly, earning a nod from Darcy.

Richard would have snorted at his cousin's certainty had the conversation not been so serious. "You should not be punished and pay the price for Anne's happiness, such as it is. Do as you will; I will support you. And if this Miss Bennet is all you claim, the rest of the family will follow."

He gave in to a smirk. "After all, you can always hie off to Pemberley and forget us all."

Darcy gave him a weak smile. "I can, indeed." He rubbed his jaw. "Richard, you will admire her as Georgiana does. Elizabeth will be a wonderful sister for her."

Richard stood and sauntered over to the table holding the brandy decanter. "Well, then. A drink to it? To you and Miss Elizabeth Bennet."

CHAPTER TWELVE

In spite of his most grievous injury, Henry had not been able to stop talking about his great adventure. Thomas, a bit sleepy from a cold, envied his brother's jaunt with the golden-haired princess, but he was placated by an extra story from his cousin and the promise of a good game of spinning tops the following day.

"Lizzy, do you know what Miss Georgiana says?" Henry confided. "Her brother is going to a kingdom of horses and sheeps to meet his friends."

"A kingdom?"

"Yes! A duke and some ladies for her brother to meet. She wishes to go as well for she likes country houses and horses."

Does she? Is he? What is he about?

"Do you think it is a castle and they will meet princesses and knights? That would be so grand."

Her cousin's enthusiastic disclosure preyed on Elizabeth's imagination that night as she lay in her bed. Questions about Warwickshire, Kent, castles, dukes, and ladies filled her thoughts.

She awoke tired and rather cranky and feeling as though Thomas's cold had found a new host. The coal grey skies did nothing to lighten her mood; she was sure it was sunny and cool in Hertfordshire, and never had she missed the countryside so much. The morning passed slowly as the gloom and her heaviness of mind held firm.

"Lizzy, your Mr Darcy is here." Her aunt peered through the curtain in the second-floor hall window.

"Aunt, he is not *my* Mr Darcy." Her heart raced even faster than her mind as she searched for a reason for his unannounced arrival. "Why is he here?" she whispered.

"Can you not guess?" Aunt Gardiner squeezed her hand. "I have seen how he looks at you, Lizzy. He admires you a great deal."

"I wonder whether he admires every girl with a quick mind or a clever mouth. I do not understand him at all."

"You have a clever mind, dear. Think quickly. He is here now." Mrs Gardiner patted her stomach. "This babe is not an easy one. Will you manage without me? Might we trust the good character of the master of Pemberley, a man who knows my beloved Lambton, for a few moments?"

Elizabeth rolled her eyes at her aunt's teasing. "Yes, Aunt. His character vexes me, but I do believe him trustworthy."

She also thought him handsome, perplexing, witty, frustrating, and perhaps a little obtuse. He had thought her promised to another—to her *uncle*!—and never thought to ask after it? What did he and Mr Bingley talk about?

Granted, she had not engaged in conversation with him over his engagement or his dead bride, but those were delicate subjects, and his melancholy demeanour fit that mood. She could acknowledge now that his mood lifted when he was with her, and he seemed to set aside his mourning when she was near—which had been noticed rather smugly by Charlotte and more gently by Jane. And then he had left after holding her and guiding her across a dance floor. He had hovered over her hand, bid her good night, and left on his hunt for a bride, a new bride to replace the one who was dead. Or alive and certainly abandoned. And now, after that fruitless search, he was off to another estate brimming with eager prospects?

He had not even gone by Longbourn to say his farewells, yet in his bedraggled state, he had jumped off his horse in a London street to greet her and request that she meet his sister and spend a day with the two of them. He had been thoughtful, polite, and even formal at the menagerie. They had parted amicably; she and Henry had exchanged fond smiles and goodbyes with Georgiana, and the sweet girl's brother had twice thanked her for her company. His eyes indicated more feeling than Elizabeth had anticipated.

He made her head ache. Whatever his purpose now, her own was clear: to seek answers to these troubling questions. Elizabeth took a calming breath and prepared to join her caller.

Darcy stood awkwardly in the front hall, wondering whether he was all too obvious to Elizabeth's aunt; however, she made him feel welcomed. He had been to the houses of the country's richest families, but the warmth and comfort of the Gardiners' smaller, more intimate abode was as pleasant as any he could recall.

His eyes roved the walls, taking in the small collection of oils. Mrs Gardiner nodded at a painting of a mother and child. "That is my favourite, I think. My children prefer paintings with horses and wild seas."

"As did I at a young age. You have some impressive works here."

"Thank you. We are quite fortunate that my husband does business with men of true discretion and taste. Henry told us you have travelled to the Continent. Did you see works of the masters during your journeys?"

"My tour allowed me time to see a few galleries in Italy before I was called home," he said softly. "My father fell ill, and I returned to Pemberley."

Mrs Gardiner looked chagrined. "Pardon me, sir. I recall hearing only the highest compliments paid to your father and your mother. Has Lizzy told you my family is from Lambton?"

Darcy's eyes lit with interest. "I do not believe she has. Lambton is a lovely village."

"It is, though I have not seen it in years."

A child cried out from another room, and she excused herself. "Please make yourself comfortable in the parlour. Lizzy will be right down."

Darcy took a step into the room and looked around. Yesterday, he had been too preoccupied watching his sister and Elizabeth meet to truly see the house. Now he could better form an opinion, and he was indeed impressed by the clean, orderly, comfortably furnished rooms. There were paintings to admire and well-used books on tables. He could smell freshly baked bread. It calmed him but not enough to relax every nerve in his body. He felt afire. The previous day had left him unsure of Elizabeth's feelings, but her giddy laughter at his stupidity, her enjoyment of his sister, and their quiet parting filled him with hope—that damned jubilant hope—once again.

Yet he needed calm. The anger from the confrontations created by his uncle's demands and his aunt's stubbornness had dissipated a bit. His need to punch something—*someone*—had been focused instead by Richard. Insisting Darcy needed to work off his anger, he had sent late word to their fencing master, asking for a room.

Loath though he was to credit his cousin's self-professed brilliance, Darcy could acknowledge that the old dry boots had been right. The parrying and thrusting had focused his mind to one thing: evading the narrow point of his opponent's foil. Richard was strong on stratagems and movement, and he had taken some advantage of Darcy who, although younger and quicker, lacked total control of his anger.

Darcy could bear Richard's jokes. After all, the man had his own troubles—war duties and injuries, his meddlesome parents—from which he could not run away. Richard, too, would have to attend the afternoon's dreaded meeting with Lady Catherine. Darcy knew it would be awful. Yet his thoughts had cleared, and his plans had formed. He was decided. He would placate his uncle by spending two days with the duke and then travel to Pemberley with Georgiana. He had neglected his estate, and the steward's letters had become rather persistent.

First, though, he had to see Elizabeth, to confirm her feelings and to ensure that she would welcome his calling at Longbourn. They had spent little time together, and while yesterday had been less than he had hoped for, it remained the happiest span of hours he had had in weeks. Darcy knew he must leave town, but he needed to make certain she would be waiting for him, thinking of him, while he was gone. He was a rational man, and it was a sensible plan.

Then Elizabeth walked into the room and all sense failed him.

"Good morning, Miss Elizabeth."

"Mr Darcy."

"I apologise for the unexpected visit. I do my sister's bidding."

Darcy gave her a quick smile, reached into his pocket, and withdrew a single tin soldier.

"Georgiana discovered this tucked into her reticule last night." He put the toy into Elizabeth's hand, his finger lightly brushing hers. "I hope that young Henry found solace with his other toys and acolytes and did not miss this valiant soldier."

"Thank you, Mr Darcy. I dare say Henry may not have missed him yet. He was quite tired after yesterday's excursion."

"And he is well? Georgiana remains concerned over Henry's wound."

"Miss Darcy should feel no fault, truly. He is well, thank you."

"Good, good. Again, Miss Elizabeth, I appreciate your attendance with us." His voice was a little more steady. "Your cousin is a fine boy, and we took great pleasure in your company."

"It was an enjoyable adventure. I thank you."

Apparently, Mr Darcy was not quite finished with his visit. Elizabeth observed him as he stood stock still except for his hands, which appeared to be exacting a violent sort of retribution on his hat. Taking a deep breath, she recollected her manners.

"Would you care to sit?"

He paused and glanced at the doorway.

"My aunt is taking a short rest, and the children are with their nurse today."

"Their nurse?"

"Yes, Nancy has been hired only these two days, but will join the household when I return to Longbourn."

"When is that?"

"In three days."

"Oh." He looked puzzled. "You are coming and going so often."

"As are you, Mr Darcy. From Pemberley to Netherfield to Warwickshire to Kent to London, and now you are off to another estate filled with eligible young ladies."

"But they are not for me." He stepped closer. "My uncle…he insists on the visit."

And you follow his direction. She sighed softly. His eyes were far too intent. Usually, they were full of amusement at something she had said or abashed at something *he* had said. Now they were dark and focused on hers. She took a step away and moved towards a chair. He followed, and as she turned to him, he plunged ahead.

"Miss Elizabeth, I go against my family's wishes, and by my actions, I may further aggravate a family scandal, but my heart will not be still. You must know I admire you."

She blinked and sank into the chair. "You do?"

"Very much. I…I should like to court you."

At this, Elizabeth closed her eyes. The buzzing in her head, which had been faint, rose to a dull roar. This was not at all what she had anticipated.

Darcy stood above Elizabeth awkwardly before slowly sitting on the settee across from her. He leaned forward, his elbows on his knees, feeling hopelessly inept at sweet talk. *I know Greek and Latin, but where does one go for instruction on conversations of the heart?*

"What?"

"I wish to court you," he said haltingly.

"I see."

"My family will learn to admire you in spite of it all, as I do."

"As you do what?"

"Admire you. Love you."

"You love me? In spite of it all?" She shook her head. "Pray forgive me. You have praised my quickness of mind, but it fails me at this moment. You love me and wish to court me?"

"Yes." His lips moved but he stayed frozen, near dizzy, and grateful to be seated. His mind felt slow, as if all of his energy was directed towards his heart, which was beating faster than he could ever recall.

"To say the least," she said in a thin voice. "Pray, if there are no obstacles from your imaginary engagement or mine, what is 'in spite of it all?'"

Darcy sighed, feeling sheepish. "My family. They are complicated in their expectations and require much of me."

"And your former betrothed?"

"I was never promised to Anne nor to anyone else. Nor would she have married me." Darcy groaned. "Did Charles not clear that up?"

"Not entirely." Elizabeth closed her eyes and took a deep breath. "Forgive my curious nature but I must know… In Meryton, you talked to me as a familiar friend, you teased and laughed. Was it because you were thought to be betrothed or because you thought me promised to my uncle?"

Darcy's mind raced. His cousin's 'death' had been no one's business in that country town, and his mourning for Anne had rendered him safe from being fawned over for his wealth and as a potential suitor. He had enjoyed the respite, knowing nothing of his status as the Grieving Groom until Bingley informed him just days ago.

He was an ass.

"My family business is private, but I should have addressed the misconception among friends such as yourself. Most importantly, I was disappointed in thinking you promised. The more time I spent in your company, the more I regretted my chance with you."

He closed his eyes, recalling their first conversation during which he had done the unthinkable for Fitzwilliam Darcy: he had bantered with a lady. *About burned books, of all things.*

"But believing you engaged *did* in fact lessen any of society's expectations that I might have felt." He smiled at her. "Truly, I was so happy to learn of my stupidity and to discover you were not promised…so that I could openly court you."

"Stupidity, indeed," she said quietly. "So, to clarify: while I have never been betrothed, your situation confuses me. Were you betrothed?"

"I was not."

Elizabeth delicately put forth the paramount question. "The bride you were *not* to marry is dead? Or is she not?"

"She is not." Darcy paused, unsure how to explain, yet certain this was not the time to confide the sordid tale. "Anne was never my intended."

Her eyes narrowed at his reply. "Did you abandon her affections for another?"

"No, I did not!" he cried. "There was no promise, and there was no affection beyond that of two cousins. There has been no other—none until you."

"A country girl with whom you might dance but to whom your family will object."

"Not to you, not to your character!" Darcy protested.

"To my social standing—or lack thereof."

Darcy jumped up and paced around the room. "No…it is not *you*," he said in a low, urgent voice. "I am not at liberty to explain myself. It is true your family is not of the *ton*, but that is of little concern to me." He sat down in the chair beside hers, so close their knees almost touched.

"It is of concern to your family," she replied quietly.

"Much has occurred in my family these past weeks, events of which I was not aware when I met you. While the Fitzwilliams are a proud, sometimes truculent lot in the best of times, these have been the worst of times. My uncle wishes me to uphold the family name at this time as he determines the best way forward…"

"I see." Elizabeth drew in a sharp breath. "Visiting estates and raising hopes is standard practice for those of your station."

"Please. I do not explain myself well. I cannot. Even to you." Darcy cursed his uncle, his aunt, his cousin, and every member of the Fitzwilliam family who were causing him and this dear lady such tumult.

"My family situation is not an easy one. But you, Elizabeth Bennet, can merit no objection that cannot be surmounted in time."

"This is madness…you are mad."

"I am not, most assuredly not," he said with a soft smile. "It is all, alas, complicated."

Elizabeth looked away from the man sitting so close to her. She had seen that smile before, and it could weaken her righteous disappointment and anger. "Love, as you call it, often is complicated," she murmured. Straightening her shoulders, she stared across the room, letting her gaze slowly drift back to settle on his face.

"Mr Darcy, everything I know of you has shifted in the past day. Your idea of me has as well. I thought you a grieving groom; you thought me near my wedding day." Elizabeth laughed, and it sounded bitter even to her own ears. She paused and looked down at her hands, staring at a small cut on her finger, the victim of an errant needle, to focus her thoughts.

"Sir, I fail to understand: Why did you not ask about such an event? Why assume it? In what manner did I behave as a woman promised to another?"

Darcy leaned closer and stared at her hands. His fingers trembled as though yearning to grasp hers.

"These are difficult questions."

"They are not difficult; they are important," she insisted. "Why would you not enquire about an event so momentous?"

"I am not in the practice of speaking with a young lady of little acquaintance about personal matters."

She stared at him coldly. *Or asking Mr Bingley for clarification?*

"It…it creates expectations…in my experience."

Ah, the poor, hunted, eligible master of Pemberley emerges again.

Protecting himself against the huntresses. "So you spoke to me of books, flora and fauna, history, and politics?"

"Yes," he breathed out, as though relieved that she understood his direction.

"As you would with a gentleman of little acquaintance?"

"Um, no. Yes. I…I had rarely, if ever, met a young lady with whom I could speak of such things. You have such great intelligence, more so than many a man." He gazed at her intently. "It was more than diverting. I greatly enjoyed our conversations. I have missed them."

"Yet now you speak of courting me even as you set off on another wedding tour?" Elizabeth closed her eyes. Her head hurt. "I am sorry for you that your estate visits have not produced a lady of equal conversational arts. Mayhap, you will find your equal in income and social standing on this new journey."

Darcy reached out and grasped Elizabeth's hand. "There is no one for me but you."

Her eyes flashed as she pulled her hand away. "I cannot think that true. What depth of feeling can you have for me? You tell me your family will not accept me, and they are near impossible to please. You say I diverted you as a gentleman friend might do. You speak words of love, yet you are off to continue your marriage hunt."

She bowed her head. "Your imagination is very rapid. It jumps from admiration to love, from love to matrimony, in a moment."

"No, Elizabeth, you misunderstand."

"Yes, as do you. You are too familiar, sir, and you mistake my feelings, and I mistake your character."

"My character?"

Abruptly, she stood and walked across the room, turning to pronounce her verdict.

"I heard the words spoken by Mr Collins and Mr Wickham, but I believed better of you. Still, although I give them no credence, I do not understand you. I am not certain whether—"

His face paled. "Wickham? How do you know that man?"

"He was with the militia in Meryton."

"Good lord," he spat out. "He is not a man to be believed nor trusted."

Elizabeth faltered. "As I said, I did not give his spiteful words credence, but others did. Yours fail to appear trustworthy as well." She walked to the doorway.

He stood and approached her. "Please, we need to discuss what has been said."

Her head hurt. "No, I cannot. No more."

"Eliz...Miss Bennet, please." His voice conveyed an urgency unfamiliar to her. "I must know what was said. I accept and regret my own mistakes, but my name and reputation have been impugned."

"As have mine," she said quietly. "There are those in Meryton who think you a terrible man, who look at me and wonder whether I too fell under your spell. They saw us converse. They saw us laugh. They saw us walk together. Some assumed it was a declaration of affections. And then they saw you leave—in pursuit of a bride, it was said."

Her hand that had firmly gripped the doorknob fell to her side. Her heart longed to reveal that all of Meryton thought him a man who abandoned one bride to pursue another, but she was afraid to say it aloud. How could she explain her attempts to quiet rumours even as she did not understand him?

Darcy stared at her, shocked. "No, that is not how it was." He sounded desperate to his own ears. *How had this gone so wrong?*

"I defended you then as a gentleman. Yet now we are to repeat that history."

"No," he said roughly. "I shall not leave you this time."

He grasped her hand and looked at it as he stroked her palm. When he raised his eyes to her face, he found her eyes glistening with tears. His heart broke.

I did this. "Please, do not weep. We must simply talk, and all will be well."

Elizabeth pulled her hand away. She opened her mouth to respond, but a scuffle in the hall drew them apart.

"Lizzy, is the golden-haired princess here?"

Henry and Thomas ran into the room, Lily and the nursemaid quick on their heels. "Apologies, miss," the girl said breathlessly. "We were on our way to the kitchen, and Henry heard a man's voice."

A hand far smaller than Elizabeth's slipped into Darcy's. He looked down at the tiny girl.

"Pwince?"

Before he could reply, Henry was tugging his sister away from Darcy's. "No, Lily. His sister is the princess." He looked up at the tall man. "Is Miss Georgiana here, Mr Darcy?"

"No, Henry. She is at home."

"Please may we see her?"

Mrs Gardiner came into the room. "Mr Darcy, I see you have drawn an audience."

He smiled, albeit weakly.

"My Henry enjoyed your excursion yesterday. Please, might you and your sister join us for dinner, perhaps tomorrow night?"

Darcy looked away from Mrs Gardiner's expectant face and glanced at Elizabeth. She appeared as senseless as he felt. Seeing him surrounded by her adoring cousins seemed to have softened her opinion of him. She offered a small smile and shrugged.

"I am sure Mr Darcy's small acolytes would like that."

He exhaled and offered her a grateful smile. "I believe we have no engagements, but my sister and I have now imposed on you twice. We would like to host you tomorrow evening, Mrs Gardiner. With the children, of course."

"It would be our honour," Mrs Gardiner replied after a glimpse of her niece's astonished expression.

Noting Elizabeth's attention focused elsewhere, he said his farewells and moved towards the door, followed by the children.

"Goodbye, Mr Darcy."

Darcy's heart was pounding. How little did she know of him? How little did he know of himself? He had not known enough of her circumstance and misjudged that she was betrothed, and thus, he had used her ill. Not once had he considered how she might be viewed in his company. He thought she was engaged to someone else and they were merely chaperoning his friend and her sister. He had thought himself safe in her company, and she in his, and he had taken more pleasure in their time together than he remembered sharing with anyone.

Of course, she was angry that he had used that confusion to enjoy her company. Her friends and acquaintances—and perhaps even her family—had whispered and gossiped about her behaviour. *"Some assumed it was a declaration of affections."* Good lord! To think that he had hurt her name and affected her standing grieved him deeply. It was wrong of him. It was not the behaviour of a gentleman.

But worse, far worse, was that she had been obligated to protect him, that this wonderful, intelligent, lovely girl whom he had hurt had defended his name against the scurrilous likes of that blackguard Wickham!

I do not deserve her.

To think Wickham had been to Meryton and spoken about him. Impugned him! He had not thought of that cur in months, had not seen him since he was banned from Pemberley and Darcy House well over a year ago. Mrs Reynolds had discovered him in Georgiana's sitting room holding the pearl and emerald necklace left to her by her mother. It had been the final deceit; Darcy had spent years patching up and paying off the worthless man's mistakes and, years prior to that, protecting his father from knowing too much about the dissolute ways of his steward's son. He had paid off Wickham for the living at Kympton that he neither wanted nor was fit to have.

Finally, the revolting news came that the tongue-pad had dared enter Georgiana's rooms. Mrs Reynolds had said it was the second instance of Wickham being sighted in the family wing, but nothing was missed on the previous occasion. The thought of his mother's jewels being stolen, of Georgiana's possessions touched by that man, had infuriated Darcy and made for an easy decision he vowed never to regret. He had thrown the sponging fellow out of Pemberley and cut all his ties to the Darcy family, barring Wickham's entry to their homes and to any of London's decent establishments. *Worthless hell-hound—he always was able to cut a wheedle and better his situation.* No more, Darcy had determined. He would do all he could to deny the man access to society.

Yet now, he was returned to society by the wearing of a red coat, and he had slandered the Darcy name. The uniform was more than Darcy would have expected. Richard would be aghast, but Darcy burned with fury. *That man has been near Elizabeth, spoken to her. Has he been in her home? Who is in his confidence? Is he still there, spreading his lies?*

Darcy stared sightlessly out the window of his carriage, desperate to reach his home, his only refuge from everything that was crashing around him. *She does not return my affections; she thinks me no better than a rake. Me! My name and reputation are in tatters among her family and neighbours.*

He was ashamed. He had not cared what the people of Meryton had thought of him. They had left him alone, respected his privacy because they knew he was in mourning, and he did nothing to relieve them of their misconception over exactly whom he was grieving. His cousin, not his betrothed. *And I was grieving for a lie, a mistruth told by my aunt after she was deceived by her daughter.*

Angry though he was at his family, he thought only of Elizabeth and the tears he had caused. When she recited the list of his travels, he had been strangely heartened that she had followed his whereabouts and had been thinking of him. But, of course, she had wondered about them; his leaving Meryton had been the talk of her neighbours' dining rooms and card tables.

She thinks I dallied with her heart. I was careless with mine as well.

Darcy stormed into the house and headed for his study. There he could think and determine the words he must say and actions he must take to repair their friendship. He nearly ran into Richard standing by his desk with a drink in one hand and a letter in the other.

"Damn it!" Darcy cried. "You? This cannot be good."

"Smart man. Cambridge was a good investment." Richard thrust the letter at him. "It is not good. It is yet another sordid chapter in the demise of the Fitzwilliam fortunes."

Cousins,
An alarming event has occurred. Mr Collins, the vicar at Hunsford, arrived on our doorstep this morning. He was seriously displeased with our residence in his home. He first spoke to my dear Peregrine, demanding his ouster, and he claimed Hunsford and Rosings have been closed due to fever.

I fear I did not recognise his voice as I often had stuffed my ears with cotton bits when Mother made me attend tea with him or go to services. He is a dreadful man. Peregrine likes everyone, but he too was vexed by Mr Collins's demeanour. Might I mention that my dear husband was quite impressed by both my cousins and made particular note of your fine manners, impressive hair, and straight posture?

I digress. In feeling that I, as heiress to Rosings, must assert my authority and ensure that he understood the primacy of Peregrine's residence with me, I made the grievous mistake of showing myself to Mr Collins. His tirade shifted from one of angry displacement to one of astonishment and suspicion. It is you, Fitzwilliam, who now have become the chief suspect in my mysterious disappearance. Mr Collins could hear nothing but his own voice and insisted that you are the spiteful, cuckolded groom who has created this sham of death to preserve your own reputation. He wondered aloud how I escaped your fiery temper and pistol!

I must say, he seems to be reading from Lady Matlock's hidden novels. He had the further temerity to call Peregrine and me sinners, and he warned us that he was God's servant and would be off to advise my mother of our circumstances. I must say, sinners would not have offered the officious man food and lodging, though we did. Instead, he preferred to travel in the pouring rain; thus, I cannot report on his fate nor on his success in reaching Mother with news already known and disparaged.

I am a selfish creature who has asked much of you. Peregrine wishes to visit Mother and demand that she recognise our vows, but I fear a scene. I fear for our child and for any further slur she could make on the family. This situation can be laid at my door, but inasmuch as it is true love, I cannot regret the result.

Your cousin,
Anne Dumfries

CHAPTER THIRTEEN

If Darcy's morning at the Gardiners' had been difficult, his afternoon confrontation with his aunt would prove little better. At least with his family, he could defend himself: he was not at fault for the awful predicament created by the ladies de Bourgh, the foolishly venal vicar, and the peculiar yet earnest painter. He could set aside his despair at his own stupidity and blindness, forget the ache in his heart, and just be dutiful in resolving this ridiculous state of affairs.

The identical letters Anne had written to Darcy and Richard could only further ignite anger. For if Lord Matlock had been seething over his niece's folly and his sister's lies, he was positively furious over the insolence of the good Mr Collins. He had crumpled one copy of the letter and hurled it into the roaring fire in his study. When he demanded Darcy's copy as well, his nephew had prevaricated and claimed it remained folded on his desk at Darcy House. Instead, a tumbler, thankfully already drained of an excellent port, was sacrificed to the flames.

Tempers were beyond simmering when the cousins and the

earl arrived at Lady Catherine's London residence. Moments after the trio walked into her drawing room, where she was perched, imperious and unyielding, on a thickly cushioned chair, the indignant clergyman was announced. He pushed past the elderly, shuffling footman and prostrated himself to offer aid to his patroness in winning back Rosings.

"Who is this ass who says Rosings is lost?" Lord Matlock yelled angrily as Collins begged Lady Catherine's assistance in cleansing the parsonage, which had become, he claimed, a place of sin and fornication.

His cries did not hit their intended mark. The lady reared her head and commanded the parson repeat his words. He did, haltingly, before she demanded he retract every one of them. Her eyes narrowed, and her voice turned quiet and cold.

"My daughter is no fornicator! She is a married woman, a *lady*, who sits far above your lowly position." She frowned more deeply. "But she is dead to me."

"Enough!" the earl roared. "Shut it, Catherine, before I have you sent to Bedlam!"

Collins stepped back from the increasing acrimony, hunched down, and slowly moved away. Never a graceful man, he stumbled on the long tails of his coat and rolled off to the side of the rug. The elderly footman looked away from the cleric sprawled near his perch. Darcy sighed and leaned over to hoist him to his feet.

"Unhand me, sir!" Collins cried, his voice a mix of fear and disgust. "You are the cuckolded stallion behind this scheme of death and deceit! First your cousin and now mine, their names and reputations besmirched!"

Darcy scowled and released his grip, sending Collins crumpling back to the floor. "You are a fool, you lying, totty-headed dolt."

"Sir, I am a man of God," Collins said feebly as he got to his feet, "and I speak the truth."

Richard leaned close to him. "Shut it, or your tongue could have an accident with my sword."

Collins whimpered and tiptoed away.

The earl reached over to thump his son on the head before chastising the heaving, petrified-looking Mr Collins.

"I would have thought you a yea-and-nay man, but you are a pudding head if ever I saw one," he growled. "Now obey your betters, and my son will not have your gossiping tongue."

Collins swallowed and bowed his head.

Richard snorted. "If my aunt would pay for more household help, that jingle brains would never have made it in here."

"Do not dare insult me, young man," scolded Lady Catherine. "No estate in the country is run as well as Rosings." She sniffed, and then quick to her purpose, she focused her ire on her youngest nephew who, weary of the drama, was quietly watching events unfold.

"As for you," she cried, pointing at Darcy. "Your sister will come live with me. You abandoned Anne and your promises to her, breaking her heart and spirit and hurtling her into the arms of that catamite, that awful little painter."

"Bloody hell," murmured Richard. He glanced at his father to ensure the earl's angry fists were not within reach of his head. "She speaks a truth at long last." He noticed his cousin stood perfectly still, his expression bland and unreadable. Darcy's attention was focused on their aunt as she neared them, waving her hands in the air and screaming angrily about his character. *How does he stay silent?*

Lady Catherine's diatribe against Darcy continued. "Now you are off gallivanting in the marriage mart, pushing up skirts and spilling seed," she hissed. "That is no example to set for a young, wide-eyed girl. Your sister must not turn out like Anne, ruined by a low-born man."

The room fell silent. Collins turned and peered at Darcy as though seeing him for the first time. "So murder was not your plan, and Miss de Bourgh lives in lustful sin by her own choice? You have been cuckolded, in truth, but you frolic about as a ladies' favourite."

"You are an ass," Richard choked out angrily before a raw laugh rippled out of his throat. "Where is my sword?" His father glared at him and then at Lady Catherine, whose face slowly shifted from fury to incredulity as Collins's words dawned on her.

"This is insanity." The earl shook his head as his son's bitter laughter grew louder.

"There is no humour in this story! This is a tragedy!" Lady Catherine cried. "My Anne is the victim of a grand schemer, lost to me and to her inheritance. If Darcy had done his duty, none of this would have occurred!"

"Insanity," the earl repeated loudly, as he often did when feeling his opinions were being overlooked.

Collins stood to his full height and neared his patroness. "Lady Catherine, this is an outrage. Miss de Bourgh is a victim of greed and sinful lust, and she is beyond saving. But my parsonage! My parishioners need me. I need my home!"

Lady Catherine stumbled backwards towards her chair. She shook her hand at the vicar. "You! You are as selfish as my nephew! And you are an idiot! I never said she was dead. You assumed it and spread your slanders."

Collins stepped back as though she had slapped him. "No...I was—"

"Reddington!" the earl bellowed.

The ancient footman hobbled over to the red-faced patrician.

"Take this man to the study, where he will remain until I deem his company *necessary* to the conversation. Lock him in." Lord Matlock glared at Collins before sending his sister a withering stare. Collins meekly followed Reddington, throwing but one beseeching look back at the assemblage.

"My parishioners...my lambs need my guidance," he whispered to himself.

When the doors closed, the earl turned to his sister and spoke in a steely voice.

"Catherine, your daughter is alive."

"I never said she was dead—it was that fool who misunderstood. I said she was 'dead to me.'"

"He is an idiot, as you say, but you knew what he assumed and did nothing to stop the lie from spreading. The fault is yours, Sister. Anne is married and with child. It is well past time to issue an edict that a mistaken communication circulated whilst you were away from Rosings, and Anne and her husband have returned from their extended wedding trip."

She stared at him. "No. I forbid it."

"Catherine, I warned you of Bedlam. Be reasonable. They cannot live in the parsonage. My son and nephew report filthy conditions and limited food and funds. Do you wish Anne to sell her possessions in order to eat? Her jewels?"

When his sister remained impassive, the earl sat down next her. "Cathy, she carries your grandchild, the heir to Rosings. Lewis's grandchild."

For a moment, the fierce expression on her face softened. Just as quickly, the anger returned. "No! I shall not have Anne's fancy man and that base-born child in my home."

"Well, then it is a good thing the dower house is at your disposal. The boys have secured maids, footmen, and cooks for Rosings. Mayhap your daughter and her husband, fancy though he may be, will lend you one or two."

"Rosings is *my* house!" she roared.

"No, madam, it is not."

All heads turned as Darcy stepped forward, speaking in a low voice.

"I have toiled for years with your stewards, all four you have employed over the course of the past eight years. Your late husband's will provides for Anne at the age of nine and twenty, an age she attained just days ago. Rosings is hers, and neither your angry temper nor stubborn will can alter that fact."

"But—!" she sputtered.

"Ah yes, argue with me, fight with me, slander my family name," Darcy spat out. "It is by your word that good people who know only that name look upon me as a seducer of women and, how did you say it, 'spilling my seed'?"

He shook his head in disgust, barely holding onto his self-control. "Your own vicar has spread lies about me and about an innocent lady." He could not bear to think on the pain Elizabeth might have experienced by his own thoughtlessness. "You used me, my name, to justify your actions, your lies. To cast off your daughter."

"I did not claim you as the child's father! I did not claim *any* child."

"No, you simply encouraged the view of me as the Grieving Groom, bereft of his 'beloved betrothed' and cavorting about country estates *pushing up skirts*. Have you no shred of decency?"

"I did not say those exact words, Nephew! Idle people will talk, create explanations, and—"

"Gossip. Which begets lies and ruins reputations." Lord Matlock glared at his sister. "You have brought shame on the family."

"Anne brought shame," she retorted in a wild voice. "Not I."

Darcy held steady, a severe expression on his face, his body near motionless. "You wished to cast off Anne? You cannot. She is soon to Rosings, by my estimate. When and if Mr and Mrs Peregrine Dumfries or their steward has need of my advice, I shall give it. But as for you, dear aunt, sister to my beloved mother—I cast you off."

"How dare you—!"

Darcy spun on his heel and nodded at his male relations. "Uncle, Richard, I am for Darcy House."

He needed to be away from this madness. He needed to fix his mind only on Elizabeth, on how to improve her opinion of him, on how to mend their friendship and make her amenable to not only continuing it but to see him as a better man, a more honest man. *A man who loves her and is worthy of her love.*

It would begin tomorrow evening. He was to see her—to dine in civilised company after a day of mendacious accusations and bitter revelations. He now knew what that damnable simkin Collins had said about him, had whispered to everyone within earshot, and if it had slandered *him*, the injury was far worse to Elizabeth.

"First your cousin, and now mine, their names and reputations besmirched!"

Worthless, malicious little fool. Could Wickham have said even worse? Elizabeth said she believed neither man. She did believe in *his* good character but lacked the truth about his situation. Yet, in spite of her anger, disappointment, and hurt, she had believed in and defended him. That was something to think on and appreciate. It might be more than he deserved, but it was a beginning. It must not be an end.

Elizabeth waited until the door closed and Mr Darcy's carriage moved away before sinking into a chair. She was shocked and miserable. He had thought of her as he would a man: likeable for easy conversation. Somehow, that had led him to think her worthy of courtship? He *loved* her, yet would leave her once again for an estate where better-situated marital prospects awaited? She tempted him?

It was nonsense, all of it.

He could not love her. He might claim enjoyment of her company as he would Miss Bingley's—as an acquaintance without claim on his affections or intentions. *A poor country maiden who reads Defoe and Milton must be such a novelty in the grand world of Fitzwilliam Darcy. And he thinks I would fit into his world? He wants me to?*

He is so stupid. But he loves me. Or so he says.

"Lizzy, are you well?"

Elizabeth put down her book and smiled at her aunt. "I am well, simply fatigued and perhaps a bit touched by Henry's cold."

"So, Mr Darcy played no part in prompting this quiet demeanour?"

"Somewhat, perhaps."

"I am not unaware of conversations at Longbourn. Jane has written of her happiness with Mr Bingley and of her concern with your mother's favourite, Mr Wickham."

Elizabeth sat up straighter. "Her favourite, she says?" *Oh, Mama, you are a fool.*

"Your sister and Mr Bingley have done their best to quiet her since you left, but she seems to believe you were wronged by Mr Darcy." Mrs Gardiner peered closely at her niece. "Do you agree?"

"No, not as my mother sees it. He misunderstood my…my situation, but we were nothing more than friends and chaperons to Jane and Mr Bingley."

"That is all? It goes no deeper?"

"We…" Elizabeth searched for the words. "We enjoyed a rapport and shared many interests." She added softly, "It was unusual for both of us, I believe."

"I know a little of the Darcys and their estate near Lambton. Every word I hear is complimentary. Mr Darcy's parents were kind and generous to Pemberley's tenants, and he has continued that tradition since becoming master."

Elizabeth cringed at the reminder of the man's earlier sorrows. "Mr Bingley mentioned that Mr Darcy's parents had died."

"Yes. I was perhaps sixteen years of age when his mother died in childbirth. He would have been a young boy. His father passed not five years ago."

"Oh." This knowledge did not surprise her; he *was* master of Pemberley, was he not? Mr Bingley had made mention of Mr Darcy's role as guardian to his sister, but had he ever spoken about his parents? Elizabeth had never truly considered his mother or how losing her when he was but a young boy might have affected him. It seemed, perhaps, that his wish for a family beyond the small one formed by him and his sister was genuine and heartfelt. As thankful as she was for her aunts, uncles, and cousins, Longbourn, filled with her parents and her noisy, oft-time irksome sisters, was the centre of her life. The Darcys' quiet demeanours now made more sense.

"Lizzy, he is a good man. He is far above us, yet he has twice come to our door to seek you out."

"Yes." Elizabeth blushed and looked down. *Stupid and in love.*

"And we are to dine with him and his sister tomorrow. Do you mind my accepting his invitation?"

"No, I suppose I do not."

The sound of a wailing child caught their attention.

"Do think on why he comes here, Lizzy," she added, her eyes twinkling. "And do not think me like your mother when I ask you to smile a little more at him."

"Aunt Gardiner!"

"He could use a little liveliness, and you could use a little happiness."

"I also could use a bit of explanation from the man—some answers to his many mysteries."

"Ah, but that is the best part of courting and love: the mutual and happy discoveries." With a wry smile, Aunt Gardiner squeezed Elizabeth's hand and went off in search of the increasingly loud, unhappy child.

Elizabeth groaned and mumbled at her aunt's retreating back, "My mother would be proud of you!"

Darcy's nerves remained turbulent the day after confronting Lady Catherine. He had tossed and turned all night, pondering Elizabeth's rejection and his aunt's unspeakable, implacable attitude.

Now, as the morning sun peeked through the curtains, he stared at the wall, determined to put the de Bourgh disaster out of his mind and think only on the problems affecting his heart.

He regretted not following Richard's parting advice to smash out his frustrations with his fencing foil. "Imagine a melon to be Lady Catherine's head. Or mayhap a sour lemon would be a better fit?"

Ah, the rotten fruit metaphors… Richard could find sick humour in their aunt's madness, but it was no joke to Darcy. He had become increasingly determined to protect his sister from this appalling branch of his mother's family. Were the roots decayed and dying, taking his mother's life, his aunt's mind, and Anne's reason?

As happened so frequently, Elizabeth's blushing, glowing face appeared before him. She was so full of health, happiness, intelligence, and kindness. Of course, he was drawn to her. He had thought her drawn to him as well; in fact, he was sure she enjoyed their conversations. Yet he had been a wiseacre not to recognise how others might view their friendly rapport and a fool to assume she was betrothed. Damn it, he was a man who demanded answers from his steward, his solicitors, his housekeepers, and his servants, so why had he been unable or unwilling to ask questions about her? Fear? Cowardice? Envy? Did he wish to avoid knowing too much of her happiness with another man?

She made him both weak and foolish. It was an astonishing feat, yet she was entirely unconscious of it. She prompted emotions in him that suppressed his natural actions, and he knew he was lost. He had everything to prove to this woman who had suffered gossip and rumour but stood up to those back-biters who impugned him.

Wickham. Good lord! Hearing that man's name cross Elizabeth's lovely lips was infuriating, but it was the final push Darcy needed —in spite of all the risks involved—to once again change his travel plans. How had he ever dared think it was appropriate to visit Marlbourn, play out his aunt and uncle's wife-hunting fantasies, and then inform Elizabeth of his plans? His thoughtlessness made him shudder in disgust. He deserved her anger. He must prove that he was a better man than he had shown her.

Richard would laugh at his foolishness and mock him for his ding-dong ways, but he determined that before he and Georgiana could head to Pemberley, they would pay a visit to Longbourn. They would go to Hertfordshire, and he would face down the whispers. He would show Elizabeth and her family every courtesy, act as a friend, and prove that he had not deserted her nor made promises he would not honour. He would continue courting her. No matter her reaction, he would remain her friend. Oh, what a bleak prospect mere friendship would be.

He penned a note to the duke informing him that a family issue would suspend their plans to visit Marlbourn. It would be, he scowled, attributed to Anne's 'death' and her mother's need for him. He was sickened by the thought and let his mind wander, imagining what his mother would have thought of the situation. In light of all that had occurred, he hoped she would have approved of his cutting ties with her sister. She might also, as he had, question the Fitzwilliam bloodlines and wonder whether her sister's weakness was in the head rather than the heart.

Darcy wrote a second note, this one to Bingley, informing him that he and Georgiana would pay a short visit on their way to Pemberley. Then he began idly jotting down thoughts he wished to convey to Elizabeth. Ten minutes of pen to ink, and he had begun a letter explaining his family's delicate situation, his aunt's deception, and the careful subterfuge they had undertaken to protect Anne and the Fitzwilliam name. As he wrote, he felt lighter, as if he were in actual conversation with the intended recipient and mindful of her response to his words. He hoped she would be pleased by his adjustment of his travel plans.

Darcy's 'just slightly older but impressively more worldly' cousin burst through the doors near tea time. Somewhat annoyed at the man for his constant presence at Darcy House, he leaned back in his chair.

"Have you nowhere else to be, Richard?"

"I escorted your sister here. I believe that arduous work merits a tumbler of brandy and perhaps a dinner away from my parents."

"You need more friends. Georgiana and I have an engagement this evening."

"An engagement? Do tell."

Darcy did not respond. Richard took a new approach.

"What are you writing there, Cousin?"

"I am sending a note to my solicitor. We have one or two outstanding matters to address before Georgiana and I leave town."

"Ah yes, Marlbourn." Richard furrowed his brows. "I thought I might join you there."

"Or go yourself, as we shall not."

"What do you mean? Buxom ladies await!"

"You are a single-minded man."

"Double-minded, actually." Richard smirked. "My mind prefers a dual cup of bounteous goodness."

Darcy snorted in disgust. "Yes, oh son of Venus."

"You truly mean to disregard my father's marching orders?"

"Yes."

"And leave me alone here?"

Darcy looked at his cousin and sighed. "Seriously, why are you here? What do you want of me now?"

Richard sank into his favourite chair, a roomy, reddish brown one moulded just right by his many days and nights relaxing in its fine leather. "I am here, as ever, to support you. I know my father pressured you, but I had thought to accompany you to Marlbourn and…you know…provide assistance when the fawning ladies and eager misses become too much for your tender sensibilities."

"My tender what?"

"Those lovey feelings currently—and mayhap forever—occupied by Miss Elizabeth Bennet."

"Do not mock me, you ass." He fixed his eyes on the ceiling.

"I do not. I envy you."

Darcy shifted his attention back to his cousin. To his surprise, Richard looked sincere.

"You and Anne each seem to have found someone to truly and deeply care for. Madly care for, in her case, which I fear will not turn out well." Richard stretched out his legs. "That Dumfries does not sit right with me. Anne is too altered."

"You do not believe love capable of instituting great change in character and behaviour?"

Richard barked a laugh. "Zooks, man, she was a younger version of her mother: irrational and bordering on tyrannical."

"People change."

"Yes—a fevered kiss, her skirts tossed and lower bits caressed, and Anne is a new woman."

"Why do you insist on imprinting these images in my mind?" Darcy groaned and rubbed his eyes.

"It is a simple question: Did love change Anne, or was it the act of love that changed her?" Richard stroked his moustache, a sure sign he was either deep in his cups or deep in morbid thought—or perhaps both.

Darcy cleared his throat. "Events, good and bad, alter behaviours and a person's point of view."

"Ah, life is war, a series of battlefield skirmishes requiring constant vigilance and retrenchment?"

"Or advancement." Shaking his head, Darcy leaned forward in his chair. "You deal with your parents every day you are in town. Do you not adjust your temper and your conversation to their moods? Just yesterday, I saw you anticipate your father's wrath—and his throwing aim."

"Ha! You have the right of it. Damn that university education!" Richard jumped up and walked to the window. He stared out at the street below before turning. "Still, I trust neither our aunt nor Dumfries."

"Agreed. But as I have cut ties with her, she is your problem. I shall continue to oversee the situation at Rosings."

"You have the better of it, I believe. It is a Gordian knot, Darcy."

Darcy smiled. "Gordian knot, you say? I knew you paid attention to your history lessons."

Richard crossed his arms and smiled. His smug expression was long familiar to Darcy. "I pay attention to your sister's enthusiasms as well as to the fish and flower deliveries. Interesting engagement you have here tonight. I believe I must join you and become acquainted with the magical Miss Bennet. The 'perfect woman,' is she not?"

Darcy felt all the weight of being the younger man in need of his cousin's support. Richard admitted he had never felt Cupid's arrow, but he had never made the acquaintance of a woman as fine as Elizabeth. He would like her; Darcy was sure of it. He was equally sure that his cousin would require frequent reminders to temper his inclination to flirt.

"You will behave, Richard," he said sternly. "This night is important, and if you fail to curb your eyelash-fluttering ways, you will be sent to the nursery with the children."

"Children? Rug imps? Oh, this is too great a temptation. I must play with them. Ha! Imagine when my mother smells their biscuit crumbs on me. She will be mad for my brother to toss out his official calendar of marital coitus and get to the baby making."

Darcy was grateful he only turned slightly green at these words.

Elizabeth thanked Lucy, her aunt's lady's maid, and stared at her reflection in the mirror. Her eyes, while puffy from a lack of sleep, bore only a slight trace of redness. Her nose, now powdered, appeared normal. If the Darcys dined by low-burning candlelight, they would never see her symptoms of melancholia and head cold. She hoped to keep them innocent of her other ailments: the heart that ached with regret and the head that pounded with anger at herself for flinging blame and accusations at Mr Darcy.

She knew she must communicate tonight the message that she did not blame him. That her anger was, if not ceased, now more accurately aimed at others. He had behaved stupidly and unthinkingly but not maliciously. In fact, she finally had been able to find some humour in his mistake; however, it did not absolve him for his thick-headed lack of initiative in determining the truth. The very idea of confusing her kindly but somewhat paunchy uncle as her true love now prompted a quiet giggle.

How she wished to curl up with Jane and plot out The Case of the Gullible, Grieving Groom. Oh, if her father ever learned of Mr Darcy's blunder in judgment, she would never hear the end of it. Nor would Mr Darcy, if he spent time with her father in the future. But that now appeared unlikely unless Jane wed Mr Bingley and they settled at Netherfield.

She did not think Mr Darcy would resume his courtship; after all, he was a dizzying man setting out to meet more eligible ladies at another estate, but at the least—*at the very least*—they could remain friends. He had invited her family to Darcy House, a great honour for a tradesman, even as Mr Darcy behaved as though their presence would be an honour to *him*. She would never understand him. Was he still hopeful of her sentiments or hoping only to smooth over his *faux pas* for when they met on future occasions? He had his faults, as did any man, yet his seemed so much less defining than those of other men with whom she was acquainted—or related. Yes, Mr Darcy could be stupid and proud, but no one could dispute that he was a man of good character with a mind that was clever and a manner so gentle. His temperament was defined by experience, education, duty, and conceit.

'There is no one for me but you.'

How could he say those words when his carriage was likely packed for his next journey into the land of ladies hoping to win him?

Only if she could overcome the foggy buzzing in her ears and the dull pain in her heart would she believe tonight could be a success.

CHAPTER FOURTEEN

Darcy House was large and impressive, handsome to the eye and furnished with sculpture, paintings, vases, and so many artful luxuries that Elizabeth felt overwhelmed. It was formal yet comfortable, exuding wealth, strength, and intelligence. It was very much Mr Darcy.

The only fragile object Elizabeth noticed was Georgiana, who exerted herself flawlessly but ever so carefully. After warm greetings and a short tour of the public rooms, the group sat down to a sumptuous dinner that Elizabeth and her relations found easy to overpraise. Her cold might have dulled her senses, but even she could taste flavours cooked into the dishes created in the wondrous Darcy House kitchens. *How Mr Collins would swoon.*

She saw Georgiana's eyes often drift to her brother's as though seeking approval or perhaps simply his notice. His attention seemed focused solely on Elizabeth, much to the amusement of the Darcys' cousin. In a manner quite different from Mr Darcy and all of his complications, the colonel puzzled her. There was something oversized about him, as if he could burst at any moment, though whether into laughter, a bawdy story, or anger, she could not say. Sadly, she was not as sharply honed this night, as such a dissection would require.

Elizabeth's fog had lifted only slightly. She was a dull thing. Rarely ill, she cursed the timing of this cold. She had relied on the burst of energy she felt as they left the carriage, and it had carried her through conversation with Georgiana. The soup was helpful, but the steaming heat loosened her wits along with her breathing. If she looked as awful as she now felt, Mr Darcy should be well pleased with her earlier dismissal of his romantic sentiments.

She noted he seemed uneasy, and she was pleased to recognise that it was not because he found himself hosting lesser society but because too much was unknown to him. She wished for a means to let him know that her aunt and uncle remained unaware of his previous confusion about her and her uncle's marital status. But her throat was scratchy and her thinking a bit too thick for determining such an approach.

Fortunately for all parties, the Darcys' cousin was loquacious, and Mr Gardiner was an able conversationalist like his sisters. Unlike his sisters, he could speak on a broad range of topics beyond fashion, sauces, and weddings, and so it was that he and the colonel spent a good deal of time canvassing recent news from Parliament and the battlefields and on her uncle's latest business ventures, while her aunt spoke quietly to Georgiana and Mr Darcy about Derbyshire.

For a broad-chested, long-winded man, Elizabeth found Colonel Fitzwilliam to be delicately wry in his conversation. He teased his cousins about their trip to see the wild animals and pouted a bit when Mrs Gardiner explained her children's absence.

"A never-ending case of sneezing."

"Sadly, I am left bedecked and beribboned with no moppet to marvel at my medals and exploits," he opined, his hand to his uniformed heart.

"I am sure we could round up some street urchins to swoon over your every word," Mr Darcy replied drolly. "Especially after I drop them each a shilling."

Mr Gardiner led the laughter. "My boys would enjoy your tales, sir. Like all young lads, they love the idea of danger and swordplay—"

"Until one of them is hiding his head in my skirts with a scratch on his cheek or a wound to his valour," her aunt interjected.

Colonel Fitzwilliam nodded. "That is always the way of it! Ask Darcy, poor chap. I honed my fencing skills and knife thrusts on him for years when we were boys."

"You still do," Mr Darcy responded drily. "And those three years of age you have on me are no longer such an advantage, old man."

They were, Elizabeth marvelled, like brothers, as though they had said these very words before and knew how the other would react. Her eyes shifted between the two men. Mr Darcy's fellowship with his cousin was full of warmth and humour and not as she had expected. She appreciated that the colonel, smart and well informed as he was, was unlikely to ruminate over clouds, philosophy, and poetry. *Few men are...*

With a start, she realised she had been staring at the uniformed man. She blinked and glanced at Mr Darcy. He was looking at her, a concerned expression on his handsome face that she tried to alleviate with a small smile.

Their interaction did not go unnoticed by the colonel.

Fortunately for Richard, Darcy was unaware of his cousin's wildly ranging thoughts. Since welcoming his guests, Darcy had been respectful to all and especially attentive to anything said by Elizabeth. He noticed immediately that she was out of sorts. She might not be unhappy, but she was at least a bit uncomfortable. Her eyes lacked the sparkle to which he was accustomed, and he could only hope that yesterday's disastrous encounter had played no part in her less spirited demeanour.

No, he knew that he was fully responsible for her mood, for hurting her. He had behaved badly, without thought. He had been stupid, and his stupidity led to her pain.

He missed her joy in teasing him, her smiles, her witty repartee.

He wanted nothing more than to recapture that and to regain her trust and friendship. And he did not want to see her staring at his cousin, whose charm, in his opinion, was wearing thin. *She smiled at me, but it did not reach her eyes. And she was staring at Richard. Blast him!*

Mr Gardiner's voice interrupted his self-chastisement. "My brother found you a fine competitor at his chessboard, Mr Darcy."

Darcy nodded. "I enjoyed myself as well. It is a rare thing to be so fully engaged in both the match and the conversation."

"Samuel does like to keep his opponents off guard," Mr Gardiner said with amusement. "Lizzy too has recounted some stimulating conversations with you while walking the lanes with Jane and Mr Bingley. What thought you of Hertfordshire?"

"I found it a charming landscape. The view from Oakham Mount was especially fine." He ventured a look at Elizabeth. "We did not want for birds to shoot nor intelligent conversation."

She met his eyes and smiled, and he felt everything shift within: his hope and happiness surmounting the fear and regret. His chest filled with a contentment he had not known for weeks. He returned her smile, and she blushed.

"You enjoyed the society?" Mrs Gardiner voiced.

"Very much," Darcy replied in a warm voice. He managed to pull his eyes away from Elizabeth.

"My brother said it was a pretty area, less wild than in the north. Derbyshire is quite rugged," Georgiana supplied, eager to add to the conversation.

"You must miss the country," Elizabeth said.

"Yes, although London has tigers and peacocks, and I have enjoyed my new friends."

"I regret that some of those new friends were too out of sorts to join us tonight, but I do hope you will see Lily and her brothers again soon." Mrs Gardiner smiled at Georgiana and turned to her host with an enquiry. "Did you encounter Lizzy's cousin Mr Collins while in Meryton? He seems a busy man, bursting with ideas, however not always wise in sharing them."

Elizabeth spoke up hurriedly. "Aunt, Mr Collins is an odd fit for a clergyman. Modesty is not one of his virtues nor one he aspires to, though he would beg to differ."

"Repeatedly and with great excitement," Darcy added quietly.

All attention swung to him. His cheeks reddened, he begged their indulgence for his comment. "Mr Collins is vicar at Hunsford, my aunt's parsonage, and he has proved himself difficult these past weeks."

"Much has proved difficult these past weeks," Georgiana said.

Mrs Gardiner squeezed her hand. "I am sorry for the loss of your cousin. She was but a young woman."

As Georgiana nodded, Elizabeth and Darcy both busied themselves with all the activities that eating can entail, from the cutting of meat to the chewing of bread to the drinking of a long draught of wine.

"She was," Georgiana agreed. "'Tis all a great mystery to me. My family is wonderful but so complicated."

Darcy cursed inwardly. Richard had urged a delay in telling Georgiana the details behind Anne's so-called death and the drama presently occurring with her mother, her husband, and their unborn child. How he wished he had not agreed. It had been awkward not to apprise Elizabeth of the sordid tale—or inversely, the happy news, if one focused solely on Anne's return to the living. At this moment, silence and a talent for changing the conversation were both his best allies and his greatest trials.

"Oh, Georgiana, all families are complicated, and each is happy in its own way," Elizabeth said in a bright voice. "That is both the joy and the disaster of family."

Darcy stared, awed at Elizabeth's social finesse as she leaned closer to the wide-eyed girl. "Has your brother told you of my four sisters? All so different in their own particular ways."

"Four sisters." Georgiana sighed. "You are so fortunate, Elizabeth. I am sure they are all as pleasant company as you have been for my brother and me."

"Indeed," asserted Mr Gardiner. "My nieces are not peas in a pod, but each is a singular person."

"What my uncle means to say is that the Bennet girls of Longbourn are a motley mix of personalities. My eldest sister, Jane, is being courted by your friend Mr Bingley. Two kinder hearts could not be found."

Georgiana smiled. "How lovely."

"My next younger sister, Mary, is a great reader who enjoys sharing her knowledge. Lydia, the youngest, loves to dance and to laugh." Elizabeth rolled her eyes. "She is a bit of a merrymaker."

Who knows her metaphors from her similes, Darcy thought.

"Those three are indeed quite different, but all sound so interesting," Georgiana exclaimed. "What of your fourth sister?"

Darcy found himself unable to keep his eyes away from Elizabeth. He revelled in hearing the teasing lilt returned to her voice with her eyes shining and her lips curved in a small smile.

"Oh, Kitty is but a year older than you are, and like Mary, she is quite earnest. Rather than literature, however, she has applied herself to bettering her deportment and manner. In this, she is guided by Miss Bingley."

"Oh dear," Georgiana gasped. A moment later, she clapped her hand over her mouth.

Darcy gave his sister a reassuring smile. "Miss Catherine is, like all Miss Bennet's sisters, intelligent and quite pleasant." He paused, feeling Elizabeth's eyes on him. "I believe she finds Miss Bingley a fascinating creature of study, and she is gaining knowledge of fashion and social customs from her."

"Miss Bingley does possess great familiarity with social customs, fabrics, and fashions. It is kind of her to lend her expertness," Georgiana said doubtfully. "She is eager to offer me similar advice."

"You and Miss Catherine may find it advantageous to combine forces," Darcy said, "should you ever meet."

Finally, he looked directly at Elizabeth. Her eyes were merry, but her expression was one of disbelief. He smiled a small, gentle smile and enquired of Mrs Gardiner whether Thomas and Lily were, like their brother, to visit the menagerie.

The colonel found his cousin's friends greatly to his liking. The

Gardiners were intelligent, well mannered, and good-humoured, an exceptional combination and one rarely found in his own family. Miss Bennet certainly was not the sort of lady Darcy was expected to marry and the complete opposite of spindly, wheezy, wanton Anne. *That dress is not responsible for that figure,* he mused in appreciation before quickly reprimanding himself. *She is Darcy's. Do not look there.*

He had fallen quiet at times during the meal, marvelling at Georgiana's eager conversation and Darcy's smiles. *The smiles of a smitten simpleton.* Richard was no schoolboy; he had seen the dark glance Darcy sent his way when he gazed too long upon Miss Bennet. She was an object of much fascination, and he fancied himself a man of science puzzling her out. Apparently, Darcy neither required nor appreciated his deductive skills. *Jealous fool, and such a fortunate one. She is a gem.*

Although the party was small, the sexes separated when the men adjourned to Darcy's study to peruse his books and enjoy his liquor. After accepting a glass of his host's best port, Mr Gardiner noted the finely tooled chairs and revealed his familiarity with the Italian leather house that created them. Darcy was impressed, and Richard appeared amused as he had all evening.

"Quite a collection of books you have," Mr Gardiner said, comfortably ensconced in one of the fine chairs. His eyes were focused on one particular volume. "We share some titles in common. After my wife and children, nothing is closer to my heart than books: the smell of ink on the page and the feel of soft paper as I sink into the author's thoughts."

"While I believe my sister and mementos of my parents would rate more highly should I be forced to choose, the books in my library are the items I most cherish." Darcy suddenly chuckled.

"What amuses you, sir?"

"Your niece—she told me the story about Mr Eggleston, the gentleman who had owned Netherfield, the estate my friend now leases."

"Ah yes. Mr Bingley, the young man who is courting our Jane. What is the story?"

"During an especially difficult winter a few years ago, he saved himself the trouble of chopping wood and burnt his books in order to stay warm."

"The savage!" Mr Gardiner gasped.

Richard shrugged. "You book lovers lack survival sense. One does what one needs to do during wartime."

"It was winter, Richard, not the battlefield." Darcy glared at him and turned back to Elizabeth's uncle. "My immediate thought as well, sir, but as your niece told the tale, it affected me less."

He trailed off, his cheeks reddening as he realised he had said too much. He saw Richard bite back a smirk and settle in his seat. Apparently, watching Darcy squirm in his own house was beyond delightful.

"She revealed Mr Eggleston's dastardly folly in a light-hearted manner, so I found some amusement in it. In spite of the injustice done to literature, of course." Darcy took a quick sip of his port and stared at his boots.

"Lizzy is a bright, happy girl," Mr Gardiner said. "She rarely speaks an unkind word but, like her father, can voice amusing bon mots about nearly everything." He smiled. "Lizzy's observations, although true, are less biting."

"Yes." Darcy struggled not to agree too enthusiastically.

"Not everyone values nor understands that gift, and it *is* a gift."

"Indeed." He found it difficult not to break into a foolish grin.

"You remembered your conversations with her?"

Darcy nodded and sipped more port.

The older man glanced at the silent Richard before turning back to level a serious look at Darcy. "Sir, might I ask, is it your enjoyment of Lizzy's company and conversation that brought you to our doorstep twice this week and led you to tender your most generous offer of dinner?"

When he considered it later, Darcy realised he could have sparred and joked and passed off the question; however, in the moment it was asked, he was all sincerity.

"Yes, sir, it is." He paused and looked solemnly at Mr Gardiner.

"I care deeply for your niece. I wish for her friendship with my sister—and with myself."

"Friendship," Mr Gardiner repeated.

"Yes, at the very least. I shall accept what she offers."

The older man expressed surprise. "This is a sudden event—or was it spurred by your visit to Netherfield? When you were mourning your betrothed?"

Darcy sighed.

"Sir, I mourned my cousin, not my betrothed. We were not engaged. Due to some unfortunate events and mistruths by others, I have a series of misunderstandings to unravel and explain."

Mr Gardiner's eyebrows rose. "As this story affects my niece, I must ask how much she knows."

"Very little. I need time to talk to her. We have been subject to many misunderstandings."

"So you did not leave my niece in a difficult situation when you left Meryton, subject to gossip about your lack of a declaration?"

"To my everlasting grief, I did, but most unknowingly."

"She was surrounded by rumour and half-truths."

Never one to enjoy a foxhunt, Darcy suddenly realised he would never again chase down a creature for sport or pleasure. He could feel only sympathy for the poor frightened animals. He sighed. He had gone from being pursued for his money and name to being tracked and hunted for tales of his enormous blunders.

"It makes for a long tale. If it will make you think better of me, I must tell it, but I beg your confidentiality. My sister remains unaware of many details. The colonel and I, who share guardianship of Georgiana, shall have a long conversation with her tomorrow."

Mr Gardiner rose and refilled their glasses. "This sounds as if it is one of Scheherazade's tales."

"I agree," Richard added in an expectant tone. "Like you, I am in possession of only half the story." He eyed Darcy, clearly wary about revealing details of the family's simmering secrets.

A minute ticked by in silence. "Mr Darcy, I do not see the need for you to reveal secrets and confidences to me. It is your sister and Lizzy who need to hear them—if you wish to be my niece's *friend*."

Darcy gestured at an envelope on his desk. "If I might beg your assistance, sir?"

The stories being exchanged in the drawing room were less dramatic, but the three participants were equally engaged.

When Mrs Gardiner delicately asked Georgiana about her late summer sojourn in town, the girl sighed. "You have heard about the fate of my cousin Anne. She was not a happy person, really, but to die at a young age is tragic."

"It was sudden?"

"Oh, Anne had always been ill…and discontented. Richard oftentimes mutters something about a chicken and an egg when that is said." Georgiana shook her head in confusion, her blonde curls bouncing around her shoulders. "He is so funny, but I do not always follow his jokes and gibes. My brother tells me it is best to look at him disapprovingly as that will put an end to Richard's behaviour."

"Indeed?" Elizabeth tried not to laugh at the girl's confusion.

"Yes, though it rarely dampens his fun. Fitzwilliam says Richard inherited all the family's silliness, Anne all the sourness, and I all the sweetness." Georgiana reddened, suddenly aware of the compliment she had paid herself. "I do not mean I have *all* the sweetness…"

Mrs Gardiner gave her a gentle smile. "Ah, but you have much of it. What of your brother? What does he have?"

"Strength, I think, and intelligence. Oh, and kindness, though that would make my cousin laugh."

"Well, *he* is silly, after all." Elizabeth smiled mischievously.

Georgiana laughed nervously. "In spite of their differences, Richard and my brother are quite close. Fitzwilliam has been fighting with our family, especially Lady Catherine, for weeks. He wishes to keep the particulars from me, but Richard has supported him throughout and told me not to fret over Fitzwilliam's dark moods. I worry it is my fault."

Elizabeth stared, horrified, at the young girl. *He has been at war over his affections for me, for his behaviour in Meryton, for whatever he did or did not promise to his family about Anne. And I berate him for it.*

Her aunt quickly spoke. "Miss Darcy, your brother would be your greatest defender. I cannot believe you could be the source of any disagreement in your family."

"But..."

"However, I do believe my two sons have had some jealous conversations over who would be the valiant knight to save the 'golden-haired princess.'" She smiled at the girl, whose gloom vanished instantly upon hearing the pet name given her by Thomas and Henry.

"Oh, I do wish your children could have accompanied you tonight. I hope to visit them again."

Mrs Gardiner glanced around the finely furnished room. "I think my sons are best confined to the schoolroom, the nursery, and the kitchens."

After a moment, Georgiana announced that she would like to take the children to the park before she and her brother left for Marlbourn. "That house will be filled with adults and young ladies too interested in my brother to be a true friend for me."

Elizabeth was relieved when her aunt redirected the conversation to one of music and the gentle pokes her babies had given her when her nieces played or sang. "I hope this one kicks a bit less than did Henry." She touched her stomach and laughed. At the light blush on Georgiana's face, Mrs Gardiner smiled. "We are all ladies here. I hope you do not mind such a comment."

"Oh no, babies are so sweet," Georgiana assured her. "Your children are wonderful." She appeared pleased to have been included in a discussion of such intimacy.

Elizabeth smiled along with the conversation but stayed silent. She had summoned her resources to remain on alert and focused during the house tour, the many courses served, and now with the ladies. She could not play or sing tonight. The lightness in spirit she had felt when Mr Darcy spoke of Hertfordshire and her sisters faded when Georgiana shared her confidences about her brother's struggles and their plans for Marlbourn. She could not recall a time when her emotions travelled so abruptly from delight and joy to sadness and loss. It pained her to think how she would feel if this man truly mattered to her future happiness. *He does not, much as he once thought he should. His thoughts again tend elsewhere.*

When the group reunited, she hoped only to make it through coffee and dessert. Her goal was to tell Mr Darcy that she regretted her angry words and wished to part as friends. She was impatient for that moment, and it was especially difficult when her aunt and Mr Darcy discovered a mutual interest in Derbyshire history. Elizabeth was weary in body and spirit, and she clenched her fist and dug her nails into her palm to keep awake. She enjoyed Georgiana's playing and was saved from exhibiting a poor display of her talents only by the thoughtfulness of her aunt, who, noting her fatigue, prompted the colonel to tell an especially dramatic tale of battlefield bravery that he assured them would inspire the Gardiner sons to greatness. Soon, and finally, it was time to leave.

Elizabeth thanked her hosts warmly and wished Georgiana well on her journey. The colonel bent over her hand and looked up to wink at her, saying it was a great pleasure to finally make her acquaintance. It left her concerned that he was yet another member of a rather strange family who assumed greater intimacy with her than was wise.

Mr Darcy drew near, and they were left alone when his family abandoned them to escort the Gardiners to their carriage. He looked down at her with a soft, worried expression. "I thank you for coming tonight. Are you well?" At her nod, he said gently, "I worry for you, knowing I have hurt you."

"You need not worry for me."

"Do not ask me to do the impossible."

"Do not do this," she whispered. "Your family is at war, let it be. Your heart belongs elsewhere."

He looked at her, his eyes dark and serious. "Please, hear these few words, all of them true and all of them much delayed in the telling: I was never to marry Anne. She is not dead; she has married another." When Elizabeth gasped, he leaned closer and whispered. "My family is never easy, but these past weeks have been a trial as we have grappled with the web of deceit and confusion her actions have created. They have distracted me from the true aim of my heart: you...and earning your love and respect."

She gazed up at him, confused and shocked. "She is alive? And married to another?"

He nodded. "It was a surprise to us all. I learnt of it, of her well-being and her wedding, just a week ago."

"Oh my."

If Elizabeth felt dazed earlier, she was positively overcome now as his words sank in. *"...the true aim of my heart: you...and earning your love and respect."*

She looked up and met his gaze. Darcy's eyes widened, and his finger rose to brush back a loose curl. Aware that the Gardiners were in the carriage and awaiting her, she took a step back from their intimate posture.

"May I see you off in the morning?" Darcy's voice was hoarse.

Elizabeth shook her head. "I do not know what to say...you do not listen."

"I hear what I wish to hear. I wish to hear a 'yes.'"

"You are an impossible man." *And so very persistent.*

She looked away but smiled shyly and quietly said, "Yes."

His eyes alight, Darcy called to the footman, who stepped forward with a package. "This book is for you, Miss Elizabeth. Your uncle was amenable to my giving it to you. I thought we might discuss it and other...subjects...when I visit Netherfield."

"You plan to return?"

"Yes, of course I do. I must attend to some business here, and"—he pressed her hand and looked at her intently—"I hope my sister and I shall arrive at Netherfield by week's end. With your permission, of course."

"Week's end?" she repeated. "You and Georgiana? What of your friends...at the estate...?"

He shook his head and gave her a hopeful look. "There is nothing, no one, for me there."

Elizabeth felt a warmth spread through her. She took the package and briefly closed her eyes. *And so we begin the next chapter.*

"I thank you. Your presence at Netherfield would be agreeable, Mr Darcy."

He looked dismayed. "Merely agreeable?"

In spite of the shock she felt from his disclosures, Elizabeth knew his pain in facing them these past weeks must be greater. As he continued to put forth such a great effort with her, she felt he deserved more consideration. Besides, although his furrowed brow conjured warm thoughts of him as a worried little boy, she so preferred when he smiled. He was such a handsome man. She had never much cared for cleft chins; all the Goulding ladies had prominently cleaved chins, which gave them less than pleasing faces. But Mr Darcy had a strong jaw and shy grin, and when his eyes brightened with happiness, Elizabeth had often found herself nearly undone.

"I hope you will call on us at Longbourn," she said softly. "I look forward to further conversations on topics neither of us canvass with others." She gifted him a bright smile, and he beamed and squeezed her hand.

Shaken with joy, she walked with him in silence towards the carriage. Each was able to supply a few courteous words to the Gardiners but little more. Elizabeth managed to avoid the indulgent looks of her relations, and she offered them one or two observations on the moon's particular glow.

Her mind was filled with thoughts of Mr Darcy's family struggles, his mysteriously wedded and quite troublesome cousin, and his desperately quick telling of it. It prevented her from settling into bed until quite late. She had been right about him from the beginning: Mr Darcy *was* a puzzle, only now she urgently wished to piece him together.

It was not until she was under the covers that she peeled the wrappings off the book. A letter fell to her lap, and she gasped at the neat handwriting that formed her name. Elizabeth ran her fingers over the thick black ink. She took a breath and looked at the book, nearly laughing at the familiar title: *On the Modification of Clouds*.

They would have at least one easy topic to canvass after all.

CHAPTER FIFTEEN

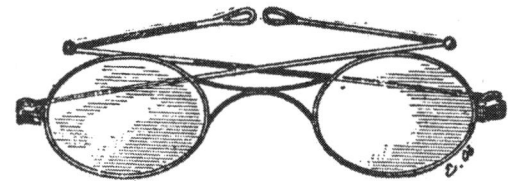

Only two months earlier, Fitzwilliam Darcy would have described his life as routine. Rise and ride, bathe and shave, dress and dine. Read the post and write letters, address whatever estate issues required attention, spend time with his sister, and ride some more, fence, or walk—anything to wear off excess energy. Lord knew, he had far more energy to wear off these past couple of years than he had had since he was at Cambridge.

Yet, since the day nearly two months ago when Mrs Reynolds had reported discovering the too-friendly footman huddled in conversation with lonely, innocent Georgiana, he had not been able to enjoy the rolling hills, riding trails, and walking paths of Pemberley. Whether in town or on another's estate, he instead was sentenced to a new routine: jumping on his horse and riding hither and yon to deal with the family's latest outrage.

Of late, he never knew what news might be delivered with his morning coffee or who might leave a card or pound on his door. But he knew it would be connected to his aunt, her daughter, or the still-unfolding spectacle they had created, ably assisted by the curious Peregrine Dumfries and the odious William Collins.

Elizabeth's cousin... It seemed they both had their lives made more difficult by a cousin. He smiled to think it was perhaps the only connexion they shared that he wished they did not. He had found it difficult to sleep the previous night, thinking of all that had passed between them and recalling her words desperately pushing back against him.

"You need not worry for me."

He was grateful he had been able to summon his wits and convey the truth to her. It had changed everything. His letter, which further explained the events of the past month, could only fortify that change.

He took strength from remembering her parting words to him; they rolled back and forth in his mind. *"I look forward to further conversations on topics neither of us canvass with others."*

Had he ever anticipated a visit with the Bingleys with such eagerness? He would lock the door to his rooms, close his mind to Caroline's mewling, quell—violently, if necessary—any slander on Elizabeth and her family, frequent every shop in Meryton, and stroll every lane in Hertfordshire. He would pay any price necessary to have Elizabeth Bennet on his arm with neither of them promised to anyone else—at least until she was promised to *him*. Then he would speak to her father. He laughed at his giddiness. Was this what it felt like to be Richard, smiling and joking and weak in the head? How long would it take for his face to ache from the smile that even his manservant had noticed? It was the first time a smile had ever caused Smith to pull back his razor and awkwardly request a return to his master's normal impassivity.

He needed to get to her and say another farewell; last night was not enough. He had held her hand, kissed her fingers, and gained her smile, but it was not enough. He was not sated of Elizabeth Bennet, and worse still, he needed more affirmation. Confirmation. She had given him no indication that she shared the strength of his feelings, but she had ceased fighting his expression of them. She wished to see him at Longbourn. Those were positive signs in his favour, were they not?

He was a wealthy man who had never been greedy, but he had never before been in love. How was he to focus on crops…and tenant issues…and water rights…and his breakfast when he needed to think about a beguiling dark-eyed woman? Could not the master of Pemberley—a man who could not manage to free himself from family responsibilities and ridiculous bride hunts—reclaim time to think on the most pleasing subject of all?

Of course not. As a man educated at the best schools, Darcy should have known better and understood that the never-ending Fitzwilliam Family Saga would have at least a few chapters left. He nearly cringed when a note was delivered to him from Richard, and he sighed at the sight of his cousin's scrawl on the paper lying open by his breakfast plate. It was nearly as awful anticipating the man's appearance before the first meal of the day; it never boded well. Darcy perused the brief note and sighed again. Doctor Percival Dumfries was in town, and Richard was bringing him to Darcy House. He took a last bite of toast. This was going to take some fortification and patience. *Blast!* He had some place he wished to be…needed to be. Instead, he told the footman to expect the colonel's arrival and headed for his study. He would keep their meeting brief and then ride straight to Cheapside.

Honestly, he had had his fill of Richard's teasing. The man could be glaringly sincere when necessary and horribly galling when the mood struck. Such a mood and a few too many tumblers of brandy had hit last night after his guests' departure, and his cousin had enjoyed ruminating over the beauty, intelligence, and manner of one Elizabeth Bennet.

"She is nothing like your true love, Miss Bingley, nor your previous devotees. Miss Bennet is a refreshing change but perhaps too lively for a dull, bookish old man such as you."

"Dull?"

Richard's eyes had gleamed as his barb finally roused the bear. "Your Miss Bennet seems as inclined to debate Dante in the original Latin as she is to challenge you to a game of mumblety-peg or beat you at a game of Graces."

Darcy had scoffed. "And these would be bad things?"

"Such interests make her equally suitable for a rough and tumble sort like myself."

"Hmm," Darcy had growled. "Rough and tumble, in spite of your bad knee?"

While some men might have been alarmed at such a challenge, Darcy had seen—he always saw—the grin lurking under his cousin's alarmingly bushy moustache. *Would he never trim that thing? Likely not. Should I tell him that the lady reads Cicero? No.*

"First, Richard, I wonder whether any lady is willing to risk a close encounter with whatever is growing above your lip. Elizabeth is certainly no fool there. In fact, I believe you were cowed by her wit and her sure knowledge of both Cowper and Bach."

"Ah yes. Your Elizabeth is both pretty and smart; thus, she is no match for you, as you are far prettier with those dark eyes and cleft chin; ask any lady in town." Richard had roared with laughter. "Sadly, you are not as pretty as the fine Peregrine Dumfries, so it is a good thing that Anne snared him first."

Yes, his cousin was an ass of the first order. Darcy looked forward to his first tumble into love; the man could tumble into ladies' beds but one had yet to enter his heart. He promised himself he would tease Richard only a little when such an event did occur. After all, he was as close to a brother as he had. When Darcy had been a boy and made sad by the babies his mother lost, he had sometimes wondered whether a brother would have been as he was: quiet and studious, equally fond of books and nature, tall and dark like the Darcys. Family members differed, this he knew, especially those of opposite sexes. Like him, Georgiana was tall, fond of dogs, skilled in maths, and unsettled by spiders; but opposite to him, she was light haired, unsure of herself, excited by novels, and averse to exploring woods and nature. Richard and his brother shared a devil-take-it approach to life; he might have enjoyed experiencing such a bond, though not at the expense of losing his beloved sister.

Georgiana had been so happy last evening. Darcy recalled more smiles and laughter in these past few days than he had seen from her in weeks. *She likes Elizabeth, and Elizabeth clearly cares for her. I shall have to be honest with my sister about my hopes when I tell her we leave for Netherfield rather than Marlbourn.*

Such thoughts ceased as his cousin strolled into the room, trailed by a rotund man wearing spectacles.

"Darcy, we were fortunate," Richard said quietly. "The good doctor left his card, which I seized before my father saw it. I brought him over as soon as I could. The earl would have too many questions and accusations."

He glanced over his shoulder and lowered his voice another notch. "He seems a normal sort…nothing like his brother." He cleared his throat and gestured to the man to step forward.

"Cousin, I give you Doctor Percival Dumfries."

It was as if his earlier thoughts had taken on the form of scientific enquiry, and the Dumfries brothers were Exhibit A. Unlike Peregrine, whose sharp features were softened with powder, accented by a beauty mark, and framed by waves of blond hair, the older brother was wide, dark, and hirsute, a bear of a man with paws for hands. Percival Dumfries certainly did not have the delicate hands of a painter or a doctor. He did, however, share Peregrine's fluid movements and quick mind.

"Mr Darcy, as I told your cousin, it is you I hoped to meet, but I had failed to gain the location of Darcy House." He looked around the room with its globe, shelves of books, and neatly rolled maps. "Peregrine tells me you are the least fearsome member of the family." The doctor glanced at Richard, who looked fairly placid beneath his great moustache and furrowed brow until he caught the insult.

"Pardon?" Richard said, clearly annoyed.

In spite of the delay the doctor was causing him, Darcy thought he might grow to like the man. He sent his cousin a warning glance and gestured for them to be seated. "What is your business here, sir?"

The doctor sank into one of the chairs Mr Gardiner had so admired, and he began to tell them of his earliest meetings with Lady Catherine and the treatments his father, and then he, had provided until her husband's death eight years prior. "Last year, she requested my presence at Rosings with certain medications, some of which had been prescribed for her late husband."

The doctor looked straight at Darcy as he continued. "She wanted them for what she called a 'preventive' for Anne."

He went on to express his belief that the lady had been dosing her daughter for years with watered-down versions of the remaining medicines. Peregrine—notorious in the family for saving small creatures—first wondered about it and then became her rescuer. Dumfries straightened in his chair and looked from one man to the other. "Do not doubt my brother's love for your cousin. He is not a perfect man, and he has his eccentricities. I grew up desiring to fix what was broken, to create curatives and salves to heal people and animals. Peregrine cares deeply as well but in ways that are different from mine."

"How different?" Richard growled.

Dumfries shrugged and waved his large hands. "He likes to tame creatures, create beauty, and capture moments and images in paint. Almost always, he sets things free or moves on to a new challenge, so marriage will be a test for him. But he does love your cousin."

"Marriage is for life. It is a chain that cannot be broken or unlocked," Richard growled. "We shall not see her hurt or her name sullied."

"Nor will Peregrine. His name and reputation as a painter matter to him."

Darcy rolled his eyes. "You do recognise that the de Bourgh and Fitzwilliam names already have been sullied?"

"I understand."

"Your brother appears unwilling to distinguish that fact. He does not appear to be a serious man."

"Well, yes," Dumfries agreed. "His appearance and affectations belie his manhood."

Richard guffawed while Darcy frowned. "Are you aware our cousin is with child? That she was compromised?"

"I am, though I question the reference to a compromise. Their thoughts came together rather swiftly, and their bodies followed."

The doctor stared at his red-faced host and glanced at Richard, who made an odd noise in his throat.

"Peregrine has asked me to care for Anne."

"How? You are a physician in Surrey," Richard said sharply. "If Lady Catherine goes to the dower house and is near her daughter, must we worry lest she influences her local surgeon to treat Anne as once was done?"

"I left word with Doctor Cummins that he is to consult with me." Dumfries's expression pinched when he said the man's name. "Peregrine and Anne have little money until this situation is sorted out, but my brother has assured me that Anne will take no medicines until we have communicated by express."

"When did you last hear from him?"

"Yesterday. He said that, thanks largely to you, all should be in place by tomorrow for them to move into Rosings."

"Good." Darcy glanced at the mantel clock and groaned. Elizabeth would be leaving in a quarter hour. He might not make it there in time but a message could. He summoned a footman and handed him the sealed note he had written before breakfast.

Richard eyed Darcy and smiled. "Love is detected everywhere we look," he muttered before adding that he and his father were likely to make the journey to Rosings to ensure the smoothness of the transition. "Darcy wishes this disaster to end. He misses the country and wishes to return north to his estate."

The doctor appeared affronted. "While events have been unfortunate and the circumstances made worse by high emotions, neither my brother nor his bride would consider their marriage and child to be a 'disaster.'"

"Then they are the luckiest people in all of this," Richard said gruffly. "The rest of us must restore the lustre to the Fitzwilliam name. Not to mention, we must paint our cousin's wedding and impending motherhood as occurring on a path that was planned and celebrated by the happy family, and we must determine whether these circumstances demand my aunt be led off to Bedlam!" He shot Dumfries a bitter look. "And those are among the smaller of the complaints."

Darcy waited for the doctor's reply, but when none came, his annoyance rose. "Your brother, my aunt, and my cousin have done a fine job of breaking things and creating havoc. Peregrine may believe he has rescued Anne, but he did so without consideration for her family. With neither a letter nor a meeting with my uncle, the colonel, or me, *he* determined that he knew best. Marrying her was a rash move, and marrying a Fitzwilliam without speaking to a male relative is not a rational act. I wish your brother well when he meets my uncle."

Dumfries's eyes narrowed. "As do I, sir, but do ask yourselves why it took my brother to see clearly what the family had overlooked."

"Anne has been sickly since childhood, always racked with fevers and coughs," Richard said glibly. "There was nothing to overlook."

Darcy stood, indicating the doctor's dismissal. "Your brother noticed something of grave importance but informed no one in his wife's family. That is hardly a responsible or rational act. His lack of common sense has required all of us to set aside our own duties and attend to his and Anne's self-made troubles."

He walked to the door and opened it. "I appreciate the intelligence you have given us, and I hope you and your brother keep us aware of any changes. Excuse me; I have other business to attend to."

The two men watched Darcy move quickly through the entryway, grab his hat, and disappear through the front door.

"He will never make it in time," Richard muttered. He turned to Dumfries. "God save Peregrine if his mess further muddles Darcy's plans."

As the hour of her departure from Gracechurch Street neared and Mr Darcy had not yet appeared, Elizabeth had wondered whether she had been correct about their starting a new chapter on the same page. Now, back at Longbourn and experiencing the hysterics, worry, anger, and laughter surrounding the news of her impending proposal from the odious Mr Collins, she could only wonder whether she and Mr Darcy would ever have the opportunity to read from the same book. Elizabeth most certainly did not wish to turn pages with her cousin, and she was feeling impatient for Mr Darcy's return.

She had read and re-read his letter. While he was cautious and gentle in his expression—and his words were couched carefully with pronouns or initials rather than names to protect his family—his feeling for her shone through. He was clever in his telling, using the letter to recommend a 'novel' whose metaphorical plot clearly laid bare details of his tense relationships with Lady Catherine and her daughter and revealed that Anne was living a life straight from the pages of a real and lurid novel: married in secret, with child, banished from her home, and declared dead. 'The landowner,' as he referred to himself in the letter, felt no shame for his family, just frustration and anger.

'One's happiness owes much to family, but one does not owe family one's happiness.'

Even more important, he said, was how news of Anne's 'death' had both freed him from one household's expectations and burdened him with another's hopes. That burden, and his desire to simply be away from his family, had prompted him to set out on what he admitted was little more than a quest for a wife. Meeting *her*, the beautiful, intelligent daughter of a country gentleman, had irrevocably changed his outlook and, he hoped, the direction of his future life.

'My happiness is centred on and owes much to you and the feelings you have evoked in me. You warm my heart. I desire only to earn some small place in your heart and to bring you equal happiness.'

The man who had talked to Elizabeth in Meryton as he might a man, who pointed out clouds and debated passages of Milton, could write a love letter of unimagined passion. His sentiments shocked and thrilled her.

'Our moments of shared thought and laughter warmed me; it was then I knew how cold I had been. I wish for a lifetime filled with such moments.'

How could she not read such a letter over and over again? There was more, unwritten on paper, that she nevertheless read between the beautifully inked lines. *'A lifetime filled with such moments'...with you. With him.* She had never had such a declaration; he had expressed similar sentiments now on two—or was it three? —occasions. He was an ardent lover, a man who had been misunderstood and maligned as mendacious. And he was in pursuit of her heart. How would she explain his intentions to her family when she could scarcely grasp his passionate devotion? How could she broach the subject of their nearly secret friendship with Jane, whose foot was beginning to tap in impatience for Mr Bingley's proposal? Her sister and Mr Bingley seemed well matched, but Elizabeth had wondered at times whether their mutual bent towards steady politeness might be rather dull. Mr Darcy had done little more than touch her hand, and he gave her shivers and goose flesh. Did Jane have those feelings, those sensations, with Mr Bingley?

I love my sister, but I wonder whether, in this as in many things, we are more different than alike. Jane might be more frightened than thrilled.

She was rather enjoying the tumult of emotions Mr Darcy prompted in her. They had made each other laugh until laughter gave way to deeper feelings; then hurt and confusion set in. But trust was there as well as a strong belief in his goodness.

Elizabeth would heed his concerns about her family's friendliness with Mr Wickham. He said little but referred to a life of scurrilous waste and reckless, venal behaviour, and he revealed the man's banishment from all Darcy properties. Darcy did not trust his childhood friend and did not want him near those he loved and respected.

Those he loved. Elizabeth recognised Mr Darcy had no improper feeling, merely a surfeit of it and an untried manner of expressing his emotions. Small wonder that his former friend could smear the oils on the portrait she and others were painting of him. Now, however, she knew Mr Darcy's outlines, and she was growing to understand his colours and shadings.

A note—just a few lines hastily written and delivered nearly as her carriage pulled away from Gracechurch Street—had only reaffirmed her new confidence in the man.

Apologies, I am delayed by an unexpected visitor: the brother of my cousin's new husband. My absence is one only in body, not in spirit. If I fail to reach you in time today, trust that I shall be with you within the week.

—FD

His feelings for her were clear. She had to determine her own and decide whether his, however genuinely felt, were of the moment. He had been wrestling with family crises—loss and duplicity, anger and frustration—and he was in need of some happiness. She had diverted him and provided that happiness. She feared his feelings for her were ephemeral, his happiness fleeting. She could not judge him too severely; the heart was a strange and uncertain thing, and his recent life events bore similar description. In fact, Elizabeth knew she liked him a great deal, but did shivers and admiration mean love?

With his words still fresh in her mind, she felt some pangs of remorse. He knew not how she felt about him. She had judged him harshly, leaving him to press his case in a letter. It was awful to think he was in London, wondering whether she still thought ill of his behaviour and dreaded his arrival.

No, he could not think so. He must not. Not just as her feelings were forming. How she wished she had seen him one more time before she left London.

At least, she had had the presence of mind to take a moment and read his note, and she had left one in return in the event he did go to the Gardiners after she and her uncle had departed. Her words must give him some hope, some reassurance.

Sir, although we missed your presence this morning, we look forward to your arrival at Longbourn as well as your company and your conversation on a morning walk. As you know, in all things of nature, there is something of the marvellous.

—EB

It was likely his family still occupied his time. Mr Darcy had implied that no cordiality was left in his relationship with his aunt Lady Catherine de Bourgh, and in expressing his feelings for *her*, he would defy his uncle's wishes. Elizabeth wondered whether this man must always have a new family crisis.

And some would think my *family difficult?* Such a family he had! A devious, lovesick cousin. A malicious aunt. A loyal if rather improperly mannered and flirting cousin. She would await Mr Darcy's arrival at Netherfield and see how he reacted to the newest twist in the endless saga of who was betrothed to whom.

She looked down and sighed. *Mr Darcy is not the only one of us with a difficult, mercurial cousin. Nor is he the only man who writes letters of intent to those who reside at Longbourn.*

The cursed Mr Collins had written a grandiloquent letter, full of self-regard for his self-sacrificing intent to save the Bennet name from its association with the nefarious Mr Darcy. He would, he vowed, burnish the family lineage with children of his loins. His bride awaited him there, and he would speak to her father upon his arrival two days hence.

His bride. Such a terrible fate.

Elizabeth could hardly bear to count the hours or meet the laughing, pitying eyes of those who knew through her mother's loud exclamations that it was she, Elizabeth, who would be redeemed and Longbourn would be saved. Such a notion could be true only if her stomach did not turn at the thought of Mr Collins's face, loins, and horrid fishy smell and if she had not stood mere inches from Mr Darcy, feeling his warm breath and looking into his dark, expressive eyes.

Oh my.

Perhaps with such thoughts, she too could write a lurid novel worthy of being buried in drawers and under mattresses. After all, she had two men wishing to save her name and reputation. She could only hope one man—the better man—arrived sooner than the other. Why did her cousin assume she needed her name redeemed and her reputation restored? He was the one responsible for slandering Mr Darcy and perpetuating the mythology of the 'Cuckolded Mr Darcy's Malfeasance and Great Perfidy.'

"Lizzy, do not be missish," her father had said upon welcoming her home. "Come, read this letter from my dear cousin, and tell me all I have missed in your great and tragic love story. It is worthy of the Bard."

It was indeed a horror story. Mr Darcy might have a cousin risen from the dead and married to an odd, inappropriate man, his aunt might be bound for Bedlam, and the rest of his family might be waiting for him to finish playing saviour in order to ruin his plans for his own personal felicity, but *she* was facing the prospect of a proposal from the increasingly odious Mr Collins.

Granted, she realised she might not be his intended…victim. In his letter, he wrote of his plans to return to his parsonage and his need for a wife by year's end. "The man has a mission," her father said with a chuckle. Year's end was but seven weeks away, and he would be at Longbourn within two days to declare himself. Who was his intended? Was it one who wished for his address, such as Mary or even Charlotte? Could it be the Widow Toomey, who set a fine table and whose creamy turnips had so excited the man's palate that he had asked Hill and Cook to recreate them at Longbourn?

Yet Elizabeth's father teased that it was she who was the devout man's intended. The suggestion sickened her, pleased her mother, reduced Lydia to hysterical laughter, confused Kitty, and angered Mary, who pounded hymns furiously on the pianoforte and refused to listen to Elizabeth's denials of mutual affection.

"Lizzy, stay inside. Mr Collins will not want a wife with sun-browned cheeks." Her mother eyed her as carefully as she might a plump goose or an especially fine piece of lace. "A stitch or two in your gowns would tighten them here," she added thoughtfully, pinching the fabric across her daughter's chest.

Elizabeth fled and sought peace behind the closed doors of her bedroom or in the stillroom with her one trusted supporter. Two days after her arrival home, and but one day before the appearance of the wrong suitor, she beckoned Jane to help plait her hair.

"Jane," she said, appreciating the confident serenity that a courtship and firm affection were having on her steady older sister, "shall I speak to Charlotte? I am sure Mama has told Mrs Lucas the news of Mr Collins's visit and his business here."

"Oh, Lizzy." Jane grimaced, which her angelic countenance wore more as compassion than pain. "Mama is so eager for an engagement. She worries for Longbourn and her future. We could avoid this uncomfortable situation if Charles were to propose, but he waits, I think, to speak to Mr Darcy and to have him at Netherfield to help assuage Caroline's worries about losing her position in her brother's household."

Elizabeth was startled at the turn in conversation. Was Caroline still undermining her brother's courtship of Jane? But it was true that if her mother was busy worrying for Jane's hoped-for engagement, she would not be speculating on the prospects of her second daughter.

"Is Kitty not some consolation to Miss Bingley? My sister appears as her pet project, adorned in feathers with her cheeks pinched and her back straight as she primly mutters inanities about teas and Belgian laces."

"Lizzy!" Jane giggled. "I should not laugh. One is my sister, one is likely to be my sister—and I should hope for that connexion, yet I prefer to think only of the one to be forged with Charles."

Elizabeth pulled her hair away and turned to look at Jane. "Oh, how radiant you are. You are so happy." She twitched an eyebrow. "Is your Mr Bingley glowing as well? Is there colour in his cheeks and a bounce in his step? Does he hum while walking and daydream during breakfast?"

"Lizzy! Turn around and let me finish your hair." Jane pulled, brushed, and plaited her sister's hair in silence before pausing in her ministrations. "As I said, Charles awaits Mr Darcy. I believe he seeks his blessing."

"But why? He should not need any 'blessing.' Mr Darcy has done nothing but express his happiness for his friend."

"Has he, Lizzy? While you were in London, I listened to the words being spoken about him and about the circumstances in which he left you. It is the reason our neighbours think so poorly of him."

"Jane…"

"I do not think Charles needs his blessing; he should not wish for it." Jane cleared her throat. "I am sorry, but I wonder at their friendship. Charles supports Mr Darcy while he goes off to his… his adventures, and you and Miss Bingley are left wondering at his motives."

"His adventures?"

"His estate visits. To find a bride among the ladies."

Elizabeth thought of the letter she had hidden in a reticule stuffed behind books on her shelves. *His motives and his character are clear to me. What has happened here in my absence?*

"That is not quite what occurred. Mr Darcy is my friend. He was kind to my aunt and uncle and their children. He is Mr Bingley's friend."

A sigh escaped Jane's lips. "Yes…but you did not hear what has been said. I have had to defend your behaviour." Her tone sounded harsh to Elizabeth's ears. "He hurt you. He damaged our family name."

"He was the victim of gossip and misunderstanding, as was I."

"His lack of grief over his cousin's death did not reflect well on his character," Jane replied, her fingers busy plaiting her sister's thick, dark hair.

Elizabeth said nothing.

"I know my heart, Lizzy. I understand love and allegiance. Charles has given me his."

Yet there is no proposal. Because the man you do not trust for me is the only one trusted by Charles.

"Do you resent the trust that Mr Bingley and I place in his friend? That his absence means you must wait for a proposal?"

The room was quiet for nearly a minute before she responded. "I question Mr Darcy's absence and his intentions towards you."

"Oh, Jane…but you do not question Mr Bingley, a man of three and twenty, needing a friend's 'blessing'?"

"No, I do not."

Elizabeth clenched her teeth. Jane was pulling her hair and bruising her feelings. *There is so much I cannot say. When did you learn to form, let alone voice, such an opinion?*

"I know Mr Collins can be tiresome, Lizzy, and somewhat too

pleased with himself. But he will inherit Longbourn and has the means to be a good husband and father. Would he be so very bad a match?"

Elizabeth stilled, shocked at her sister's sentiment. "For *me*? Is this one of Lydia's riddles? *You* desire less of a connexion with Charles's sister because her temperament is so difficult, but you do not see how ill-formed a marriage is between me and that awful, slanderous man?"

"He is not so terribly awful." Jane shifted behind her, her voice hushed. "Mr Collins would not be my first choice for you. But he *is* a choice, a good possibility, and marriage to him would clear your reputation, make our mother happy, and keep peace in our family."

"Then *you* marry him, Jane, because not one of those considerations matters to me."

"Lizzy…"

Elizabeth pulled away, tears springing to her eyes when her hair caught in Jane's hand. "Do you not care for my feelings? For my future happiness? Mr Collins will be here and demand a wife. If I am his choice, I shall not marry him. I hope for your happiness with Mr Bingley, but it seems I shall not have your support for *my* choice."

"Your choice is Mr Darcy?"

Elizabeth began fixing her hair in a furious manner, uncaring of the tangled disaster she was creating. "I thought never to marry, to be a spinster and live with you and your husband and your ten children and torment Caroline with my liveliness and carelessly stacked books and muddy boots. That seems a less happy, nay impossible, proposition to me today. My cousin may wed Mary or Charlotte or Hill for all I care; they seem to like him, and his words have not hurt *them*."

Jane looked up solemnly at her sister, but Elizabeth would not meet her eyes. "Not every woman finds felicity. Caroline will not; Charles is sure Mr Darcy will not marry her as she wishes, and she will remain a burden to him and Louisa."

They talk of others' marital prospects as though solving tenant disputes. Kitty is not the only one under Caroline's influence.

"Of course, Mr Darcy would never marry her. Caroline Bingley is not the sort of wife he seeks."

Jane sat back and looked at her sister curiously. "I am not familiar with the sort of ladies who interest Mr Darcy. You have an intimacy with him that has worried Mr Collins and Mama. You must be careful."

Elizabeth gathered her hair up under a bonnet and opened the door. "I have been judicious in keeping my own counsel these past weeks. I must return to doing so."

"Lizzy, your hair!"

"You worry more for my hair than for my heart."

Elizabeth choked back an angry sob. She could not hear Jane's voice over the din of the music pounding from Mary's angry fingers. She ran outside and was but a step away from the far garden when Kitty hailed her. She could not bear it; she needed to be away from this house. She needed to think, to understand how Jane could care only of her own happiness and assign her 'most beloved sister' to a dreadful marriage.

"Lizzy?"

Elizabeth looked up, tears stinging her eyes. Kitty stood before her, twisting a feather in her hands. "Lizzy, I must talk to you. I need your advice."

Elizabeth had never felt less able to provide wise counsel. "Kitty, this is not the time—"

The younger girl pulled her into the shelter of the garden and began to speak in a hushed, hurried voice. "Miss Bingley is fluttering over Mr Darcy's return. She is certain he comes to seek her hand. She plans to ensure he does!"

"Oh no." *Hunted and in danger of compromise!*

"And Charlotte and Mary are so angry that you have won Mr Collins's heart."

"No, I have—"

Kitty squeezed her sister's hand. "I think all of them are so horribly wrong. Let me help you run away and hide from our cousin. I shall tell Mr Darcy where you are hiding, and he may come rescue you and marry you, and all will be well."

Elizabeth stared at her younger sister, astonished and impressed.

"Honestly, Lizzy, I have decided that Miss Bingley is an unpleasant sort of lady. She does not like my drawings. She never looks at clouds, she always talks to Jane rather than to me, and she hates it when I cough. Mr Darcy likes you ever so much more than he does her. I heard his cousin call him a smitten simkin when he thought no one was listening."

Kitty grinned and leaned closer. "He is coming here for *you*, Lizzy, not to bless Mr Bingley's proposal. I am sure of it."

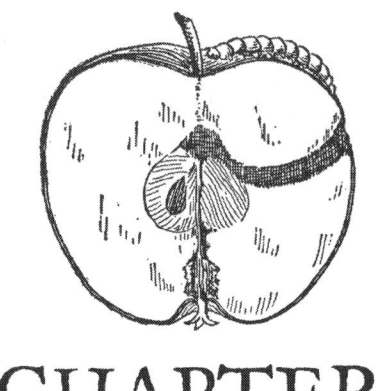

CHAPTER SIXTEEN

By half past four on a bright but windy day in London, Darcy was just beginning to see relief. He had spent the day with his solicitor: reading documents, signing papers, writing letters, and revising all of the above. All of the legalities concerning Rosings and Anne's rightful ownership had been thoroughly inspected, every detail attended to, and all possibilities for the future considered. By full rights, the new mistress of Rosings should have been present. But since Sir Lewis de Bourgh's death, Darcy had been granted nearly complete decision-making rights with only his aunt's signature necessary.

Now, with the estate fully in Anne's name, he retained authority even after the birth of her heir. Apparently, his Uncle de Bourgh was a wiser man than his choice of wife would indicate; he had trusted the Darcys over the Fitzwilliams when it came to his family's estate. With the assistance of Darcy's keen-minded solicitor, and some musty papers filed away with his dead uncle's former solicitor, they had ensured that Peregrine, pleasant man though he might be, would have neither authority nor dominion over Rosings.

Lord Matlock had made but one demand: "Emasculate the beau bird." Richard's outburst of hysterical laughter over 'Peregrine's plume plucking' had given Darcy the impetus to manoeuvre the wished-for enfeeblement into an intricately worded separation. In spite of his status as Anne's husband, Peregrine Dumfries would have no legal standing over Rosings or his child. The purse strings remained firmly in the hands of Darcy and the earl.

The duties of the day had been exhausting, and Darcy dreaded the months ahead as the vexing trio of Rosings Park recognised their loss of control. But at this moment, none of that mattered. By tomorrow, Georgiana and he would be at Netherfield, just three miles from Elizabeth. Everything was prepared for the journey and for their travels north to Pemberley. He needed to return to the estate. Autumn was upon them; winter would soon creep in.

Four days at Netherfield, mayhap a se'nnight. No, strike that out, and damn his steward's incompetence. He would stay however long it took to revise the town's opinions of him, to state his intentions to Mr Bennet, and first, of course, to ensure that Elizabeth wished his attentions and shared his desire for an attachment. He was not entirely confident but neither was he discouraged. He had seen her smile; he thought he had sensed her desire. He had declared himself to her, and although she had not replied with like sentiments, her shy smiles had filled him with hope.

'I look forward to further conversations on topics neither of us canvass with others.'

How he wished to know her feelings as she read his letter. Did it change her opinion of him and help her to understand how his family situation had affected his behaviour? The pained look in her eyes and the tears he had prompted tore at his heart. Yet they had parted on far warmer terms, leaving him with ardent hope.

Does she return my feelings?

He was a ridiculous, besotted fool; he had never committed such words to paper and had only felt these sentiments since meeting Elizabeth. If the town thought he had declared himself before and walked away, now he had pledged his heart to her in ink, above his signature. He would not allow any further confusion to come between them.

Her note, handed to him by a slyly smiling Mrs Gardiner, should have cleared any doubts. It was full of sweetness and intelligence. *She tells me she was sorry not to see me, looks forward to my arrival, and quotes Aristotle?* His heart swelled to think on it. Reading the note, as he had done at least a dozen times already this day, left him weak in a happy sort of way. Last night, he had fallen asleep with her note in his hand and finally enjoyed the vivid, lovely dreams of her that he worked so hard to repress during his waking hours.

> *Elizabeth lounged in the grass, Pemberley in the distance, and smiled as he approached. It was a hot sunny day, cloudless 'til an hour earlier. Her light summer gown fell loosely off one shoulder, its thin fabric shielding her soft skin from the sun's rays but not protecting her lovely figure from his interested eyes. Suddenly, the wind picked up and stole her bonnet. He took a step, intending to run after it, but she stopped him with a wave. "I despise bonnets. Kiss me instead." He fell to his knees and touched his lips to hers. So soft, then they turned demanding. As he pulled away to catch his breath, Elizabeth rose to her feet and reached her arms to the sky. The wind billowed, and her gown flew up and followed her bonnet. He looked up at her, naked in the sunlight, as she laughed and watched the runaway dress flutter in the currents towards a grouping of clouds. He reached up, tenderly touching her, and she fell into his arms, ravenous for his kisses, hands everywhere. As they tumbled to the grass, she whispered his name...*

Darcy had awoken with a start, and once he had regained his bearings, he lay abed re-living the visions and relieving himself of his hard agony.

He could not be ashamed of his passion for her. He had confided his feelings to Richard. Had Elizabeth confided her thoughts about him to anyone? Would no one know why he went to Longbourn?

Did she tell her father or her sister of my declaration, of my hopes?

He thought not, but Darcy anticipated her father would be approachable, and Mr Bennet would not laugh too much at the great hill of misunderstandings over which his daughter's suitor had tripped and stumbled.

Once Elizabeth's affections were secured and he had her promise, then he and Georgiana must head to Pemberley. Or must they? His resolve to go there if only for a week or two was sinking. How could he leave Elizabeth once he had won her heart? What if he still had much work to do to win her? Could his steward perhaps rise to the occasion of his master's desperate situation? *So many questions...* How he hated uncertainty.

"Where is Georgiana?" he said aloud. Darcy glanced at the mantel clock. It was near five. She had missed tea. *How long can it take to retrieve sheet music?* Lady Matlock was likely the culprit, plying her niece with questions about their journey. Mrs Annesley was not with Georgiana to help her navigate an interrogation; she had absented herself for the day to visit her niece, and his sister had taken her lady's maid with her.

Some questions would not be asked by his aunt, for he knew Richard had been silent about Elizabeth. His cousin would not hand over Darcy's heart to be dissected and discussed. His parents' appreciation for their nephew's diligence on the Rosings estate matter was tempered by their continuing resentment that neither man would consider Anne for his bride. To them, his day spent with solicitors was nothing more than due penance.

Feeling ill prepared to see his relations, he sent over a note asking Georgiana to return to Darcy House. He wished to show her the drawing young Henry Gardiner had given him two days earlier when he had arrived too late to see Elizabeth and her uncle drive off to Meryton. Darcy had tried not to show his deep disappointment, and he was much heartened when Mrs Gardiner presented him Elizabeth's precious words. Before he could react with more than a stunned half-smile, the young boy tugged his sleeve and handed up a folded sheet of paper. Henry had drawn a picture of Georgiana with a tiger to thank her for returning his tin soldier.

"Lizzy says to thank you for helping as well, Mr Darcy."

Thinking on it made him smile in spite of his concern for his sister. He wandered the house, waiting for Georgiana's arrival, pushing thoughts of Elizabeth to the back of his mind. His impatience for their trip and his growing disquiet over his sister's absence finally drove him to call for his horse.

He rode the four blocks to his uncle's home on Park Lane and knew within moments that something was terribly wrong. His uncle and Richard had returned from Rosings not thirty minutes prior, and his aunt was in her rooms. The footman said Miss Darcy had received two notes. His note had arrived some thirty minutes ago, but she had received one an hour earlier from Lady Catherine.

"The lady's coach waited, sir." The footman looked nervous. "Miss Darcy got into the carriage."

"What did the note say?" Darcy demanded.

The man could tell him nothing. "Miss Darcy was quite proper and said nothing to me, sir. All I understood was that her aunt required her presence."

"Why was I not informed? Did my sister leave no note? Where is her lady's maid? She did bring a lady's maid here, did she not?"

The footman, already grey-haired, turned ashen. "I do not know, sir."

The sound of Darcy's angry interrogation stirred the household. His aunt appeared on the stairs. "Darcy? What is it, dear?"

"Georgiana has not returned to Darcy House."

Her eyes wide, Lady Matlock hurried down the stairs. "She had gathered her music and was to leave for tea with you. That was some time...at least an hour ago."

"Lady Catherine sent for her," Darcy replied grimly.

"Oh no. What does that woman want now?" The countess frowned and told the footman to fetch her son.

"Your uncle has gone to his club. He arrived home from Rosings in quite a bad temper. The...the meeting with Anne and her husband put him in great need of some gruff conversation." She looked at him sharply. "You and Richard did not prepare him for Anne's frightful connubial happiness. He lost his ruddy cheeks in the telling of it. That awful Peregrine person..."

"My sister, Aunt. I must find her."

Richard suddenly emerged on the stairway, pulling on his coat. "We shall follow you to the blighted bat house."

The door to Lady Catherine's ornate London house was barred to visitors, but Darcy's low-voiced reminder to the butler that he oversaw the budget and paid his wages prompted Reddington to open up.

It took little time for Darcy to encounter his aunt, though Georgiana's whereabouts remained a mystery. Lady Catherine strolled into the entryway, tapping her walking stick on the worn marble floor and looking as if she smelled something especially awful.

"You, again? I thought you had cast me off," she sneered.

In the calm, controlled voice he tried to affect when he was close to a heated eruption, Darcy enquired, "Where is my sister?"

"Your sister belongs with me, Darcy. She needs my guidance to avoid Anne's mistakes."

"Anne's mistakes?" he uttered through clenched teeth. "You created those conditions from which she so desperately needed to escape!"

The wiry woman scoffed. "Your refusal to marry her set this ball of deception into motion. You are not worthy of raising my sister's daughter."

Darcy stepped forward, his fury at last boiling over. "I shall tear apart this house and pack you off to Bedlam today."

Richard and his mother entered the house. Lady Matlock took in the scene and, eyes flashing, used the shrill tone her younger son knew well as a warning to stand down.

"Everyone," she cried, "into the sitting room. Now!"

Darcy and Richard walked briskly into the cramped, stale room. The ladies followed, one quite angry and the other quite impatient.

"Catherine! Where is Georgiana? Why have you brought her here?"

Lady Catherine sighed dramatically and rolled her eyes in Darcy's direction. "Darcy, you are a pathetic little man. You fail in your duty to Anne and now must bring reinforcements to a parley?"

She turned back to address the newcomers. "Martha, your nephew means to take the girl to the wilds of the country where the heart of the deception continues."

"Featherfield?" Richard said, puzzled.

"You have always been the dim nephew, Richard," Lady Catherine snapped. "Pemberley."

The atmosphere in the sitting room went from cold to icy. She scoffed at the affronted colonel. "Georgiana has no discernment. She is an innocent whom her brother places in frightful situations. I warned the girl of the dangers of returning to Pemberley, the site of her sordid affair with a bran-faced footman."

"Catherine!" Lady Matlock cried.

Aghast, Darcy yelled, "How dare you! You sent my sister, only fifteen years old and your niece, a threatening, slanderous note about a supposed 'sordid affair'?"

"Of course, Darcy. I do my duty as her family. I have it on the best authority." Catherine gestured at the doorway where the shame-faced Pemberley footman stood shaking.

"Oh, hell," Darcy muttered. He felt sick with anger.

The footman stepped forward, looking terrified and embarrassed. He did his best to stand straight as duty required, but his trembling caused him to slump under Darcy's glare.

"It was my c-cousin who got me this p-position, you see," he stuttered. "You wrote me such a nice letter when I left P-Pemberley, Mr Darcy. Mary's friend Lieutenant Wickham advised me of this place of employment."

"Wickham?" Darcy paled. "Damnation…"

"He was to marry my cousin Mary King in Hertfordshire, but my uncle—he doubts it, you see." The young man glanced nervously at the lady of the house. "The lieutenant passed on his knowledge of this position to show my uncle he was a good man, true to his word."

"Oh, did he now?" Darcy spat. "Where is my sister?"

Richard, his face a furious shade of red, nearly growled. "Wickham is a lieutenant? That cur is in uniform?"

The young man neared Darcy. "Well, sir, I—"

Catherine pounded her cane. "Speak no more, boy! And go wash your face. You have been stealing biscuits. The crumbs are all over your cheeks and nose!"

The footman blushed, which nearly concealed his freckles, and lowered his head.

"Where is my sister?" Darcy loomed over his aunt.

"I shall not tell you, Darcy. Begone from my house!"

"Sir?" the footman squeaked. "Miss Darcy never got into the carriage. It was her lady's maid."

Lady Catherine turned to glare at the trembling young man. "Shut it, boy! You speak in riddles."

"Her abigail, Irene?" asked Lady Matlock.

"My cousin sent another in her place? Smart girl," Richard said in a sharp voice. "Not 'dim' like me."

"Then where is she?" Darcy demanded.

"You have deceived me, boy!" the great lady cried.

"The miss said, 'Tell my brother I am doing as I believe Anne has done.'"

"You see!" Lady Catherine roared. "She is to be a barque of frailty as my Anne became! She veers towards the path of licentiousness and aberrant sexual congress!"

"Catherine, you have always been spiteful, but now you are cruel and insensible," Lady Matlock snapped. "Peter has just come from Rosings, and Anne is a happy bride. Her husband is good for her."

While Richard rolled his eyes at his mother's shaded retort, Darcy suddenly grabbed his shoulder. "Georgiana is not here. I know where we can find her."

He turned to the footman. "Young man, what is your name?"

"Andrews, sir."

"Andrews, where is my sister's maid?"

The young man gulped. "Upstairs, sir. Hiding."

Darcy nodded and softened his glare. "Bring her to me. We shall all return to my uncle's house."

"Boy, begone from this house!" Lady Catherine cried. "Do not collect your things. Throw him out, Reddington. Give him no letter of praise. He has discredited my home."

Richard glared at his aunt and then at Reddington, who quaked, wide-eyed. "Stand down, sir. Andrews, fetch your things and the girl. You deserve better. We all do."

Darcy took a deep breath. Although his worry was subsiding, his fury was not quite spent. "Lady Catherine, yesterday I told you I was done with you as a relation. Since that time, I have learnt of your interference with Anne's doctor and the malfeasance done to her by his medicines at your direction."

"Goodness!" Lady Matlock gasped. Her son reached a hand to steady her.

"My business with you is finished," Darcy said, his voice cold. "Do not attempt to speak or write to my sister, or I shall support my uncle and send you to Bedlam."

"You would not dare."

"Will you require assistance tomorrow in packing your things?" Lady Matlock's voice dropped to an angry whisper. "You have lost, Catherine. Lost everything dear to you, and all by your own choices."

"Anne's choices! She chose to spread her legs for a mincing man who covets my estate."

"Blast! Does every woman in this family read those awful novels?" Richard mumbled.

Darcy stepped closer and leaned over his furious aunt. "For the final time, think on your position. You will be a grandmother in the spring."

The small lady quaked then slapped her ring-laden hand hard across Darcy's cheek. "Never mention that mongrel to me again."

Holding his cheek, a trickle of blood emerging through his fingers, Darcy shook his head.

"Bedlam it is, then."

Upon their return to Matlock House, the colonel sent Andrews below stairs. A trusted, long-time footman was instructed that the newcomer was to remain in either the kitchens or the room to which he had been assigned.

It took Richard and Darcy but a minute to find Georgiana hiding in a closet cupboard in her bedchamber 'as Anne might have done.'

Her brother enfolded her in a hug. "Oh, sweetheart, such a smart idea to hide yourself and send Irene instead, but that is not what Anne did."

Georgiana stifled a yawn. "It was so dark and quiet in there; I could not hear or see a thing. Thank goodness, you found me." She rubbed her back and stretched. Her eyes widened when she looked at her brother and his reddened cheek.

Richard squeezed her shoulders. "A fine hiding place, though I believe behind the curtains might have been the more comfortable choice."

The three returned to Darcy House where the men slowly and carefully revealed the full story of Anne and the happiness she seemed to have found beneath—and then away from—her mother's ever-watchful eye.

Neither man could hold still while relating the tale. One would pace behind the settee while the other sat, tapping his knee and trying in vain to maintain eye contact with Georgiana. Darcy's face was pink-hued for much of the telling while the colonel's was a dark angry red. Painful though it was for him, Richard curbed his tendency for exaggeration and funny voices, leaving Georgiana to form her own opinion on Peregrine Dumfries.

"Oh my." The girl looked past the two men and stared at the opposite wall. "Anne is alive, married to a painter, and with child. Does everyone know?" she asked plaintively. "Everyone in the family?"

Darcy glanced at his cousin. "Just we three, and our aunt and uncle..."

"My brother is aware, though Robert knows less, as usual," Richard added in a sardonic voice. "It is a small circle, dear. Six, seven in total...dotty Great-Aunt Minnie knows nothing. Not that she ever has known much, as one can surmise by spending an evening with that muttonhead of a son she raised."

"Cousin Rufus? He is a bit odd," Georgiana agreed.

Richard groaned at his digression. *Darcy will kill me for bringing up the damn Fitzwilliam bloodlines. Sickly, dotty, spotty, or dead. Or mad with lust or anger, in the case of Anne and Lady Catherine.* He smiled at Georgiana, hoping she had not seen him flinch at the reminder of his family's weaknesses.

"The woman is near ninety years of age," Darcy said with a glare at his cousin. "She hardly can remember anything past that tea towel she says you speared to shreds with a fork back when you were in leading strings."

"My cruel brother was to blame. Leading strings…blast it, I was but five." Richard sighed in mock outrage.

"Yet still in leading strings." Darcy affected a solemn mien.

"Against my will, and only when she visited."

Georgiana might have fallen prey to the buffoonery playing out in front of her, but the shock of her cousin Anne being not only among the living but now married and bearing new life appeared to render her more thoughtful. Yet her confusion remained unabated.

"Why is Lady Catherine so set against Anne's happiness? She never wanted our cousin to be happy. If Anne laughed, it was a cough. If she smiled, it was a seizure."

Richard patted Georgiana's hand. "Our aunt has been angry and bitter for a long time, poppet."

"I cannot fathom such feelings," she murmured, turning to her brother. "Was she kind to Mama?"

Darcy looked as though he had received a physical blow at his sister's plaintive question. "Yes, sweetheart. Mama said she was."

Richard knew that Darcy hated to prevaricate, especially to his sister. Lady Catherine could be kind when it served her purpose. But as much as she grieved when her sister died, her jealousy of Lady Anne's beauty, charm, talents, and happy marriage to George Darcy had emerged in petty sniping and grumbling for nearly his whole life. She had never been a pleasant relation.

"I do not like Lady Catherine, Fitzwilliam." Georgiana turned to Richard. "She is cruel and smells of sour apples."

Richard burst into laughter. "Ah, you are a smart girl. I thought only I noticed that rotten fruit stink about her, and as you know, I am quite dim."

Georgiana frowned and leaned over to hug her cousin before turning her worried eyes to her brother. "Fitzwilliam? Your cheek...you are not a man who bumps into walls. Did my aunt strike you?"

"'Tis only a flesh wound," he assured her quietly. When he could not meet her eyes, Georgiana moved to his side, murmuring, "Sour, rotten apples full of worms."

Richard's tears of laughter soaked his handkerchief and most of Darcy's.

Later, as they sat down to their evening meal, Georgiana turned to her brother. "Will you be angry with me if I tell you why I trusted Andrews?"

He managed an encouraging smile. "No, sweetling, of course not." Darcy waved the footmen out of the room. "Go on then."

"At Pemberley, he was nothing more than a nice young man able to tell me the names of flowers. It was lonely there for me, especially when you were away. He has many brothers and sisters, and his stories made me laugh."

Darcy shook his head. "You were too often alone, Georgiana. Mrs Annesley is kind and a good companion, but you should have friends around you, cousins your own age."

"Or a sister. I wish Elizabeth Bennet and her Gardiner cousins could come to Pemberley."

Richard laughed while Darcy frowned and gently took his sister's hand. He cleared his throat. "Was Andrews your friend?"

"Yes, he was nice." She took a deep breath and, in a tremulous voice, began to stutter. "He...he was at the menagerie the day we were there. He was the man who picked up Henry's soldier. When I recognised him, he whispered, 'Beware your aunt.'"

Darcy sat frozen while Richard was stirred to anger.

"He said that? How does he know anything of your aunts?" Richard cried indignantly.

The girl started crying. "I knew which aunt, Richard. I knew he did not mean your mother!"

"There, there, my dear." Richard gave her a tender smile. He had an unfortunate tendency towards gruffness, resulting in an uncanny ability not only to discipline soldiers but also to elicit his cousin's tears and his mother's fury. *Why are women so complicated when I am all charm and kind-heartedness?*

His sister's tears provoked Darcy to react. "How did he know you—we—would be at Pidock's?" Darcy asked in a gentle voice.

"I do not know. Coincidence, I suppose," she speculated.

Darcy was watching her carefully, and Georgiana seemed to sense his worries.

"Andrews is not my secret correspondent, Fitzwilliam," she cried. "I have known nothing of him since you banished him!"

He grimaced. "I believe you."

"The whole thing was so odd until the note came today. I just knew something was wrong." Georgiana took a breath. "I asked Irene to wear my bonnet and pelisse and get into the carriage, then go straight upstairs to the blue bedroom and hide in that great closet."

Richard guffawed, heedless of the crumbs that flew into his moustache. "The one with the hidden door?"

"Yes! I knew she would be safe. I told her to trust the footman with the freckled cheeks."

"And so you did." Darcy beamed at her, though Richard wondered at the origins of Andrews's information and of his very presence at Pidock's. Darcy looked equally perplexed. It took all of the colonel's self-control not to spout something unsuitable in front of Georgiana.

"You are not angry with me?" she asked quietly.

"Not at all, my sweet," Darcy reassured her. "I am proud of you. There are too many secrets that turn into lies and rumours around this family." He smiled and pulled a child's drawing from his pocket. "I have nearly forgotten to deliver your post."

Georgiana sighed. "Henry is such a sweet boy. I like the Gardiners. And Lizzy is so nice."

Richard's eyebrows rose. He crossed his arms and stared expectantly at Darcy. "'Lizzy'?" he mouthed.

Darcy scowled and turned back to his sister. "Have you gathered all your music and books for your trunks? I believe we have a journey to make."

"We leave tomorrow for Marlbourn?"

"Um, our plans have altered. We go to Netherfield and then home to Pemberley."

Her eyes widened. "Pemberley? Truly? Oh, Fitzwilliam, I have missed it."

"As have I."

Georgiana's happy smile slowly faded. "You will not visit the duke and duchess?" She looked stricken. "Is it my fault you will not go?"

"Not at all, sweetheart. I have travelled enough on Fitzwilliam family business these past weeks. I wish to go home and see to Darcy lands."

"So you will not meet any more ladies."

Richard barked. "On the contrary. Miss Bingley is at Netherfield, my dear."

Georgiana's look of horror expressed her thoughts.

Darcy sighed dramatically and gave his cousin a dark look. "We shall stay at Netherfield but a few nights. Longbourn, the estate where Elizabeth Bennet and her family reside, is nearby."

Georgiana's face brightened with excitement.

"I shall meet her sisters!"

Her squeal of exuberance hurt Richard's bad ear. Its origins, traceable to his days as a greenhorn officer standing too near to cannon fire, involved an elaborate tale he never tired of recounting.

After embracing her brother and cousin, Georgiana disappeared to her rooms to see to her trunks and recount her day to Mrs Annesley.

"She is a sly one, Darcy," Richard barked. "Nary a question about the lady you will visit? How unlike my mother. Georgiana seems more a Darcy than a Fitzwilliam."

"Thank goodness," Darcy muttered. He turned to Richard and

grimaced. "We need to learn more of the footman's connexion to Wickham. Mayhap, he is under orders to create more havoc or steal my mother's jewels."

"The boy is an innocent, I believe. Just a pawn. What is Wickham up to? Tupping country girls and situating footmen with Lady Catherine?"

"He best not still be in Meryton. Can you find out where he is placed? If he remains in uniform?"

"Hmm, of course." Richard stared at the painting on the wall opposite his chair. "Meryton? In Hertfordshire? Has your Miss Bennet made the acquaintance of our old friend?"

"Yes," Darcy replied, his face grim. "She read his face quite easily, but he is quick. Although he was taken unawares of the rumours and the truth swirling around Rosings, he was swift to support and spread any slanders against me."

"Good for your lady," Richard said, smirking at the blush his words brought to Darcy's cheeks. "Is he simply making merry, lacking power and freedom of movement, and being devious?"

"He has never been capable of making a plan. He careers and crashes." Darcy rubbed his neck, a clear sign his mind and body were near exhaustion. "Wickham is a dim one."

Richard glared at Darcy, but his cousin's comment appeared innocently made.

"Yes, well, I shall speak to Andrews," he replied. "Your mind appears to be elsewhere—already in the country, dreaming of your sweetheart?"

"Her beauty outstrips yours, Richard." Darcy squinted at him. "Perhaps if you shaved off that monstrosity, I could be tempted to stay…"

"Ha! You would desert me even for Miss Bingley." Richard collapsed into a chair and threw his leg over the stuffed arm. "I am bereft."

"I think you have a secret admiration for Charles's sister." Darcy smirked. "I am sorry to break your heart, but I have much work to do in Hertfordshire. Even without determining what mischief Wickham might be up to, I have many steps on the road towards achieving my goal."

"Your *goal*? How dreadfully droll you are, Darcy. Perhaps you are a romantic after all."

"Hmm."

Richard watched his cousin, fingers steepled and brow furrowed, deep in thought. *Always with the thinking. Does he never tire of it?* The more he pondered it, the more Richard recognised that his cousin had not truly changed from the ever-watchful, slightly diffident boy he had once been.

He was never a woolly-crown, and I am not dim. That venal old bat. I knew she hated me. Did not even consider me for Anne, thankfully. Ha! The old witch got what she deserved for a son-in-law.

All this staring at and thinking about Darcy hastened Richard's need for a drink. *Drink. Think. They were such opposites.*

Even when on horseback or when swimming in Pemberley's ponds, Darcy was always thinking. *Why?* Richard recalled the hungry looks his cousin had bestowed upon Miss Elizabeth Bennet. *Does a man in love and lust need to bloody think? One should be taking direction from below, damn it, not from the brain. Instinct, man!*

Darcy said quietly, "It surprises me, but I think I am."

"You are what?" Richard had forgotten what they were discussing. Miss Elizabeth's lovely figure could cause any man to lose track of a conversation. Damn it, now he was the one off thinking!

"A romantic," Darcy replied. "I rather like it." He stood to follow his sister from the room.

Fascinated, disgusted, and perhaps slightly envious, Richard stroked his moustache.

"You will see yourself out? I have letters to write." Darcy smiled. "Thank you for your assistance today, Richard. As always."

The colonel stood and shook his hand. "Bloody besotted fools. First Anne, now you. I must be resigned to my fate as the family's sole bon vivant."

Darcy laughed as he strolled off. Richard stared at his back and then turned to the empty room.

"Damn it, another long Thursday evening lies ahead. My cousin is in love, and my brother is busy relishing his wife. Where is the port?"

"Go home, Richard!" came a deep voice from the stairway.

The colonel returned to Matlock House, where he headed downstairs to see the shaky young footman.

Try as she might, Elizabeth could not keep her mind on her stitches; they were as disordered as her thoughts. Nothing held firm nor straight no matter how she pulled her needle.

She despised such needless tasks assigned simply to keep her seated under her mother's sway. But she was trapped with her sisters, ordered to sit and wait for the arrival of their Most Important Relation, the future husband of a Bennet daughter and father to the future heir to Longbourn. His parsonage was even now being readied for his triumphant return as a betrothed, perhaps married, man. *For goodness' sake!* Her mother was readying her campaign.

Elizabeth had only seen her mother plan so far ahead when it came to choosing a Christmas goose from among a gaggle of newly hatched goslings. Her behaviour these past days was frighteningly disciplined. The menu was planned, the rooms fully aired, the silver polished, and the stays lifted and tightened on gowns. Only Jane's wardrobe had been spared. Hill had been ordered to serve creamed turnips at least three times during his visit. *Oh joy.*

While all of Longbourn waited with bated breath for the entitled man's arrival and his choice of bride, the return of Mr Darcy remained privileged information. Kitty's knowledge had been gleaned from her time spent as a former worshipper of Miss Bingley; Jane's understanding arose from Mr Bingley's anticipation. Only Elizabeth had the full intelligence, and her information was closely held, the better to head off the gossip and rumour that seemed to follow, or precede, the master of Pemberley.

Elizabeth's concern was made worse when Aunt Philips came to call. She braced herself for false tales of rich men with wandering hands and roving eyes, and she wished she could count on Jane to be her confidante again. They scarcely had spoken since the prior day. Her sister had drawn closer to her mother's thinking, and while not further questioning the intentions or morals of Mr Darcy, Jane remained doubtful that he was the match meant for her 'most beloved' sister. When she glanced over at her mother, sister, and aunt, Elizabeth thought the trio made for a lovely matched set of bobbing heads and hands, pushing needles and points of view. She turned and looked at the closed door to her father's library.

How has it come to this? The dual looming threats of Mr Collins and Mr Darcy had angered two sisters, amused another, and made one her great ally. It was a shame, truly, that her father remained unconscious of the shifting sands of emotion and allegiance in his own household. His dusty books could not be half as interesting as the 'Macabre Tale of the Five Bennet Sisters.' *I could write quite a companion volume to Mr Darcy's hand-lettered novel.*

The excitement only heightened an hour later when the Great Heir arrived, settled in for a plate of cakes and tea, and began describing the improvements now being made to the cosy parsonage he soon would share with his wife. Fresh paint and thatching for the roof! Well-aligned shelving and new mattresses! At the last, Elizabeth felt her stomach lurch, and when she met Kitty's eyes, she felt strength in their newfound conviviality.

As Mr Collins chattered on about copper pots, Elizabeth discerned little of what he knew about the Fitzwilliam family events occurring at Rosings. She feared and anticipated the first enquiry.

CHAPTER SEVENTEEN

Darcy adored his sister. Georgiana had a sweet disposition, and she was intelligent, pretty, and gifted on the pianoforte. Yet, if pressed to name an imperfection, he could cite her tendency to be late for excursions, meals, and departures—especially the latter. When he was kept waiting for her yesterday, his concern rather than his patience was tested. But now, his nerves, his forbearance, and his wits were all at an end. He owed Georgiana's tardiness to her excited anticipation, but he was so conscious of his own that he could do nothing but smile tensely when his butler knocked and ushered the Fitzwilliams into his study. And then he cursed quietly.

No quick escape after all. This house needs a moat filled with crocodiles to save me from the onslaught.

"Oh, hell," he mumbled before greeting his relations. He requested tea be served and then he smiled. Grimly.

"Oh dear, look at your cheek," his aunt admonished as she settled into a chair.

"It is a dashing mark of battle, Mother. The ladies will swoon."

Richard chuckled, sending his cousin an apologetic look and a shrug. "I must conjure up some dashing tale for you to tell, Darcy. A slap from a wizened old bat is not quite manly enough."

"Richard, shut it!" Lady Matlock cried.

Darcy bit back the smile threatening to erupt and nodded. Grimly.

"Darcy, my boy. I have news to share," his uncle boomed. "I have made the arrangements for my sister. We, and all of society, shall be rid of her by week's end."

"Scotland? The Glencoe estate? You have acted, truly?" Darcy had not been convinced that his uncle would follow through on his threat to send Lady Catherine to Bedlam, but he had to be certain. An angry, obstinate relative committed to a hospital for the insane in the heart of London certainly would be a dangerous circumstance for the family's standing and his sister's future marriage prospects. Although greatly relieved that Lady Catherine would be sent instead to the family's most remote estate, Darcy could not but feel sorrow at a final estrangement from his mother's sole sister.

Lord Matlock tilted his head and stared at his nephew. "She leaves a mark on your face, and you ask me whether I have acted? Damn it, boy, she struck you!"

Darcy nodded, his tension slowly uncoiling. "Yes. She did me more damage than anyone has managed since Richard."

"Ha!" His uncle snorted and slapped his knee. "The Great Biscuit Incident of '94, was it? Or was it over that girl he claimed you snubbed the following year?"

"The biscuits were mine, and your son was a pest, following her about," Darcy said coolly. "He could have compromised himself with such behaviour."

"When he was a boy of twelve?"

Richard coughed. "I was protecting the girl from Robert. He leered at her, and Darcy laughed."

"Must you always place blame on your brother?" Lady Matlock challenged. "He was of an age then to notice young ladies."

"He did more than notice," Richard mumbled.

"Hmm." Lord Matlock glanced at the satchel and stacked

papers on Darcy's desk. "Where are you off to now? Marlbourn, is it?"

Disinterested in tea, the earl strolled over to the tray of spirits to pour himself a drink. Darcy stared at his back and noticed his stance looked remarkably like a stouter version of his two sons, though with far less hair. *Will Richard be bald as well? How he will hate that. Ha! His moustache will likely grow larger as a result.*

"I am pleased you are taking Georgiana with you," Lady Matlock said. "Watch how the ladies befriend her. She will help you choose a bride who is kind as well as beautiful." She laughed at Darcy's blush. "Come now. I know men. A dowry and title are important, but you all wish for a desirable woman."

"Martha, this is Darcy. He knows his goal." Lord Matlock collapsed heavily into a chair.

My goal. He took a deep breath.

"I am not off to Marlbourn. We are to Hertfordshire."

His uncle coughed. "To buy a horse? Is that on the way?"

"We go to visit friends. Charles Bingley is there."

"What are you about, Darcy?" Lady Matlock sat up a bit straighter and peered closely at her nephew.

"We shall stay for a few days and then head north to Pemberley. I am late in attending to the harvest accounts."

His uncle's eyes narrowed. "Yes, yes. We are for the north as well," he said, waving his hand in dismissal. "But you are to journey to Marlbourn and see the duke and duchess. You will find yourself a bride and divert attention from Anne's farce."

Darcy stopped pacing and leaned against his desk, one that had been used by his father, and his father before him. "It is not my duty to save the Fitzwilliam name. I did not marry Anne as her mother wished, and I shall not marry some unknown lady with a title and a dowry as *you* wish. I shall live my life."

"You will go to see that Bingley chap, the one with the sister?" His uncle grimaced and misunderstanding dawned.

"Oh no, Darcy! Not that woman. Anyone but her," Lady Matlock gasped.

"Anyone?" Richard smirked. "Oh, such a list I can make."

Darcy sighed. "Caroline Bingley will never be my wife."

"Is there someone else? Darcy?" When her nephew did not answer, Lady Matlock tapped her son on the arm. "Richard, tell us what you know."

He shook his head, stood, and followed his father's path to the spirits. "Mother, can Darcy not have a private life?"

"No," replied the earl. "Anne did, and see how that turned out."

Richard and Darcy stared at each other. The former shook his head in disgust, while the latter shrugged.

"I am not interested in, nor in the habit of, shopping for a wife," Darcy said quietly. "Ladies are not merchandise to be handled and picked over and compared. For years now, I have been placed in that position, and these past weeks have soured me on the exercise. I need time away from it."

He cleared his throat. "I wish to spend time with Georgiana. I shall retreat from society's marriage market, but I promise you, Aunt, I shall do all I am able to be happily wed next year."

Richard smirked at his cousin's clever wording. Both watched the earl warily; one of his hands was clenching his glass, the other flexing into a fist. Surely, a violent outburst was due. Instead, Lord Matlock surprised them with his controlled manner.

"I am disappointed, Darcy. The family should not like to wait so long. No one in town will miss your aunt or cousin, but we need some happy occasion to overshadow recent events."

"Oh, think bigger than a mere wedding, Father," Richard replied as he took his seat. "Perhaps Robert and Harriet might make good on that promised heir, or mayhap I shall take down old Bony by myself."

"Richard, no talk of war or your brother's…troubles!" Lady Matlock swatted her son and turned to her nephew. "I am not pleased, Darcy, but I shall not take on Catherine's role as judge and jury of your actions."

"Thank you, Aunt." Darcy gave her a small, pleased smile. His mother had always preferred the company of her brother's wife to her own sister. All her quiet admonitions about Catherine's bad temper and Martha's kindness had come to fruition.

"However, I shall count on you to be present during the Season next spring."

Ah, kindly, but she still holds expectations.

"Yes, ma'am." *With Elizabeth on my arm.*

The arrival of tea, accompanied by a happy and excited Georgiana, stilled the conversation. The party of five—one amused, one relieved, two confused and irked, and one effusive and impatient—enjoyed polite conversation until it was time to leave.

Richard and Darcy lagged behind their relations as they walked out.

"Andrews knows little of Wickham," Richard said quietly. "Our old friend helped secure him an interview for the position, but it seems to be only as Andrews said: Wickham wished to improve his standing with the uncle who is guardian to a young lady who has come into some wealth."

"Of course." Darcy bit back a curse. "Wickham would plan to call in that favour."

His cousin nodded. "Yet Andrews's presence at Pidock's appears to have been a coincidence on a rare day off from his duties. He knew from his cousin in Meryton that Miss Bennet had enjoyed a visit there."

"A fortunate coincidence," Darcy replied. "How did he know of my aunt's plans?"

"Within days of his arrival at Lady Catherine's home, he had taken her measure and possibly cleaned up a thrown vase or two. As you learned at Pemberley, Andrews is quite observant, if naïve. He knew your sister was lonely… I believe we have concluded his intentions there were honest?"

Darcy nodded in agreement.

"He knew Georgiana feared my aunt," Richard continued, "and in the past weeks, he heard the old bat's angry rants about Anne. Thus, when a housemaid mentioned orders to prepare a room for our girl, he feared the worst and wished to protect his friend."

Darcy glanced down at his boots and then up at Richard. "'His friend?' He is certainly mistaken and must be dissuaded of such a notion. Georgiana is his superior, the mistress of Pemberley and Darcy House."

"Knife it, Darcy. He knows that. Apparently, she reminds him of his younger sister." Richard adjusted his cuffs and eyed his parents walking ahead with Georgiana. "I do not fear his intentions. He is no Wickham, nor is he under that blackguard's sway."

"Thank you." Darcy felt relieved. "What shall we do with him now?"

"Matlock could use a man or two. Andrews has family in Birmingham. His brother is there, made lame by a skirmish with the French but apparently quite good with horses and his hands." He cleared his throat before adding, "Father has agreed to place them at the estate."

"Truly?" Darcy looked shocked.

Richard chuckled. "All is well on these counts. Now you must attend to your business of the heart."

Darcy's footsteps slowed to a halt. "I find myself forced too often to thank you for your assistance, Richard." He swallowed. "You serve as more than Georgiana's guardian; you are protector to us both. I thank you."

A deep blush crept across the cheeks of the military man. "As you do for me, Cousin. You know I need a little brother to both defend and torment," he said in a low voice before returning to his customary gruff demeanour.

"Now go fetch yourself a bride. Our girl needs a sister, and I wish to welcome a lovely new relation lacking both a beauty mark and a damp hand."

Darcy choked back a laugh. Richard clapped him on the shoulder and pushed him forward towards the waiting trio.

"We shall see you up north next month," Lady Matlock assured her niece and nephew before the Fitzwilliam carriage pulled away.

As soon as they were out of sight of Darcy House, the countess turned to her son.

"Why are they going to Hertfordshire? Tell me everything you know."

Richard weighed his choices. His afternoon was to be spent packing his aunt off to Scotland. Darcy House would be locked by tonight. It seemed wise to allow his mother—a clever and good-hearted but rather fearsome lady—at least some intelligence on the course of things.

He gave her a small smile of the kind that endeared him to her as the younger son and charmed widows into inviting him over for late dinners. "Darcy and Georgiana will visit a young lady they have befriended—an intelligent, pleasant, quite handsome lady. Her family has a small estate in Hertfordshire. Charles Bingley is courting her sister."

"You have met this person?" his father demanded.

"What is her name?" his mother asked.

"Yes, I have met, conversed with, and been charmed by 'this person.'" Richard rolled his eyes. "Her name is Miss Elizabeth Bennet."

His parents exchanged looks. "What are his intentions?" his father growled. "To save our name by marrying some country girl? He has been bewitched by a country nothing?"

"He *should* be bewitched. Elizabeth Bennet is like no lady I have met here in town. She has no disguise, no silliness about her. She is not 'nothing.' She is quite intelligent, and she and Darcy match wits and converse."

Lady Matlock looked affronted. "They converse? What does that mean?"

Her husband rubbed his chin. "Who is her family? Tell me they bear no similarity to those loathsome Dumfries your cousin has married into."

"Lord, no. You have no fear of a female Peregrine," Richard replied with a shudder, willing away vivid memories of the goatish dandyprat and his swive-mad cousin. *Who knew Anne would be so eager a participant in bedroom schemes? Had her mother provided her instructional, nay enlightening, materials?*

He took a cleansing breath to erase the thoughts.

"This is Darcy; there are other considerations. They talk about books and all those dull things he likes to go on about. She is his friend and Georgiana's. They have few acquaintances to enjoy without fear of society's expectations. Let them be."

He glanced between his parents and found them intent on his words. *Once more unto the breach.* "If he chooses to court Miss

Bennet, she will bring charm, wit, beauty, and interesting conversation to our family."

"Court?" his mother murmured, shocked. "A courtship? This is a friendship of serious consequence."

"Mother..."

His father coughed and gave him a knowing look. "Little dowry, but other considerations?"

Richard nodded, and his father smirked in approval.

"Oh, goodness, you two." Lady Matlock sighed. "Can you think of nothing but the swell of a woman's chest?"

"Books, my dear. I meant books."

It would take a clever eye to notice the difference in Mr Collins since his previous visit to Longbourn. His pomposity had shifted from praising his connexion to the Great Lady Catherine de Bourgh and worrying over her grief to the personal subjects of his parish's need for his guidance and the necessary touch of a lady for his parsonage. His bride-hunting expedition was in full swing.

Fortunately, as all attention was fixed on the unseasonable warmth in the air, the militia's imminent leave-taking, and the reasons behind the growing plumpness in a farmer's large-nosed daughter, there were few clever eyes focused on the visiting vicar and his quest for a lady.

Mr Bennet—never a man to speculate on weather or unfortunate female predicaments—noted the man was slightly diminished. "Our worthy cousin," he chided Elizabeth, "has likely been rejected by his true love and has returned to Longbourn only to choose a second-best bride."

Elizabeth smiled awkwardly. She was not certain what Collins knew but felt she was likely more familiar than he was with the intimate details of the Rosings scandal that had driven him from his parsonage. In no way did she wish her cousin to become aware of her privileged knowledge; she wished for him to feel no familiarity or kinship between them. His cow-like eyes drifted to her face and then well below often enough that she simmered in a permanent sort of indignation in his very presence. (Unbeknown to Elizabeth, her anger gave her cheeks and other exposed skin a becoming blush that easily could be mistaken as excitement. And so it was misjudged by the bachelor cleric.)

She worried that the man's enjoyment of attention and of the tones of his sonorous, perhaps monotone, voice might lure him to say too much. He might reveal a sliver of what he knew, and Elizabeth was sure he knew that Anne de Bourgh was not dead. Did he hold to his belief that Mr Darcy was his cousin's betrothed? What would occur when Mr Collins learned of Mr Darcy's planned return to Netherfield? And how could she convey to Mr Darcy how dear she held his words? How she wished to write him a letter telling him that her feelings had changed and how much she welcomed his company.

She had one further concern. When her cousin's eyes were not roving her person, she felt them judging her worth. Did he feel her sullied by her friendship with the man whose name he had maligned? Would he take it upon himself to rescue her from her presumed depths of depravity? Would he make her an offer before Mr Darcy arrived? What could she say to him to fend off such a proposal? Kitty, suddenly bursting with ideas and schemes, had suggested carrying a knitting needle at all times. The idea had a touch of the dramatic Mrs Radcliffe, but Elizabeth appreciated the suggestion. She already had discerned that hatpins were smaller and more comfortably concealed.

Each time her cousin simpered in her direction and attempted a tête-à-tête, Elizabeth would turn the conversation to topics such as Fordyce or gooseberry jam, provoking effusions from the vicar and much comment from her mother and the other ladies. Three of her sisters, however, had had enough of the man, and they were eager to change the discussion to one more to their liking. Kitty, returning with Jane from tea at Netherfield, found a topic that diverted everyone when her whispers to Elizabeth were overheard.

Mr Collins looked at the girl. "Miss Catherine, did you say that Mr Darcy is returning to Hertfordshire?"

Mrs Bennet rolled her eyes and waved her handkerchief. "He is not welcome at Longbourn. His betrothed dies, and he comes here and toys with our Lizzy."

"Mama!"

"That is what Mr Wickham has told us, as little as he liked to turn on his former friend."

"And you are quick to join him, Mrs Bennet." Her husband stared at her over his newspaper.

Elizabeth had felt the stares and heard the whispers of her neighbours, and at this moment, a cold certainty swept her, confirming who had woven the tales and who had made sure to repeat them. Her mother was more than a simpleton; her loose tongue rendered her dangerous.

"Mama," Elizabeth whispered loudly. "I thought you understood that Mr Wickham's word is not to be trusted."

"I grant you that Mr Darcy is a handsome man of large fortune, but we know nothing of his character." Mrs Bennet glanced at Aunt Philips. "He was betrothed, he threw her over, and she died. He had another sweetheart waiting for him elsewhere, but he bided his time here, charming Lizzy and Miss Bingley until his so-called mourning was over."

Mr Collins gasped and shifted in his chair to peer at Elizabeth. He nodded his head as though he finally had confirmation for his beliefs. She suddenly feared he had mistaken her for a rotten sweetmeat and turned away from him.

Mrs Bennet exchanged a knowing glance with her sister before issuing her final edict. "For all his riches, Mr Darcy is not a gentleman."

"Mama!" Jane cried, her indignation finally lit. "He is Mr Bingley's friend, and Mr Bingley would not place his trust in a man who acted as you allege."

"Indeed, he would not," Elizabeth said bitterly. "He is an honourable man." Her eyes, flaming with anger, settled on her father and silently pleaded with him to stop the conversation. Mr Bennet nodded and turned to his wife, levelling a harsh look in her direction.

Lydia waltzed through the front door and clattered into the room, laughing and swinging her bonnet. She stopped and looked around the silent group. "What is the matter with all of you?"

"We are well, Lydia," her mother replied in a tight voice. "Did you enjoy your walk?"

Lydia grinned, delighted with herself and scarcely able to contain her news. "Oh yes. Maria and I saw Mrs Forster in Meryton, and as we spoke, a fine carriage went by, heading towards Netherfield."

"Mr Darcy has arrived…" was murmured by more than one occupant of the room.

Lydia stomped her foot, angry that she had been interrupted. "He was not alone," she said loudly, sending a sly smile towards Elizabeth. "He has a young lady with him."

"A young lady?" Mr Collins gasped. His eyes narrowed and settled on Elizabeth. Noticing his intense stare and flared nostrils, she felt slightly ill. *I fear he is marking me.*

"Oh yes. She is quite handsome." Lydia laughed. "And such a fine bonnet!"

"The lady who caused him to throw over Miss de Bourgh?" cried Mrs Bennet.

"Oh, he is a rake!" agreed Aunt Philips.

Elizabeth spoke, willing to give herself away to protect her friends. "Mr Darcy is here to visit the Bingleys and the Hursts at Netherfield. He was to bring his younger sister with him. He is devoted to her."

All eyes not already boring into Elizabeth now shifted to her.

"You know this with some authority, Lizzy?" her father voiced.

"Yes. We met in London with Aunt and Uncle Gardiner."

Mr Bennet frowned at his second daughter. "Did you?"

"And contrary to what Mr Wickham has said, Mama, I have learnt that the man was never betrothed to Miss de Bourgh, and in fact has been of great service to his family, the Fitzwilliams."

"Mr Darcy was never engaged to his cousin? Truly?" Mrs Bennet's tone betrayed her excitement.

"No, he was not." Elizabeth stared at her father, beseeching him to throttle Mr Collins and demand his eyes move elsewhere. *Why does he not look at the honey cakes? They are his favourite!*

Instead, her father asked a simple question. "He is an eligible man, Lizzy? Able to marry?"

At Elizabeth's nod, Mrs Bennet swooped in with the Looming Query: "And with ten thousand a year to his name?"

"Ah yes." Mr Collins spoke up. "I cannot vouch for his character, but he is a wealthy man. And it is true," he added quietly, "that he and Miss de Bourgh were never formally promised to each other. There was some confusion…someone misheard my words last month."

"Mr Collins!" Mrs Bennet admonished.

"Or you misunderstood things and misled your eager audiences," Mr Bennet said in a withering voice.

"And gossiped." Kitty waggled her fingers at him.

"That was not very Christian, Mr Collins," Mary scolded.

The cleric grumbled, "I was misled."

"Misled by creamy turnips," whispered Lydia. She and Kitty broke into giggles.

"Ah, so tell us, sir." Mr Bennet had folded his newspaper and leaned forward with a keen and avid interest. "In addition to being wrong about Mr Darcy—I believe you called him the Grieving Groom—you were misled as to the majesties of Rosings, the tragic beauty of Miss de Bourgh, and the brilliant mind of her mother?"

Mr Collins looked rather like a gasping fish when Mr Bennet finished speaking.

Mrs Bennet pulled her eyes away from the sulking man and settled her gaze on Elizabeth. "Hmm. None is as it seems. You are a clever girl, Lizzy."

Jane appeared vexed while Kitty beamed at her sister. "Miss Bingley thinks Mr Darcy to be wondrous, a man among men, and *she* dislikes nearly everyone."

Aunt Philips gasped. "None of it was true? The town has besmirched his name without cause?"

"Well, he is not an innocent," Mr Collins averred, regaining his wits as well as his need to opine. "He has quite a bad temper, and in fact, should have done his duty long ago to his cousin to save her from—"

"From what?" Lydia cried. "An early grave?"

"So to speak."

"Mr Collins!" Elizabeth jumped up, her arms frozen at her sides and her hands fisted to keep her from swinging at the man. Her cousin clearly knew more than she had suspected, but she would not let him strut about as a peacock and do further damage to Mr Darcy's and his family's reputations.

"Is it considered within the Christian way to discuss the character and personal business of another person?" Elizabeth said coldly. "Would your esteemed patroness approve of such behaviour?"

The man's eyes widened, and he sank into a chair next to Mary. He shook his head. Mary watched him carefully. All other eyes remained on Elizabeth, who stood angrily at the window, staring outside and away from the chaos within her home.

Then Mary's voice broke through the silence. "Proverbs 20:19 says, 'He that goeth about as a talebearer revealeth secrets: therefore meddle not with him that flattereth with his lips.'"

Mr Collins sighed and nodded.

Mr Bennet snorted behind his newspaper. "Nicely said, Mary."

"Oh, Mr Collins. Just marry her already! You are such a perfect pair!" Lydia cried out before dissolving in laughter.

Elizabeth swallowed a bitter laugh. *It is so easy to ruin a good man through careless chatter and misheard words.* She had no doubt that Mr Darcy's arrival and his polite demeanour would quickly put to rest the rumours and slanders, though she wondered how soon she could forgive those friends and neighbours with cruel tongues. Her gaze remained settled on a distant point beyond the orchard. Elizabeth heard footsteps cross the room and approach her. Suddenly, she felt a hand on her shoulder. *No. He would not dare touch me.* She tensed and readied a sharp retort.

"Lizzy," Mr Bennet said quietly. "Come to my study. I believe we have a mystery to solve, and you are holding all the clues."

"How are you, old friend? You bring me no wedding news?"

Bingley laughed and clapped Darcy on the back.

"I believe it is your wedding I am here to discuss, Charles." Darcy smiled and made his way to a chair. He sat, crossed his legs, and brushed a bit of dust from his trousers. "You are making progress with your courtship?"

Bingley sighed and slumped down across from his friend. Darcy tried not to laugh and gave a serious ear to his friend's unfolding romantic soliloquy. It went on for some three minutes but revealed nothing new about Jane Bennet's goodness, kindness, or beauty beyond Bingley's surer grasp of her affections.

"So," Bingley said, out of breath from his effusions of his angel's loveliness. "I thought to speak to Mr Bennet when we call at Longbourn tomorrow and then walk with Jane to the gardens to ask for her hand." He leaned closer and nodded knowingly. "The trees are bare of leaves, but the shrubbery yet affords some privacy."

Darcy was overtaken by this knowledge. *Tomorrow. Elizabeth. Shrubbery.*

"Darcy, do you agree with my plan? Darcy? Are you in there?"

Bingley tapped his arm, finally bringing his friend back to the present.

"Um, yes. Sorry," Darcy said sheepishly. "I had a sudden recollection of some business with my steward."

"Hmm. I believe your mind had drifted to the shrubbery."

"Bingley!"

The younger man jumped up and announced the necessity for a toast to his future happiness. Darcy, still chagrined by his woolgathering, heartily agreed.

"You have been industrious, Bingley. It is a fine plan. Miss Bennet has been awaiting your proposal for some time, I think."

"I have been certain for some time that I wished to marry her." Bingley handed Darcy a glass and raised his own in the air.

Darcy cut off his toast. "Then why have you not proposed?"

"Caroline had objections, which she said you shared." Bingley lowered his arm and levelled a stare at Darcy.

"To Jane? For you?"

"Do you?" Bingley asked plaintively.

"Of course not, you idiot. She will make you a fine wife." Darcy raised his glass, dipped his head, and smiled. "Propose, marry, and send your sister to live with the Hursts. Her opinions should not weigh on the matter."

Bingley grinned and took a long sip. Both men were startled by a loud roar.

"Now just a minute!" Hurst's red face emerged from behind the room's long sofa. "She is not to live with us."

"Oh, Hurst. I did not see you there." Frowning, Darcy watched the man totter over to the spirits and pour himself a tall glass of brandy. Hurst took a long draught and turned to inspect the new arrival.

"I say, man, what happened to your face? An unwilling, yet merry widow?"

Bingley laughed and looked at Darcy.

"No. Well...actually, yes," he confessed. "An unwilling, angry widow—Lady Catherine. For a small woman, she wields some power in her right hook."

The other men burst into laughter.

"Caroline mends pens rather well. She could fix you right up and kiss it and make it all better." Hurst chuckled.

Darcy shook his head in mock agony. "Must I lock my door to you as well with your evil schemes?"

"And here I thought it was a fencing mishap," Bingley mumbled.

When Hurst's laughter died down, Darcy enquired as to what else might be happening at Longbourn. "They await you daily with great expectation, I am sure."

"Oh yes." Bingley replied with alacrity. "Although her sister has just returned from London, Jane is pleased to be away from the house as much as possible."

Darcy thought that odd. "She is not pleased to spend time with Miss Elizabeth?"

"Well, yes. But Miss Elizabeth is often occupied with her cousin Mr Collins."

"Collins is at Longbourn? Why?" *Why is he near Elizabeth?*

"Um, he wishes for marital felicity with one of Jane's sisters."

"Miss Mary? It would of course be Miss Mary." Darcy realised his voice sounded desperate. Was he stuttering?

Bingley's face turned from hesitant to grim. "Jane believes it to be Lizzy. Miss Elizabeth. Her mother wishes for that."

"What? Why?" Darcy stood up and began pacing the room.

"She feels Lizzy is in need of a husband." Bingley's face showed his distaste for the subject. "Jane says she has been tainted by your earlier leave-taking. You showed some partiality and then you left."

"Oh lord." Darcy sank into the window seat. "She would never marry that toad."

"Toad?" Hurst barked. "He *is* rather a toad-eater, I grant you."

"Collins has not been a friend to me or to my family. He is a mendacious cod's head, unworthy of the Bennet family," Darcy finished bitterly.

"Sharp words, my friend!" Hurst cried.

Bingley glanced at Hurst and shrugged. "Mayhap you can run him off, then." He poured Darcy a drink and took a long draw from his own glass. "Darcy, you know I am glad to have you, but truly—why are you here and not at the duke's estate?"

I have work to do. I have to make a good impression. To win hearts and charm Mrs Bennet while showing I am serious and intent on one thing, one person: Elizabeth. And now I have to thwart her mother and that pig of a parson.

Darcy managed to clear his throat and choke back his frustration over Bingley's news. "To clear my name, of course. And to support you, my friend, in your courtship of Miss Bennet. To play a chess match with her father and to show that I am a friend to Miss Elizabeth."

And to safeguard her against her odious cousin.

Bingley looked at him carefully. "That is all? To be a friend?"

Darcy felt Hurst's eyes boring into his back. *Am I so easily read?*

"A better friend to some than others," he said in a disinterested voice. "Georgiana began a friendship with Miss Elizabeth in London just last week and wished to see her again before we travel to Pemberley."

Hurst smirked. "I say, that is a sharp-witted sister you have, Darcy. At least one of you is honest about your reasons for being here."

CHAPTER EIGHTEEN

The maids at Netherfield were relieved that Mr Darcy's companion was in fact his sister and not his mistress. The footmen were pleased that he had no heavy trunks of books. The stable hand was happy to groom such fine horses. The cook was delighted to host a man who had always made sure to compliment her dishes. Yet all of them wondered at the swollen cut upon his noble cheek.

"Protecting his sister from highwaymen."

"Slapped by his lover when he threw her over for a new one."

"Tumbled out of bed."

"Pecked by a mad raven."

"Hit by a jealous ex-suitor of his mistress."

"One of his thick books of big Latin words fell from a shelf and hit him."

"His betrothed rose from the grave to wreak her revenge."

"Horse threw him."

"Ran into the wall fleeing a lady's bed when her husband arrived home unexpectedly."

"Fencing accident."

Bingley sighed. Rarely had a one-inch scratch resulted in so many rumours, but alas, Darcy was a rare man and a rare friend. As likely the most prominent person to ever spend time in Meryton, he was subject to much speculation on his wealth, his supposed dalliances, his connexions to royalty, his fencing skills, his opinions, and his habits. In Meryton, the whispering had grown louder when he was perceived as 'the Grieving Groom gallivanting about,' and unfortunately, Lizzy's name often was attached to the gossip.

Bingley hoped desperately that all the rumour mongers had ceased their chatter. Jane had been unhappy that Darcy's friendship with her sister was misconstrued. She said little but did allow that Darcy confused and concerned her, and Bingley—though he suspected Darcy had strong feelings for Lizzy—lacked confirmation to convince his angel of his friend's good intentions. Darcy was overrun with family matters, the particulars of which he had not shared with his friend, though his offhand comment that his cousin was in fact alive proved Caroline's inquisitive footman to be an accurate source.

I should not have allowed her to let Woodley go. That was unfair. He was a good man...though he did appear to be a bit obseque— What is that word Darcy uses?

He hated when Darcy's rich vocabulary stumped him. His friend read too many damn books and remembered too many of the words in them. *Hmm. Was Woodley obsidian? No! Blast it, Woodley was too eager to linger in rooms where interesting conversations took place. Obsolete. That was it!*

Relieved at this thought, Bingley straightened his cuffs. *We did the right thing, letting him go.*

He was happy that Darcy had come back to Netherfield; otherwise, he would have had to write to him and announce his intention to propose to Jane. He assured himself that Darcy would approve; after all, his friend admired Jane, and Bingley believed that he *more* than admired her sister and had similar hopes for his own marital felicity. He must tell Darcy his deeply considered theories on love—how he and Jane both had blue eyes and light hair and shared a taste for roast partridge and a joy in dancing reels. Darcy's and Lizzy's darker eyes and colouring and their mutual enjoyment of books and walking made them a fine match as well. It was elementary, really, this love logic. *Why was Darcy so damn tortured by romance? Because the answers did not lie in a book written by a dead Greek?*

Oh, and he must tell his brooding friend as soon as possible what it would mean to him to be brothers. First, though, he had to talk to Darcy about the theories being bandied about the town regarding that marring of the man's near-perfect visage. *Damn it, can nothing be as pleasant and simple as Jane's sweet smile?*

Much as he dreaded the impending conversation with Darcy, Bingley was pleased when his butler came to him with the gossip. It truly was quite outrageous that his friend could provoke this range of scurrilous stories. In some ways, he allowed that it was rather amusing, and he wished Colonel Fitzwilliam were at Netherfield to make sport of it. *He*, at least, could tease Darcy, a feat that Bingley—lacking both the imposing moustache and the family connexion—tended to avoid. The problem was that he now had to tell Darcy about the rumours. *Damn it. He will not be amused, and we are due at Longbourn this morning. This will ruin his good mood.*

Perhaps Cook had some of that bacon Darcy so enjoyed during his last visit. Bingley smiled. *We shall be brothers who love bacon.*

Mr Collins had spent too many years in sacrifice to his Lord and Saviour, staring at bowls of lumpy breakfast porridge and sipping weak tea. During these past weeks as a guest with his aunts in Epsom and then at Longbourn, he had discovered that muffins and toast heaped with more than a fair portion of black butter or raspberry jam made for a far tastier breakfast. He could rhapsodise about the ragouts and roasts, tarts and cakes he had consumed while in Hertfordshire, but proper piety prevented him from such boasting. Usually. Avarice and gluttony were sinful, and while he could never be deemed as a sinful man, the vicar did his best to praise the tables he graced with his presence. He, William Josiah

Collins, was a man of God. He was full with His blessed goodness. Very full, he acknowledged. That would explain why his trousers felt so tight about the waist.

The delicious aromas of the dishes emerging from Longbourn's kitchens—and his determination to secure that last bit of perfectly sweetened jam—took Mr Collins's attention away from the oddly charged air around the elder Bennet sisters. His eyes, usually absorbed in deciphering the strikingly confounding Cousin Elizabeth, were instead engaged with scraping the last fruity remnants from the jam pot. Therefore, he did not see the anxiety that consumed his cousins.

However, Kitty, the self-appointed Overseer of Happiness and Romantic Felicity, did see. Lizzy might have smiled and laughed away the offer to help her run away and hide from their jam-splotched cousin, but Kitty had gained sharp eyes these past weeks. Miss Bingley had indeed proved herself excessively prideful, but she was a most attentive lady.

"*Heed the conversation and keep your eyes open,*" she would say pointedly in Kitty's general direction. "*People often act stupidly, and you can easily best them by gleaning their intentions through every word not spoken and every movement restrained.*"

It was confusing advice. Kitty quickly understood that her mother required no deep observation as she spoke every word that entered her mind. The motives behind most of Papa's words, voiced or not, remained beyond Kitty's comprehension. But her sisters?

She glanced at Lydia, who was staring at Mr Collins and stifling her laughter. Briefly, Kitty wondered whether her sister had pulled a familiar childhood trick and salted the jam. Watching her cousin's enthusiastic chewing, she determined Lydia was innocent of *that* at least. *No, I believe she is merely diverted by our cousin's resemblance to a starving pig.*

Mary also stared at their cousin, but it was with an expression that had become all too familiar to Kitty. Her quiet, plain, moralising sister had fallen in love, and no one—most especially the object of her regard—was the wiser. *Only I see it.* Kitty was impressed by her gift of insight. Beyond her distress at Mary's misguided affections and what it could mean for her family's happiness, Kitty fretted over the words Maria Lucas had confided just yesterday: *"Charlotte is desperate for her own household. She is determined to marry your cousin."*

In spite of the living he held at Hunsford and the entail promising him Longbourn, Mr Collins deserved neither of these ladies. Yet for the sake of preserving the family estate and saving her mother from the hedgerows, it seemed that Mary must have him. Kitty needed a plan to ensure her sister's success. *It would be nice to see Mary happy and smiling. Though that contentment may not endure long after they wed.*

She needed to consult Lizzy, who was eager to shed their cousin's purported affections. Besides, this sister was the most clever of them all and would know how best to bring together awkward, misguided, and perhaps unwilling lovers. Lizzy, however, appeared concerned with her own love story. The worried bits of uneaten toast and the half-finished tea testified to her restlessness. Kitty hoped for some resolution for her sister; surely, if he loved her, Mr Darcy would soon be at their door. *Hmm, perhaps she does not know best about love.*

Elizabeth felt too many eyes focused on her. The attentions of Mr Collins, his appetite nearly sated, seldom strayed from her person. It had reached the point where she could appreciate this rare occasion when they dwelt on her face rather than her bodice.

Jane, she noted, sat calmly; her plate was empty but for scattered crumbs, and her interest kept drifting from the window to her sister.

What is she thinking? Would she appraise Mr Darcy and measure his character and his ardency against that of their cousin? Mayhap, she should compare their incomes and their bathing habits as well. Mr Darcy would win on every count. She would not care whether the handsome master of Pemberley smelled of mutton and tobacco, was penniless, or had French blood coursing through his veins. He was the one she preferred, and if he came today—*when* he came today—she would convey those sentiments, though perhaps not with any mention of mutton.

Elizabeth sighed at the wasted breakfast before her and again glanced across the table at Jane. It was an odd feeling to have her beloved sister withholding her affection as if all of that warmth and energy must now be aimed at securing Mr Bingley. *How like their mother, and how disturbing an insight!* She wrinkled her nose and shuddered, drawing scrutiny from both her mother and Mary.

Ah, Mary... She remained the inscrutable sister, though somehow different than she had been mere weeks ago. Then she had seemed desirous of Mr Collins's affections, but now she appeared to view him with some disdain as well. Or perhaps it was merely clarity; Elizabeth could not be certain. It shamed her to admit that her middle sister had always bewildered and wearied her. She had tried to determine the direction of her sister's feelings, but her enquiries to Mary regarding her distraught letter to Gracechurch Street were met with a shrug and a solemn recitation of Proverbs 16:28. "A froward man soweth strife, and a whisperer separateth chief friends."

Does Mary know her own heart, or is she as confused as I had been? Mr Collins is certainly no equal to Mr Darcy, yet both are men and equally vexing. I shall ask Kitty. Of late, she seems to notice everything.

At least her youngest sister was constant. Lydia the Stalwart continued to be ever amused by everything around her; *she* would feel the absence of Mr Collins's daily displays of folly.

Kitty, though, had changed, proving herself especially devoted since Elizabeth's return to Longbourn. She had drawn closer with silly but well-intentioned offers to protect her sister from their cousin. The girl might have read too many novels, but at least she had some sense of the current situation. Elizabeth watched Kitty stir her tea in a thoughtful manner. *What is she thinking? How could a drawing of animals best capture this tableau? A weasel, some chickens, a goose, an owl, a hound, and a pacing cat?*

Sighing, she pulled her eyes away from the table and looked

longingly at the window. It was a sunny morning. She wondered that no note had arrived from Netherfield.

Will he come today? Or have I frightened him away with my vehement stupidity and misplaced anger? What happened to his face? Did someone strike him?

After weeks of confusion over her friendship with Mr Darcy, three days of frustration with her cousin, and one perplexing conversation that had prompted an odd estrangement from her favourite sister, Elizabeth longed to see the man himself.

The time she had spent with Mr Darcy had been brief, but their friendship proved more genuine, interesting, and stimulating than any she had known before—just as he had said it was for him. Few men would tolerate, nay encourage, a self-taught country girl to converse about books and debate ideas. Yet, Mr Darcy respected her enough to engage with her and to pursue her company for conversation.

In the aftermath of his declaration, their oft-heated conversation, his confession at Darcy House, and then his heartfelt letter, Elizabeth recognised that she more than knew the man; she liked and admired him as well. And although she had but one happy model with which to compare, she suspected she could love him, and he her, as a man and a woman might love each other. Someday, she would laugh at her denials to Aunt Gardiner, but that was far in the future. She and this man had much ground to cover, and this first meeting would tell her whether his feelings remained ardent.

The ride to Longbourn took a forever minute. Darcy wished to race to the Bennet home yet worried over his reception there. The townspeople had spent weeks pondering lies and half-truths about him, and they had spent the last day determining the origins of a one-inch cut on his cheekbone. How confined were the interests of these people to spend their time dwelling on his dull business. *His?* Did they mistake him for a Beau Brummel? His clothing was tailored from the finest cloth, but he was no dandy, and he certainly did not share that man's love of the Prince Regent or his propensity for lascivious behaviour.

Why did Bingley not write and tell him the stories that had circulated about his comportment and the slurs cast upon not only his reputation but also Elizabeth's? Yes, the man's handwriting skills were woefully unequal to his education, but he should have put aside his lovemaking and made the effort.

The shopkeepers and door dwellers of Meryton unspooled nefarious opinions and cruel falsehoods about a young lady who had grown up among them, smiled at them, and cared for them. But rather than protect her good name, they sullied her reputation by misjudging her kindness and intelligence.

How much had Elizabeth been tormented by the whisperers and their sly looks? Had she been able to withstand three days in a house with her horrid cousin? One night at Hunsford with Anne and her goatish beloved had nearly killed Richard's will to live. And *he* was a battle-hardened soldier.

Richard can lie in bed and imagine his 'perfect woman.' He does not have an Elizabeth Bennet to think and dream about. And there is all the difference.

Darcy, followed by Bingley, walked to Longbourn's front door. His hand nearly trembled as he raised it to the knocker. Had Longbourn always had twisted vines growing up around its doorframe? Was a basket of squashes customarily sitting on the path? Had Elizabeth heard all the ridiculous rumours about him? Was she exhausted from defending his name and character, and did she suffer from the insults to her own?

Is she angry over all the distress I have caused her? Angry with me?

All of his questions and worries faded when the parlour door opened and Darcy saw the face of the woman he loved. *She is so beautiful.* He took a quick, shaky breath. She did not look vexed or angry; she did not appear displeased with his presence. He sighed in relief. In fact, she looked pleased, nay happy, to see him.

She was.

"Good morning," she breathed. "You are here."

"As soon as I was able," Darcy replied, his voice rough. He returned her small smile with one of his own. "Good morning."

Salutations mixed with warmth, curiosity, and suspicion welcomed the visitors. Elizabeth disregarded the sharp-eyed look Jane gave her when she eagerly greeted Mr Darcy. Mr Bennet remained ensconced in his study, while Mrs Bennet and Mr Collins lacked expression beyond furrowed brows and stammered effusions. The sisters exchanged a look, and at Elizabeth's pronouncement that they must enjoy the fine weather before any afternoon storms arrived, they swiftly ushered the two men out the door and on a walk down the lane. In their rush, neither sister remembered her gloves, nor observed a few minutes later that Mr Collins and Mary followed them from the house with Kitty lagging behind.

The group smiled and waved when Mr Parker and his wife drove past in their curricle. A moment later, they nodded to Mr Little astride his horse. "Word of your arrival at Longbourn will spread quickly, Mr Darcy," Elizabeth said quietly.

"As I had hoped," he replied, his voice laden with meaning.

Elizabeth felt the knot of tension that had settled in her stomach and weighed upon her heart these past weeks lift up and float away. She looked up at him and smiled, forgetting everything around them.

Bingley, intent on his errand, soon hurried Jane away. So absorbed were they on the words they needed to say that neither Darcy nor Elizabeth noticed nor cared where their own wanderings took them. Although Elizabeth had walked this path hundreds of times, she managed to stumble on a forgotten tree root. Darcy steadied her when she fell against him, and her grip on his arm tightened; he did not loosen his hold even when the path ahead appeared clear.

"Georgiana is at Netherfield?" was her first question once they cleared a small embankment.

At his nod, she continued. "Why did she not accompany you?"

"She hopes to see you and your sister for tea today at Netherfield. I was not certain of my reception by your family"—Darcy glanced at her and saw her face fall—"given the endless gossip."

"Yes, some of my family members have been less than intelligent in their understanding or circumspect with their opinions."

"Please, they are blameless. Much, perhaps all, fault for the gossip lies with me." Darcy's relentless head shaking loosened his hat, and before it could topple to the ground, he pulled it off and gripped it in his hands. "It is just, um, I was not certain whether Mr Collins would be with your family. I do not wish for my sister to make his acquaintance, not at this time."

Elizabeth grimaced. "You are a clever man, Mr Darcy. None of us wished for his acquaintance, let alone to maintain it. I have made it my business to avoid him since my return home."

Darcy heard more than exasperation in her tone. "Has he said something to you? Does he concern you?" When she remained silent, he tried again. "Why is he here and not at his parsonage?"

She coloured. "He will return there after choosing a wife, presumably from amongst me and my sisters."

"He has announced his intentions?"

"Oh, he never ceases practising the art of conversation. I never quit my efforts to avoid it."

Darcy was caught between horror and hysterical laughter. "He has determined you as the object of his pursuit?"

"He believes he must rescue my tattered reputation and utilise my knowledge of the estate to restore the lustre of Longbourn."

"He says this to you?!"

"No, but I hear murmurings. My father laughs at him while my mother and Jane see value in his reasoning."

Darcy froze. "Jane? Your sister?"

"She has tired of the talk swirling around you and our friendship." Elizabeth said quietly. Darcy could hear the trembling beneath her words. "Mr Bingley has withheld his proposal until your arrival, and it has bred some impatience in her and my mother."

The angel was impatient and aimed her frustration at her favourite sister and closest friend? Things have been awful here, indeed. Darcy could kick himself for his thick-headed behaviour, but if he injured himself, he was likely to start a new round of taradiddle about his wounds.

What a thankless place this is!

Darcy looked around for a log or a rock on which they could sit. They needed to talk, just the two of them. *A thankless, seatless place.*

Elizabeth touched his arm and gestured towards a rough wooden bench ahead.

"Mr Goulding built benches here and in the meadow nearer his house so his mother could rest on her rambles. She was a great walker too in her day."

They sat, and with their heights more evenly matched, she turned and looked closely at him. Frowning, her hand rose and her fingers fluttered but did not touch his face. Unconsciously, he leaned towards her, yearning for her caress.

"Your face?" she said softly. "There have been many theories. I hope you were not attacked by books or highwaymen or pirates."

Darcy sighed and smiled at her sheepishly. "Nor an angry cow or jealous lover." He paused and shook his head. "School friends who yawned at my dull attention to my studies would laugh to know I have become the most interesting man in England, at least to the people of Meryton."

Elizabeth bit back a laugh. "I found the suggestion of a mad goat to be a most plausible suggestion."

"You are not far off." He leaned forward, his arms on his knees. His fingers worried the band on his hat. "Lady Catherine was angry, as usual, and refused to listen to reason."

"She struck you?" Elizabeth paled, seemingly horrified by his disclosure.

He nodded.

"You wrote of her stubbornness," Elizabeth said softly. "She blames you for the choices her daughter has made? Does she also hold you responsible for the lies they both have told?"

His shoulders slumped.

"My aunt is the great and all-knowing mistress of Rosings—or was, I should say. Under the law and the terms of my late uncle's will, the house and estate pass into Anne's hands. As to the rumours, Lord Matlock has concocted a fairly plausible story for Anne's 'rise from the dead,' her marriage, and her child." Darcy laughed bitterly. "We are a ridiculous lot."

Elizabeth shook her head sadly. "You have had much to do these past weeks."

"Yes, and much more to tell you," Darcy agreed quietly. He straightened and turned to her. "You read my letter? Did it explain my actions, my mistakes?"

Elizabeth laid her hand on his arm. "What mistakes? You took responsibility when others did not…"

His heart pounding, he looked at her with eyes full of emotion. "My mistakes affecting *you*, Elizabeth. I was so occupied with my own thoughts and the actions of my family that I failed to see how you might be touched."

He looked down at the mossy soil beneath their feet and let out an exasperated sigh.

"I was stupid."

The sound of Elizabeth's tinkling laughter filled his ears. "Stupid? Well, then stupid men who are kind, witty, and well-read are the only ones worth knowing."

His head shot up, and he stared at her, amazed. "You are remarkable. Simply astonishing."

"And you are quite generous with your indulgence for my conversation as well with your bestowal of compliments," she said lightly. "Such sentiments would prove a lively topic for debate among those who know me."

Her words coaxed a soft, tender smile from him. "Your value is not up for debate. But I do wish to apologise for any distress I have caused, knowingly or not."

"All is well," she replied softly.

Darcy dropped his hat and took her hand; with his other hand, he gently traced her fingers, so small and delicate in his. He could feel her shiver as she looked down at his motions before her attention shifted and she found his eyes intent on hers. They held a steady gaze while their fingers continued to play.

"Yet I hurt you. I beg your forgiveness."

"There is nothing to forgive," she insisted. "You meant well."

"I did mean well, poorly though I might have shown it." His voice was less than steady. "You are well?"

"I am," she whispered. Her eyes fell away from his and she stared at their entwined hands.

Darcy was no less affected. "I have worried," he said gently. "The gossip here, made worse by my thoughtlessness, has been difficult for you."

"Interesting and frustrating, but not too difficult," she replied, before adding in a light-hearted voice, "Of course, I have not had to dance with Mr Collins since my return home; I simply elude him at every turn."

He stared at her, astonished. "You can laugh at all of this?"

His fingers slowed and clasped hers tightly. He wished to kiss them, but he had learned to move slowly; he would wait for Elizabeth to show her feelings.

"I must laugh," she said. "As injurious as some of the gossip has been, it was short-lived and, truly, rather absurd." She shook her head. "Yet I do not understand some of it."

"Elizabeth, please tell me if my presence offends you." At her look of surprise and the forceful shake of her head, Darcy continued. "Are you pleased I am here? You did not anticipate my…my declaration at your aunt's home."

"It took me by surprise," she said softly, "but I no longer find your words unwelcome."

Darcy eyes lit up.

"I do appreciate that you came here with Georgiana." She smiled at him, the first look of pure happiness he had seen since he arrived. He returned it and finally brought her fingers to his lips. Elizabeth closed her eyes.

"My uncle's goals do not match mine," he whispered. "There is nothing for me at Marlbourn."

"No?"

"Only here, Elizabeth. Only here."

They sat quietly, caught in the other's gaze.

She yet has summer freckles.

His hair is freshly shorn.
She should wear blue every day.
Does he always wear black?
Her lips look so soft.
His eyes are so dark.

Their unspoken ruminations caused each of them to lean with slow intent towards the other. Elizabeth's hand rose to his cheek, and she gently touched the mark left by his aunt. He trembled at the intimacy permitted by her lack of gloves, and she blushed.

"Does it hurt?"

"Not at all."

"A badge of valour for your cousin to envy."

"Richard envies other things far more." Darcy swallowed. Their faces were mere inches apart. "Elizabeth, may I be the man to rescue you from your cousin?"

"Yes," she breathed, a small smile playing on her lips. "I would like that very much, Mr Darcy."

Oh, he could not bear formality and manners. Not when she smiled that way.

"Elizabeth…may I kiss you?"

"Please…"

Her hand fluttered from his cheek and fell to his shoulder. Darcy's fingers tenderly smoothed a strand of hair behind her ear as he drew her face towards his. There was but a whisper of distance between them when he tilted his head to one side and gently pressed his mouth to hers. Her lips were soft, full, and welcoming. He pulled away briefly, opened his eyes to glimpse the glow on her face, and returned his mouth to hers. She shifted a bit, and her fingers slid from his shoulder to his neck. As she tightened her grip, he pulled her closer and opened his lips. Someone moaned, though neither was ready to claim it.

Slowly, achingly, their eyes still closed, they pulled apart. Darcy shook off his stupor and gazed upon her face.

She is so beautiful.
Oh. Oh. That was lovely.

With his fingertips, Darcy softly traced her face, from her

temple to her chin. How he wished to kiss her again. To marry her. Instead, he asked, "You are well?"

Elizabeth opened her eyes and gave him a shy smile. "Oh yes, very well. I was thinking of a poem."

At his confused expression, Elizabeth squeezed his hand. "I was thinking that I now disagree with Donne's premise: 'More than kisses, letters mingle souls.' I treasure your letter, but I think I might prefer the kisses."

It was all he could do not to fall to his knees, propose, and commence more kissing.

"Lizzy? Where have you gone off to?" Kitty burst through the trees, startling the lovers apart.

Darcy stood quickly before bending down to fetch his hat. "Miss Catherine, I did not realise you had accompanied us."

Kitty looked past him at her blushing sister. "Lizzy," she said in a loud whisper. "Mr Collins is coming. He worries he will catch you in some improper act. He means to save you from Mr Darcy!"

Although her face remained a charming shade of pink, Elizabeth had regained her wits. "Thank you, Kitty. I believe Mr Collins is too late to secure my regard, and there is no need to rescue me from Mr Darcy."

When Mary and Mr Collins appeared a few minutes later, he was not only too late to save his cousin from Mr Darcy's affections but too slow to secure her arm for their return to Longbourn. Elizabeth and Kitty each held one of Mr Darcy's arms as they strolled back to the house.

He does not smell of mutton or tobacco, Elizabeth thought, sighing. *I can think only of how he tastes.*

She felt witless yet astonishingly attentive to the man at her side. She was too happy to gasp at her wickedness.

CHAPTER NINETEEN

The group, including two rather flushed, distracted couples, strolled slowly back to Longbourn. Although Darcy intended to seek out Mr Bennet, he was waylaid by another Bennet relation. He had felt the clergyman's eyes boring into him during their walk, and now, when Collins entreated him, Darcy nodded. The sooner he held certain conversations, the sooner he could move ahead with other, more pleasurable activities.

Collins. Mr Bennet. Mrs Bennet. Darcy had secured Elizabeth's affections. Now he need only swat down her ridiculous suitor, inform her father of his intention to propose as soon as may be, and charm her mother, who would ensure the truth of the past weeks would spread far and wide. Then they could again seek out the shrubbery.

As the rest of the group filed into the house, Darcy's eyes searched out Elizabeth's. Her nose wrinkled most becomingly as she gave him a puzzled but encouraging smile.

He followed Collins to the side garden—a pretty but rather

overgrown bit of wilderness—leaned against a tree, and crossed his arms. *I would rather be thinking on the lips I just kissed than listening to the words coming from the bottle-headed vicar with the flapping jaw. How Richard would enjoy this interrogation.*

"What is it you wish to address with me, Collins?" he asked in a cold yet polite voice.

The clergyman rose to his full height. Although he often relied upon his imposing size to remind others of his worth and wisdom, the master of Pemberley outstripped him by a few inches. Somewhat subdued, Collins began to speak.

"As cousin to all the Bennets, but most especially to Miss Elizabeth, I must importune you to recall yourself, sir. Your reputation here and in town is muddied by tales of skirt-chasing, by the sins committed by your cousin in Kent, and even by the low behaviour of your aunt."

Collins looked at Darcy reprovingly, prompting a low laugh from the man he had chastised.

"You dare censure my family while rebuking those who would find *your* behaviour extremely objectionable?" Darcy loomed over the cleric and lowered his voice in a deliberate manner.

"Oh, do tell me how I have misbehaved, Collins. Please, enlighten me as to where the appellation of the 'Grieving Groom' arose." Darcy scoffed. "From your brain, sir. From your lips to God's ear and onto all of Hertfordshire. You are a mendacious gossip."

Collins quaked but remained firm. "You must leave here and not further besmirch my cousin's good name. I am to take my future wife from Longbourn—"

"You may have your pick of ladies who do not go by the name of Bennet, but it is you who will besmirch their names." Darcy stared at the man with disdain. He had always felt he was a gentleman—and a *gentle* man—but he was speaking in the voice of an imperious Fitzwilliam. He did not know whether to be amused or horrified.

"Mr Darcy, I must refute your words," Collins began, his voice betraying some uncertainty.

"No, you must listen to them instead," Darcy replied as if

speaking to a petulant child. "My family's business is not yours to make public, and Miss Elizabeth is not for you."

"But I have spoken to her father."

"I am certain he laughed at such a notion," Darcy snapped.

Collins gasped. "I shall be marrying her to save the family's good name."

"The Bennets need no saviour, nor would you be the man for such an endeavour." Darcy rolled his eyes. "Miss Elizabeth is a lady of gentle birth and has a say in the sort of man she may marry. She has been quite emphatic in refusing your attentions."

"I am heir to Longbourn," Collins whinged. "The Bennets have great need of my grace."

"Ah, but I do not," Darcy growled, "nor do I have business with you. You have disgraced yourself and brought shame to this family. You must depart, wife or no, and leave the Bennets in peace."

"Alone?" Collins was ashen. "'Though I speak with the tongues of men and of angels, and have not charity...'"

"Yes, yes, yes...you have become a 'sounding brass, or a tinkling cymbal,'" Darcy parried in a sardonic tone. He eyed Collins, his exasperation now warring with some small glimpse of sympathy. As hapless, stupid, and unpleasant as he appeared, the cleric was not completely cruel and mean spirited. He toiled at the mercy of Lady Catherine, yet Richard had reported his parishioners respected him; no wonder his impulses towards staid common sense were uneven and awkward. Anne had certainly been damaged by her mother, yet she emerged to find joy in her life. Perhaps there was hope for the cleric.

"You are a man of God quoting Corinthians. You have a gift, sir." Darcy prevaricated with only good intent. "I recall your worries for your parishioners. You said your 'lambs' need you."

"Yes, they do," Collins replied with no small amount of eagerness. "I am needed at Hunsford."

"Then go," Darcy urged. "Make haste. You retain your parish, but you have a new lady to please. My aunt no longer resides at Rosings nor runs the estate. She has taken ill and is gone to a family estate to recover." He paused, waiting for Collins's nervous fluttering to taper off. "I suggest you curry favour with my cousin.

She has a good heart and far more to offer you than your former mistress."

Darcy leaned closer, affecting some intimacy with Collins to better enforce his point. He sniffed. *Good lord, the man smells of fish and soured cream sauce.* "We both are gentlemen who care for Rosings and its parish. Let me confide this to you: my cousin has long been in poor health. It was fear of the pox—a rumour we have yet to trace to its origins, mind you—that delayed her return to Rosings with her new husband. My aunt's misplaced ire created a host of problems and gossip circulated by many—but originating with *you*."

Collins looked at him, wide-eyed and slightly trembling. "Lady Catherine said her daughter was dead to her."

"To *her*, you ass. To her. Did Lord Matlock not explain this to you in London?" Darcy shook his head in disgust at the buzzard clergyman. *So much stupidity in one man, yet he felt himself worthy of my Elizabeth? Deluded fool.*

He took a breath and prepared to elucidate his uncle's white-washed account of the still-living Anne and her unlikely nuptials. His audience was such a malleable, frightened little man that he would believe any words said by the master of Pemberley.

"Lady Catherine was unhappy with my cousin's choice of husband and their delayed return from their wedding tour. You misunderstood and discouraged my aunt from clarifying the truth"—Darcy's eyes narrowed as his voice deepened—"and proclaimed me to be the Grieving Groom!"

Collins gulped. "She said it had been arranged whilst you slept in your cradles…"

"Another untruth. My mother and father agreed to no such attachment."

"Oh my," Collins croaked in a small voice. "So much deceit and unwarranted grief."

Darcy refrained from rolling his eyes. He had done far too much of that lately. He gave Collins a grave nod. "My aunt is not well, but she deserves neither scorn nor slanderous musings. Your new patroness is my cousin and my friend. She has a generous heart, and she always has my ear. I can be of assistance in assuring your success at Hunsford, or I can do differently. In this, Collins, I give you a choice."

It appeared that the cleric finally had grasped the finer points of his situation. His eyes grew wide, and he began to tremble. "I am truly rejoiced that your cousin's sad business has been so well hushed up, and I am only concerned that their rush towards marriage should be so generally known."

Darcy's voice dropped to a harsh whisper. "Collins, you wear on my patience."

"I wish to be of service to your cousin and to you, sir, of course. In fact," Collins went on, blushing in a most unbecoming manner, "I have received word from Rosings that my parsonage is under improvement, and I may soon return."

Collins bowed dramatically, catching his coattails in the briars of a thorny bush. He began to jerk this way and that to pull himself loose.

Biting back a smirk and fully exhausted from such a long tête-à-tête with the grovelling man, Darcy sighed. *Elizabeth awaits me, for goodness' sake.* He leaned over and pulled the cleric's coattails free from the shrubbery.

"Be warned, then. Do not set foot again in the viper's nest you created. Do not lie nor gossip."

Collins looked properly shamefaced. "Indeed. I am a man of God, and I shall follow His word. You, sir, have been maligned. I am sorry for my part in what has occurred. Be assured, I shall spread no slanders."

"Nor haunt Miss Elizabeth?"

Darcy thought he detected a slight hesitance, but then Collins shook his head with such vigour that Darcy feared the man would knock himself out. He bowed deeply, excused himself, and wandered over to Longbourn's beehives.

At long last. Satisfied with the persuasive success of his conversation and eager to return to the person who most mattered, Darcy turned heel and headed to the house. Elizabeth was waiting just inside the doorway. He took a sharp breath as his memory seized on the kisses they had exchanged. *Mine. She is mine, and I am hers.*

Elizabeth gave him a warm smile. She had seen the cold manner in which he had spoken to her cousin but now saw the possessive look in his eyes. She had felt his lips on hers, and she knew his heart. *Mine. He is mine, and I am his.*

"My father is in his library. I believe Mr Bingley awaits an audience as well."

He leaned nearer her ear and spoke a few words as his fingers traced her wrist. Then he pulled away, gave her a soft smile, and walked into the library.

Elizabeth watched the door close and sighed. Suddenly she heard Kitty's voice in her ear.

"Lizzy, if Mr Darcy has not yet asked you to marry him, he had best get to it. All that kissing will only lead to rumours and gossip."

Elizabeth turned to Kitty and found her sister smirking at her.

"I do not believe I shall need to help you hide after all," the younger girl declared. "You and Mr Darcy have discovered such a fine spot in the shrubbery."

With her sister gone home, Mrs Bennet's attention was focused on the conversations occurring in her husband's library and the daughters on whom those conversations centred. Yet, she was clever, and she would say nothing; she would listen and observe. Kitty had talked nearly endlessly about Miss Bingley's cunning ability to absorb knowledge simply by watching. Well, that girl was not the only one who could play at such a game. And how proficient was Miss Bingley at the art of observation, anyway? Four or five Seasons out and one foot already on the shelf.

Not like her own clever daughters. Jane would have Netherfield. Elizabeth would have Longbourn. And Kitty, sly one, would have Pemberley and a house in town. Yes, Mrs Bennet had seen how Mr Darcy escorted both girls back to the house. *Kitty has stolen him away from Miss Bingley!* Ten thousand a year would more than suffice for being married to a man with a slippery past and murky tastes. At least, he was pleasant to the eyes, mayhap even more than Mr Bingley. Although he had mourned carelessly, he had been quite handsome while doing so.

But Longbourn's mistress would think on this quietly and await the announcement. No one would know what she knew. Not yet. Her Lydia now had years to enjoy the company of redcoats before making her debut in London through her sisters' connexions. And Mary? Well, she had lost her chance with Mr Collins. He preferred Lizzy, and the match would settle things nicely for them all. The gossip about that girl's behaviour would be quieted when she was betrothed to Longbourn's heir.

Mrs Bennet shook her head and glanced over at her eldest daughters in the corner of the room.

"Lizzy," Jane whispered. "Charles wished to speak alone with Papa. Must Mr Darcy attend their conversation?"

Elizabeth, stirred from the happy memory she had been enjoying, allowed a little annoyance to seep into her reply. "Jane, I am so happy for you and Mr Bingley. Yet if Mr Darcy's approval was so necessary to achieving it, there should be no concern that he sits with Mr Bingley as his friend asks for *Papa's* consent."

Jane eyed her sister. "Is Mr Darcy in there with a question of his own?"

Elizabeth answered her with a smile.

"But did not Mr Collins already receive consent to speak to you?" Jane looked alarmed. "Mr Darcy cannot have it as well."

"Jane, our father would not give consent to any man without first gaining *our* consent. He knew of your feelings for Mr Bingley before now. My father knows I share his opinion of Mr Collins."

"And does he know what you think of Mr Darcy and that your information differs from the impression left in the neighbourhood?"

Elizabeth had never before heard conceit in Jane's voice. She responded with narrowed eyes, her anger overriding her despair at losing the good opinion of the only sister who had mattered.

Before she could find her voice to form a response, the library door swung open, and the three men emerged. One beamed, another radiated intense joy, and the third and eldest appeared both amused and relieved. Mr Bennet's eyes rested on his daughters. He cleared his throat and drew Elizabeth's attention from that of the young man standing beside him. She rose and joined her father; Jane followed.

"I have given permission to your young man, Jane. I could not part with you to a worthier man than Mr Bingley. Your happiness is certain." He added quietly, "It would be wise to keep your families nearby for contrast."

The betrothed couple, arm in arm, beamed in confusion. Mrs Bennet leapt up and began to rhapsodise over the shopping and planning and sewing that lay ahead.

"Mrs Bennet, I must tell you that while we have a wedding to plan, we must rely on the three silliest girls in the country to serve as chaperons to a second pairing as well. Mr Darcy is courting our Lizzy."

Kitty squealed, Lydia screeched, and Mary beamed. Mr Darcy, always clever and quick, caught Mrs Bennet before she hit the floor.

Spending some weeks apart from Miss Bingley had not changed her in any fundamental manner, Darcy reflected at Netherfield later that day. Elizabeth claimed her as the least pleasant woman of her acquaintance, though that was likely a temporary status. Once his relations learned of his attachment to Elizabeth, she was certain to experience even worse treatment.

My attachment. They were courting—not engaged like Bingley and her sister but only a few steps behind. Darcy felt he had a deeper understanding of the woman standing beside him than his friend had of his betrothed. *They smile and blush; we laugh and talk.* How was it that Bingley remained so tongue-tied around the woman he was to marry, the woman Darcy assumed his friend had kissed in the shrubbery? Was awkwardness a sign of love? He felt just happiness and relief. Elizabeth glanced up at him, and he rolled his eyes to mask his apprehension of Miss Bingley's likely greeting. "She does not frighten me. After all, you and I have seen a yawning tiger, and I have faced an angry, sharp-tongued peacock."

Elizabeth smiled. "Be prepared, Mr Darcy. Catching my mother in a faint and being struck by your aunt are trials indeed, but Miss Bingley is a bit more sharply angled. I would prefer you avoid further flesh wounds."

His eyes lit up, and he bit back a smile just as Georgiana arrived in the entryway with Miss Bingley hard on her heels. Darcy immediately saw the relief on his sister's face.

"Oh, Lizzy, it is so nice to see you again!"

"Mr Darcy, we feared the worst." Miss Bingley's voice masked her obvious surprise at Georgiana's intimate address to Elizabeth. "Do come in." Her eyes were hard as she stared at the Bennet girls attached to her brother and his friend. "Good afternoon, Jane, Eliza."

Disregarding the previous acquaintance between his sister and Elizabeth, Miss Bingley instead performed a grandiloquent introduction of Georgiana to Jane Bennet. She led them into the sitting room where the Hursts sat deep in conversation and unaware of the group's entrance.

Darcy, suddenly overwhelmed by his recognition of the similarity between Miss Bingley and Lady Catherine, felt his sister's eyes upon him. He gave her a soft smile and nodded, pulling her into the small circle of knowledge. Georgiana stared at him, her mouth open in happy surprise and looking as though she would leap into his arms in excitement if they were alone. In light of his sister's suppressed joy, Darcy determined he must hasten events along, no matter how much he now wished to slow them down. After weeks of denying and wondering about love, of reeling from and dealing with his family, the past hours had moved so quickly. He wished for a few moments to savour them, to gaze at Elizabeth and relive the happiness they had so recently shared. Her eyes had such a sparkle when he looked at her, and her voice held a new warmth; it seemed as if their minds had mingled as intimately as their breaths.

Darcy exhaled and brought himself back to the moment. His sister sat beside his Elizabeth. *Our happy future.*

His shoulder ached a bit from the well wishes, effusions of joy, and fainting ladies at Longbourn, so when he was certain that everyone was firmly seated in Netherfield's sitting room, he cleared his throat and shot a look at Bingley, urging him to announce his news.

Bingley gazed at Elizabeth's sister and took her hand in his. "Miss Jane Bennet has agreed to be my wife," he said, beaming.

To their credit, both Miss Bingley and Mrs Hurst praised the engagement. Hurst chuckled. "Finally, another lady of good sense in this family. We need a toast!"

Miss Bennet appeared unable to stop her cheeks from pinking, and Bingley seemed overwhelmed by the effusive sentiments.

"We all are quite pleased with your brother's happy news," Darcy said. "Charles could not have found himself a kinder, better-suited lady."

Miss Bingley's smile nearly faltered at his earnest words. "The Bennets must be quite pleased. Charles will be a wonderful husband to Jane and a comfort to them. Shall we expect more happy news soon, Eliza? Mr Collins is likely quite impatient with his suit."

Georgiana gasped, too quietly and too politely for anyone but her brother to hear.

"I scarcely think I try my cousin's patience in any manner, Miss Bingley," Elizabeth replied. "We have been so fortunate as to be out of the other's company these past weeks, and I daresay, we both are happier for the separation."

"It is my understanding—" Miss Bingley began.

Hurst snorted. "Understandings are often prone to *mis*under-standing, Caroline."

"I quite agree, Hurst," Darcy said, rising and moving to stand by the fireplace. "I fear I am too happy not to encroach on your brother's joy; I too must share."

He moved his eyes away from Miss Bingley's and smiled at Elizabeth. She beamed back, and he fought the urge to wink at her. *I am not Richard. I shall be proper.*

"I am pleased to tell you that I am courting..." hearing a gasp, his eyes shifted to see his sister smiling and Miss Bingley reeling.

"...Miss Elizabeth Bennet."

"But..." Miss Bingley croaked.

"Hear, hear," Hurst bellowed. "Now who is giving the toast?"

Longbourn was in an uproar when the foursome returned for dinner. Darcy and Bingley escorted their ladies inside only to find Mrs Bennet being assisted to her room. Kitty and Lydia were perched on the settee flanking a weeping Mary while an ashen Mr Collins was being led by his host from the library. All the inhabitants looked up in hysterical relief when the group entered. Mr Bennet urged them to be seated and then sank into his favourite chair. He announced that there was to be another engagement. "Before the gossip can begin," he said gravely, "Mary is to wed Mr Collins."

Jane flushed a deep red, shocked by her pious sister's unexpected fate and bewildered by the tumult of emotion roiling the room. Although a touch annoyed at once again sharing the glory of what she had hoped was *her* day, Jane almost immediately felt shame for her selfishness.

Bingley sighed, wishing to express his congratulations but wary of the sombre atmosphere. His sisters never cried, and he was at a loss whether to console or congratulate Miss Mary. Instead, he patted Jane's hand and nodded encouragingly at any who met his eye.

Darcy was struck by the irony of Collins the Gossip forced into marriage to *avoid* gossip. Another truth hit harder and cut deeply: *I am the last man in the world to gain engagement to a Bennet.* It was insupportable, but at least Mr Bennet was aware of and approved his intentions. Now, to get Elizabeth to agree. He made a silent vow: *I shall not share my wedding day. This will be the world's briefest courtship.*

Meanwhile, Elizabeth dwelt on the reference to gossip. What had Mr Collins done now? She was torn between joy for Mary, who had long admired their toad-eater cousin, and her anger that her sister—who had never been the object of attention or desire—would accept so meagre a man. A man who apparently had compromised her! She searched for understanding and kind words to say and found none.

Mr Bennet looked grimly around the room and sighed. "I believe I shall see to your mother." He wandered towards the stairs, but instead, retreated to his library.

Elizabeth's eyes flared. "How did this come about?" she murmured quietly to no one in particular. Mr Darcy took her hand and clasped it tightly.

With their father in retreat and their mother absent and unable to speak beyond calling for her salts, Kitty and Lydia took turns unspooling the tale for a reluctant though rapt audience.

"After all of you left for Netherfield, we walked to Meryton to buy ribbon and share the happy wedding news," Kitty said breathlessly.

"And courtship news," Lydia interjected. "Mr Darcy is a bit slow exhibiting his adoration of Lizzy, I think." Her attention focused on her storytelling; she overlooked Mr Darcy's flaming cheeks and Mr Bingley's quiet chuckle.

"Mary and Mr Collins walked with us," Lydia continued. "He was bothering Cook about her berry tarts, and Mama hoped to distract him from his earlier worries over Lizzy's *disreputable* courtship with Mr Darcy."

"Disreputable?" Mr Darcy murmured angrily. "'He who has a head of glass should beware of any hostile stones that pass.'"

Mr Collins slumped further in his seat and moaned, "No, my good sir. Those worries were at an end. All has changed…"

Elizabeth smiled a little in spite of herself at Mr Darcy quoting from Chaucer.

Lydia began speaking again, but Kitty shushed her. "As I was saying at the beginning, we went to Meryton, where we found delightful red ribbons. Charlotte and Maria joined us, and we shared the happy news. They determined to return with us to Longbourn and congratulate Lizzy and Jane."

Lydia sniggered. "Maria had bought herself a nice piece of blue lace to trim her bonnet, but it would better suit me as it would set off my lovely eyes."

Mr Darcy cleared his throat, and Kitty resumed the story. "As we left Meryton, we saw Mr Wickham! Lydia was so pleased until—"

"Let me tell it, Kitty! It happened to me!"

"No, it did not! It happened to Mary!"

"But I was a witness," Lydia cried, stomping her foot. "The very first witness!"

Elizabeth could feel the tension radiating through Mr Darcy. She glanced at Jane, who appeared frozen in shock, and then observed Mary, who stared wide-eyed at her pale-faced betrothed. Hill entered and set down the tea tray.

"Girls," Elizabeth said quietly, "is this a story that should be told here?"

Her youngest sister glanced past the empty doorway to their father's library and nodded briskly. "Wickham is always so pleased to see me although his misrepresentations about Mr Darcy have made *me* less pleased to see him." Lydia gave the slandered man a fond look, prompting a rather nervous half-smile in return. "But today, he looked cross. He was walking from the Nortons' little milk house, and their kitchen girl, Amelia Brown, was behind him. Wickham was buttoning his waistcoat."

Kitty shook her head. "Oh, his face was quite red. His lips were swollen, like all of yours were this morning." She nodded smartly at her sisters and their suitors. Suddenly aware of her error, Kitty cringed and averted her eyes. No one took notice as all eyes were occupied in the canvassing of walls, floors, boots, and lace trimmings.

"Amelia is an ugly girl," Lydia assured them. "And there she was, having her way with Wickham. He is pleasing to look at, but he behaved so badly!"

"When he heard Lydia scream—"

"Gasp, Kitty. I gasped."

"When she *gasped*, Mr Wickham became quite angry," Kitty said, a bit irritated at the interruptions. "He did not run away but walked towards us and, without even the courtesy of a greeting,

Mr Wickham asked whether the rumours were true about Lizzy and Mr Darcy."

"There have been so many rumours, as you know," Lydia said. "So I asked him to be more specific in his enquiry."

In spite of her consternation, Elizabeth felt a small glimmer of pride at Lydia's comedic sense of propriety.

"He demanded to know whether Lizzy was to marry Mr Darcy. I am not a liar," Kitty assured her audience, "so I told him they were merely courting. Nevertheless, Mr Wickham was not pleased."

"His eyes swept across all of us, from Charlotte to Maria to Mary to Kitty to me. He was looking at me in an odd way," Lydia whispered. "In a delicate place. At my neck."

Jane and Elizabeth gasped. Mr Bingley and Mr Darcy growled.

"Mr Collins asked him to remove his eyes from my person, and he attempted to step in front of us. Then he tripped and fell onto Mary, who tumbled into Wickham's arms."

"His clutches!" cried Kitty.

"Mr Wickham seized my person, and laid his lips upon mine," Mary said meekly.

"He…oh! The scurrilous cur!" Mr Bingley cried. "Oh, pardon my language."

Jane's hands flew to her heart. "Oh Mary."

Mr Darcy said nothing but sat very still. His hand fell from Elizabeth's and folded into a fist. Elizabeth looked from Mary's drawn face to his hard, impassive one. She leaned into his shoulder, awakening him from his fury. He regained her hand and held it between his own larger ones. It was not the caress of lovers but of repressed anger and anguish.

Lydia sighed. "Poor Mary. Her first kiss came from a handsome man, but he is wicked."

"He smelled of spirits. I believe, in his deluded state, he supposed I was Lydia." Mary closed her eyes and drank her tea.

Kitty patted her shoulder and resumed the tale. "'Tis true, I think. Suddenly, Mr Wickham began shouting, and he pushed Mary back into Mr Collins and they tumbled to the ground. Mrs Goulding and Mrs Norton came from the house and saw us all."

"And Mr Wickham claimed our cousin had compromised poor Mary?" Jane asked quietly.

"Oh yes," Lydia said. "He called him a 'sinful spreader of seed!'"

"Lydia!" Elizabeth cried. "Hush!"

"Lydia, mind yourself and stop upsetting your sister!" Mr Bennet roared. His appearance in the doorway, brandy bottle in hand, stifled the uncomfortable coughing and throat clearing. Looking rather bleary, he strolled into the room.

"From the looks on your faces, I should assume there has not been talk of ribbons, lace, and weddings." His gaze settled on his youngest, still unclaimed daughters. "I expect you two have made everyone privy to the details of Longbourn's latest news?" he asked in a tired but angry voice. "Even as we rejoice in the engagement of such a like-minded pair, this is not a tale that bears repeating. *Ever.* And certainly not outside this house.

"I believe we are all family here," he added, prompting Mr Collins to cringe, Mr Bingley to nod gravely, and Mr Darcy to tighten his grip on Elizabeth's hand.

Mr Bennet took his seat after pouring a generous serving of brandy into Mr Collins's tea. After a moment, he added a few drops to Mary's cup and then to his own. Mary's upper lip quivered. Mr Collins drained his tea and sighed heavily.

"Poor Mary," Jane said. Mr Bingley gave her a warm smile that showed his unwillingness to embrace the sadness and drama of the day.

Darcy held himself in check. He had questions to ask and a man to hunt down and send to debtors' prison—after he had damaged his face once or twice. *A few hours. Elizabeth and I had but a few hours to savour our understanding before that worthless ass had to involve himself in our lives by ruining Elizabeth's sister. Had he wanted to tie himself to me as family? He grabbed the wrong Bennet and tossed her to a different fate.*

"There is more to Mr Wickham than we know, is there not?" Mr Bennet asked, his attention focused on Darcy.

He nodded. He had thrown Wickham from the Darcy properties before he could become a thief; he had supported the children he knew Wickham had thoughtlessly spawned; he had done his father's bidding and paid Wickham the promised three thousand pounds. Wickham had skirted the law and common decency for too long, and he was not good enough for the uniform. He soon would be a desperate man without recourse. *His wiles have been dulled by drink and dissolution.*

"Wickham may pretend, but he has never been a gentleman," Darcy said in a cool voice. "I am sorry for the pain he caused you, Miss Mary. I did not know he remained in Meryton."

"He knew much about *you*," Miss Catherine averred. "All lies, I believe. He is a gossip and inventor and spreader of tall tales."

"One among many," Mr Bennet said, his eyes resting on the man who would soon be his son, the trembling heir to Longbourn.

"Wickham saved himself and doomed my sister," Elizabeth murmured.

"Poor Mary," her elder sister said quietly.

Miss Mary found her voice, shaky though it remained. "I am not 'poor Mary,'" she stated. "Nor am I doomed. In spite of the circumstances, I am to be married to a good man. Mr Collins tried to defend us all from Mr Wickham's wicked behaviour."

Mr Collins stirred, his attention moving from his empty teacup to the face of the woman to whom he would be married. Darcy caught a glimpse of his dawning apprehension of his future wife's worth. Elizabeth, watching them closely, clutched Darcy's hand.

"'Tis true he would not have fallen if his coats were better tailored," Miss Lydia agreed. "They are far too long to be fashionable or wise." All eyes dropped to the torn hem of Mr Collins's flowing coat.

"Indeed, Miss Mary is fortunate that her cousin was there to protect her and to save her name," Bingley offered.

Mr Bennet stared at him and laughed ruefully. "Not everyone is the author of their own love story, but all in all, it has been a rather romantic day."

Miss Lydia turned to Darcy. "As my father says, we are all family here. What shall we do about Mr Wickham?"

CHAPTER TWENTY

After a Sunday of rain and separation of young lovers, Monday's post brought timely news, but as the roads had been muddied and horses slowed down, it was not timely enough. The inhabitants of Netherfield moved slowly through the sunny November morning, save the one who rode through the muck to meet his morning maiden.

"Mr Darcy."

"Miss Elizabeth."

The dew was fresh, the air was crisp, and the conversation suspended while they stared at each other. A gentle pull on his horse's reins rallied Darcy's attention. He dismounted and tied Orlando to a fence post. Then he reached for Elizabeth's hand.

"I believe I prefer your hands without gloves," he murmured.

"Ah, but that would be most improper, sir. Just two days past, I neglected my gloves, and within sight of my own home, a handsome gentleman captured my hand with his lips." Her voice was soft yet lilting with humour. "It was most careless of me."

"Do tell." Darcy bent over her gloved hand and kissed it. He wished to kiss other things as well. In all his years in London, Derbyshire, and Cambridge, he had never before noticed how the English air could colour a cheek, rouge a lip, and brighten an eye. Elizabeth radiated happiness, health, and all that could be good and wonderful.

Is one day enough for a courtship?

"Pardon me?" Elizabeth was staring at him, a blush spreading across her cheeks.

Ah, I said that aloud.

"I wonder at all that has happened since I spoke to your father but two days ago," he managed. "Is your mother well?"

She smiled. "Yes, Mama is quite overcome, welcoming two sons and a suitor."

"She has set aside the gossip and rumours about me?"

"Oh yes. You surprised her most pleasingly," Elizabeth reassured him. Her words provoked a wry smile.

"A feat of which I am rarely accused."

Elizabeth laughed quietly. "Forgive my mother if her manner veers from distraction to effusion. We are quite busy at Longbourn. I am gaining two brothers, both eager suitors as it turns out. And I am being courted by a fine man who loves books but disdains gloves."

He glanced at her and noted her eyes were focused on his lips. His thoughts muddled. *Richard is right to mock me; my brain empties of thought when I am near her. Might I just kiss her and be done with it? That would secure an engagement without tripping over my tongue...uh, words.*

He coloured and looked away. The temptation she presented was too great. He tucked her arm in his and began to walk.

"Collins is eager, you say?" he rasped. "How is Miss Mary?"

Elizabeth's eyes brightened. "Quite well. Although my family is exultant that Mr Collins has had to remove himself from Longbourn, Mary is most happy with the attention and pleased with her groom, on whom has dawned recognition of the Bennet bride best suited to his temperament. While I think it ungenerous that Jane's happy day was halved and then shared yet again, I cannot deny my younger sister's joy."

"Glory to your cousin for his enlightenment," he said in a droll tone. "Will your sisters share their wedding day?"

"Oh. Oh dear." Elizabeth sighed. "I am not certain of the merit of such an idea. My mother would like to see her eldest daughter marry first from home, yet with the circumstances of Mary's engagement, her wedding is likely to precede it. Mr Collins has expressed a wish to be wed in his own church." She peeked at him from under the brim of her bonnet. "He wishes to have his patroness attend."

Darcy's head dropped to his chest. "My lord. Elizabeth, I have much to tell you. My family is rather complicated."

"Do you mean to warn me away from you, that I have not the courage to accept a cupboard full of relatives akin to Colonel Fitzwilliam?"

Darcy smiled and quelled the flutter her words had stirred in him. How he loved her! Her beauty, sensibility, and wry sweetness were as necessary to him as air to breathe. How had it taken so long for him to understand that he needed her, how well they fit together as perfect lovers and companions? There was so much he needed to say to this woman. He shook his head and cleared his throat.

"How do you make light of such things? Will it frighten you to learn that Richard is my favourite cousin and often in residence at Pemberley or Darcy House? That in spite of his oft-embarrassing jokes, he was the champion of my admiration for you?"

She laughed lightly and gave him an arch look. "I had assumed he admires nigh every lady he meets."

Darcy raised his eyebrows. "Perhaps, but he knows that I do not."

Elizabeth turned her eyes from him and sighed. "You have met my family. None are yet hidden in the cupboard. I have two silly sisters and a gossiping mother. My father is often disinterested, and my vainglorious cousin is soon to be my brother. Pray, how can you best me?"

He stopped their progress, chuckled softly, and lifted her chin. "Elizabeth," he said, willing her to meet his eyes and seeing the vulnerability in hers. "I like your family. I like mine as well in spite of the difficulties their behaviours create. I told you a little of it while we were in London and in my letter." Darcy looked at her in earnest. "Now I think I must tell you the long and twisting tale of my aunt, to whom I have no allegiance; my cousin, to whom I was never betrothed; and her whisk of a husband."

At her nod, Darcy pulled Elizabeth closer before leading her on the path nearer the trees. Under the warm autumn sun, he took a deep breath and began his tale. Even while losing his thoughts many times whilst staring into her laughing eyes, he remembered to include the story of his sister and the now somewhat heroic footman, which Elizabeth—as he knew she would—found endearing.

Elizabeth had exhausted herself of questions when Darcy ventured the one he had neglected to ask Bingley "How soon will the first wedding take place?"

"Both of my sisters will marry before year's end."

"That is a generous amount of time. If Collins and your sister are first to wed, it would matter little to Bingley. I believe he would share his happiness with any bride and groom as long as your sister graced his arm and took his name."

"Your friend is a good man. He sees all that is good and happy with the world, as does Jane." *Mostly.* She recalled her sister's impatience but a day ago. Jane had offered sincere and happy congratulations on Elizabeth's courtship, but the topic of Mr Collins's bride had not been broached between the sisters. Elizabeth did not want to appear missish, but she had had to temper her desire to show off Mr Darcy and remind Jane that an intelligent, handsome man of ten thousand a year could appreciate her worth.

"Such optimism is an enviable trait, though one that requires caution equal to its application." Darcy smirked. "My approach to the world is often remarked upon by Bingley as quite the *opposite.*"

Elizabeth touched his arm. "I have seen little that is disagreeable in you or your approach, Mr Darcy."

"Fitzwilliam," he said softly. "You could, if you are so inclined, use my Christian name."

"Oh."

"When we are alone," he said, his voice low, "or with your sister and Bingley?"

"I would like that, Fitzwilliam." Elizabeth watched his eyes darken and his face light up with happiness. She said it again, this time more playfully. "Fitzwilliam."

He smiled at her. "Forgive me; I am rather stupid at the moment."

"Oh dear. Will you burst forth in poetic raptures, or shall I recite a psalm to soothe your nerves? Mr Collins has been quite helpful in broadening my knowledge of verse."

"He is a learned man," Darcy replied solemnly. "And, as of yesterday, a romantic hero."

"Now, now. We must not mock my cousin-turned-brother." Elizabeth paused, fully realising what her family had gained. Last evening, as Mr Collins packed his valise for his move to the Philipses', Lydia had congratulated Mary on her service in moving their cousin into matrimony and out of their house. Elizabeth had done little more than frown at her youngest sister and hope her concurrence did not show in her expression. The knowledge that Mr Collins would be her brother—and brother to the man she would marry—had created a brief flare of fear in her as she lay abed, sleepless in the long, still hours. This man she loved already had a difficult family tree. Could it be weighed down by one more twisted branch?

"I apologise," Darcy voiced.

She gave a little shake of her head. "No, no. All is well. Truly, Mary is quite pleased with the turn of events. As for my mother, little needs be said. 'Two daughters married.'"

Darcy bit his lip. "Your sisters are to be married, but I hope you are happy as well."

"Of course, I am very happy!" she exclaimed and squeezed his hand. She rather liked this careful, shy version of Mr Darcy. Courting was full of unexpected pleasures; she wondered how she might inspire him into more kissing. They had at most ten minutes before she would need to return to Longbourn.

"Good. I am happier than I can ever recall. I fear, though, that I have neglected to ask whether you wished for a long courtship or a short one."

"Fitzwilliam, we have only minutes left before my mother sends one of my sisters to seek me out. In less than two days, she has had two daughters betrothed and has seen me being courted." She bit her lip and looked up at him. "I fear she cannot bear more happiness before breakfast. If I could, I would flee it."

He closed his eyes and said quietly, "Pemberley has hundreds of acres to roam and rooms in which to hide."

She stared at him. When he had whispered in her ear two days earlier, she had been so intent on the sensation of his lips and the thrumming feeling it created that she had barely been conscious of his words. It was not until later than night in her bed that she had been able to consider them.

"I cannot wait to show you Pemberley."

"It sounds wonderful." She steeled herself, recalling something else he had said. "Are you…you just arrived…are you to go to Pemberley now on family business?"

"Until a day ago, I thought I must head north and attend to my duties there. Elizabeth, I despise the thought of it. I am so tired of traversing the countryside away from you." He sighed heavily. "A fortnight in Pemberley is beyond my patience. My steward and housekeeper are intelligent and capable. My business can be conducted by letters and messengers, and by a short trip to London. The weather will turn, however. We must go before the snows."

"Oh, I see." She knew she sounded miserable. "Will you and Georgiana depart directly after the wedding?"

"No. Not without you."

She looked up sharply.

"Elizabeth, do you not understand?" Darcy shook his head, grimaced, and looked down at their joined hands. "I am courting you and cannot leave unless I carry your promise with me."

Oh my. Elizabeth felt warmth spreading through her. She was sure her cheeks were flaming; she knew her heart was.

"I do not wish to return to Pemberley without you." He lifted her hands to his lips and gently kissed her fingers. "I wish to marry you. I love you."

Everything around them—the air, the trees—was still. Darcy took a deep breath, and Elizabeth tightened her grip on his hands.

"I am not a perfect man," he said haltingly. "But I am a man of honour. And my heart was pure and untouched until you."

Elizabeth looked up into his dark, pleading eyes. "As was mine," she said, resting her hand on his heart.

"Marry me."

"Yes," she whispered. "I shall." Her hand drifted to his cheek and pulled him down, nearer to her. She kissed the wound given him by his aunt and left her own mark there. "I love you."

"Elizabeth," he murmured in a tender voice before capturing her lips. His hands clasped her close while her arms curled around him.

Neither a sister nor a wandering sheep interrupted them.

The afternoon wore on as two blissful lovers—and one man's joyful sister—paid calls at Longbourn, where the Bennets and their neighbours were happy to greet them, feed them, and assess the changes soon to be forthcoming. The three who were left behind at Netherfield stared at walls and unfinished needlework, leafed through magazines, and plotted billiards tournaments. The Hursts found separate pursuits while the Highly Tormented Caroline stared forlornly out the window.

"I despise it here, Louisa. The people, the food, the deceit…"

Her sister sighed. "Caroline, those are the same things you love and despise in London. You must quit this pouting over Charles's engagement. Jane will be a kinder, more generous sister to you than many would be."

"I know that," Caroline snapped.

"Then what distresses you? Mayhap, you miss the inquisitive company of her younger sister Kitty?"

"That girl was a hopeless case. Her attention wandered just as her mind and her fashion were showing signs of improvement." Caroline turned and stalked over to a chair. She stopped and stared down at it. "This is a hideous shade of blue. Look at the pattern. It must be replaced."

"Leave the chair be, Caroline. You resent Eliza Bennet and regret losing your chance with Mr Darcy." Louisa gave her sister a sympathetic smile before returning her attention to polishing an errant spot of spittle off her bracelet.

"That clergyman was supposed to marry Eliza, not her squinty-eyed sister. I do not understand Darcy's attachment to her and her country manners. Mayhap, it is all just another rumour." Caroline saw she had lost her sister's attention and briefly wished Kitty would visit and elucidate the details of the awful arrangement of couples. She cleared her throat.

"You are altered, Louisa. You think yourself so clever and so settled with your own marriage. Do you think I do not recognise the reason for your titters and sighs and teasing ways?"

Louisa froze.

"It is those…Thursdays. Do you think I am stupid? I know why you retire early those evenings," Caroline sniffed. "What I do not understand is why you continue to allow such attentions when they do not produce a child. How do you tolerate it?"

Her sister stared at her, a tense smile on her face. "I tolerate many things, Caroline, and suffer the attentions of many people; however, Cornelius is not among them. I long ago ceased closing my eyes and humming hymns, and I have discovered he is more than a dutiful husband."

Caroline sank into the hateful blue chair. "Yes, I understand husbands are quite in fashion now."

She looked up at the sound of footsteps and laughter in the hall. "They are returned," she said quietly, her fury and frustration seeping out.

Georgiana took a deep breath. These two days spent with Elizabeth and her family had been exhausting yet exhilarating; there were five sisters, and the two nearest her age—out yet unclaimed—were full of observations, witticisms, and questions that left her breathless. Her cheeks hurt from nervous laughter and genuine smiles, giving her confidence enough now to walk into a different kind of atmosphere.

How was it that Kitty referred to our host? 'Poor Miss Bingley, alone with her bitter beauty.'

Georgiana appreciated her new friend's sympathy for the aging yet fashionable lady and commiserated that Miss Bingley would be sister to the Bennets when Charles married Jane. Georgiana wished for sisters, but her desires were quite specific and verging on impatient. In two days, they were to Pemberley; would Elizabeth be promised to Fitzwilliam? Would she accompany them north? Or would more time pass before their happiness, and hers, was assured? *Selfish girl*, she scolded herself. She knew her brother wished to wed Elizabeth. If he had secured her hand, he would tell his only sister, would he not?

We cannot go to Pemberley, not without Lizzy.

Georgiana was heartened by the thought. Her brother's affections were deep and true. Nothing could stop his attentions to Elizabeth or affect his pursuit of her hand. *It would be so terribly unfair.* After all, Anne had married *her* true love, and rather than compelling the rest of the family to make more distinguished marriages, did it not instead free them to follow their hearts? It must, she concluded, unless it meant a footman or a soldier...or another painter. *Peregrine Dumfries.* In spite of Richard's jokes and Lady Matlock's pained expressions whenever the name was raised, Georgiana looked forward with great anticipation to her first meeting with Anne's husband. She had never seen a man with a beauty mark.

For now, however, she lingered in the hall outside the drawing room, looking back over her shoulder at her brother, bright-eyed, red-cheeked, and reading an express. Mr Bingley hovered nearby, smoothing down his hair as he spoke to the butler. They were happy men, and she so hoped to learn that her brother's happiness soon would be permanent.

When will he propose? Soon, I hope. Three Darcys we shall be. And they will not send me away or leave me to hide in cupboards.

Fitzwilliam might be her brother's Christian name, but he was a Darcy—honourable and kind rather than perverse and angry. He was the best brother and would be the best husband.

Hearing voices through the open doorway, Georgiana was confused by the meaning of Thursdays and rather bemused to learn that Mr Hurst carried such an imposing Christian name. *Truly, Cornelius?* But she felt no small sympathy for Miss Bingley's wistful declaration on the currency of dutiful husbands. She herself knew little of marriage and had observed only that her aunt and uncle enjoyed each other's company and her cousin Robert and his wife seemed...content.

One could hope for far more; she had learned that in the novels hidden in her aunt's sofa cushions. Those pages spoke of passion, lust, and forbidden desires. Truly, it was not appropriate to think of her always-proper brother in this way, but she saw how he gazed at Elizabeth. He was in love, and Elizabeth was perfectly suited to him. They would be beyond happy—already they glowed. Mr Bingley appeared just as besotted with Jane; she supposed that his cheeks ached from his incessant grinning, bobbing, and quiet chuckling. Love was in the air, was it not?

"Georgiana? Shall we go in?"

Startled by her brother's deep voice from her admittedly improper eavesdropping, Georgiana nodded. Fitzwilliam led her into the room of expectant hosts, and she smiled a greeting to the ladies of Netherfield.

"Good afternoon, ladies. Hurst." Fitzwilliam nodded to the other new arrival. Mr Hurst wandered over to the settee and dropped down next to his wife. Mr Bingley stepped into the room a moment later.

Her brother enquired, "May I request accommodation for Colonel Fitzwilliam? He will be arriving this afternoon."

"To meet your lady?" Miss Bingley asked in a brittle voice.

Fitzwilliam smiled, the full force of which the Bingley sisters had rarely seen. "Oh, my cousin and Miss Elizabeth formed an acquaintance when she and her London relations dined at Darcy House." He did not seem to notice the shocked expressions his words elicited. "It should make for a lively evening here."

Mrs Hurst sputtered, "Of course."

Mr Bingley smiled. "Your fearsome cousin is always welcome at Netherfield."

"He can go shooting with us," Mr Hurst exclaimed.

Fitzwilliam nodded solemnly and gazed at Georgiana. "Prepare for your cousin in full regalia. He—"

"—is here, you dolt." Amid a thunderous stomping of boots and jingle-jangling, the colonel strode into the room. He flashed a broad smile at Georgiana and the Bingley sisters before slapping Fitzwilliam on the shoulder. "Darcy, you would be an utter failure in the militia. The enemy would cut you down in a flash. You want for fox sense."

"Oh, Mr Darcy would be an excellent soldier, sir!" scolded Miss Bingley. "The military is the lesser for not having its share of his intelligence and sense of honour. His posture, too, is quite impressive."

"Quite lofty and erect," Mr Hurst agreed. Mr Bingley burst into laughter; then, glancing at Georgiana, he began coughing.

"I believe I have lost my peace hours earlier than I had hoped." Fitzwilliam sighed and wandered away towards the window to stare outside, a small smile on his lips.

Richard stared forlornly at Georgiana. "How do you put up with this starry-eyed man, my dear? Must you repeat and explain everything to him? Love's arrow is indeed sharp and dangerous."

Mr Bingley chuckled. "Love's arrow cannot pierce the clouds he and Lizzy gaze at." Noting the incredulous glance Darcy was sending him, he protested. "It is true! It is a wonder neither of you has tumbled down the paths you walk. Jane and I cannot keep pace."

"Nor do you wish to, Bingley."

"Pot and kettle united again, I see," Richard murmured, gazing at Mr Bingley's dreamy expression.

Sighs, groans, and throat clearing erupted.

Richard tapped the mantel. "Walk with me, cousins. I have news from London."

Darcy followed Georgiana and his strutting cousin to Netherfield's library. He glanced at the gleaming, nigh-empty bookshelves and sighed. He missed Pemberley and wished desperately to take Elizabeth there and keep her there.

Richard walked over to the long reading table, devoid as always of books, and sat upon it. "Lady Catherine will soon be travelling with my parents."

"To Scotland?" Darcy scowled. This was suspicious. "Why have they not yet left?"

"Doctor Dumfries called in an associate to examine Lady Catherine in London, but she fell ill shortly afterwards. Bad cheese, she claimed." He stifled a snort.

"It is a trick. She cannot be trusted."

"No, she truly was ill. Perhaps with regret," Richard assured him. "Dumfries had her examined by some expert on the head." He shrugged his disbelief. "Her head was found to be oddly shaped, and he believes that her anger and outbursts could be assuaged by medical work—kneading and rubbing of the scalp or some such."

Darcy, incredulous, guffawed. "Her head?"

"If they squeeze it too hard, lemon juice might pour out." Obviously astonished by her own words, Georgiana clapped her hand over her mouth. "I…I did not mean…I apologise."

Darcy stared at his red-faced sister, stunned by her joke. *She has been spending too much time with Richard. Or Miss Lydia.*

"Do not worry, poppet," Richard said, laughing. "It was a keen observation. Your brother has been less than kind in his similes and metaphors about the 'fruity' Fitzwilliams."

Darcy glared at him before touching his sister's arm. "Sweetheart, you are a Darcy; you are but one-half a Fitzwilliam. Please be kind to your less fortunate cousins and aunt." He earned a slight nod from Georgiana before turning back to Richard. "Why on earth is Lady Catherine's misshapen head suddenly the focus of so much attention? Is she diseased? Will this cure her bitter, irrational anger?"

"It is a ridiculous notion that touching my aunt's waxy head might make her happy. She despises being touched. When I was a boy, she would smack me when Mother made me kiss her chalky cheek!"

"You have established that Lady Catherine is both chalky and waxy, Richard." Darcy rolled his eyes. "Now tell us, is there a bump of some kind? A tumour?"

"No, simply a series of odd protrusions, some scabbing. Rather monstrous, really. An expert in Edinburgh will address it." Richard glanced at Georgiana and realised he had exposed too much to an innocent girl. He gave her a smile. "Lady Catherine always has been a difficult woman. My father tells amusing stories of her childhood tantrums. He and your mother called her Crabby Cathy."

Georgiana gasped and bit back a giggle.

Darcy leaned back against the bookcase and crossed his arms. "Georgiana, you, as my mother, are nothing like Lady Catherine. It is a blessing to us all."

"Very true, my dear," Richard barked. "The lady has no peer in pomposity and self-importance. Or, apparently, head lumps. Mayhap Anne has them as well. It could explain her odd behaviours."

Richard shuddered before strolling over to the side table to pour a glass of brandy. "My father will write when there is a verdict on her health. Neither pen nor paper is within the grasp of our aunt; these matters will remain private. But there will always be rumours about her disappearance and about Anne's curious wedding."

"And curious husband." Darcy added, looking at his sister. "You must disregard any letter or any gossip that reaches your ears, my dear. I would advise you to think of the past only as it gives you pleasure, but I believe we have few such pleasurable memories when it comes to our dear aunt."

"She cared for Mama—you said so," Georgiana said in a plaintive voice.

Brother and sister stared at each other—one uncomfortable, one sad.

"I would like to think on Cousin Anne's happiness," Georgiana said. "She wrote me a delightful letter about settling in at Rosings. It would appear her husband has decided opinions on Lady Catherine's choice of decoration."

"Do tell." Richard smirked.

"He has declared the house is to be rid of all animal heads and hides. The elephant-footed table is to be burned."

Aghast, Richard scowled. "The trophy room? That is the only respectable, liveable room in that mausoleum. Damn it, I knew he was a—"

"Richard!" Darcy shook his head. "We shall talk later about other mutual acquaintances. For now, excuse me. A letter needs to be written."

He turned to walk away then whirled around. "Georgiana, we do not yet go to Pemberley. I have some business in London. You and Mrs Annesley may remain here or return to the city with me."

"Yes, Brother," Georgiana said, her eyes wide. "I shall have more time with Lizzy and her sisters?"

Darcy nodded and went off to his rooms.

Richard was confused by his cousins' melancholy about Lady Catherine. *My aunt cares for no one other than that foul little spaniel. Cromwell, was it?*

"What is it, Richard? Is something wrong?" Georgiana asked worriedly.

"Not at all." The colonel stared at the empty doorway. "Your brother is love-struck. I wonder whether he has won Miss Elizabeth's hand."

"Proposed? And not told us?"

"The man might have some fox sense after all. I shall question him later."

Georgiana sighed and sank into a chair. "Richard, is everyone like this when they fall in love?"

"Yes, poppet." He sagely stroked his moustache as he always did when pretending deep thought. "Or so I have observed, having never been under such a spell myself. Mark my words: I am not, nor shall I ever be, a besotted pig-widgeon. But nigh on every man I know falls under a lady's spell sometime."

Georgiana sighed. "How does it happen? Is it always so sudden? I never imagined my brother could be so...full of blushes and smiles."

You have yet to see Anne and meet her 'dear Peregrine.' Love is an epidemic in this family. He squeezed his eyes closed as the recollection of the Wretched Night of Headboard Shaking and Moaning swept over him. He needed to have a woman soon to dispel the horrific memory.

"Oh, it is simple, my dear," he explained. "Your brother might be a stiff and proper man, but he never saw it coming. I do not know of their first encounter, but he likely was riding or walking along, minding his own business—*or Bingley's*—when suddenly, there was The Lovely and Wondrous Elizabeth Bennet. Time stood still, the air became thick, his head swam, and he became weak in the knees. His head whirled. And then he was in love. Simple as that."

"But—"

"Well, of course there were complications, but at the heart of it, the love was there. An undeniable truth."

Georgiana sighed. "You know so much about love, Richard. I cannot wait until you meet a lady who turns you upside down."

CHAPTER TWENTY-ONE

Loath though he would be to admit it, Darcy felt a bit let down by Mrs Bennet's subdued response to the news of Elizabeth's engagement. He had prepared himself for raptures, shrieks of joy, and the likelihood of uncomfortable pats and squeezing. He thought he could endure them as a counterpoint to his own family's likely violent-shock-turned-silent disappointment. However, the momentous events of the past days had seemingly sapped the lady of her shrill energy. She had been elated at Jane's engagement, shocked by Mary's, and now, it appeared, merely content with Elizabeth's.

His betrothed, his lovely and beautiful bride-to-be, merely smiled when he looked at her, surprised.

"Too many salts?" he whispered.

Elizabeth bit back a laugh. "Too many weddings," she replied.

It was only after the squeals, hugs, and questions from Miss Catherine and Miss Lydia were properly heard, returned, and answered, that Mrs Bennet quietly asked Darcy about his favourite dishes. He had never seen her so restrained.

"Mr Darcy, make no mistake. I am well pleased with you and our Lizzy. Your shared affection is a surprise to me, but already I can see the harmony of your minds."

She gazed across the room, and Darcy was afforded a view of her that he did not anticipate: a pensive woman. Her brow was furrowed, and she wore a sad smile. It was the first time he had noted any resemblance between Elizabeth and her mother.

"I am reserved in my joy for Mary," she continued. "We shall keep Longbourn, and she is more contented than I thought possible. I wish to be equal with my happiness for all my daughters…"

Darcy was impressed. This was not the Mrs Bennet with whom he had become familiar.

"But it is difficult, you know, because of the rumours and the gossip. Everyone is watching to measure which daughter's marriage should be best celebrated and whether Mary's is suspect."

Ah. There she is.

"Your ten thousand a year will provide such gowns and jewels and carriages for Lizzy," Mrs Bennet said dreamily. "Poor Mary is well prepared to be a parson's wife, though I dread the moment Mr Collins discovers she despises fish."

He smiled. It was his duty, after all.

When freed from the politely intemperate society of Longbourn, Darcy took advantage of every opportunity to be alone with Elizabeth. Even before Richard drove over with Georgiana—Darcy's unfounded worries over Mrs Bennet's fervour had brought out the protective older brother in him—the ardent suitor was regretting the sheer number of Bennets and servants roaming about Longbourn. He and Elizabeth managed a brief turn in the garden with Jane and Bingley; both couples sought out privacy within its confines for whispered conversations and displays of affection.

The weeks they had spent apart had led Elizabeth and Darcy to more than an examination of feeling and the sorting out of mistaken understanding. While they had long felt themselves to be friends, their newfound knowledge of mutual regard had prompted a deeper appreciation of each other's appearance and a desire and confidence to touch the other. Carefully and respectfully, of course.

It might have been an engagement of but a day, but Darcy had long found his thoughts dwelling on Elizabeth's more-than-pleasing figure, the soft curve of her neck, and the temptation of her lips—and other places. For all his past thinking that he would be her guide, Darcy found himself nigh unable to think cogently in the rare moments they were alone. Instead, *she* led him. He would like to think his vulnerability was intentional, and he was determined not to allow his cousin to see how deeply he was in her thrall. At least not until she wore his ring.

Elizabeth had no comprehension of her power over him. After endless days when she felt alone and apart from those who would toss around rumour and conjecture about a man they did not know but whom she called friend, she was content simply to touch him and know he was real. Yet she was a lady who cared for knowledge and sought proof in all things.

Thus, on this escape from the maddening crowd of Longbourn, it took little time for her to discover that Darcy liked her fingers in his hair and her lips just below his ear. She quite enjoyed the way his hands held her—gentle and warm yet chaste—and the manner in which he had quickly determined their mouths best fit. *Tongues? Who knew such things?* Elizabeth Bennet had never been prone to sighing, but Fitzwilliam Darcy had changed that. He made her sigh.

Our mouths, our minds. Our bodies and souls to come. Elizabeth, always a quick study, chose to tuck away such thoughts. Her future husband was clearly more experienced than she was, and the quickness with which desire could come to overrule rational thought unsettled her a little. Perversely, it took but a memory of how Mary had gained her haplessly mendacious betrothed for Elizabeth to recall herself. With their sense and appearances restored, they returned to Longbourn where little intelligence could be spared. Mr Collins was expounding on the beauties of Hunsford for his "most glorious nuptials to his good lady."

Darcy's discomfort was not noticed by his beloved as she was busy being pleased. The decision about Mary's wedding location had been perhaps the second happiest moment of Elizabeth's day. Her father had agreed that Mary would be married from Hunsford within three weeks, and her sisters would marry a week later from home.

"I would wish for a longer engagement for you, dear Lizzy, but I have no desire for the sighs and melancholy that accompany a winter-long epistolary love affair," he had said in a woeful voice. "Your aunt is well-practised assembling wedding clothes for her other nieces and will likely be delighted to do so for you and Jane. The price for her kindness will be a quick marriage here before she can no longer travel."

The announcement of the wedding dates had Bingley nearly bouncing with excitement. Darcy steadied his friend and smiled at Georgiana, whose countenance shone with happiness. Elizabeth stole a glance at her elder sister. Ever serene, Jane was glowing. She squeezed Elizabeth's hand and turned to her. "All is as it should be, Lizzy. The best of men have claimed us to be their wives. I regret speaking in haste and so unthinkingly about Mr Darcy. I was so anxious for my own happiness that I neglected yours. I beg your forgiveness."

"Jane, all is well."

"We will share our day, Lizzy," she said fiercely. "As it should be."

Elizabeth looked away, her trust and faith not yet restored, and discovered Darcy's eyes settled on hers, waiting to be found. She let go of Jane's hand and walked to his side.

As subdued as Mrs Bennet might have been to the latest nuptial news, Richard more than compensated with a boisterous guffaw of congratulations.

Although he pouted that he had not been the first to hear his cousin's news, he happily welcomed it and declared that, as Most Favourite Cousin, he would partner Mrs Darcy for the second set at every ball for the rest of their days.

He reacted less well to the news of Darcy's future brother.

"Him? That foul-smelling cod's head of a cleric? *Him?*" Richard stared dumbfounded at Darcy. "Anne has gifted us with bloody Peregrine Dumfries for a relation and now this? The clubs will bar their doors to us!"

Darcy rolled his eyes. *Richard has a filthy mouth, and Miss Lydia will be a great audience.* He too had needed time to make peace with the notion of a family connexion with Collins; yet, he had known without asking that Elizabeth had set aside her own repulsion to support her sister and was likely more worried for his feelings.

"I cannot begrudge my sister her own bliss when I am so happy," she had said. "But you cannot be pleased. Nor will your family find much to praise in the connexion."

The distress in her voice had pained him. "You have yet to meet most of my family and my wide array of eccentric relations. Their wealth and lineage protects them, but they are truly little different from their peers in their quirks and behaviours."

Elizabeth had stared at him with a doubtful expression. "You will meet them in London and judge for yourself," he had assured her before stealing a kiss. "As for Mr and Mrs Collins, we shall keep them tucked away in Kent. My cousin and her husband will have great need for your cousin's theological advice and your sister's common sense. I believe they will make a happy foursome for whist."

Now, a day later, visiting Longbourn and witnessing the cleric's smug joy, Richard required similar reassurance, though Darcy refrained from embracing him or stealing kisses.

"Calm down, your moustache is jerking about." His eyes drifted to Georgiana, who sat in a circle of Bennet girls, laughing and chattering happily. He blinked quickly and inspected the wall.

"Damn it, Darcy," Richard snapped. "Who has cursed our family with such a man?"

"They spend no time in London; your marital prospects will not be tainted."

"Be serious. Is there no other solution for Miss Mary?"

"She seems to care for him," Darcy replied, shrugging. "And, I think, he for her."

"Such husbands these women choose!" Richard shook his head.

Darcy cleared his throat. "Bingley and I shall assume you refer to Miss Mary and my cousin Anne and not all of the Bennet sisters."

Richard, arms crossed and body coiled, grunted. "What they will do to the bloodlines alone…"

"Please, Richard. No further comment on the marital felicity of our cousin or my future sister. Remember, I must prepare Elizabeth to meet the Dumfries."

The colonel's moustache twitched—lately, a frequent occurrence—but he remained silent. Finally, in a tone that almost broached levity, he replied, "You must buy my father a case of the finest French cognac. Only that may alleviate his anger."

Before Darcy could reply, Collins appeared before them, his face contorted in a mix of fear and pride. "You have heard my happy news, Colonel Fitzwilliam? I came to Longbourn to extend an olive branch, and I have chosen a bride. New leaves will sprout and strengthen our family tree."

"So to speak," Darcy said drily. "You are a fortunate man. As Pope said, 'Just as the twig is bent, so is the tree inclined.'"

"Enough of your damn Latin nonsense, Darcy," Richard growled. "Go buy a new ride and talk to me of saddles and horseflesh."

Collins nodded in eager confusion. "I do not ride, sir. I am a man of God, and my feet remain planted on His soil." He leaned in and bent his head closer to the colonel. "I look forward to returning to my parsonage and becoming acquainted with your cousin's new husband: the master of Rosings."

Richard's eyes narrowed and his face turned a deep red. "Have you not met? I recall a letter from my cousin expressing her dismay and outrage at *your* dismay and outrage. You were displeased to find she was alive?"

Collins caught the colonel's menacing expression and excused himself.

The two men watched the cleric hasten to the side of his beloved, who received him with more warmth than either thought warranted. Richard shook his head in disgust. "This is a sorry business and no way to extend an olive branch. Why didn't my father simply have the toad beaten and trundled off somewhere?"

He stalked across the room to the window and looked at the landscape until a giggle caught his attention. As ever, only the joyful laughter of giddy young ladies could cheer up a bachelor losing his cousins to marital felicity and unpleasant family relations.

Darcy took up his old post as a haunter of walls. He remained ever watchful of his sister, now speaking earnestly to Elizabeth and Jane; it was a sight that once again affected his eyes and compelled him to blink rapidly. He felt safer in his emotions by watching his cousin deluged with questions and flattering observations. Few sights were more amusing than seeing his gruff cousin blush at the attentions of curious yet guileless girls. After an especially loud squeal of laughter, he caught his cousin's eye and called him over.

Richard excused himself while Miss Lydia and Miss Catherine huddled, deep in discussion.

Upon reaching Darcy's side, he drawled, "Do your duty as my favourite cousin and co-guardian to your sister, and swat these girls away from me. I am defenceless to their charms and insults."

Darcy scowled. "But not to their endowments. When speaking to my future sisters, do repress your basest instincts as a Fitzwilliam and draw on your mother's genteel stock."

Richard chose the route of an imp and debated the point. "My mother reads novels. These girls read novels. Their father is a gentleman, my father is a gentleman. So far, we are equal."

"And you are better than twice Miss Lydia's age." Darcy rolled his eyes in recognition that his cousin would never stop teasing him on the matter of romantic love. "They are pleasant young ladies, Richard, but natural and unsophisticated. I shall be their brother, and I shall relish calling you out. If you need to flirt, you will find opportunities in London. If you need a wife, let your mother ply her matchmaking talents."

Richard groaned. "I have you and my commanding officers to order me about and send me hither and yon. What need have I for a wife? I need a woman."

"Your absence would be alarming, Colonel Fitzwilliam. Who would my put-upon and oft-besieged husband-to-be turn to for escape from this endless talk of wooing and weddings?" Elizabeth slipped her arm into Darcy's and smiled brightly at the startled men.

"I…um…we did not see your approach, Elizabeth." Darcy glared at his cousin.

The colonel, his cheeks flaming, cleared his throat. "You must call me 'Richard,' you know. Informality becomes us all as family."

"Yes, and as you can see, my family is deeply informal in its behaviour," Elizabeth said wryly, her gaze sweeping Longbourn's crowded sitting room. "Will you make me privy to all Fitzwilliam and Darcy family secrets, the hidden lore, and the many misadventures of my betrothed and his merry band of cousins?" She glanced from one man to the other. "Richard, you must have an abundance of tales to reveal, and I expect to hear them all, no matter their suitability for a lady's ear."

Richard straightened. "Indeed, I do, Elizabeth. Your dullish man has a less lively past than some; he must thank me for nigh all fun and adventure in his life." He winked at Darcy and smirked. "He will avow that his bookish interests kept him from trouble-making. I say all those books kept him from a life more interesting."

"Ah, but a life more interesting is mine now." Darcy directed a smug smile at his cousin before shifting his attention to the lady by his side. His expression softened with his voice. "I shall soon be wed to the most captivating woman in England."

"Yes, yes, yes," Richard replied. "So happy, so in love." He watched as the couple became lost in each other's regard. Darcy wore that simpleminded grin he used to have as a wee pup eating cream cakes. Elizabeth simply…swelled with happiness. *Swelled? Bad word choice. She glows.*

He was a second son, destined to earn his way in the world and marry—or preferably just bed lonely widows and wealthy lady friends. The joy and felicity emanating from the couple before him was staggering, like one of the puffy clouds the two of them stared at and tittered over. Was there some way to capture this happiness in a bottle, to boil down its essence, sell it, and make his fortune? His mother would think him so clever. The scent of amorous love, wafting about all of London, and her son raking in gold. Love in a bottle. *Eau de Joie.*

Richard sighed. He was no chemist, and they were a hopeless pair. *You two may wrestle in the sheets and play spillikins while discussing Latin poetry in French, but I shall be on my horse, sword at my hip, keeping you and your family safe. Then I shall come drink your brandy and teach your children to tease you. Yes, that will be my way.*

In the meantime, he still needed a woman to relieve his suffering. It was time to go.

"London is calling," he mumbled cheerfully.

Mr Bennet sat in his chair, newspaper lowered, quietly observing The Daily Spectacle of Lovers and Oglers. His wife was settled across from him, sorting through a box of lace while Mary watched with more patience than she felt. She had declined the following day's shopping trip to London, preferring to spend her time in study and preparing for the duties of a vicar's wife. Mr Collins would be leaving in two days to open his parsonage and announce his engagement to his congregation. With a wedding in not much more than a fortnight, she had much to do.

"Mary, a bit of lace here and a pull of some thread and one of Lizzy's old gowns will do you nicely. Mr Collins will appreciate it." Mrs Bennet furrowed her brow and peered closely at her daughter's chest. "We shall pull the thread very tightly."

Mary stared down at her chest and up at her mother. She

sighed, looking relieved that her mother's attention already had moved on to lecturing Lydia and Kitty about their future happiness. Did they mourn the absence of Colonel Fitzwilliam, now back in London on what he called Very Official Military Matters?

"Men with moustaches do not make good husbands," Mrs Bennet declared. "I have heard tales of hirsute men and their cruel indifference to their families. Why, that Mr Larkin in Hatfield was rumoured to have—"

"Rumoured, Mama?" Kitty smiled prettily. "But the best rumours are always unfounded, and they are always about the best men and meant to inspire envy and ire."

Lydia chimed in. "'Tis true. The only fabrications we heard about Wickham were those he told, and the things said about Mr Darcy were obviously untrue. He is wonderfully nice to Lizzy, and I rather like his smile."

She lowered her voice and leaned towards her mother. "You need have no worry of my admiration for his cousin, Mama. His moustache is rather fearsome, and I believe I saw jam and biscuit crumbs hiding within it. I suppose it would be dashing if it hid a battle scar or two."

Lydia exchanged looks with her sister. Kitty's face lit up with excitement. "I believe I have a new scheme," she cried. "Where is Georgiana? We must ask her to convince her cousin to shave!"

The two girls jumped up from the settee and wandered away to plan their mission.

Mr Bennet stifled a chuckle. "Mrs Bennet," he said quietly. When she looked up, he continued, "I have not encouraged your matchmaking nor complimented your skills, but today, I must commend you on your mastery with these girls. All of our daughters are cleverer than I had realised." He smiled at Mary and leaned back in his chair.

"I like Bingley, of course. He is a man who must be liked, and those who fail to do so will lose a loyal and generous friend. Collins will amuse me for years and maintain Longbourn as it always has been, albeit with fewer books, better gardens, and more disciplined hives." He winked at Mary before gazing across the room at his second daughter, her head bent to Darcy. "But Lizzy's groom, now I believe he may well be my favourite. So many entertaining and sordid tales preceded his first appearance, and he left so many more in his wake. Add to that his skill at chess, love of books, and a fine talent for arguing with both Lizzy and Lydia. With these three sons, I look ahead happily to my years as Longbourn's old toast."

"Papa! Language!" Mary cried.

Mrs Bennet fastened a stern look on her husband. "I must ask you, Mr Bennet," she began. "If any man comes to Longbourn before the New Year and wishes to court Lydia or Kitty, please stay closed up in your library. I cannot part with another of my girls for now."

"Ah," he replied, "at least until they are invited to London or to Pemberley?"

After dinner—and before Darcy, Georgiana, and Bingley returned to Netherfield to join an ailing Miss Bingley, her loyal sister, and a disgruntled Hurst—Elizabeth walked with her intended along Longbourn's walled wilderness.

Despite the darkness, Darcy could see the dying vines that wrapped the walls. He smiled, thinking that the walls of his heart had surrendered to the tendrils of love. *Oh lord, Richard is right: I am a complete idiot! Yet he misses so much without such love in his heart.*

He gathered himself to speak sensibly. "In spite of the little time she has been given for it, your mother is pleased to have three weddings to plan."

"Her perch atop Meryton society is secure. Neither gossip nor rumour will besmirch the Bennet-Darcy-Bingley-Collins families."

He stopped and stared at her, blinking.

"You look like a fish, sir." She squeezed his arm playfully. "Are you well?"

Darcy sighed. "You must allow me time to reconcile that my future happiness requires accepting Mr Collins as my brother."

A sympathetic smile greeted his confession. "He is a sour bite to swallow, is he not? Are you certain your uncle and aunt will not resent me for his connexion to you?"

"Elizabeth, you are marrying into the strangest family in all of England. I have a lumpish-headed aunt estranged from her love-crazed daughter, a cousin who cares too much for silly jests and ladies' figures, an uncle whose abuse of glassware breaks his household budget…"

He shook his head, half-amused and half-appalled by the blank truth of it. "Truly, after the blending of the de Bourgh, Fitzwilliam, and Dumfries bloodlines, my aunt and uncle can have little to say on the matter."

Elizabeth patted his hand. "We must steer Georgiana towards a manly sort when she chooses her husband: a great shooter of guns, swinger of swords, and reader of books. You deserve such a brother, and in the meantime, together we shall face the unpleasant spoonful known as Mr Collins."

He laughed quietly and kissed her cheek. "Yes. And then on to meet the Dumfries. Such a large dose of grudging acceptance we must swallow."

"You promised we shall be equal in our marriage." Elizabeth's fingers played with his waistcoat. "Our families are kind to facilitate it."

"Oh yes," he agreed. "We shall strengthen our marital felicity by sharing incredulous laughter and horrified glances." Darcy held his breath and glanced down at Elizabeth's hand, slowly tucking a thread back through a buttonhole.

"And this," he gasped. "You weaken me and make us stronger."

Elizabeth grinned up at him. "These are important matters, fixing the wayward tailoring of your clothing."

"Ah, remind me to fire Smith. And my tailor."

"Fitzwilliam, be serious," she cried. "Let your brain idle a while rather than creating a new family crisis."

He drew her hands to his lips. "My brain is never idle whether you are near or far."

"I shall believe that to be a compliment," Elizabeth said in a playful tone. She stared up at the sky. "The stars are especially bright tonight."

"Absolutely stunning," Darcy replied quietly. He heard her indrawn breath.

The trill of Miss Lydia's laugh sounded behind them. Quickly, Elizabeth pulled Darcy around the corner and into a walled thicket.

"You, sir, owe me an explanation. Your cousin tells me you once were dullish. Your sister tells me you have been known to gift the world with your smile only once a fortnight." Elizabeth leaned against the thick vines. "Who is this dour Darcy? I do not know him."

"Nor will you ever. He is a man of the past. I am a work of your heart and your goodness." He stood before her, his eyes searching hers in the moonlight.

Her small, gloved hand caressed his cheek. "You are a poet, my love," she whispered.

Darcy bent down and kissed those teasing lips. He pulled back just a fraction. "And you are my happiness." When Elizabeth responded with a shiver, his dutiful Darcy sensibilities kicked in. He wrapped her in his arms and kissed away any vestige of the cold.

It was most fortunate that the Matlocks remained in London and thus could meet their nephew's betrothed whilst she was in town shopping for her wedding clothes. They would leave two days hence for their home in the north, and then the earl would escort his sister to Scotland. Or, as Richard liked to say, "The land without a fruit tree. Seems likely to cure my aunt of her afflictions."

"Oh, Dickie," his mother said sharply. "You should be kinder to your aunt and to Scotland."

His father's voice cut more deeply. "Boy, you are an officer in the king's forces. Did you pay no attention to your geography lessons? Apple, pear, and plum trees grow in Scotland!"

"Yes, well," Richard responded, more grumpily than he would like them to note, "the worms inside them likely freeze."

He despised when his parents worked together to deliver him a set-down. He paid no attention to his brother's scolding, and Darcy's admonitions never wounded in the same way. Richard would miss his cousin's company once Darcy was married. In the short time he had spent at Netherfield, he had seen the devotion and the attraction between Darcy and Elizabeth Bennet. He had never seen his staid cousin so full of smiles and sheepish grins; in fact, Richard had felt terribly well behaved for almost never mentioning the twisted cravats, swollen lips, or dreamy expressions. Even more impressively, he had never chanced even a glance at any one of the Bennet bosoms. This was difficult work, as Elizabeth was captivating and her two youngest sisters eager to hear stories of his adventures.

His adventures. Yes, he would be off to his regiment soon enough. Just one day after the wedding, but he would not dare tell his cousin and provide him with worry. *Though perhaps it might be just what Darcy needs to keep his mind occupied and his breeches looser. Ha! He is a lucky sort of lovesick fool.*

Any further thoughts were set aside in calming his parents' anticipation and anxiety for meeting Darcy's future wife.

They were to gather for tea at Matlock House on a cold Thursday afternoon. The countess wore her lesser jewels, donned her favourite afternoon gown, and adopted a hopeful countenance; Darcy was determined and in love, and she could do nothing but hope that Richard's reports on the lady were trustworthy. Her younger son was a talented twister of the truth, but some years ago, she had discovered that the disciplined officer had developed a twitch in his eye when he misled her. She attributed it to guilt, mayhap to maturity, but certainly to yet another flaw in the Fitzwilliam family tree. Peter and Catherine had the odd twitch as well. Her older son, Robert, did not, but while he had always favoured her family in looks, his staid dullness was of unknown origin. Harriet was his perfect complement, and she anticipated they would leave before dinner. It was Thursday, after all.

Lady Matlock examined herself in the mirror as she recalled that Richard's eye had not twitched once when he had spoken about Miss Elizabeth Bennet. He had reminded them that Anne had chosen a husband of rather questionable value and uncertain character, but there appeared to be deep—though unpleasant to witness—affection between them. Darcy, on the other hand, *had been chosen* by a lady of prodigious value and character, and they should appreciate his great fortune.

At such times, the colonel's parents were at a loss to understand their son. Did his loyalty to Darcy run so deep that he would shield a woman unworthy of the Darcy name? He praised few people and almost never a lady. They could not wait to meet Miss Elizabeth Bennet, her sister, and her London relations. Still, Lady Matlock made sure to admonish her husband to behave himself.

Not ten minutes before the Darcy carriage arrived from Gracechurch Street, Richard gathered his parents and brother and filled their glasses from the brimming carafe. Harriet was indisposed, and Richard felt she likely was either preparing for her evening of baby making or sickly from a previous Thursday's success. His brother's face betrayed nothing. His parents looked expectant. He must do all he could to aid Darcy.

"Darcy is pleased you will meet Miss Bennet before leaving town."

"He may be less pleased if we are not at his wedding. The rush of it all, Richard…" Lord Matlock raised a fearsome eyebrow.

"It is a bit of a hurry up," Robert said drily. "Not like the old, dutiful Darcy."

"Not like you to wonder so at another's private affairs, Brother," Richard retorted. "You have no cause to think badly of Darcy or Miss Bennet. I have told you nothing but good things about her. She and Darcy have much in common, with books and music and such. She is lively, and that is a good thing for him."

"Richard, we never suspected she could be quite as unsuitable as Anne's choice, but you praise her quite highly."

"I have a high regard for her, Mother, and rightly so. She is all that Darcy needs and deserves."

His mother gave him a wistful smile. "In his letter, he said his parents would more than approve; he said they would adore Elizabeth Bennet."

The earl leaned over and patted his wife's hand. "Anne wanted the best for her son. She wished him happiness. As do we."

"Good, good," Richard said. "Darcy and Elizabeth are perfectly formed for each other. One more thing they share in common is difficult relations," he added slowly. "Darcy has Lady Catherine, and Cousin Anne has never been easy…"

"And you, of course," Robert said, chuckling in the way that so annoyed a younger brother. "By the by, thank you for finally taming that forest over your lip. It was a fearsome thing, that moustache."

Richard turned beet red. "Regulations and such, dear brother," he muttered.

Their mother eyed her younger son strangely but cut to the matter at hand. "One uncle is an attorney, another is in trade. You have told us this before, Richard. Is there more?"

"A loon in the attic, perhaps?" Robert laughed at his joke. No one joined him.

"Her mother is boisterous but sets a good table, and her father enjoys books but not his estate duties. Her sisters are admired by their neighbours."

"I sense a 'however' is dangling, dear," Lady Matlock said.

Richard grimaced. "Father, do you recall that clumsy cleric, Collins? The one who prostrated himself to you at Lady Catherine's."

"Who could forget that obsequious little toad. Why do you ask? Will he perform the vows?"

"No. He is cousin to the Bennets and holds the entail to their estate, Longbourn."

"How dreadful to be father only to daughters." Lord Matlock shook his head as if faced with the greatest tragedy of his life.

His wife reacted wistfully. "I should have liked a daughter. Richard will be my favourite son when he makes his marriage to a kind, gentle, witty, and wealthy lady."

"Mother!" Robert groaned. "Must you always strive to be so kind to my half-wit brother?"

Richard, recognising that his family could be slow and his father could react violently, set out to explain matters in a deliberate manner. "Just as we have had to accept an unlikely new relation in Peregrine Dumfries, Darcy will have two new brothers."

"Yes, yes." Lord Matlock said carelessly. "His friend with the fortune made in trade. Charles Bingley seems a pleasant fellow. Always has made Darcy laugh, and that alone gives the man value."

"You spoke of two brothers," Lady Matlock commented. "These two Miss Bennets have three sisters. Another is to marry?"

"Yes. The eldest three will marry next month, including the third sister, Mary. She is to wed Collins." Richard looked dolefully at his father. Thankfully, he was holding no glass, nor were any sharp implements within reach.

"The toad-eater parson?"

"Yes, Mother."

His father remained silent. *This is not good.*

"Our Darcy is to be brother to that awful little man?" his mother cried.

"The one who referred to my nephew as a cuckolded stallion?" The earl sat down hard in a chair. "How can this be?"

Richard grimaced. "Your shock and dismay rivals that of Darcy and Elizabeth. She loves her sister, and her sister appears to care for the parson. But you should know that neither love nor the Bennets' desire to retain the entail led to this engagement. There was a mendacious matchmaker."

His mother gasped.

"You know his name, I fear: George Wickham."

"Wickham, the rutting goat of renown?" Robert looked appalled.

"That boy the maids called 'Peaches'?" cried the earl. "I always knew he was a worthless mutton monger."

All thoughts of rotten fruit and mendacious matchmakers were forgotten moments later when the butler announced the arrival of their guests. Lady Matlock, the family's quickest learner, immediately took to Elizabeth Bennet and her relations. Georgiana's happy telling of her visit with the Gardiner children and their joy in welcoming a 'golden princess' as a cousin softened any gruffness left in the earl. Witnessing the adoring looks exchanged between the betrothed young couple brought a shamed blush to Robert's cheeks and hastened his hearty congratulations. He vowed a swift ride home to his wife.

"You look well, Richard," Darcy said, staring at his cousin's face. "Have you given up drink? You look different, but I cannot quite capture what it is. More…something."

"I believe it is less, my dear," Elizabeth said, smiling at the colonel and steering a confused Darcy off to join his uncle's conversation.

Richard chuckled, pleased by the quickness of the ladies in his family. Before he could hide his expression, another lady came to his side.

"I think your moustache looks most dignified, Richard," Georgiana said slyly. "Its smaller shape is quite becoming. Kitty learned much about fashion from Miss Bingley."

He could do no more than sigh in surrender. He truly was dim. *Thank the lord that I am the charming one.*

Lord Matlock rarely shrugged off his glower long enough to reveal his silver-haired charm. Pretty ladies, however, were a weakness. From afar, of course. He loved his wife and feared her ire should he ever dwell too long on another's allure. Yet he found the Bennet sisters a lovely pair—one beautiful, one beguiling—and was chagrined that his younger son had missed his chance with such fine ladies. Of course, it was for the best as they brought neither fortune nor connexion to marriage. Neither mattered to his nephew, but it mattered greatly for a second son. The earl sat back in his chair, sipped his tea, and learned some particulars on Darcy's courtship of Miss Elizabeth from her aunt and uncle.

"A book on clouds? Darcy?"

"Oh yes," Mrs Gardiner replied. She smiled and glanced over at the rest of the party.

Lord Matlock contemplated his nephew standing just behind the chair where Miss Elizabeth sat speaking of lace or kittens or some such to her sister, Georgiana, and an enthralled trio of Fitzwilliams. Understanding dawned as he gazed on the fine-eyed, perfectly formed lady and the besotted young man who towered above her.

Ah, the Fitzwilliam blood bubbles to the fore. He smiled with no little satisfaction. *Darcy, too, is a breast man.*

CHAPTER TWENTY-TWO

The engagement between Darcy and Elizabeth had lasted but three weeks, long enough to dampen rumours about the supposed scoundrel, his dead bride, and the local lass whose heart he had broken. And it was long enough to clarify the truth about various matters of the heart, beginning with the belated news of the wedding of the mistress of Rosings to a celebrated portrait artist. Of course, of especial importance to those with the need to know, discuss, gossip, and ruminate over such things was the reading of the banns of marriage for the eldest three Bennet sisters. Praise, wonder, and tongue clucking ensued around Meryton's sitting rooms and kitchens. However, the one *actual* marriage stirred fewer conversations in London salons than the Fitzwilliam family had earlier feared.

The family name had taken a dent or two but bore no lasting scratches or scars. Lady Catherine had been little seen in London since her husband's death and little liked before it. Her recent removal to the family's Scottish estate was scarcely noticed, and her nearly unknown daughter's marriage to a man familiar only to a few admirers of his work was perceived as advantageous, if a bit odd. All in all, few commented or cared about the news. Other personages stirred far more curiosity.

Although gossip had settled down, the past and present of the future Mr and Mrs Darcy was of high interest during those weeks. Twenty-one days had done little to dampen the couple's ardour or their private demonstrations of affection. Whispered asides and titters were confined to ladies sighing at the romance playing out in front of them and to the servants at Netherfield and Longbourn, any number of whom had espied a flushed Mr Darcy with his cravat askew or Miss Elizabeth's hair looking not quite as it had mere minutes earlier.

An assembly the week prior had found all eyes riveted to the Bennet ladies. Their mother preened under the attention; no one dared look untoward and question the reasons for Mary's hasty wedding when the eldest girls were marrying fine gentlemen with houses in town, impressive carriages, and access to the finest shops and salons. No one could miss the looks of affection that passed between those two couples; the awkward but well-meaning conversation between Mary and her betrothed went unnoticed beneath the glare of her sisters' great love affairs. All was as it should be, Mrs Bennet thought to herself when she was not saying it to her neighbours. Not all shared her point of view.

"Young love," muttered Mr Bennet, staring out the window at his daughters and their swains. Jane and Bingley sat on a bench, staring into each other's eyes and speaking of topics Mr Bennet was certain would be of little interest or substance. "'Gooseberry or blackberry jam? We must think as one in our love of jams.' Bah!"

He shook his head and moved his eyes to the beehives, where Mary stood listening to Mr Collins expound on whichever bit of knowledge he had deemed best suited to the day's theme. "Ecclesiastes or Deuteronomy, today's dinner or tomorrow's dessert?" he grumbled.

In the distance, he could make out Elizabeth and her betrothed gesturing at the sky above and clearly debating the significance of some cloud before coming to agreement and sealing their intellectual felicity with yet another quick, furtive kiss. Mr Bennet's eyes narrowed.

"These empty-headed lovers have full hearts, but it is all quite a trial to one's patience. And here I thought Mr Darcy would be my favourite."

Mary's wedding in her new husband's 'most glorious parish' brought neither surprises nor new and unwelcomed suitors for Lydia and Kitty. While the elder sisters had been away in London shopping for wedding clothes, Lydia had enjoyed her father's need for company in his library and her mother's desire to shop. Kitty, meanwhile, had determined that Miss Bingley's advice and fashion stylings lacked wisdom and taste. Among other events, she decided Samuel Lucas was not beneath her notice. Although she could admit that his appearance was nothing to the dignified handsomeness of Mr Darcy or the ever-present smiles of Mr Bingley, Kitty now thought that Mr Lucas's faded freckles and kind expressions were of great interest. His work as a law clerk and hopes of advancing himself also proved worthy of admiration. After one especially engaging conversation on contracts, she found enjoyment in sketching the details of a land dispute, and she determined that a talent for drawing trees, logs, and rock formations could lead to an improvement of her skills as well as be of use to the legal profession.

Even better, Miss Darcy had mentioned the lovely views at Pemberley and, with her brother's permission, extended an invitation to Elizabeth's sisters for a summer visit. Kitty was determined to avail herself of the opportunities offered by at least two of her soon-to-be brothers. There was no advantage to be gained in Kent from Mary's betrothed, though she was interested to learn that a painter of some renown was newly married to Darcy's cousin there.

In spite of his ill-conceived first meeting weeks earlier with the Dumfries, Mr Collins had since worked diligently to insinuate himself into the graces of the new mistress and master of Rosings.

Influenced by Mary's example of patient fortitude, he endeavoured to admire rather than admonish, praise instead of preach, hold his tongue rather than hold forth. His patrons' appreciation was made easy by their own mutual felicity.

The spindly, petty, and unpleasant Anne de Bourgh had blossomed into the plump, rosy-cheeked, and exultant Anne Dumfries. Her mother seemed a forgotten ghost, and all traces of her existence at Rosings were disappearing as new colours, fabrics, carpets, and paints transformed the manse. All, it seemed, had been renewed at Rosings, and Anne had seized upon her new responsibilities with some alacrity.

She had been quick to take to Mary's company when Mr Collins's wife-to-be arrived to tour her future home and even quicker to invite Mary's family to stay at Rosings for the wedding.

"We will be family," she had said, seizing on the idea of her Peregrine, her cousin Darcy, and her parson all being brothers of sorts. Anne congratulated herself often for having begun the happy revolution in her family. Weddings and babies would be the rule, and she marvelled at the thought of Darcy, the man whose heart had seemed untouchable, succumbing at last to Cupid's arrow.

Mixed with her wonder was frustration as Richard refused to reply to her questions about Darcy's betrothed, and Peregrine declined to join her in speculation about the beauty or character of another woman. "Such a thing would be unseemly," he whispered as she lay prone beneath him. "Sinful and stupid would be the man who gazed at anyone but you, my dear." Giggling with satisfied joy, she rubbed her rounded belly and counted on learning much during the family's evening at Rosings, where all were to spend the night prior to the Hunsford wedding.

Elizabeth and Jane arrived with the Darcys and Richard; the Bennets, including the bride, followed. After the ladies retired to their rooms to refresh themselves, Richard took Darcy aside to assure him that the trees were well stocked with bottles of brandy and port and, mindful of future visits, provided him some guidance as to where a few of the estate's largest hollow trunks could be found.

The cousins took a moment to appreciate the changes inside the house. Lady Catherine's rooms were being stripped of their gaudy baroque furnishings. New paintings populated the walls, most by Peregrine's hand. Yet while Darcy had found his aunt's taste appalling, he thought her son-in-law's art to be indecent and wished for his future bride to avert her eyes in every room.

"Is that a nipple?" he muttered, leaning closer to a painting hung just outside the music room.

"That is incredible," cried Richard. "A true work of art! Look at how he has detailed the small bumps on her aureola."

"'Aureola' is the radiant cloud surrounding a celestial being," Darcy replied. "You refer to the areola."

"You and your damn clouds," Richard growled. "The nipple is a celestial being worthy of worshipful attention. Thankfully, you soon will be married and rid of all of this frustration."

Darcy sighed.

"Such attention to realism." Richard leaned closer to the enormous painting. "Father would appreciate this one."

Darcy stepped backwards, attempting a fuller view of the work.

"My lord." He seized his cousin and pulled him away from the painting.

"What has got into you?" Richard glared at Darcy.

"It is Anne."

Richard followed Darcy's red-faced gaze upwards.

"Bloody hell. Bloody, bloody hell." He stepped back, aghast. "In a public area. The servants…"

"Thank the lord that your father is not here. He would forever forget his credo as a breast man."

"Mine may yet be forever marred," Richard said in a low voice. "I believe it is time to crack open that first bottle."

Even prior to his encounter with the many portraits of Anne,

Darcy had been helpless to forewarn Elizabeth about Peregrine. She had heard Richard's jokes, which he had tried to temper with helpful asides about the man's appreciation for Anne and his skilled eye for proportion. Yet the rumours and mumbled asides laid a groundwork that Elizabeth was happy to tread in the hour or two before her family arrived and while Jane and Georgiana rested. As it was, she quickly determined Peregrine to be nothing more than a fastidiously powdered version of Sir William Lucas: always pleased and always happy to please others. Only his artistic sensibility and sometime indecorous glances at his wife set him apart from Meryton's Most Illustrious Citizen.

Darcy and Richard hovered at Elizabeth's elbow, grimly supervising the conversation and paying close attention to where Peregrine's gaze fell. Whether mindful of his company or simply more of a gentleman than the cousins had anticipated, the painter was a gracious if overzealous conversationalist.

"Miss Bennet, I would like to capture your eyes in oils. I hear much of the beauty of Pemberley, its lands, and its galleries. It cannot be called the finest home in England until your portrait hangs on its walls."

Elizabeth smiled, more primly than her usual wont. Darcy tensed. Richard growled.

"I would be honoured to paint your portrait, and those of your future children. After all," he added, "we will be family in mere weeks."

Anne laughed. "Oh yes! Look about Rosings and see what my Peregrine has done! He has kept me captive in his studio. Have you seen my portraits?" She leaned forward and peered closely at Elizabeth. "You must let him capture you, my dear. You have such lovely eyes."

Elizabeth felt a slight shudder in the man seated beside her. She placed a hand on Darcy's arm and gave him a gentle squeeze. She did not like him to be anxious. "You honour me with your wishes," she said placidly to the eager couple. "Your cousin and I lack your artistic sensibilities. Fitzwilliam is liberal with his kindness and good humour but conservative in his management of his family's estate and his legacy." She smiled at Anne. "Choosing a wife who brings him happiness but does little to enrich his holdings or enlarge his lands is quite daring, as you know."

The Dumfries nodded in harmonious agreement. "A thing in common," Anne said, beaming at Darcy, who shifted uncomfortably under her intense gaze. "My cousin and I always have been of like mind."

Elizabeth slid her hand down Darcy's arm, tenderly tracing his wrist and intertwining their fingers. He squeezed her hand in return. "Yet he has long run his own estate and overseen yours, so he already has ensured that he will follow the family mandate handed him by his father."

Darcy appeared perplexed. The colonel quickly drained his tea.

"Mr Darcy's fondest wish was that Fitzwilliam's future wife and children would be portrayed in the Darcy family tradition. He desired to ensure that, no matter the bride, her likeness in the public galleries and private family rooms would be a perfect match with previous generations.

"As I am that fortunate bride, I applaud Mr Darcy's foresight and can only regret that I shall not know him." Elizabeth gave her intended a fond look and picked up her teacup. "I believe Thomas Lawrence has the family commission."

Richard guffawed and breathed a quiet, "Bravo."

Darcy smiled and nodded at his betrothed's clever prevarication.

Anne sighed. "Oh my, that is just like Uncle Darcy. He always was taking care of his duties and worrying for society's expectations. Just like his son—until you, my dear." She shrugged. "I will remain my husband's artful captive. He is a master of miniatures as well. Our babe will be well documented as he or she traverses the early months and busy years."

Peregrine nodded, looking at Elizabeth sadly but intently, as though committing her features to memory.

"Yes, Lawrence has, as always, been commissioned," Darcy said in a firm voice. "Dumfries…" He waited until the man met his eyes. "Make no mistake; you have great talent with your brush. However, I do not wish to hear from your steward—who remains under my employ—or from anyone else that my wife has been 'captured' in the same manner as you have captured yours. Do we have an understanding?"

"Yes," Richard growled. "Do we?"

The colonel was no artist and had little familiarity with oils and powders and colours. But he did rather appreciate the peculiar shade of ashen grey that spread across the face of Peregrine Dumfries as he nodded his acquiescence.

As the day wore on, Rosings's mistress, the once-thought-promised-and-then-thought-dead Anne, proved more interesting to the always-curious Elizabeth. Darcy and Richard spoke of her as she was before her marriage, but as Elizabeth could only judge her on the after, she was pleased by her soon-to-be cousin. Years ago, she had heard her mother's friends mention a girl about to wed a ne'er-do-well; they had said she would be 'the making of the man.' Over tea and then over dinner, she had gazed upon the merry couple, clearly besotted and clearly unconcerned with behaving in company according to society's expectations or propriety, and she felt they had found a perfect match in each other. The Dumfries were not an easy pair to observe in any serious manner, but they were well suited.

Not everyone could take Elizabeth's point of view. Her family arrived and were awed by Rosings but unprepared for its master and mistress. Darcy was chagrined. Mrs Bennet was flustered. Mr Bennet was amused. Jane remained pink-cheeked throughout the evening. Kitty was fascinated by the artist and his muse. Lydia appeared slightly stunned by the self-displacing beauty mark and, biting back laughter, was pulled away and escorted twice around the room by a quick-thinking colonel. Mr Collins and Mary were occupied with their impending nuptials and seemed oddly uninterested in the behaviours of the newly wedded couple. Or so Darcy assumed until Mr Bennet came to his side.

"Darcy," he said quietly. "I wonder if you might take a minute to speak to your future brother."

Brother? The younger man was confused. Bingley had journeyed to Reading to arrange for Miss Bingley's removal there to reside with their aunt for a few months after the wedding. Mrs Hurst's temperament had taken a turn for the worse, and Bingley hoped that his youngest sister, afflicted of late with a deep melancholia, would rally when ensconced in a busy family home. As he had explained to Darcy, "She has always enjoyed small dogs and quiet children, and she is better there than with me and my new bride."

"Sir?"

"Collins, it would seem, lacks the education necessary for his wedding night." Mr Bennet paled and his voice dropped. "His wedding night with my daughter."

"Sir?" Darcy's voice was strangled. *Oh, no, no, no, no, no, no.*

"I am Mary's father. I do not believe Collins deserves her, but she appears pleased with her lot. You are to be his brother, and as little as I believed of the rumours and slanders that stained your name, I assume you to be at least familiar with the mechanics of marital relations."

"Sir…" *I think I shall be sick. Now.*

Mr Bennet clapped a hand on Darcy's shoulder and leaned towards him. "I have seen how you gaze at Elizabeth. I have seen a kiss or three. You owe me this."

"Sir…I will do the best I can," Darcy stuttered.

"Your worst would be Collins's best, I believe." Mr Bennet shook his head. "Mary will thank you…um, Elizabeth…for it."

Darcy morosely watched him saunter away, clearly chuckling at the horrible position in which he had just placed the man Elizabeth claimed would be his favourite. *My uncle and now my father-in-law reduce me to a sputtering eight-year-old boy.*

Taking a deep breath, Darcy looked around and spotted the wisest man he knew.

"Richard."

It was Peregrine who raised the first toast to the newly wedded Mr and Mrs Collins. As his florid tribute wound on, Elizabeth leaned over to her betrothed. "Am I cruel to be pleased that your cousin and her husband will travel to Hertfordshire for our wedding?"

"You will not rue such attention to your person or such flowery well-wishes?"

"I believe I shall be merry watching Mr Collins enhance his mind to become a lover of art," she replied. "One can only admire closets and chimneys for so long."

Darcy laughed.

"Your cousin is now my good friend, and we shall exchange letters and, I hope, visits when her child is born."

Darcy blanched and tried to repress memories of the previous evening. He and Richard had accompanied Collins to the parsonage and had tried, calmly and in few words, to explain the small ways in which to gently consummate his marriage. Richard had helpfully suggested baths and forgoing mutton and fish. "Soft skin that smells and tastes of soap is preferable to reminders of last week's supper."

"Mine eyes should not be cast upon my wife's unclothed skin, nor hers on mine," Collins had said solemnly. "The marital bed has but one sole purpose: to beget children."

Richard had drained his brandy and handed a brimming glass to Collins. "This. Now."

He had watched the cleric gulp down the liquid and poured him another. "Damn it, Darcy," he had groaned. "I feel as if I am Lady Catherine, caterwauling and tutoring the lovers behind the bed curtain."

Darcy had poured himself another drink, and together, the cousins watched as the brandy's effects spread through Collins. Suddenly, Peregrine had burst into the house, a sheaf of papers in hand, and every possible detail of the lush pleasures of married life had been elaborated upon before Collins had turned from an excited pinkish colour to an unusual shade of green.

Now, at the wedding breakfast, Darcy observed that the cleric's skin was a shade somewhere between the two. At least the man had made it through the vows and now had only to survive this celebration, the farewells, and the long hours leading up to nightfall. Would he retain any of what he had been told? Would he remember to bathe? To refrain from quoting Scripture? Or would he simply faint when he recalled the intimate details shared about the female body and its sensibilities?

Oh lord, has Richard ever looked as startled as he did when Peregrine mentioned the joys of lush folds?

"Fitzwilliam?" Elizabeth said. "Are you well?"

He swallowed and stared at his plate. Had bacon always smelled so foul? He reached for a piece of bread and began shredding it. *Think of her, of us.*

"I am well. I simply look forward to our wedding. You and I prefer a simple ceremony with neither words nor sentiments that can be embellished or twisted." He shook his head. "We should not fear finger pointing, screams, and fainting in Meryton when my dead betrothed appears at our ceremony, should we?"

Elizabeth paused. "We are all family now, or soon will be. Our children will play together; we will celebrate and mourn together."

Elizabeth hoped she could include Jane in her picture of future family togetherness. They had sat up half the night, giggling and cringing in horror at Anne's swooning confidences about the joys of married life and the secrets of the marital bed. She was sure the blush would not fade from Jane's face before her own wedding.

Their evening sharing thoughts on Anne's breathless revelations had been their happiest, most comfortable time together since the day before Darcy arrived at Longbourn.

Their argument—if Jane's frustrated determination that her favourite sister should marry their cousin could so be termed—had shattered their closeness. Since then, they had built a fragile and polite friendship. Elizabeth felt that an olive twig rather than a solid branch of sisterly closeness was all she could extend. They remained occupied with their betrotheds, busy with counselling Mary or calming their mother, focused on planning weddings, packing their trunks, and enduring their neighbours' joy and awe. They no longer shared time in their rooms, plaiting hair and discussing the men they loved; there was, for Elizabeth, no reclaiming that intimacy they had once shared.

The two sisters seemed now to inhabit different realms. Jane remained pleased yet shy with Bingley, making Elizabeth's need and desire for Darcy seem overwhelming. It was so abundant she feared at times that she could not contain it within herself. It was not that way with Jane. Her hesitant admission that she and Bingley had shared a single kiss had stunned Anne and Elizabeth, whose eyes had drifted to each other in surprised dismay. Mary, however, had been truly shocked by her sister's wanton behaviour.

But her next eldest sister earned Mary's praise. "Elizabeth returns from her walks with Mr Darcy and appears to have enjoyed nature to its fullest. There always are bits of leaves and small twigs in her hair and about her person. They use their time alone in a fruitful manner, enhancing their understanding of nature and clouds and such."

Anne had coughed just as Elizabeth stifled one. *Fruitful? Remember this, word for word. How Fitzwilliam will treasure it.*

"Mr Collins and I discuss Scripture and his plans for the parish. But you, Jane? Kissing before your wedding day?" Mary had squeezed her sister's hand. "I shall not tell Mama."

Anne had looked at the three Bennet sisters. "Well, then. Returning to our discussion. Where were we? Pinching? Oh, my Peregrine enjoys it. In fact…"

The mistress of Rosings was full of happy feeling and a need to advise others on how best to achieve it, physically and with emotion. Mary had looked ill and soon left for her own bed. Jane had perched primly, taking in the lessons quietly, gasping or giggling as warranted. Her eyes had often sought out Elizabeth's, an expression of shock or amusement on her face.

Elizabeth had smiled in return and rolled her eyes. Anne's tales were amusing and rather shocking, but she wished to learn about intimacy with the man with whom she would share a bed. She had felt herself too much apart from him, the one she wished to be with always. For these past weeks, the feelings she had not expressed to him had not been shared with another; her thoughts were far too private. Instead, she had written them in a small journal, and she smiled and spoke more coolly than was her wont. Kitty and Lydia had seen through her disguise, and while remaining Darcy's greatest champions, they shared the eye-rolling occupation of listening to Jane's sighs about her happiness.

Elizabeth concluded that love sorted people into their best and worst selves. It made her and Darcy happy and compelled them to be better people. She saw it in the former Anne de Bourgh, and she saw it in Mr Bingley. In fact, she now hoped that Netherfield would be sold at last to him and that her sister would be made happy by staying near Longbourn.

"Elizabeth?" Darcy's soft voice broke through her wandering thoughts. "Are you well?"

She reached under the table and patted his knee. "I am so very well, my love. Quite simply, I am ready to be married."

His eyes lit up. "As am I. We have had enough of rumour and misunderstandings and obstacles in our path. I want my ring on your finger."

"Your happiness is mine." She smirked. "After all, you are now the Gleeful Groom."

And so it was that one week after Mary took the name Collins, her elder sisters were married from home. The new Mr and Mrs Collins had arrived shortly after the Dumfries, who brought along Peregrine's older brother, Percival, to attend Anne as her confinement drew ever nearer.

Elizabeth noticed little to commit to memory that day. Her father's face, sad and proud as he gave her away. Bingley's exuberant bouncing. Jane's nervous happiness. Mary's soft smiles towards her husband, who had combed his clean hair in a new style. Charlotte's melancholy, which lifted quickly upon her introduction to Doctor Dumfries. Miss Bingley's tense countenance and elaborate bonnet. Mrs Hurst's green complexion and renewed devotion to the husband who hovered nearby and escorted her outside or near a window whenever she fluttered her handkerchief.

Most of all, Elizabeth noticed Darcy. The little light in his eyes when he silently gazed at her as their vows were read. The gentle strength of his hand when he took hers. The small thread of nervousness she sensed in his posture. And the chaste but sweet kiss he bestowed on her publicly when she signed her name, 'Elizabeth Bennet,' one last time, putting to rest any rumours of the past and fomenting speculation on their future.

"A babe conceived on the wedding day is pure as the bride's dress and sweet as the cake," Mrs Goulding commented.

"Ah, but a babe conceived in the weeks before is ambitious and driven to prove itself," Mrs Long replied.

Mrs Bennet interrupted her neighbours. "My girls will do their duty, and it does no one good to speak on what occurs behind closed doors or in the shrubbery."

Fitzwilliam Darcy, new husband and besotted lover, thought he had learned all of Elizabeth's expressions these past few weeks. He was proved mistaken within moments of closing the door to their rooms that evening at Darcy House. He simply stared at the vision before him, her dark hair spilling over shoulders sheathed in something he vaguely noted had ivory lace.

She gazed at him and smiled tenderly. "Good evening, Mr Darcy."

"Good evening, Mrs Darcy." He wondered why she looked so calm when he felt his heart would soon leap from his chest. He hoped that was *all* that would leap out. He adjusted the belt on his robe and strove to think clearly about anything that would help slow the beating of his heart.

"We are alone," he said, returning her smile. "Free of Fitzwilliams and Bennets and all those I choose not to name whilst in our chambers."

Elizabeth burst out laughing. "Come gossiping dragons or preening peacocks, they will not part us." She gazed at her husband in his robe, his neck and legs bare to her for the first time, and swallowed nervously. "No more dragons to be slain, no more family crises to solve?"

"Dark clouds will always loom behind the white ones, but there are no dragons here." He was speaking nonsense but she was so beautiful and there was so much *of* her to look upon, did words truly matter? "We are home."

"Yes. Home," Elizabeth said softly. She was surprised by Darcy's neck. She had kissed him below his chin and near his ear many times; she had seen drawings and sculptures of the Greek and Roman gods and other heroic legends; but she had never once allowed herself to imagine the temptation of this man's neck. This led to his chest, which appeared to have a fine covering of hair on it…rather a match for the hair she was trying not to notice on his calves. She wanted to touch it all. She let out a shaky breath and looked towards the fireplace before forming a reply.

"We have wood for our fire, so the books of Darcy House are safe tonight."

"I do not fear being cold," Darcy responded as he drew nearer. His hand reached out, and with one trembling finger, he gently traced his wife's collarbone.

"Elizabeth?'

"Yes?"

"You are so beautiful." He leaned in and gave her lips a soft kiss. His finger lingered along its gentle path until it was joined by another to trace the shadowed hollow that led to her shoulder. As their lips parted and their tongues touched, Darcy pushed aside his wife's robe, and the ivory silk puddled at their feet, leaving her in nothing but her sheer nightgown. He pulled his mouth away as he felt her shiver. He gazed into her eyes as his fingers drifted slowly along the side of her breast, down to her hip, and then reversed their path. It was but a moment later that he brushed her nipple and she let out a gasp.

Elizabeth leaned into her husband. His fingers, now his hand, continued their ministrations; she felt his thumb caress that place, her breast, once again. She moaned and reached up to capture his lips before gently, achingly slowly, scattering kisses along his jaw until she found his neck. *Soft, yet rough.* He sighed, and she kissed him until her lips came to just below his chin and she felt the tickle of the chest hair that so enthralled her. Her hands, which had been resting on his arms, drifted lower to pull open Darcy's robe.

"Elizabeth," he whispered, his voice faltering. His hand fell away from her soft, heated skin, and with a slight shrug of his shoulder, his robe joined hers on the rug. She felt his eyes shift ever so slightly. She followed his gaze and looked down at their feet, encased in a sea of silk and flannel.

"Lizzy," Darcy said in a voice so tender, she felt her eyes well with tears.

Elizabeth looked up at the tall man who had won her heart. His hair was unkempt, his eyes wild with yearning and love. She smiled. *My husband.*

"No more problems to fix or messes for you to think on, Fitzwilliam. The maids will do it tomorrow." Daringly, she leaned forward, kissed his chest, and wrapped her arms around his neck. "There is other, far more important work to be done."

"And I am a most dutiful husband." Darcy scooped her up in a tight embrace and carried her to their bed.

They fell into the billowing sheets, which enveloped and swirled about them as their soft moans, whispers, and gentle sighs filled the night air.

CHAPTER TWENTY-THREE

"Husband, I believe I must bow to family tradition," Elizabeth said when her breathing had returned to normal.

"Which tradition is that?" Darcy enquired, his voice rough. "Do you refer to a Darcy tradition or some custom of the Bennet family?" He moved closer. His hand disappeared and began tracing lazy patterns on her smooth, naked hip.

"Ahh," his wife purred, shifting and sighing. She sank her head more deeply into her pillow. "Are there no Fitzwilliam family traditions?"

"None suitable for my wife," he whispered, resting his chin on the lovely shoulder peeking out of the sheets. "She is too exquisite, charming, soft, and warm to consider adhering to such practices."

"The wife of the master of Pemberley has no cause to repine over treasured family customs, but she is a lady new to ancient tradition and eager to learn about those old and venerated." Her hand caught hold of his and brought it to her lips. "Stop distracting me with your clever touches and whispers."

"I am attempting to create new customs and practices for us and our marriage bed." He fell back to the pillows, pouting.

"We have left this room but thrice since our arrival on Saturday," Elizabeth said, laughing. "That is a scandalous and certainly unusual practice."

"It is rainy and cold outside," Darcy replied in as haughty a voice as he could muster, unclothed, unravelled, and sprawled on twisted sheets at one o'clock in the afternoon. "We are where we belong."

"We must rouse ourselves eventually." She stretched her arms above her head, disregarding his growl. "I must tour the rest of the house. And we shall see your sister and cousin tonight."

"*Our* sister and cousin." He gazed at her fondly. "They are your family as well."

Elizabeth smiled then curled up beside him and touched her new husband's morning…uh, afternoon whiskers. "So many," she whispered. Her finger lingered on his upper lip. "I wish you to make me a promise."

Darcy turned his head and met her eyes. "I promise you everything, Elizabeth Darcy. I shall always love you. I shall adore you and protect you and ensure Cook never serves liver or mutton for dinner and always serves chocolate and tea when you breakfast."

"There, you see!" She laughed in delight. "A new Darcy family tradition."

"Indeed," Darcy replied, ridiculously pleased with himself and all the ways he had learned to please his wife of three days.

"But your promise?" Her fingers trailed through the soft hair on his chest.

"Yes?"

"I am quite fond of your lips, Fitzwilliam. They must always be visible and accessible to me. Your cousin's moustache is imposing, and I would not like the men in our family to make a tradition of wearing whiskers."

"May the women, then?"

Elizabeth quelled the urge to leap on her husband and tickle him. *No, he would enjoy that too much.* She pulled her hands away and fell on her back. "I am serious. As for the next tradition, I must follow your cousin Anne and be sure to refer to you as '*my* Darcy' whenever your name arises in conversation. Just as she must assert her dominion over 'her Peregrine,' so must I assert mine over my husband."

He turned and propped himself up on his elbow. He stared at her, mortified. "Dominion?"

"Oh yes. I am quite possessive."

He swallowed. She would never not surprise him. "Elizabeth?"

"Yes?"

"Please stop mentioning my relations by name in our bed."

"Yes, my Darcy. How simple this is!" she cried in delight. "Another tradition has been created. Chocolate for breakfast, no moustaches, no naming of relations, endearing assertions of possession…"

"Elizabeth?"

"Yes, my Darcy?"

"Never, ever call me 'my Darcy.'" He leaned over until they were nose to nose.

"No?" She stared up at him, all innocence.

"No."

Laughter bubbled up. "Yes, my love."

Darcy bent his head and kissed her lips. "Now," he whispered, "may I assert my dominion?"

He kissed her throat. "My possession?"

She sighed.

Her breast. "My obsession?"

She moaned.

Her hip. "My love?"

She trembled, curled her hands into his hair, and whispered, "And you, mine."

Arm in arm, the ladies disappeared from the dining room. Their lively chatter about the 'magnificent Mr Bach' floated behind them as Georgiana led Elizabeth to the music room.

Richard stared at Darcy. "You have taken your wife to see the library but not the music room?"

Darcy smiled sheepishly.

"Otherwise occupied?"

"Oh yes. The cards have piled up as it is known we are not receiving callers."

"None in three days?"

"No."

"And it appears there has been no grand tour of the house."

"Elizabeth is familiar with her new home," Darcy asserted. "She has yet to go below stairs, but she has met the servants and planned our meals."

"I see." Richard smirked.

"Do you?" Darcy narrowed his eyes. "What do you see?"

"Your perfect woman in your perfect home. At one time, you could not find words to describe her, and now you have exhausted yourself—"

"Richard…" Darcy's voice cut in sharply.

"—of superlatives and adjectives with which to describe your perfect wife. She is simply glowing with happiness."

Darcy leaned forward, beaming. "She is wonderful, Richard. All and everything I could wish for."

"Good lord, you are bedazzled." Richard raised his hands. Marital felicity surrounded him; his teeth ached from its sweetness. *How do they stand this honeyed fog?* He sighed in bemused resignation. "I shall make no further comment and share no more observations. I shall think my thoughts only on the purity of your happiness."

"You should try it, Cousin." Darcy rose and strolled around the room. "There is nothing else."

"I believe that is true for you." Richard smoothed his moustache and watched a morsel of dried plum tart fall to the carpet. Words he had said months ago when both men thought Anne was dead and Darcy felt overwhelmed by guilt returned to mind. *Nothing has changed. Everything has changed.*

"You are the master of Pemberley. You rule lands and lives, and you make me miserable with your endlessly happy smiling and chattering." Richard sighed. "And this poor, put-upon cousin must listen and nod, for he is dependent upon you for good brandy, a hot meal, and a decent fencing match."

Darcy laughed. "Ah yes. Put that way, mine is not too sorry a fate."

The men drifted into a comfortable silence, broken only by the bright, melodious sound of Elizabeth's voice joining her new sister's in song.

Darcy's face lit up. "Not sorry at all. Let us join our family."

The three Darcys had been settled at Pemberley but four months when the express came announcing the birth of the young master of Rosings: Rollo Lewis Dumfries. Months later, within a moment of his presentation, he would be dubbed Lardo by his ever-prescient cousin Richard. It was a nickname the boy would happily endure for the rest of his elder cousin's long life.

A fortnight after Rollo's arrival, the post brought two letters of note. Charlotte wrote to congratulate Elizabeth on the weeks-old news that she soon would be an aunt. Both Jane and Mary expected arrivals come autumn. "Ah, Peregrine's diagrams were indeed effective," Darcy said wryly upon hearing the Collinses' happy news. "My lord, that man knows his anatomy."

Baby news abounded. Already they had rejoiced in the birth of a little sister for Henry, Thomas, and Lily Gardiner to dote on.

Charlotte, however, had further news to unveil: she would be joining Elizabeth in the happy state of matrimony and soon would call her 'cousin.' She was betrothed to Doctor Dumfries, and she would make her home in Surrey.

Elizabeth paused and gave her husband the news. He smiled, took her hand, and leaned close to respond quietly so as not to disturb Georgiana and Mrs Annesley, who were busy making plans for their return to London to host a visit from Kitty and Lydia.

"May we pledge that, from the cradle, no child of our relations will be promised to another, and in fact, all will be discouraged from such an inclination?" He moved away, eyebrows raised, as he awaited her answer.

My husband does so enjoy sealing pledges and agreements when we are alone in our bed. Perhaps I shall tease him to distraction and find cause to disagree. Now there is a lovely idea.

"Such promises do lead to awful entanglements and create unpleasant situations for dutiful nephews," Elizabeth agreed, using a solemn tone of voice while attempting not to smile. "Yet while we might protect our own children, how do we thwart the hopes, dreams, and machinations of others?"

Darcy grimaced.

"Fitzwilliam, what is it?"

He handed her the letter he had just read. Elizabeth glanced at the familiar handwriting and frowned. It was from Scotland. This was no time for teasing.

Nephew—

Pay heed. My head lumps have receded. My temper has moderated. There is a de Bourgh child who requires my guidance and whose mother needs my maternal wisdom. I demand a carriage for my return to my family estate.

Lady Catherine went on to proclaim her determination that living in the Rosings dower house—replete with servants, edible meat, and access to her grandson—was preferable to the cold north of Scotland.

Elizabeth bit her lip so as not to laugh, and she nodded her farewells to Georgiana and her companion as they headed to the music room. Within a moment, one of their lately arrived visitors, Richard, strolled into the room, noted the letter, and chuckled. He said his parents had received similar dispatches prior to their journey to Pemberley for a final few days with their son before he returned to France with his regiment.

"My aunt worried you would refuse her letters?" The colonel, who had barely stopped joking about Baby Dumfries's early arrival or the imagined weight of Anne's milk-heavy breasts, roared with laughter. "Lady Catherine is well? Offering her wisdom to a daughter who has disregarded every bitter word of it? Is she preparing to hire tutors for the plump, screaming heir to Rosings to help guide his crying, spitting, and soiling himself?"

He stood straight and saluted Darcy. "It is our duty to protect Baby Dumpling."

Darcy sighed and stared balefully at his cousin. "Yes, but we are men who know little of maternal needs and feeling. I am husband to the wisest woman of my acquaintance. I shall defer to my wife for her advice. She has some distance from the family drama, after all."

Richard supplied Elizabeth with the packet of letters written to his parents; it took but a quick perusal of the tersely worded missives for her to form an opinion, which she shared when the earl and his wife entered the drawing room.

"At least Lady Catherine no longer refers to Rollo as a mongrel. That is progress," Elizabeth offered. She looked around the room and counted three of four heads nodding in agreement. "It is a simple thing: doctors must examine her, and Anne must be consulted. Despite the lingering problem of potential madness, Lady Catherine is her mother and the grandmother to Rollo."

"Yes, yes, but the father?" Lord Matlock sputtered. "How will Dumfries stand for her presence? She oversaw the dosing of her daughter into passivity."

Lady Matlock weighed in. "Can Peregrine not stand up and defend his family? Rosings is theirs, and the servants are loyal to him and Anne."

Richard laughed. "Peregrine likes everyone, especially himself. What was it the old Sun King said? 'There is little that can withstand a man who can conquer himself.'"

Darcy stared at him. "My cousin has been reading?" At Richard's indignant snort, Darcy continued, "The king also said, 'I could sooner reconcile all Europe than two women.' Yet neither sentiment is pertinent in this situation."

The colonel raised a finger to debate the point, but his father summoned all the attention by slamming down his empty glass. "Why are you two quoting Louis the Fourteenth? We are at war with the frogs. Shut it, boys."

Elizabeth held back a laugh when she saw the twinkle in her

uncle's eye as both Darcy and Richard glanced warily from his glass to the fireplace.

"Measuring the distance?" the earl asked drolly.

"Not again, Peter. Do behave," his wife snapped. He gave her a crooked smile and shrugged. "That's better, dear."

Their son disregarded his parents' odd flirtation, and their nephew chose to be dutiful. "We must write to Anne and Peregrine," said Darcy. "They are doing well at Rosings. The steward reports that he meets with them together on all matters."

"Aha, together! A lack of trust on one side, I wager," Lord Matlock cried.

"Or the inability to part ways for more than one hour," Lady Matlock replied, her eyebrows raised. "All of you observed the remarkable joy they take in each other's presence." The earl's countenance took on a light shade of green. "Catherine took pleasure in running an estate; perhaps, her daughter enjoys it as well."

"True," Darcy agreed. "It is likely that Anne takes an interest in *having* duties. Her mother certainly never allowed her to have responsibilities or even a voice."

"I learnt to care for our family estate from my father, who had no sons," Elizabeth said quietly. "Although preserving proper ditch depths held little interest for me, meeting with tenants, ensuring crop yields, and maintaining sturdy fences were quite rewarding." Elizabeth felt her husband's eyes beaming at her; neither noticed the Matlocks' smiles of approval.

Clearing his throat, Richard forged on to the business at hand. "Hmm. How will Lady Catherine, lumps or no, reconcile herself to losing her power and her voice?"

"Guards. Under my command," growled the earl.

Darcy looked at Elizabeth, and she nodded reluctantly. "Very well. We leave the details to you, Uncle."

The assemblage visibly relaxed as one difficult decision had been made—and not solely by Darcy but as a united family. As ever since childhood, Richard broke the silence.

"Speaking of war, I have word on our old playmate."

Darcy turned and gave him a curious look.

"Wickham is in gaol." Richard turned towards Elizabeth when she gasped. "He is a fool, my dear cousin. He slept with the niece of the Prince Regent's mistress then cheated a viscount at cards."

Darcy, shocked and horrified, nearly laughed in disbelief. "That is a roundabout tale, Cousin. Are you certain his fate truly wends in such a way, or is this another game of whisper down the lane?"

"Viscount Lydon, was it?" the earl asked. At his son's nod, he clicked his tongue. "Wrong man to wrong. John has a mean streak."

"Still…" Elizabeth said. "Gaol? Does he await his sentence?"

"I do not wish to make the effort to know more." Richard shook his finger and assumed a mocking air. "Any man who earned the sobriquet 'Peaches' before failing in his studies at Cambridge deserves whatever fate is handed him. Has your husband not told you the tales of those years? Wickham was always a bad one."

"A liar and an opportunist," Darcy said, his cheeks pinked. "And look where such actions have put him."

"The nickname alone boded badly," Lady Matlock said.

"I have always despised peaches," her husband commented. "I like a good juicy plum. Peaches go bad with such haste. They are too rotten a fruit to hang from the Fitzwilliam family tree. Apples and plums are the finest of fruits."

"Yes," Darcy agreed, his eyes searching out those of his bride. As always, her dark orbs sparkled, and now they followed his gaze as it drifted lower to their secret, the not yet detectable bulge that would round into a perfect shape. *Our perfect child.*

"The seed that plants the tree is essential to the creation of a good fruit," Elizabeth said in a bright, cheerful voice.

"Indeed," her husband agreed, bowing to her slyness. "The best fruit, the happiest families, all begin the same way.

"Or so goes a rumour I once heard."

Richard rolled his eyes. No, he was not dim. Something was afoot. It always was in this family.

As the years wore on, life bumped along with all of its happy highs and its base lows.

Baby Dumfries was but the first of the next generation of lovers and fighters, cloud watchers and beekeepers, totty-heads and geniuses, artists and bumblers who graced the families in this story.

The Darcys would spend their decades together watching clouds and pointing out stars, settling family quarrels, and quietly teasing and blaming each other for begetting their brood of seven children. All seven—as well as assorted puppies and kittens—slept in a nursery under a cerulean blue ceiling dotted with clouds, designed and painted by their Uncle Dumfries. Some little Darcys were dutiful; some were witty. One sang especially well, another loved ships, and the tallest one wrote poetry. One haunted ballroom walls and another screamed in terror at spiders. But all were clever, handsome, and well loved by their parents. All were most decidedly—as often declared by their father—a wonderful mix of Bennet and Darcy.

Richard, who remained bemused by the couple's obsession with all things skyward, blamed the moon, stars, sun, and clouds for causing him to be beset with so many yard imps screaming, 'Uncle Dickie.' Yet his visits to the family were of long duration, and when he was away, his letters to the children were regular and full of adventurous stories and silly riddles.

Beloved as their bemedaled cousin could be, it was their father who taught the Darcy children their favourite hiding game of Lost and Found. All vied to be the last one discovered, earning an especially heartfelt hug from their beloved papa as he happily pronounced them found. Their mother taught them to laugh and to make believe, to chase a cloud but never a butterfly. Their Aunt Georgiana taught music to those willing to play; she encouraged the others to listen or to sing.

Although Lord Matlock once had urged Richard to marry Georgiana, Darcy threatened to break every glass and brandy bottle at Matlock House if such an idea was ever again proposed. The fear of fusing the Fitzwilliam bloodlines into a new generation and unleashing said offspring onto London society was all the reminder Peter Fitzwilliam needed—though he needed to hear it from his wife, his nephew, and both sons before he gave up on his idea.

Instead, Georgiana married a young earl and lived happily in the country with her horses, dogs and cats, lineage charts, and pianoforte until they began their own family.

Richard sniffed at domesticity but never took the bait set by his many lady friends. He rose to the rank of general and enjoyed the respect of the men stationed below him and the exertions of the ladies lying beneath him. All who met him quaked at or admired the presence of the man and his moustache.

Rather than marrying one perfect lady, he preferred the role of lover to many women and grumpily indulgent uncle and cousin to the dozen or so children (he lost count by 1820) produced by the Darcys and their spouses and, at long last, Robert and Harriet.

Thursdays had not been fruitful for the stoic couple. It took a hot June day visiting Rosings, with a tour of Peregrine's paintings and his collection of Italian sculpture, for a Monday to prove itself as the fateful and productive day—again and again, in fact, until they had three sturdy sons. None was named Richard, but two had his teasing, rather combustible Fitzwilliam nature; the other was easily his father's favourite.

Doctor and Mrs Dumfries remained in Surrey but spent a month or two every summer at Rosings with their three hirsute children. The Collinses also were frequent visitors to the estate. Anne had drawn close to the couple and their children as, by all reports, Mary's influence on her cleric husband had been greatly to mutual benefit. She smiled more; he talked less. She oversaw a strict household and ensured bodies and clothing were cleaned. He ate less as well, though his desire for smaller servings often was attributed to Mary's careful discipline with spices.

The bond between the two women was especially strong and useful when dealing with Lady Catherine, who, ensconced under quiet guard in the dower house, wished to be heeded by her grandchildren and thus declared all small persons to be under her purview. However, Peregrine Dumfries had taught his children to laugh at any rule and person they found ridiculous, and Rollo and his three sisters quickly learned to turn tables and instruct their grandmother in the fine arts of mud pies, tea parties, and puppetry. Lady Catherine—her head free of lumps, her bad temper spent, and her heart seemingly open—was a champion of the gifts of all her grandchildren, taking a keen interest in Theodosia's love for the harp, Florentia's skills at painting screens, and Patience's gift for poetry. Of Rollo, she could find no fault.

The Bingleys remained at Netherfield, close to the Bennets and at the centre of Meryton's fine society. Bingley found himself many friends with whom to laugh and shoot and to advise him on dam construction and fallow fields. He had love and joy but no one to remind him of common sense and firm decision-making. He received Darcy's letters with alacrity but failed to write cogent, legible replies; nevertheless, his friend and brother remained his stalwart adviser. Jane had never enjoyed letter writing, but she maintained correspondence with her sisters and her aunts in which only happy events were mentioned and glorious thoughts were recounted. She spent much time with Louisa Hurst and less with those she could call her own.

The couple was blessed with sons and daughters so plentiful that they wished for sisters to help teach them. Instead, it was Mrs Bennet who did her best as tutor, for although sisters were abundant, they were not available, not capable, or not interested. Until her marriage to a disgraced duke's son in Brighton, who preferred ornithology to balls, Caroline Bingley divided her time between the Hursts' London house and the Bingleys' country estate. The boisterous joy found in both households verified her theories on the foul nature of children, and she proved skilled with sponges, lemon juice, and headaches to protect herself from the role of mother. She also grew fond of parrots.

Kitty preferred the company of the Darcys. She continued to draw cow-like horses, but after many lessons with the master Darcy had retained for her and Georgiana, it was clear that Kitty could boast of a decided talent for landscapes; she had a special gift for sketching beech trees. Upon her return to Longbourn after a long stay at Pemberley, she found that Samuel Lucas had stopped smiling at her quite so openly and had transferred his admiration to a girl more pleased to stay rooted in Meryton. Years earlier, the tongue wagging would have disturbed her, but Kitty Bennet had been out in the world. Hoping to further advance her painting, she moved into Rosings and became a pupil of Peregrine. Three years after her sisters were wedded, an introduction to one of his best customers brought Kitty marriage to a London solicitor.

Lydia, who had immersed herself in Darcy's collection of sky maps and cloud books, found a sea captain who shared her passions. They sailed to Africa in 1819 and sent gaily wrapped gifts to the nieces and nephews they did not know. Her mother especially missed her, but it was Mr Bennet who was her most faithful correspondent. Many of his letters were written from Pemberley, where he wore out the seats of at least two finely upholstered chairs in the library.

Darcy not only became Mr Bennet's favourite son, he long had been Peter Fitzwilliam's favourite nephew. The earl would always see him as Anne's boy, quieter than his own sons and almost withdrawn after his mother's death. He knew Richard was a blessing for Darcy, and it had been no surprise when Darcy had turned to him for support upon choosing a bride of whom the family might not approve. Years ago, when Lord Matlock had first met the young lady, he had observed her exchanges with Darcy and the smiles she elicited from Georgiana, and he understood her value. She would be good for Darcy and excellent for diluting the often-extreme strains of the Fitzwilliam bloodline.

Yet he had believed that there was one aspect of their family mantel Darcy should accept and wear proudly, and thus when his nephew married, it had been time to acknowledge him fully as a Fitzwilliam. Lady Matlock had chosen the couple's wedding present, but Lord Matlock made sure another, more private gift awaited Darcy in his library.

"Not every man would give another an embroidered pillow," the earl stated as he gazed, beaming, on the fine needlework and awaited Darcy's response. "But blast it, we are Fitzwilliams. We have traditions we must honour."

Let her be as the loving hind and pleasant roe; let

> *her breasts satisfy thee at all times; and be thou ravished always with her love*
>
> — PROVERBS 5:19

And as it was the Darcy tradition to be both amused and appalled by the Fitzwilliams, Darcy and his future wife had swiftly determined certain family gifts and customs were best kept private. So there, at Pemberley, the pillow sat, warmed and then faded by the chequered sunlight that fell across the bed they would happily share for five decades.

— The End —

ACKNOWLEDGMENTS

This story was hilariously fun to write and share with others. I owe much gratitude to my unknowing family, blissfully going about their business while I wrote it, and who were sweetly considerate and supportive as I went about editing it. They're the best.

I had some knowing and encouraging friends and fellow writers as well, especially Cat Andrews, Julie Cooper, and Anniina Sjöblom, who read this story and laughed and sighed in all the right places (and told me when they didn't), and Jessie Lewis and MJ, who happily shared some naughty Regency vernacular with me.

Hugs and thanks to Gail Warner, a lovely person and a gifted and supportive editor, for parsing my sentences and knowing a chortle from a chuckle; and Amy D'Orazio for all of her creative help and 24/7 support.

I cannot thank my parents enough for allowing me to read at the table. My deepest thanks and love to my family, who read books and screens, make me laugh, and give me time to write.

And of course, this book wouldn't exist if not for the words of Jane Austen. I'm not sure what she would think about the cheeky liberties I've taken with her beloved characters and story, but I do hope she would get a laugh from it.

ABOUT THE AUTHOR

Jan Ashton didn't meet Jane Austen until she was in her late teens, but in a happy coincidence, she shares a similarity of name with the author and celebrates her birthday on the same month and day *Pride and Prejudice* was first published. Like so many Austen fans, Jan was an early and avid reader with a vivid imagination and a well-used library card. Her family's moves and travels around the United States and abroad encouraged her to think of books and their authors as reliable friends. It took a history degree and another decade or two for her to start imagining variations on Jane Austen's books, and another decade—filled with career, marriage, kids, and a menagerie of pets—to start writing them. Jan lives in the Chicago area, eats out far too often with her own Mr Darcy, and enjoys membership in the local and national chapters of the Jane Austen Society of North America. In 2019, she and Amy D'Orazio co-founded Quills & Quartos Publishing.

To learn more about new releases from Jan and other great authors, please join the mailing list at www.QuillsandQuartos.com

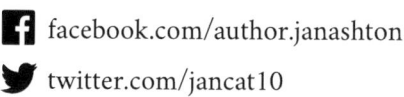

facebook.com/author.janashton

twitter.com/jancat10

ALSO BY JAN ASHTON

A Searing Acquaintance

"I don't know why I ever thought we made sense."

Smart, educated people are fools in love, especially when they're mired in denial and misunderstanding. In this modern spin on Jane Austen's classic tale, Elizabeth Bennet, a grad student with literary aspirations, has found her big career break and broken up with yet another forgettable boyfriend. Fitzwilliam Darcy is a man accustomed to living his life in the spotlight even as his heart dwells on the dark side of loneliness. When he first meets Elizabeth, he thinks she looks like "a bloody pumpkin," but he soon sees so much more. She, however, can't even decide what to call him. "So, it's Fitzwilliam, right? That's an amazing name, you know. Which came first-the name of the accent? He looked at her. "Oh, come on. It's like the name of a subdivision or a sofa at Pottery Barn. 'Please note the extra firm cushions on The Fitzwilliam.'"

Can an accidental encounter that leads to shocking intimacy change the course they've both set and bring them into love's light? Or will they stay mired in cold words and angry misunderstandings, overshadowing the deep connection they each feel? Getting beyond their own mistakes to find each other again is one thing; they also have to heal the wounds of their pasts. Can they do that together?

The Most Interesting Man in the World

A novella with Justine Rivard

Charles Bingley is a man who relies on Darcy's judgment in all things yet understands very little of it, at least when Darcy is speaking Greek to a horse who only understands Latin or staring at the quick-witted sister of his own angelic Jane Bennet. What was happening behind the scenes at Netherfield, Pemberley, and Darcy House, and just what did those men talk about over billiards and brandy? A generous, kind, and always hungry Bingley sheds a little light on keeping company with the most interesting man in the world, and shares his thoughts on puppies, his dreadful sisters, and the meaning of happiness.

Manufactured by Amazon.ca
Bolton, ON

44097767R00199